Ravensoul

Ravensoul

LEGENDS OF
THE RAVEN

James Barclay

GOLLANCZ

LONDON

Copyright © James Barclay 2008
All rights reserved

The right of James Barclay to be identified as the author
of this work has been asserted by him in accordance with
the Copyright, Designs and Patents Act 1988.

First published in Great Britain in 2008 by
Gollancz
An imprint of the Orion Publishing Group
Orion House, 5 Upper St Martin's Lane, London WC2H 9EA
An Hachette Livre UK Company

A CIP catalogue record for this book
is available from the British Library

ISBN 978 0 575 08200 7 (Cased)
ISBN 978 0 575 08199 4 (Trade Paperback)

1 3 5 7 9 10 8 6 4 2

Typeset at The Spartan Press Ltd,
Lymington, Hants

Printed and bound at CPI Mackays,
Chatham ME5 8TD

www.orionbooks.co.uk
www.jamesbarclay.com

For Oscar, who brings such joy to my life

Chapter 1

Blood sprayed across Geskard's chest. He grunted in satisfaction and stepped back out of range. He needn't have bothered. His strike had beaten his mark's defence and bitten deep into the shoulder, carving through leather jerkin and flesh before smashing the collarbone.

The uneven contest was done. Their eyes met. The victor and the unfortunate with too much money on his belt and too little skill with his blade. This city was no place for such imbalances. Never had been.

'You should have given me your purse when I asked you,' said Geskard. He smiled, recognising the dismay at approaching death that contoured the man's face. 'But I am much obliged you chose to fight.'

The man dropped to his knees, his sword falling from his right hand, which then clutched at the wound in his left shoulder. Nothing he could do would staunch the blood. His eyes dimmed and regret was his lingering, final emotion. He slumped forward, face in the dirt.

Geskard took a quick look about him. Again he blessed the chaotic sprawl of streets behind the north edge of Xetesk's central market-place. A man of his profession had surely designed it. In the warm light of early evening, tenements threw shadows across the alleyway. Above him, tatty washing hung on rotting lines. The sounds of the market day winding down rolled gently over him. If anyone had heard the brief exchange, they preferred not to make themselves known.

'Very sensible,' said Geskard.

He cleared his throat then cleaned and sheathed his sword, humming tunelessly. He knelt down by the body of the erstwhile merchant who had been just too eager to make one more deal in the day.

'This wasn't the sort of killing you had in mind, was it, my friend?' said Geskard.

One big hand had reached for the man's belt and bound purse, the other for a knife to cut it clear when Geskard shivered and paused. He looked round. A shadow had moved across the light behind him, making a shape like a man tattered by wind. He had seen it quite clearly, though just for a heartbeat.

No one there. He shrugged and returned his attention to his prize. The merchant moved. A tiny twitch but there nonetheless. Geskard started then chuckled.

'Fight in you yet, is there? I'm impressed.'

Geskard felt for a pulse at the neck. Nothing. He moved his fingers and pushed harder. Still nothing. It didn't matter. The man wasn't about to offer any resistance. Geskard looked about him once more. He remained alone. He smiled to himself, shook his head and reached a third time for the purse.

The merchant abruptly pushed himself up on his hands, coughed and spat blood onto the hard-packed ground. Geskard scrambled backwards, his heart thumping. He dropped his knife and put his hand to his sword hilt.

'Why aren't you dead?' he asked, backing off a pace.

The man looked at him as if for the first time. Blank dead eyes met Geskard's. The merchant's body rose to stand, a little unsteadily at first. Geskard watched slack-jawed while the man looked himself over, scraped ineffectually at the blood soaking his clothes and rolled his good shoulder with a cracking sound.

'Hmm. It'll do for now,' said the merchant, light entering his eyes. 'I can't wait any longer anyway.'

'For what?' asked Geskard not knowing why he had uttered a sound.

'There are people I need to see,' said the man.

Geskard was not a man normally prey to fear but when those dead eyes fixed on his and the sagging mouth tugged into a smile, something let go inside. He could feel his legs shaking, his crotch warm.

'Oh. Dodgy bladder?' said the merchant. 'Now then.'

Geskard wanted to run. To scream his terror. But he still couldn't place why he was so afraid. The man was a head shorter than him and half as powerful. He posed no threat. And yet, and yet. Geskard drew his sword, watching the merchant stoop to recover his own, the wound in his left shoulder gaping hideously, exposing raw flesh, sinew and bone. Fresh blood ran over his jerkin.

'There is no honour in murder, so we will make this fight again,' said the man. 'But this time you will find out something new. That you aren't quick enough to beat me.'

'You're dead,' said Geskard. 'I killed you.'

He backed away another pace and swallowed on a dry throat. He'd have fled but he'd never run from a fight in his life. His reputation was based on it. So he brought his blade to guard.

'You murdered a man for a few coins, that's true. And now you face me.'

'What?' Geskard couldn't suppress the laugh. 'I don't have time for this.'

He already knew the man's weaknesses and they were many. He crossed the space between them, a two-handed grip on his long sword, and wound up a strike to sever the left arm completely at the shoulder. But the merchant didn't try to defend like before. He merely swayed to one side and had jabbed his sword into Geskard's midriff even before Geskard's blade hit the ground.

Geskard gasped in pain and jerked back to give himself some space. He clutched at his belly. The cut was not deep but it should have been. In front of him, the merchant smiled but the eyes remained so bleak.

'Told you,' said the merchant.

'Don't dare to toy with me, boy,' said Geskard.

'Hmm,' said the merchant, moving in. He switched his sword between his hands three times. 'I'm used to greater reach in my right arm.'

'Grea—' Geskard swallowed. 'What is this? A game?'

'No game,' said the merchant.

The sword hilt settled in the man's left hand. Geskard wasn't ready. The blade came across him, carving into his right shoulder and thudding into his neck. The pain was exquisite but brief. Warmth, then cold. Geskard felt himself falling.

Auum stared up into the rainforest canopy and let his gaze travel over the dripping foliage. The sun that had emerged from the latest bank of cloud would bless the treetops until the rains returned. A sniff of the air told him that time was already very close.

Everywhere, spears of luminescence bore down through the

shadow, sparkling on raindrops and forming pools of bright light that warmed the forest floor. It was a time to drink in the glory of Yniss, God of all creation, Father of the rainforest and all that drew breath there, grew there and died there.

Yet Auum did not kneel to pray. Instead he listened to the sounds of bird, beast and insect. All muted, fearful. His gaze came to rest on the temple of Varundeneth, the last home of Shorth, God of the dead. The glorious structure sat in a clearing four days travel from the nearest settlement. Deeper inside the rainforest than any other. Hidden so completely from the unwanted eye that only those called, or those blessed like Auum, could ever find it.

A great hand, carved from a single block of marble, grasped at the sky. It sat atop the towering green dome of the temple and was protected by the statues of seated panthers set at each corner of the compass. Fashioned from obsidian, these sentinels had watched for enemies over the long centuries. No storm could etch them, no rain could wash the glint from their eyes. Thirty feet and more they rose, half the height and girth of the Hand of Shorth.

At the base of the dome, the stone doors were open on their wheeled rails and stood against the walls of the temple. Inside, darkness was broken by the flicker of lantern and brazier light. And from within, only silence. This was the time of Shorth, when he rose to bless the living and give succour to the dead; and when Communion between the living and the dead was eased and the pain of loss was lessened.

'So where is everyone? Where is the lament?'

Auum turned. Rebraal, leader of the Al-Arynaar, the army of Yniss, stood nearby with five of his people. Auum's TaiGethen cell were at his shoulders, both elves quiet and contemplative. Their faces were camouflaged with deep green and black paint.

Rebraal was showing the effects of his efforts to rebuild his people after the wars on Balaia and the scourge of the Elfsorrow that had claimed so many of the elven nation. Tall, powerful and quick, he was dressed, like the TaiGethen, in greens and browns. About his shoulders, he wore a cloak in the deep blue of the Al-Arynaar calling.

Auum sympathised with every line on Rebraal's once youthful face, the depth of the dark under his eyes and the vague tremble that occasionally afflicted his voice these days. Auum suffered the same way.

'If there is no call, then no one will come,' he said.

Rebraal stiffened. 'How can that be? Choice is not a word entertained by Shorth.'

'Nonetheless, the temple is empty of the summoned. And the wanderers too have found no path here. Call it what you will, the effect remains the same.'

'But what does it mean?'

Auum stared around him again. The rainforest and all its sounds and smells held a haunting quality, almost mysterious. He couldn't tell how far the strangeness extended into the canopy. The hairs stood up on the back of his neck. He felt uneasy. Not an emotion he had ever experienced before in this place that he knew so well.

'Shorth is silent. The temple carries no lament.' He shook his head. 'Elven eyes are turned from the triumph of death. And like Tual's children, they are afraid. It should never be this way.'

'I don't understand,' said Rebraal.

A cry torn from the heart of a terrified elf echoed from within the temple. Auum was running before the echo had died.

'Come with me and you will,' he called over his shoulder. 'Tai, Al-Arynaar, guard the entrance. No one enters until we return.'

Auum ran hard. The cry had turned into a wail and another voice had joined it, clogged and weeping, pleading. Auum's heart was pounding. The sounds from within were his darkest fears given voice. Rebraal fell into step behind him. Together they entered the cool of Varundeneth.

A short entrance hall led directly into the centre of the temple, beneath the dome. The vaulted ceiling sat high above them, the light from its multiple coloured windows casting gentle shapes and shadows on the stone-flagged floor. The walls were covered in murals of great deeds and heroism and of the path from life to death. The welcoming embrace of Shorth was depicted as glowing tendrils outstretched from the darkness of the unknown.

A round grey marble altar sat under the centre of the dome. It was placed on a circular marble platform with white marble rails and posts running around its edge. Two steps led up to a gap in the rail. Auum stopped short of the altar. A figure was slumped face down across it, arms thrown forward, hanging limp over the near edge, covering part of the carving of clasped hands that ran its circumference. The figure was in the grey robes and green sash of the temple priests. There was a slight tremble in her hands. Another priest was trying to swing her legs onto the altar, his grunts of exertion punctuated by sobs.

There was a smell in the air. A scorched smell. Magical, not mineral or wood. Auum held out a hand to stop Rebraal approaching further.

'Ryish,' said Auum quietly. 'What are you doing?'

The High Priest of Shorth raised his face to the TaiGethen leader. The rims of his eyes were bright red, bloodshot in the whites. His pupils were tiny despite the gloom.

'What I have seen,' he whispered. 'She is dead but she is returning. The mana fires burn our resting place.'

'You may not place the living on the altar of Shorth,' said Auum. 'You must remove her.'

Ryish showed no sign that he had either heard or understood. He was a very tall elf, looming over both Rebraal and Auum from his elevated position on the dais. His large, oval face was partly turned away from them now but Auum could not fail to see the confusion written there.

'She will attempt travel again. I must prepare.'

'Ryish.' Auum's tone was sharp, cutting through the priest's rambling and startling him. 'She will travel nowhere. She is not dead. Remove her from the altar or we will be forced to do it for you.'

Ryish stared at him once again. 'Do not let her movement fool you.'

'You are our friend,' said Rebraal. 'Trust us. Trust Shorth who will not turn away from you. You are the High Priest of Shorth. What you are doing cannot be allowed.'

'Shorth is already hidden from us,' whispered Ryish. 'Before you denounce me, behold my torment.'

The priest stooped, grabbed the woman's legs and swung them onto the altar. Before Auum could move to stop the sacrilege, the smell of burning magic flooded the temple. Deep green flames engulfed the altar. The two warrior elves backed away, leaving Ryish bathed in the fire, chanting prayers and exhorting Shorth to hear him. His skin was beginning to blacken where the burning mana breached his natural defences. His robes were ablaze. Yet he did not flinch nor cry his pain. Ryish's agony ran deeper than fire.

'Hear me, Shorth. Find a path for your daughter. Let her rest; do not—'

The priestess sat bolt upright. Green flame writhed and twisted about her body. Her clothing ignited yet her skin was untouched. Pale and delicate as the morning to which she had awoken. Her eyes opened slowly, revealing orbs black as night, destroyed by mana fire. She turned to face Ryish. Her mouth opened and she uttered a wail that shattered glass in the roof of the dome and shivered through Auum's body like a plunge into an icy pool.

'O Shorth, find a path for your servant. Ease her passing to your embrace.'

Ryish's cries boomed into the temple above the priestess's wail. The stench of mana fire, burning cloth and scorched flesh grew stronger. Smoke billowed up around the beams supporting the dome. The heat compressed the chests of the elves and brought sweat to their brows.

The priestess fell back, body contorting, hands reaching towards the sky. The flames deepened in colour, gained intensity and then were gone, leaving nothing but a flare in Auum's eyes when he blinked. Still, the priestess trembled. Her mouth closed, opened once more and a single word was whispered.

Ryish slumped to the floor. Auum and Rebraal ran to his side, Rebraal dragging him into his arms, trying to comfort him.

'Rest, my priest,' said the Al-Arynaar. 'We will tend to you.'

'Nyluun!' shouted Auum. 'Healer mage inside now. No one else.'

Ryish's burns were extensive but he would live. Though when he turned his eyes to Auum, the TaiGethen wondered if living would be a mercy.

'Now you see,' Ryish said, croaking through a cracked throat. 'We are lost.'

'I don't know what I saw,' said Auum.

'There is no path for the dead to travel,' said Ryish. 'Nowhere for the soul to rest. Shorth deserts us.'

Auum glanced at the priestess, whose body was quivering on the altar.

'She is . . . ?'

Ryish was nodding. He grabbed Auum's arm. His fingers, red raw and black from the flames, gripped hard, smearing the TaiGethen's ritual camouflage.

'She cannot walk the rainforest yet she cannot rest with Shorth. Her doom is the doom of any who now die. Neither dead nor alive. No end to pain. Only fear.'

Ryish broke down and Rebraal rocked him in his arms as if he were a child in distress.

'Her soul will find rest.'

'It will not,' sobbed Ryish. 'It cannot stay within her body and it cannot find a path to the embrace of Shorth. It will be cast adrift. Lost for eternity, never to know the Communion with the living, never to feel the strength of the dead.'

'That cannot be,' said Auum. 'We cannot exist if we fear to die. There must still be a path to the dead.'

All three were silent for a while. Ryish composed himself and sat up again, nodding his gratitude, wincing his physical pain.

'And what of the dead?' asked Rebraal.

Ryish shook his head. 'My mind is a desert, my soul a dry ocean bed, my will a forest blackened and destroyed. I cannot feel them. I cannot speak with them. The heart of Calaius is rotting away.'

Rebraal wanted to ask more but Auum stopped him.

'Ryish, what did she say? What was the word she uttered?'

Ryish took a deep breath and swallowed before he spoke. The word was jagged glass dragged through flesh.

'Garonin.'

Auum and Rebraal shared a glance. Garonin. A word that denied hope.

'I have not saved my people from the Arakhe merely to lose them to this evil,' said Auum. 'We must call a Harkening.'

'There is no salvation if they have truly seen our hiding places,' said Ryish. 'All we can prepare for is extinction.'

'If there is a way, I will find it. If there is not, then we must seek a new place for our people. A new home.' Auum turned to Rebraal. 'Summon the ClawBound.'

Chapter 2

But it was a shifting grey and an indistinct horizon this time. Not like any other time. Yet the same. The abject helplessness still ripped at his soul and the cries for aid speared his head like needles driven into his brain. And the hands reached for him and the faces were of those he loved drawn into pictures of torment. Their desperation bit deep inside him.

He reached out for them as he always did, to help as he always had done and always would. Though when he did he could not reach them. A barrier he could neither see nor sense kept him from them, kept their fingers from locking together. And the more he strained and grasped, the further they were from him. He shouted for them to come back but the smoke engulfed them once more.

Sol was bolt upright in bed. The sweat was slick on his face, on his shaven head and across the powerful chest on which grey hairs had begun to dominate. He knew his eyes were wide, sucking at the half-light, desperate to see. He tried to drag in his breath quietly. Failed.

'Sol?'

Sol looked down at the shape next to him in the bed. Earlier that afternoon, they had been as close as he had remembered for a very long time. Like a memory of a decade past. Now, the veil of disappointment had risen once more. One word was all she had said. And it carried so much frustration.

'I'm sorry, Diera.'

'Same dream, huh?'

'What would you have me say?' he asked.

'That you believe it *is* a dream. It's all I ever want you to say.' Diera whispered the words.

Sol reached out a hand to her, touched her bare shoulder where the sheet had fallen from her soft skin.

'I won't lie to you,' he said.

Diera shrugged off his hand, threw the covers aside and stood up, her back to him. He watched her take in a deep, relaxing breath before she reached for her shirt and skirt. There was nothing more to be said. There never was. But he couldn't let her leave the bedroom like this. It was a mistake too often repeated.

'I've tried to tell you how real the vision is. How intricate the detail is that I have seen and, Gods drowning, I have seen it so many times. How can it be a dream?'

'How can it be anything else?'

She wouldn't face him.

'It's a message.'

Now she did and on her face, still beautiful and framed in fair hair streaked with grey, was the contempt that had become depressingly familiar.

'And one day you'll be able to tell me what it says, right? And when will that be? Right now? Tomorrow?' She picked up a shoe and threw it at him. 'Never?'

Sol caught the shoe and dropped it onto the bed. He pushed back his covers and stood. They stared at each other for a time from opposite sides of the mattress. Diera snatched her shoe back off the bed and rammed a foot into it.

'The visions have been more vivid of late,' he said into the void. 'But I still don't understand it all.'

'Don't say it,' said Diera, expression a warning, the bed an inadequate barricade. 'Just don't.'

'They're in trouble. I cannot ignore it.'

'Trouble? How can they be in trouble?' Diera jumped onto the bed. She raised her fists to beat him but he snared them easily enough. 'They're all dead, Sol! Dead. Their troubles are over.'

Sol caught her gaze and held it. He could see the pain within her. The desperation for him to be other than he was. As for the love, that was fading. He let go her fists and her arms dropped to her sides.

'Death is no guarantee of peace,' he whispered. 'The demons taught us that.'

Diera sobbed. Her face crumpled and she held the sides of his head in the palms of her hands.

'But the demons are gone,' she said. 'You of all people know that. The threat is finished. It's over.'

'I want nothing more than to believe that is true,' said Sol. 'But I don't.'

Diera slumped to the bed and buried her head in her hands. 'Why are you doing this to me?'

'Doing what?'

'Five years, Sol. Five years of this and you've been getting worse and worse. The Raven is gone a decade past. We are your life now, me and the boys.' She raised her face to him and the tears spilling from her eyes drew some to his own. 'Please, Sol, this obsession is killing us. Let the dead be. Come back to me. I need you. We all need you.'

'And I am here,' he said. 'But I must find out what is happening. I cannot rest until I am sure they are at peace.'

'How can you ever know? They're dead!' Diera shouted the word into his face, levered herself from the bed and strode towards the door.

'There—'

'I won't hear this any more, Sol. I won't.' Diera smoothed her skirt and faced him, forcing herself to relax. 'I can't deal with it. When you were hunting the demons I understood. Because I wanted a future free of those things for our boys just as you did. But this? This is chasing shadows. It will always be unfinished and I am sorry for that. But you have to accept it. Open your eyes to what is in front of you now, don't keep them on the distant past.'

Sol sat on the bed and massaged his hip. It was beginning to ache. The spell was wearing off again.

'It doesn't feel distant. Not to me.' He looked up at Diera. She was studying him but wouldn't meet his gaze. 'I stood in that doorway and watched Hirad die. I could have done something. I could have saved him.'

'And that's what all this is about, isn't it?'

'What?'

'Redemption for you, for your imagined failings.' She shook her head. 'I'll never understand why you torture yourself. None of the other survivors are. They know what they did and they know what you did. You're the living embodiment of a hero, Sol. Why can't you see that?'

'Because heroism didn't save Hirad or Erienne, or Ark or Thraun, did it?'

'No, but it saved Balaia and me and Jonas and young Hirad. Those of The Raven died doing what they always did. Be proud, not desolate.'

'I am proud. And that's why I have to know if there's trouble.'

Diera shook her head. 'You hear but you do not listen. And you are blind to what you are doing to me and the boys.'

'No, I'm not,' said Sol, moving around the bed towards her. 'It is as much to protect you as it is to help my friends if I can.'

Diera gave a short laugh. 'Don't try and justify your obsessions using us, Sol. At least be honest with yourself even if you can't be anything else. I'm asking you one last time. Think, really think about this. Then come down and join your family or don't come down at all.'

There was a hammering on the door downstairs. Diera cracked.

'Can they not give us a moment's peace?' she shrieked. 'We're not open for three hours!'

Sol was in front of her in a moment, taking her by the shoulders and sitting her back down on the bed.

'I'll go,' he said quietly.

He pulled on his clothes and left the bedroom without saying more though his mind was drenched with words. His heart was beating hard and he was aware of a growing confusion. Sol shivered and tied his shirt tight at the neck. On the stairs, pain flared in his leg, an old memory resurfacing. The docks at Arlen. The sweep of a sword. Hirad saving his life. Again. The imagery was so intense it was within a ghost of being real. Sol leaned against the wall and descended more slowly, letting his shoulder slide along the age-smoothed dark timbers.

The hammering on the door was repeated.

'Patience!' roared Sol. 'I'm coming. The Gods save me from the curse of the impatient drunk.'

When he reached the bottom of the stairs, Sol could feel the heat from the ovens in the kitchens to his right. A clatter of pans told him at least one of the staff was already in. Evenings at The Raven's Rest were always busy. It helped that so many of the city's influential people were regular customers but Sol liked to think that both the food and the wine cellar were worthy of those he served.

Ahead of Sol, a short passage led out to a fenced yard where he could hear at least one of his sons, Jonas probably, playing a loud game with friends. And to his left, his pride and joy, if he could be said to experience joy these days. His bar. No. *Their* bar. A place of laughter, memory and reminiscence. The place where he always retreated when he tired of the attentions of state. When he was allowed to.

The place where The Raven would live forever.

But now, walking towards the heavy, bound oak door that let out on to the street, he wondered if this shrine to his past really was poisoning his mind. Diera thought so. Sol walked slowly past the portraits of his friends a decade and more dead. He didn't feel the barbs of grief as he had done in the early days but he didn't think he'd ever shake the regret that he would never stand with them again.

Sol could hear Diera's voice in his head, telling him to move on. Celebrate their triumphs, learn to smile.

He couldn't. He never had been able to, and now his head was full of disaster like it hadn't been in five years, ever since he stopped hunting demons. Sol let his gaze trail over the portraits of Erienne, beautiful of face but sad of mind; Thraun, forever troubled but so loyal; and Ilkar, sharp-featured and acerbic, before pausing as he so often did at Hirad.

The barbarian's scarred face was packed full of belief and raw power and it sported that damned smile with which he had died.

'So, old friend, what is it? I'm either right or I'm losing my mind. No in between, as you'd have said. Trouble is, I don't know what to do. I don't know where to begin. Any ideas?'

It was a moment before Sol became aware that he was actually waiting for a response.

'Talking to a picture.' Sol shook his head. 'I think we have an answer, don't we?'

Another bout of hammering on the door, and this time Sol was relieved to hear it and let it distract him from himself.

'All right, all right. I'm here.'

He strode to the door, drew back the top and centre bolts, kicked up the bottom one and turned the key in the lock. The levers moved back with a satisfying, heavy sound. He pulled the door open, stepping back as he did so. You can never be too careful.

The man who stared at him with an expression bordering on elation was young and smartly dressed very much in the style of a merchant. There was blood all over his left shoulder and chest. Sol frowned. He looked at the wound and wondered how the man was still standing.

'Unknown, is it really you? Did I really find you?'

Sol flinched at the sound of his old name. The man made to move forward, his arms reaching out.

'No one calls me that,' said Sol, his voice gruff. 'Not any more.'

'Shame,' said the man, raising his eyebrows. 'I always thought it rather suited you. It was one of Ilkar's better nicknames.'

Sol's skin prickled and his head cleared. He stepped forward and jabbed the man in the chest.

'You are treading a very fine line with the memories of my friends.'

'Don't you recognise me, big man?'

'Clearly not,' said Sol. 'And be assured that if you make one more familiar remark, I will deck you.'

'The body is unfamiliar but the soul and the shadow are mine, Unknown. And you have to help me. You have to help all of us.'

Sol felt cold. He straightened. The man's eyes held a desperate sadness, and he was frightened. Not of Sol but of something far, far more deeply embedded in his mind. There was something about him Sol couldn't grasp, something recognisable. But he'd been begged for help by passing acquaintances before. Everyone knew Sol's face and reputation.

'Who are you?'

The man smiled and a spark lit his eyes just for a heartbeat. He spread his arms.

'It's me. It's Hirad.'

Sol decked him.

'Bloody hell.' The merchant put a hand to his left eye. It was already beginning to swell. 'Didn't lose your strength when you got the wrinkles, did you?'

Sol paused for a moment and glanced up and down the street. The Thread was busy as always. Heads were turning and no doubt jaws already exercising opinions laced with ignorance. There were always stories to be invented about the first and reluctant king of Balaia. Sol stooped and grabbed the merchant by his lapels. He pulled the man upright and threw him inside the bar, where he slithered to his knees. Sol walked in and kicked the door shut behind him.

The merchant displayed no fear when Sol loomed above him.

'I'll give you one more chance. An abject apology just might save you from a few more broken bones.'

'You need to believe me, Unknown. Balaia's in trouble. The whole dimension and loads of other things only Ilkar understands.'

'Right, that's it.'

Sol grabbed the merchant by his wounded arm and dragged him to his feet. He clamped a hand around the back of the man's neck and marched him to the picture of Hirad.

'Take a good close look, you little bastard. This is Hirad Coldheart. This is the heartbeat of The Raven. A man I loved and a man I miss every single day. You will not pass yourself off as one of Balaia's great heroes. Do I make myself clear?'

The merchant nodded. 'You do. And it's a good likeness though I remember my teeth being straighter than that.'

'Fucking weasel.'

Sol hurled the merchant across his bar. The man knocked aside two chairs, sprawled across a table and collided with the back shelf, upsetting a candelabra and smashing the glass in two lanterns. He scrabbled for purchase. Sol could see his eyes. There was fear of him in them now. Too late.

Sol's cudgel for the control of the unruly was hanging in its brackets on a cross beam just above his head. He fetched it down and advanced.

'Why didn't you listen to me?' The cudgel's face slapped against his open left palm. 'No one plays with the memory of The Raven. Certainly not some puffed-up pretty boy like you. I'm going to make sure that cut on your shoulder is the least of your concerns.'

The merchant pushed himself to his feet and backed away. There was nothing behind him but the corner of the alcove into which he had been thrown. He felt the wall behind him and held out both hands.

'Unknown, please. You have to believe me. I'm not taking the piss. Please.'

'No one calls me that and walks out of here. Not any more.'

Sol pushed a chair aside and dragged the table from in front of the merchant. The back of his neck was hot. The cudgel felt good in his fist. It had been a long time since anyone had tried it on with him. It seemed that not quite everyone had got the message.

'I love that you are the protector of our memories. But we're in trouble. You have to listen. I know you've been having dreams. Ilkar's been—'

'It's about respect,' said Sol. 'And the young never seem to show any these days. I try and be reasonable but some of you just don't do reason, do you? So be it.'

Sol stepped into range and cocked the cudgel for a blow to the legs. The merchant tried to protect himself with his hands.

'Unknown, no! I can show you where you died. Where your body still lies. Please.'

It was an arrow to the heart of him. Sol froze and swallowed hard. The cudgel dropped from his hand. The fury drained from him and the strength left his legs. He sagged to his knees, supporting himself with a hand on the table top. His fingers rested on last night's candle wax.

'No one knows about that,' he said, his voice a whisper, blood pounding in his head. 'How can you know about that?'

'Because I *am* Hirad, Unknown. I know how I look. The body is different but the soul is the same. And we need you. The Raven dead need you. You are our beacon. The rally flag on the battlefield. And we have to make a stand or we are all lost. The living and the dead.'

'What are you talking about?' Sol stared at the merchant, looking for the lie in his eyes. 'A soul cannot return. You cannot be here.'

'Think I want to be? It hurts, Unknown. Badly. Ilkar will be here soon enough, I'm sure. He'll make you understand.'

Sol put his head in his hands. 'This can't be happening. Not really. I have . . . dreams.'

'Told you.'

Sol snapped his head up. So like him, those words. So typical. The merchant was standing over him, offering a helping hand.

'If you promise to hear me not hit me, I'll help you up. We could have a glass of wine. Does Blackthorne still do that red of his? I wonder if I can taste it?'

The merchant wore a crooked smile. Sol glanced over at the picture of Hirad and shuddered. He allowed himself to be helped to his feet.

'I have truly lost my mind.' Sol gestured to a chair. 'Pick it up and sit on it. I'll get us a drink. While my back is turned, you have the option to leave. If I come back and find out you're lying, I will kill you where you sit.'

'I have missed your administrative guidance,' said the merchant.

Sol jabbed a finger into his chest again. 'Don't push your luck.'

He blew out his cheeks and wiped a hand across his head on the way back to the bar. There were footsteps on the stairs. Diera appeared and treated him to a scowl as she tied on her apron. She looked beyond him into the inn.

'Been rearranging the furniture, have you? Can't say I like the upturned chair and broken glass look. What the hell has been going on? And who is that? We aren't open yet.'

Sol stared at her for a moment, considering the lie that would best placate her. He dismissed every option. He plucked two pewter goblets from the bar top and wrapped his little finger around the neck of a stoppered bottle of wine. Half empty and not the good stuff.

'He says he's Hirad Coldheart, back from the dead.'

'And you believe him?' she asked. Sol said nothing. 'My darling husband, where have you gone?'

Diera cupped her hands around his face. A single tear fell from her left eye. She sucked her lip, turned and walked out of the back door and into the yard, where the children still played.

Chapter 3

'I take it the good Lady Unknown doesn't believe me?'

Sol said nothing while he poured them each a goblet of wine. He sniffed his to make sure it was still drinkable and took a hearty sip. The Gresse red had a mellow flavour and a strong aftertaste.

'Good with stew,' he said.

'I'll remember that next time I'm cooking.'

Sol stared at the man. Young and proud-looking. Shoulder-length brown hair tied in a ponytail. Sharp green eyes stared back above a crooked nose and a mouth in which the teeth were starting to discolour. The wound in his left shoulder was deep. Deep enough to be fatal. Sol could see torn flesh and bone showing through the ripped clothing. He should have been pumping blood onto the inn floor. Sol was thankful for the mercy.

'Who *are* you?' he asked.

'I'll repeat it until you believe me, you know,' said the merchant, eyes twinkling briefly. 'You do believe me really, don't you?'

'Let's just say I'll listen to you. Give you a chance this side of doubt. But believe? What's to believe?'

The merchant took a sip of wine and a look of almost beatific pleasure crossed his face. 'Now that was almost worth coming back for.'

'Almost?'

'Another time, Unknown. But for now accept that returning from the dead isn't all it might be.'

'If you say so.'

Sol cursed himself, feeling drawn in already and wanting more. He wanted it to be true, that much he would readily admit.

'Look, think about this logically.'

Sol laughed. 'Logically? Now that is something very much in the Hirad mould. The ability to choose absolutely the wrong word at will. You appear at my door, sporting a wound that should have put you on the slab, and claim to be my friend returned from ten years dead. Logic? Please.'

'All right not logic then, just what is in front of your eyes. Rely on what you know.'

'I know Hirad Coldheart is dead. I am still counting the days, wishing it wasn't true.'

'And you also know that this wound has carved through my left collarbone and has torn nerve, sinew and artery. It's a killing blow and you've seen enough to know one, right?'

'Which means I'm looking at a fake of some sort. Because dead men cannot walk.'

'Put your finger in, then. Give it a wiggle.'

The merchant demonstrated. Sol winced.

'Isn't that painful?'

'It's fucking agony.'

'Well, stop it, then.'

'Do you want a go?'

Sol stared at the merchant yet again. Memories thronged his mind and dragged to the fore emotions long-buried. Thousands of words that should have been said. Wrong body, wrong voice. An impossible return. And yet there in the cock of his head and the manner of his speech. So much familiarity.

'It cannot be you,' he said. 'How can it be you?'

'I take it you've had your fair share of fakes?'

'You could say that,' said Sol.

'What people will do for a free drink, eh?'

'They're just the sad cases.' Sol rubbed his nose. 'It's the ones that trade on my memories for profit. They make me angry.'

The merchant reached out and patted Sol's hand.

'Well you hide it very well.'

Sol burst out laughing. He refilled both their goblets. 'Remember you're still on probation here. Though I must admit, I've never seen anyone as convincing thus far.'

'You're telling me you've had others come to you like this?'

Sol nodded. 'People claiming they were possessed by the spirits of one or other of The Raven fallen.'

The merchant straightened his shoulders, grimacing at the pain.

'Recently?' he asked.

'Last four or so years . . . until I introduced the cudgel.' Sol frowned. 'Why do you ask?'

'Anything very recent might not have been a fake.'

'You mean I might have beaten the backside out of Ilkar or something?'

'Ilkar's rather confused living host, to be precise. We were trying a number of ways to get hold of you.'

'A number?'

'Two.'

Sol sighed. 'If you are Hirad, I have to tell you your jokes have not improved.'

'It's important, Unknown.'

'All right. But you'd better surprise me or it's the cudgel and a trip face down along the river.'

'Ilkar is much better at this stuff. Basically, we've been trying to get to you through your dreams but although if we got together we could sense you, all we could do was the equivalent of wave at you in the fog. You were always so close but just out of reach. And then, when the walls of the dimension started to fall, we started to try sending ourselves out and getting hold of bodies to speak for us. They were always of the living and I guess you just found possessed people annoying. But I thought I might as well give this a try. Y'know, finding someone freshly dead and using them. Didn't have to wait too long in the north alleys to find a host.' The merchant paused. 'Are you getting this so far?'

'What? Sorry. Just trying to work out how it is you could describe my vision to me.'

'Because we sent it.'

'Who?'

'The Raven's dead.' The merchant stared into Sol's eyes. Desperation and bottomless pain flooded out. 'We need you, Unknown. They are come and we cannot stop them.'

Sol bit back on the threat of tears.

'I'm losing my mind,' he whispered.

'No you're not, Unknown. This is real.'

Sol's vision was blurred. He wiped a hand across his eyes. He couldn't stop himself. With Diera, it was too fraught. With this stranger, as natural as sunlight.

'Don't you know how much I want that to be true? Every day I walk past those paintings and I crave the company of the men and women I see. I want it so much I see movement within the frames. I crave our bond and to live by our code once more. The pride of standing in line with them. The sheer energy of our battle. The closeness that comes with facing death together day by day and living till morning yet again. The knowledge that any of them would die for me and that I would do the same for them. Things I can only embrace now when I sleep.

'I want to tell them so much. About my joy that I can see my sons grow up; that I awake each morning and see my wife. That I am living everything I dreamed of but that it is just a puff of smoke rising from the embers of the life I had, and to which I can never return. That on some days, too many days, I wish I too had fallen that day. A hero to live on in the memory, not growing fat behind a bar and dreaming of glories past.'

The merchant was silent. He drained his glass. Sol did likewise and refilled them both. He cleared his throat and stood up, needing to fill his hands with something, anything. The Raven's Rest felt a little gloomy. Apt in one sense but no good for the custom Sol expected through the door later. King or not, he still had an inn to run.

The fire needed laying but that would wait. He lifted a lantern from its alcove and retrieved flint and steel from his pocket. He was aware of the merchant's gaze on his back.

'Don't repeat any of that,' said Sol.

'You'll be able to tell them all personally before long. And you'll wish you couldn't.'

'Why would I wish that?'

Sol struck sparks onto the oiled taper which sputtered to yellow life.

'Because with the best will in the world, Unknown, we are not happy to see you. Not here, not in this dimension. We're dead, big man, and we want to stay that way. But we've been attacked. Our dimension has been plundered and we are cast out. It hurts and it is lonely.'

'And you want my help to get you back where you belong, is that it?'

'If only it was that simple.'

The Unknown chuckled. 'Sorry, I shouldn't laugh. If you're telling the truth, that is. It's just that—'

'Nothing's ever that simple with The Raven.'

Sol nodded, feeling the warmth of familiarity return. It felt like grasping an elusive childhood memory. He put the taper to the lantern wick, trimmed the wick to stop the flare of flame and replaced the glass before returning the lantern to its alcove. The light cast garish shadows in the dim room.

'Looks like I'll have to light the whole lot n—'

The taper dropped from Sol's fingers. The merchant was casting a shadow on the opposite wall. It spoke of a powerful upper body, long hair tied into waving braids and a thick fist wrapped around the goblet. It was utterly at odds with the man sat at the table and Sol knew the silhouette so well.

'Gods burning, Hirad, it *is* you.'

Sol's heart slammed in his chest and he shuddered throughout his body. His face felt hot and for a moment he thought he might faint. He strode to the table and stopped only when Hirad held up a hand.

'Best not hug me, big man. This shoulder's really starting to sting.'

'Then we'll bring Denser down to fix it. I'll send one of the boys. How could you possibly find me? How did you know I was here? How will the others get here?'

Sol felt giddy, light-headed like after his first sword fight. A mixture of excitement and fear but this time overlaid with an odd sense of detachment.

'This can't be real,' he muttered.

'I wish it wasn't,' said Hirad. 'Look, I can't answer everything. Ilkar understands it so much better. And Erienne too. It's to do with the familiarity of our souls. Almost like they are linked in some way. It meant we could all find each other when the attack started.'

Sol's elation dissipated. He sat back down and looked at Hirad in the merchant's body. He was quite still and in his eyes was an aching sadness.

'What happened?' asked Sol.

'How do I explain to the living how it feels to be thrust from rest?'

'Is that what it feels like when you're dead? Rest? What does it look like?'

'There aren't the words, Unknown. Or I certainly don't have them. There is no time; there are none of the things you associate with life. I don't know if there is colour but I do know there aren't trees, cities, any of that stuff. People assume that a glorious death will be like the sunniest day they can remember. It's nothing like that. Maybe Ilkar can describe it to you. I can't. But I do know it is peaceful and it is comfort and it is happiness. Or it was.

'We cannot fight and we cannot defend ourselves.' Hirad allowed himself a small smile. Sol was struck by how characteristic it was of him despite the merchant's face. Hirad continued. 'And that hurts almost as much as being here now. All those dead around you, you can sense them, you see? And you can taste their fear and feel their despair. They had nowhere to run. Most of them. Nowhere to go.'

Hirad's expression had become vacant and the body of the merchant wobbled before steadying. A hand gripped the table. The other put the wine goblet to his mouth.

'Fear makes you call out for those you love, Unknown. To be saved and be saviour. That's how we found each other again. And when the skin of the dimension was finally torn, we could sense you too. And Denser. You represent the end of a path and we found we could travel it, though it is like clinging to a rope in a hurricane. We dare not let go. Souls cast into the void will never be found and will roam without rest.

'None should suffer that. Not even the most evil of men.'

'But they are suffering it, aren't they, Hirad?'

A tear fell from Hirad's eye and ran down his pale cheek to drip onto the table top.

'Thousands of years and countless souls. No wonder the demons tried so hard to open the door to the dead. So many are already lost to the void and immeasurably more will follow. Any who cannot find a path back to the land where they once lived will become victims.' Hirad looked up and he was pressing his jaws together to hold back a sob or worse. 'You can hear them scream when they are torn away. Each one like a piece of skin ripped from your living body.'

Sol heard someone coming through the back gate and it reminded him he needed Jonas or young Hirad to go and ask for Denser up at the Mount of Xetesk. Just a short and familiar walk.

'What can be done?' asked Sol. 'Who is this enemy? Why do they attack you?'

'I have no answers,' said Hirad. 'We cannot see or feel them. All we know is that they are tearing our resting places apart and that they are following the fleeing dead too. We have to find a way to stop them. Should they wish to plunder Balaia too, we could all be lost.'

'But you have no reason to think that they will.'

'And also none to think they will not.'

'What do they want?' Sol's delight at Hirad's return had given way to a chill anxiety.

'I don't know, Unknown; I'm dead. We don't spend our time

gazing out at the living and being happy for your continued life, you know. Can you imagine how frustrating that would be?'

'We need Denser,' said Sol.

'Then it is fortunate that Denser is here already.'

Sol turned. Denser was walking around the bar, Diera following him. She was wringing her hands and had obviously been crying. He looked much as ever: frowning, severe and with the cares of the world on his shoulders.

'Pull up a chair. Diera will furnish you with a goblet, I'm sure,' said Sol.

He tried to catch her eye but she would not humour him. Instead she walked behind the bar and stooped to get a goblet for Denser.

'I'm here because Diera believes you have finally taken complete leave of your senses.'

Denser sat next to Sol and stared at the merchant, nodding minutely.

'But you don't think so, Denser. Do you?' said Sol.

'It is hard to know what to believe.' Denser glanced over at Diera. She was watching, listening, reluctant it seemed to come closer. 'Your wife was very upset. She didn't say much about why, just that you had caved in, just like she feared you would.'

Denser sucked his lip and turned to glare at Hirad.

'You know, I don't appreciate total strangers grinning at me like they've known me all my life,'

'Don't you recognise me, Denser?'

'No. I would have thought that was obvious.'

Sol found himself smiling and tried to cover it.

'Well, it's no surprise,' said Hirad. 'This isn't my original body after all. But I have to be honest, Xetesk-man, the years haven't been kind.'

Denser gaped. 'What?'

'Beard's gone grey, you're looking a bit paunchy in the cheeks and you're probably bald under that skullcap. Mind you, I see you've been promoted. Congratulations. Good to see you finally made something of yourself.'

Hirad pointed at the embossed bronze circle on the front of Denser's skullcap, which denoted his position as Lord of the Mount of the College of Xetesk.

Denser's eyes had narrowed and his cheeks were pointed with red.

'Clearly, you're angling for a matching wound on your right-hand side. Who is this cretin, Sol?'

'You ought to recognise the lack of tact if nothing else,' replied Sol. 'This is Hirad. Or rather, Hirad's soul in the body of a dead merchant.'

'God's falling, it's pathetic,' muttered Diera from the bar. 'See what I mean, Denser?'

But Denser didn't hear her. He was staring at Hirad, one hand absently scratching at his beard.

'It is technically possible, you see,' he said as if to himself. 'How are you doing it? Is the heart beating?'

'Not yet,' said Hirad. 'If it was, I'd die again, pushing blood out of this wound.'

'Well, we can soon fix that. Tell me how it works?'

'One soul leaves, another enters. Mine in this case. I was attracted to the body and filled it. I don't know how. Ilkar probably does. But it isn't too badly damaged or sick inside so I can hang on. Just about. But it hurts. I can make it move as if it were my own. But I need to get the heart to beat soon or Ilkar says I'll decompose.'

'Bloody hell, you smelled bad enough when you were alive,' said Denser.

Hirad chuckled. 'This body is altogether more fragrant.'

Denser stretched out a hand and felt Hirad's neck for a pulse.

'Amazing,' he muttered.

'Are you all right, Denser?' Sol put a hand on Denser's arm.

'You see, the thing is,' said Denser, 'I've got about fifty reports from around the city of dead people walking and talking. That's just in the last day or so. It's making people nervous, as you can imagine. And there's something a little closer to home too. I've got a five-year-old girl up at the Mount claiming she's Erienne.'

Chapter 4

The heat intensified still further. Steam billowed under the canopy. The orange glow of fire stretched in a broad arc east to west. Thick dust blew on a scorching wind. The flat clang of the Garonin harvesters thudded across the sky and under the earth. The roar of great beasts meshed with the crash of falling trees that signalled the death of the rainforest.

A face appeared in front of Auum's. Streaked with ash, eyes white and wide in the fire-backed half-light.

'They have breached the outer ring. We have had to fall back.' The Al-Arynaar warrior gripped Auum's shoulders. 'We have barely given them pause.'

'Yet every moment buys time for our people. What of the Temple of Ix?'

The warrior shook his head. 'Gone before those inside even knew what was upon them. Behind the fire, all is scorched and ruined. Auum, we cannot stop them.'

'I know that. We all know. Our task is to fight, die if we must, and pray our souls find the path to Shorth, though our enemies stand before us after death as they do in this life. Keep moving, keep hitting. We need to try and take down at least one of the machines. I will join you.'

Auum took the warrior's face in his hands and kissed his forehead. 'Faith, my brother. We knew this day would come.'

The Al-Arynaar nodded, turned and ran back towards the enemy, shouting others to his side. The din of conflict, screaming and fire was an assault on the ears. Auum looked about him. Everything they had was here. Every TaiGethen cell, every Al-Arynaar warrior, every ClawBound pair that answered the call to muster. And it was not enough. Ysundeneth, capital of Calaius, was only two days travel north. Beyond it, nothing but the southern ocean and seven days sailing to Balaia.

'Rebraal!' called Auum.

The leader of the Al-Arynaar was striding towards him. Blood matted the side of his face and leaked from beneath a bandage wrapped around his head.

'Auum, I thought you gone to oversee the Harkening.'

'Be assured, I will arrive there at the last possible moment. There is still damage to be dealt here. Listen to me. The Temple of Ix is gone.'

Rebraal closed his eyes briefly.

'Then we are silent,' he whispered. 'Balaia will not know what is coming.'

'They may already have arrived there,' said Auum. 'Tell me your news.'

'Everything we could retrieve from the remaining temples is nailed into crates and on wagons. All headed for the docks. The statue of Yniss at Aryndeneth has been lifted successfully and is already aboard ship. At least the Elfsorrow will not return unless the statue is broken again. All that could not be moved can only be lamented because it will inevitably be lost.

'So much of ourselves will be gone. And the people are confused and scared. They do not understand why Yniss will not act to save them. Many will perish unless the teachings of the ancients excite them to do what they have to do in order to survive. The ClawBound are doing all they can to bring the words home but I fear not all our ships will be fully laden. And there is tragedy in that.'

Auum inclined his head. 'Tragedy lies all around us already. Go to the ships. I will bring our warriors to you when we can do no more but die.'

'Do not overstay your welcome in the faces of our enemies.'

'Tual will guide my hand; Yniss will guide my mind. I will not fail.' Auum turned to his TaiGethen cell. 'Tai, we move.'

The three TaiGethen flowed over the parched ground and out of the forward camp that now lay less than a mile from the invasion front. Ahead of them through the withering rainforest were the orange glow of the burning canopy, the stultifying heat that pushed on before it and the last desperate defence against the Garonin.

Auum ran slightly ahead of Ghaal at his left shoulder and Miirt at his right. It had been hard learning to trust a new cell but he had chosen well, he believed. Now would be the test to end all others.

The land they trod was no longer their own. Auum knew they were moving south but no scent, no trail and no recognisable set to the foliage remained. He could no longer read this place. It had ceased to be their home, more alien than Balaia, to where the survivors would flee. Yniss had surely turned his back on them, unable to assist.

Smoke choked their lungs. Ash lay heavy in the air and crumbled underfoot. The green beauty was gone along with Tual's children, the forest denizens, replaced by a churned, dead land. The war had been lost the moment that Garonin had landed. All that was left now was survival.

The fight against the Garonin was confused and it had to be that way. The warriors of the TaiGethen and Al-Arynaar used the density of the canopy as best they could, keeping the enemy guessing. But with every Garonin pace forward, that density lessened and the fire that came in its wake took more lives.

Auum ran past an elf lying prone, his back a mass of charred flesh. Another tended to him but it would be hopeless. Not even magic could save him, and magic was being taken from them.

'Keep tight,' he said. 'Strike in, turn out. No hesitation.'

A series of white lights flashed through the trees at just above head height. Like teardrops but slicing horizontally, ripping through bark, sundering timber to pulp and bringing down mighty trunks. Fires leapt up where the teardrops impacted. Fire dampers ran in, those that still lived.

Warrior elves in deep green and brown camouflage clothing and paint criss-crossed his path. They were close now. The thud of the machines, the roar of the fires and the steady crump of beasts treading the ground filled the air.

'Do not be afraid to die,' said Auum. 'Our souls are promised to Shorth and he will find them.'

But images of the priestess in the temple of Shorth crowded into Auum's mind and he found himself doubting his own words.

'Yniss protect us,' he whispered. 'Your servants.'

And there they were. Garonin.

Auum stopped in his tracks, feeling a unique sense of fear. Just like before. Ancient history repeated.

'It'll never be over, will it?' said Miirt, her voice steady.

'*They* may not have changed. We are different,' said Auum.

'They do not need to change,' said Ghaal, who had stopped a pace ahead of him.

Auum followed his gaze. An arc of soldiers protected three

harvesters, each pulled by two of the great beasts. Hanfeer, the elves called them. Created for this single purpose. The harvesters were huge, bulbous skins taut with the pressure of the gas they contained. Their funnels belched waste into the sky, sensors sought new pockets of mana to exploit and the rumble of another detonation cloud built above.

The massed hundreds of warrior elves faced no more than sixty of the enemy and yet they were losing the fight here and on four separate fronts of which Auum had certain knowledge. The rainforest was being laid to waste.

'This is not as before,' said Auum. 'This level of destruction. This number of soldiers.'

'They come not just to harvest,' said Miirt. 'Their memories are long and bitter.'

God's Eyes castings struck at three enemy soldiers advancing on the left flank. One went down. The other two staggered and were driven to their knees under the force of the assault, their armour flaring a blinding white. Immediately, two TaiGethen cells sprinted in, backed by a number of Al-Arynaar warriors and mages.

Every Garonin head turned. In every hand, weapons were brought to bear, raised to the eyes and their power unleashed. Streams of white teardrops fled away. Vegetation from ground to ten feet in the air was obliterated, a path of energy driven towards the attacking elves and into their midst. Auum turned his eyes from the impacts but his ears could not block out the screams.

Elves ran in from all sides.

'Diversion,' said Ghaal.

Auum was already running. 'We are TaiGethen. We do not stand and watch our brothers die. Tai, to my mark.'

He made a curving run. Ahead and right an Al-Arynaar exploded under the weight of white tears thudding into her chest. Another lost an arm even as he raised it to strike. Auum kept his head down, pushing his legs to more speed, dragging hot, painful air into his lungs.

His target hadn't seen him yet. The soldier was moving steadily forward, his weapon still facing the initial attack point.

Auum's head cleared. He could hear his every breath and the sound of his feet on the cracked ground between the trees. He used what remained of the immediate cover as best he could. The world slowed around him. He closed on his enemy, his Tai at his heels. The Garonin saw them eventually, weapon beginning to come to bear.

Auum planted his right foot and used it to launch himself. He twisted as he came off the ground and brought his legs together. He spun in the air, his body a spear, his heels its tip.

Auum struck the soldier in the neck just above his weapon. The enemy could not absorb the blow and crumpled backwards. Auum raised his arms for balance, straightened and landed softly, coming to a crouch and drawing his twin short swords from their back-mounted scabbards. He turned.

Ghaal and Miirt were there before him, blades hacking and stabbing into gaps in the Garonin armour. Auum knelt across the enemy's neck and ripped away his helmet. The white lettering across the armour faded. What stared back at him was not human. Black orbs bulged from bony sockets. Flat nostril slits flared. The huge mouth clacked together, toothless ridges sampling the air. There was no fear in that face.

'We will find your weakness,' said Auum. 'And we will stop you.'

'Auum, you know better than that. You cannot beat us. Not in this world, nor in the next,' replied the Garonin. 'Yours will be the race extinct. None who escaped us once will do so again.'

The Garonin growled deep in its throat and vanished, leaving Auum clutching at empty air.

'The hanfeer,' he said. 'We can give them pause. Tai, we move.'

'He knew you,' said Miirt while they ran towards the great beasts. 'How did he know you? You cannot be so aged, even for an Ynissul.'

'My time is longer than you think,' said Auum. 'And it is not done yet.'

Precious few had broken through the protective arc to run towards the harvesters, their beasts and the Garonin who marshalled them. Auum tried to shut out the sounds of pain behind him. God's Eyes arced in overhead, splashing harmlessly against the shielding the harvesters possessed, doing little damage. The rumble was deafening here. The crushing of age-old timbers under the hooves of beast and runners of machine was an ugly symbol of death.

The fires at the rear of the machines ate at the dead ground and gorged at the excess gasses in the air, torching tree stumps and incinerating anything living that came into contact. Nothing would be left in the wake of their passing. Nothing.

Auum ran directly at a trio of Garonin in front of the centremost machine. His Tai were level with him. That the Garonin saw him was not in doubt, but their confidence was such that they did nothing to halt his advance. Theirs was millennia-old information. And it told them the elves would turn aside. Ten yards from them, Auum saw the first flicker of concern in the slight turning of a head.

'Split,' he ordered.

His Tai stepped aside left and right. Two paces later, all three dropped and rolled below the sweeping fists of the marshals, coming up behind them. Auum drove his blades into the gaps between boot and calf armour. The Garonin shrieked, anger and pain clashing as he pitched forward. Auum leapt on to his back, dragged his head back and drove a blade into the eye slit of his helmet. The Garonin jerked and disappeared.

Miirt and Ghaal had followed his lead, but to either side none of the other attacking elves had got any further.

'Strike and turn,' said Auum. 'Hesitation is death.'

He led them to the two hanfeer yoked to the vydosphere. Dull eyes peered from beneath heavy brows. Bone stood proud from flesh, natural armour against predators. But the beasts were weak in the legs, just like their masters. Auum moved in for the crippling blow.

This close, beast and machine were a sight to take the heart of even a strong elf. The hanfeer stood almost twice Auum's height, their massive shoulders straining against the yokes that they bore. Hawsers as thick as his thigh ran from the yokes to the machine, tensing and relaxing with each measured pace forward.

The vydosphere was a towering monument of creaking metal, raging heat and thrumming malevolence. Auum had no idea what much of it was made from. Its skin was not hide, more like expanding metal. The whole was as tall as a three-masted elven cutter, twice as broad as the ocean-going vessel and set on runners that barely settled on the ground, as if the hand of some giant were holding it just in contact. All that he saw, he logged for the future, for the time when they could strike back with an eye to victory, not to mitigate defeat.

White tears ripped up the earth in front of them. Auum threw himself to his right, the ground at his feet blistering and bubbling in the heat of the strike. He rolled and ran into the lee of the hanfeer pair. His Tai were still with him. Ghaal had fear in his face, Miirt was burned down her left leg.

'Strike and turn,' he repeated.

Auum's blades whipped down into the lower leg of a hanfeer. The beast bellowed, a primeval sound, and fell forward, its ankles collapsing under its weight. Immediately, an alarm rang out from the vydosphere. With a squeal, it halted, belching smoke. Miirt struck at the second beast, Ghaal with her. Blood gouted from deep wounds. Another scream of bestial agony.

'Run,' said Auum.

He led them right, away from the Garonin attacking them and briefly into the shadow of the vydosphere. Above him, its skin groaned and protested. He saw bubbles appear beneath its surface and a rippling that ran along a seam. Steam escaped.

The fires were close, the heat unbearable. He turned to run back into the rainforest. The remaining Garonin were all staring at the stricken hanfeer and the machine halted behind them. Some were moving, hurrying even, towards the beasts. Tears fled from weapons held high. Flesh ripped from the beasts, heads caved in. In that same moment, two more hanfeer blinked into existence. So did another thirty Garonin.

Auum glanced over his shoulder as he ran, free from attack for the moment. All the vydospheres had stopped. Every Garonin worked to shepherd the new hanfeer towards the yoke of the stranded machine. The corpses of the dead beasts were fading, taken back by their masters. Al-Arynaar and TaiGethen surged back to the attack, seeing opportunity.

But Auum knew they had already achieved what they must.

'Break off!' he yelled.

ClawBound heard him if no others could. The calls of panthers echoed across the battlefield. Warriors turned at once.

Auum raced back into the relative safety of the deep canopy, not pausing until he had reached the forward camp. Rebraal was issuing orders. Carts were rattling away towards the docks at Ysundeneth, three days distant. Squads of warriors were forming up, ready to join the attack.

'I thought I told you to leave for the docks,' said Auum. 'I need you standing with me at the Harkening.'

Rebraal smiled. 'Too many still left behind. I will leave with the last of them.'

'That time is now,' said Auum. 'We have stalled them for the moment. Precious time is ours. Use it. Evacuate the rest.'

'We can strike further. Damage them more.'

Auum shook his head and leaned in to whisper into Rebraal's ear.

'No, my friend. More have come. And not merely to harvest this time. To destroy us. More machines are arriving too. Enough to lay waste the entire rainforest. They mean to destroy us and our lands.'

Rebraal stared at him, not believing. 'They will not let us go?'

'And they will pursue us. They have not forgotten.'

Scant hundreds of yards to their left, a huge detonation. Flame swept across the horizon. Trees cracked and fell. Elves and animals screamed, broke and ran.

'How long have we lived here?' asked Rebraal.

'Three thousand years and more, and now we have no time,' said Auum. 'Miirt, have that leg healed. There is more work to do. Tai, we move.'

Chapter 5

There was an acid taste to the air. It was the sort of taint that signalled trouble for delicate grapevines.

Baron Blackthorne trusted that whatever caused it would not travel south to his burgeoning slopes. He was expecting a supreme harvest, much as Baron Gresse had been. And indeed the evening before there had been no hint of any problem. But this morning that aftertaste to every breath lingered.

The two men stood on the wide, decked veranda of the plantation lodge hidden among the hills, terraces and valleys of the Gresse vineyards. They had enjoyed a fine dinner the night before and had broken fast well this morning. But now coffee was growing cool in mugs and frowns weighted the brows of both men.

Gresse wrinkled his nose yet again.

'Stinks like old magic,' he said.

His voice, gruff for as long as Blackthorne could remember, was further deepened to a painful phlegmy rattle .

'You should have someone check out that throat of yours.'

'Hardly, Blackthorne. Damn mages have done enough damage to my land and people over the years. I'm not going to start entertaining them in my house now. Too old for that sort of thing.'

'You're what, sixty-five? A few years older than me, anyway. Never mind damage; you might even get saved.'

Gresse waved a hand impatiently. 'Cancer is just nature's way of telling you to step aside for your sons.'

'And you think that's what it is?'

'If the blood I cough up and the pain when I swallow are anything to go by.'

Blackthorne sighed. He couldn't help himself. He stared at Gresse and those sunken brown eyes stared back, the hanging skin on his cheeks quivered and the pale small mouth tugged into a smile. At least he had the decency to blush a little.

'Stubborn old goat,' said Blackthorne.

'It's the progression of life, my friend.'

'Yes, and I've lost enough to war, disease and demon to last two lifetimes. I don't need to lose any more unnecessarily. Certainly not those with a part to play while we try and climb out of the mess the demons left behind. It's not burning martyr I can smell but it surely should be, shouldn't it? What by the Gods falling is this defeatism?'

'You really want to know?'

'I'm all ears.'

'I am, as it happens, seventy-two, Blackthorne. Twelve years older than you. And I can't be bothered any more, I really can't. Look at you. I know the effort it takes for you to travel these days but you still haven't gone grey. Just a few flecks in that sculpted beard of yours. Hardly a crow's foot around the eye and think what you endured. Think what you still endure when the night releases the worst of your memories.'

Blackthorne reached for his coffee mug and found the tremble in his hand that usually only came on waking from his nightmares.

'So what's your point?' he asked a little more sharply than he intended. Gresse didn't seem to notice.

'Can't you feel it? It's not just the stench of old magic in the air. Something's on our skin. It's absorbing through every pore. I'd had enough of fighting when The Raven beat the Wytch Lords. And when was that . . . fifteen years ago, wasn't it? When the demons were defeated I thought we might actually see a lasting peace.'

Blackthorne spread his hands. 'Well, we have. Ten years and counting.'

Gresse shook his bald head. 'You know better than to believe it will last. You've had the visions and you've heard the voices. I can see it in your eyes.'

There was no hint of age or his illness diminishing his mind. Indeed Gresse seemed particularly sharp this morning.

Blackthorne studied the vines growing along the valley to the south of the lodge.

'I have nightmares, not premonitions,' he said.

'It comes to the same thing,' said Gresse. He coughed and put a hand to his lips. Blood stained the back of his index finger. 'And I can't fight any more. I just don't have the energy. Nor the passion.'

'So what is this smell in the air then?' asked Blackthorne.

'It is the start of whatever is to come. We'll know soon enough.'

Blackthorne drained his coffee, set down his mug and leaned on the veranda.

'If there's one thing I hate, it's people being mysterious and oblique. Do you know something or not?'

'It's just a feeling, Blackthorne. I've had them before and I've always been right. This is just worse than all the others and I don't have the will to face it.'

Blackthorne rounded on him. 'So you're just going to sit and rot in your rocking chair, is that it? You think any mage will rethink their morals and ethics merely because you choose to die rather than let them heal you?'

Gresse was staring right past him though, not hearing him.

'Told you,' he said.

Blackthorne followed his outstretched hand. Miles to the east, towards the mountains of the Burrs and away across rolling acres of vineyards and rich arable farmland, there was a shimmering in the air. Accompanying it was a very slight vibration beneath the feet as if the Earth itself was trembling. Up in the sky above the shimmering, cloud spewed to brief life and then burned away. A bleak foreboding settled on Blackthorne.

'We just never get a break, do we?' he whispered.

'I may not want to fight it, but that doesn't mean I don't want to see it,' said Gresse. 'Care to ride with me?'

Blackthorne nodded. 'Why not? Sight of the enemy brings with it the comfort of knowledge, so they say.'

'They, whoever they are, must be idiots. It's always struck me with dread.' Gresse clicked his finger at a servant. 'Have our horses saddled and ready at the north paddock on the instant. And we'll be needing a guard too. Half a dozen or so.'

'Yes, my Lord.'

'More coffee, Blackthorne? It might be a while till your next one.'

'Don't mind if I do.'

The riding was easy and would have been pleasant but for the dark thoughts Blackthorne could not keep from his mind. There was a noise in the back of his head too. Like a distant voice, familiar yet disconcerting. It became a persistent itch as they trotted and cantered up and down slope over Gresse's well-maintained vineyard trails.

It was a shame the glorious smells of sweet vine and young grape were obscured by the strengthening odour blowing over them from the east. Gresse was right. It did taste like old magic and more particularly like the product of something violent.

'It's a particularly painful way to go,' said Blackthorne. 'And before the end you won't even be able to eat, or drink your best reds and whites. Imagine that.'

The two men were some way ahead of Gresse's guard. Both barons wore light trail clothes and had cloaks tied to their saddles. Gresse hadn't even bothered with a weapon. Blackthorne couldn't face leaving a place of sanctuary without one even now.

'Trust me, it won't come to that. I shall sit in my rocking chair with a glass of the decade vintage and salute our enemies as they torch my vines.'

Blackthorne shook his head. 'Balaia never lies down.'

'Ah, but back then we had The Raven. Now what do we have? A grumpy man with an arthritic hip who is still unsure if he should be king or innkeeper. And a Lord of the Mount who has become far too deeply embroiled in college politics to see what is in front of his face. I've nothing against either of them personally. Sol has done some great work but the responsibility weighs too heavy on him. And he doesn't like the attention. "King" is too grand a term and Sol was right when he refused to adopt it. It's just a shame the populace didn't accept his decision. Whatever, the two of them are hardly saviour material. Not that it would matter if they were. Nothing can stop what is coming.'

'You don't know that,' said Blackthorne. 'You don't even know there *is* an enemy. All we've got so far is a heat haze and a rumble in the earth.'

But that was not entirely true and he knew it. Gresse had heard, just as he had, the clank and thud of machinery. It sounded much like someone perpetually raising and dropping a portcullis, though there was a wheezing undertone, like ten thousand Gresses drawing in pained breath as one.

'I've had the visions and the voices. And, deny it all you like, you have too. I just paid attention.'

They were riding up a steep valley side into which terraces had been cut for red grapevines. The path wound through the terraces, ascending gently. The morning was hot and the vibration under hoof combined with the shimmering air and the clanking of chain and metal to bring unease.

Beyond the valley edge, the land swept steeply down to rough grassland and, further east, fine farming territory. If whatever was coming was on the fields or open ground, they would be afforded a peerless view. Blackthorne was not convinced he wanted one. Looking to his left, he could see that Gresse was nervous. His tongue flickered over his front teeth and licked his top lip. His hands were white on the reins.

'We'll be plenty far enough back,' said Blackthorne.

'I do not share your confidence,' said Gresse.

They crested the rise.

'What in all of mighty fuck is that?' breathed Blackthorne.

Gresse would normally have chastised him for the use of language he attributed to Blackthorne's friendship with the lower classes. This time he was mute, merely shaking his head in reply.

Two miles away and advancing across the farmland, came, well . . . men, beasts and a machine, if such terms could be applied in this instance. Blackthorne had seen interesting plans for machines before, wine presses and the like. And Denser had once shown him the drawings for a machine designed to trap and hold demons. But they were nothing like this, whatever it was. Those had been relatively small devices. This was more akin to a ship on a sled being pulled across the land by beasts of burden. And whatever the beasts were, they weren't oxen or mules.

It was a while before they could see absolutely clearly, until the figures and their contraption had materialised from the shimmering in the air. Blackthorne wished they had remained indistinct. The machine was simply incomprehensible. The size of an ocean-going trader, it was principally a long, slender oval from which jutted multiple funnels, each angled differently from the next, over thirty of them and yet maintaining a sculpted poetry. From a raised spine, what looked like five masts fled skywards. Each held four spars and from these spars drifted dozens of lines that probed at the air as if seeking something.

It was a striking piece of work, and while Blackthorne had no idea what it was actually doing, the effects of its passage were as clear as they were devastating. The land in its wake was burned and ruined. Buildings were levelled and trees torched such that only broken blackened stumps remained. Flora and fauna were simply smoothed from existence as easily as Blackthorne might blow dust from a book. Man and animal eliminated without a cry. And for what purpose?

'It isn't the only one,' said Blackthorne. He pointed away to the north where more cloud smudged the sky, dark and filled with lightning. 'And see how the damage spreads in the wake of the thing. If it continues and if there are enough of these machines . . .'

'. . . then the whole land will be consumed,' breathed Gresse. 'Who are these people?'

The machine was being pulled along by a pair of massive brown hairless beasts with tiny heads, barrel bodies and enormously powerful legs. Blackthorne switched his gaze onto the figures walking ahead of them.

They were three in number, walking at a languorous pace. Deliberate, a plodding speed more like shire horse than man. Yet they ate up the ground. Behind them, the machine rumbled. Heat swept out from it in waves, creating the shimmer in the air. A cloud formed above it, shot through with flames of green, blue, yellow and orange.

The outlines of the figures distorted in the force of the inferno at their backs. They had come quite close before Blackthorne realised how tall they were. Perhaps eight feet. Huge bodies wearing ornate helms. Bone spurs jutted from shoulder guards. Ribs of boned leather layered torsos and legs. Gauntlets of obsidian and white covered huge hands. He could see no weapons.

The three walked in a loose line. The full faces of their helms, carved to depict something Blackthorne was too far away to discern, looked unflinchingly forward. Not a glance to their machine or beyond it to the annihilation of everything in their wake.

'Well, that clears it up,' said Gresse when the machine quietened and the cloud dispersed. 'Magic's involved somewhere, wouldn't you say?'

'Those colours leave little room for doubt,' agreed Blackthorne.

'Then I won't be welcoming them onto my lands.'

He swung his horse about and cantered back down the slope, shouting orders to his guard. Blackthorne chased after him, glancing to the north and south to see yet more shimmering in the air.

'I thought you were too tired to fight any more,' he shouted when he caught up with the older man.

'But the idea was to leave all my worldly goods to my children. Can't have them wiped out now, can I?'

'What do you intend to do?'

'Bring everyone I can and ask these gentlemen politely to stop and turn back. That or get carved up. The choice will be theirs.'

'I don't share your confidence,' said Blackthorne.

'And nor should you, as I have none to spare.'

'We've been monitoring some very odd movements in the mana flow all over Balaia. Research on inter-dimensional magics has had to be suspended because the streams have been rendered unstable by something we are trying hard to fathom . . . sudden huge dropouts in the density of mana. Like someone's blotting it up and leaving nothing behind. Am I boring you, Hirad?'

'What do you think?'

'Your ignorance is not my concern,' said Denser.

'Gods falling, Denser, I've been dead ten years. There are gaps in my knowledge.'

'There were plenty of those when you were alive.'

'It was part of my charm,' said Hirad.

'So what's with the sighing and the tapping of your foot? Or the foot of the dead man whose body you have appropriated.'

'I just don't see what it has to do with our problem.'

Hirad felt hot. It was not a sensation he was familiar with any more. He felt like his body wasn't big enough to contain him, like he was pushing at the skin from within, threatening to burst out. And his head was thumping madly, blurring the merchant's already poor vision still further. Hirad didn't know how to stop it. Maybe he needed a bigger body or something. Ilkar would know. If Ilkar ever made it here.

'You're telling me you fail to see a connection between the mana shield around the dead dimension being ripped to shreds, and disturbing changes to mana flow pretty much everywhere else?'

'I'm telling you I don't much care. I just want to go back but I can't. It's all any of us want.' Hirad couldn't fail to notice Denser's cheeks colouring. 'All right, all right. Tell me what it all means.'

'It means our dimension is under attack too.'

'Strange thing but I thought that's what I came here and said.'

Hirad scratched his head. Everything felt wrong. It was like someone was trying to pull him out of his body. He glanced at his shadow. It was shredding like paper in a gale. He put his hands over his ears.

'You all right, Hirad?' asked Sol.

'Dear Gods drowning but it hurts,' said Hirad. 'I think I'm going to explode out of this skin.'

'That'll be your ego trying to escape,' said Denser.

Hirad laughed and the pain eased a little. 'Not bad. Not bad at all.'

'Never mind that,' said Sol. 'What does the pain mean?'

'I don't know, Unknown.' Hirad couldn't keep the exhausted whine from his voice. 'I'm not supposed to be here. I think I need to be with the others. It always felt easier when our souls were close.'

'You should bring Erienne down here,' said Sol.

Denser shook his head. 'We should all go to the Mount. You need to open your bar and then join us. There is already unease on the streets. We need as much normality as possible. We need you on the street doing kingly things.'

Hirad screwed his eyes shut. There was a lengthy silence.

'So,' he said to Sol eventually, 'you got a promotion too, did you?'

'It's not how it sounds,' said Sol. 'I'm just an occasional spokesperson for the ordinary Balaian. People come to me with problems; I try and sort them out.'

'I think you're being a little modest,' said Diera. 'He brokered peace with the Wesmen; he's set up trade agreements with the elves on Calaius that brought us the food and wealth to rebuild; and he chairs the meetings between the colleges, lords and barons. Someone has to see fair play.'

Sol smiled at her and she stroked the top of his head, pride in her eyes for a change.

'Shame I believe in dead people walking though, right?'

'*King*,' said Hirad. 'Well that sounds about right, I reckon. And in how ever many years it is they haven't built you a palace? Very poor. And what's more, you're still working behind a bar.'

'All right, Hirad,' said Sol.

'I suppose it keeps you in touch with the common man. What do they call your courtiers? "Bar staff", is it?'

'Hirad. Enough.'

'And no crown, either. For the best. Must be hell trying to keep it on that slippery bald head of yours.'

Denser cleared his throat. 'The point is, Sol can calm people down by being outside and strolling around. Making it seem like nothing untoward is happening until we have a plan of some kind.'

Hirad snorted. 'And you think dead merchants possessed by old Raven souls is out of the ordinary, do you?'

Denser smiled. 'Maybe just a little.'

'I just can't believe you are swallowing any of this nonsense,' said Diera.

'I know what this must sound like to you—'

'I'm sure you do, *Hirad*.'

'I'll prove to you I am who I say I am, Lady Unknown, I promise. I can't ask you to trust me but do one thing.'

'What's that?'

'Be ready to leave.'

'No one's leaving,' said Denser.

'Just be ready,' said Hirad. He glanced at Denser. 'Just in case.'

Chapter 6

No one wanted to get so close but the men and their machine were not going to stop.

Gresse, Blackthorne and thirty riders drew up on the downward slope of the outermost of Gresse's vineyards. The invaders had not paused. Behind the machine the devastation stretched as far as the eye could see and the totality of it was breathtaking. The expansion north and south continued, like a creeping disease. Nothing but scorched soil, blackened trees and broken walls was left behind. Of people and animals, there was no sign whatever. Consumed in the fires that burned so terribly hot.

'And do you still feel your tactic is right as you stand here?' asked Blackthorne.

The debate had gone on for the entire ride. Both men had to raise their voices. The clanking of the machine was echoing from distant valley sides and its alien rumble underfoot made the horses skittish. While they watched, another cloud formed. Another wash of heat. More obliteration of Balaia's beautiful land.

'Look at them, Blackthorne. A bunch of Wesmen waving swords is something I understand. This . . .' he waved a hand at the approaching party '. . . casual harvesting is something else. It suggests supreme confidence, does it not?'

'So why would they stop to talk to you?'

'A couple of reasons. One, everyone is open to a bargain of some sort and I cannot believe we have nothing to offer them. Two, if they don't, I will attack them. They are not setting foot on my land.'

Blackthorne raised an eyebrow. 'So you've said a dozen times. But we are not equipped for a fight. Gods drowning, I'm here on a relaxing wine-drinking break. I have none of my regular soldiers with me, and my armour is trail dusty at best.'

'What choice do I have?'

'Well, let my mages take them out from a distance. We need never get involved. You know it makes sense.'

'I'm surprised at you, Blackthorne. You were always a man who liked to negotiate.'

'That was before the demons came.'

'These are not demons,' said Gresse.

'How can you be sure? And if your feelings are to be believed, they're even worse.'

Gresse's eyes narrowed. 'This isn't like you, Blackthorne. How would it be if they were approaching your vines, eh? Kill from a distance, is it? It's like you've lost your nerve.'

Blackthorne felt a surge through his body and bit back his first words. He leaned close to Gresse, his eyes boring into the older man's bright gaze.

'Damn right I lost my nerve. I watched the demons take my lands, my town and the souls of my people. I heard them battering on the doors of my castle. I had to stay strong for the ever-dwindling number of survivors. I lost my dearest friends, my closest advisers and I lost my Luke. Taken from right under my nose.

'Right up until the end they hammered and picked and gathered ground. Each day they gained strength while we weakened. We were alone, barricaded into the kitchens in the final days. Twenty thousand reduced to a paltry handful. Men so terrified by the relentless grind and the knowledge that a single touch meant perpetual torment that it was only memory that kept them going, kept them fighting.

'All the while, the demons delighted in our suffering. They knew our souls were as good as theirs and they waited for the inevitable. They could taste the fear; they breathed it, exulted in it. Day after long, tortured day. Night after desperate night. No respite, no rest, no salvation. No hope.'

Blackthorne's hands were clutched tight around the reins of his horse and trembling violently. He straightened in his saddle, trying to calm himself. But the visions flooded him. The masses outside his defensive spell ring, clawing to get in. The demon master, Ferouc, chilling and determined. The hordes of baying minions waiting their chance. His people standing with him even though they must have known he could not save them. Fighting and falling at his side. Luke, cold and dead in a place Blackthorne had told him was safe.

'But you did it. You won.' Gresse's voice was quiet and gentle.

Blackthorne scoffed. 'Won? It was not victory. Not for us. Survival of the very few because The Raven did what had to be done and laid down their lives for us all.'

'It is what we all had to do,' said Gresse. 'Just try to stay alive and pray someone would do something to free us. We had to make sure there was still a Balaian people to rebuild. We had to make sure there was something left.'

'I cannot shake the nightmares, Gresse. I have forgotten what a peaceful night's sleep is. They left so little behind. And that is why we cannot afford to talk to those who would take what we still have. That is why you should be pounding them with Cleansing Flame and Winter's Touch. Ripping their flesh with IceBlades.'

Gresse reached out a gloved hand and squeezed Blackthorne's forearm through his riding coat.

'I will be forever sorry I was not standing with you, old friend.'

'You had your own battles to fight. Though I would have gained strength from your presence,' said Blackthorne. He sighed. 'You must do what you feel to be right. These are your lands.'

Gresse nodded. 'But all the same, should I fail, at least you have a plan, eh?'

'Yep. Cast everything I have and run for it. Some plan.'

'See you back at the lodge for that fine dry white I was talking to you about.'

'Don't die,' said Blackthorne. 'After all, I don't know where you keep your best cut crystal.'

Gresse took his twenty men and set off down the slope. So easy to be brave when you had the advantage of height and the buffer of distance. But this was like riding into the shadows of mountains. Gresse had not grasped quite how big the invaders were, how vast their machine or how immense their beasts.

His horses, a quarter the size of the other animals, would not close further than a hundred yards. Gresse couldn't blame them. Down here, on the flat and even, the reason for the invaders' confidence was clear enough. They dwarfed everything else. The vibrations through his feet shook the vertebrae in his back. Each footfall of a beast rattled the earth under his boots. Each drag of the machine was like the thrum of a thousand horses. Each blast of the machine's infernal workings was a rake of fear dragged across his heart.

The stench was powerful, nauseating. It brought tears to the eyes and a turning of the gut. This close, the ambient heat of the machine brought sweat to his brow. But he walked as steadily as he could to within fifty yards and stopped outside the line of his first vines. His men gathered about him, some casting guiltily envious glances at the three left behind to keep hold of the horses.

Watching the men and their machine approach, Gresse was acutely aware that, should they decide not to stop, there was little he could realistically do to save his party from being trampled underfoot. They might be able to bring down the walkers but halt the machine? Hardly.

Gresse was too in awe of the scale of those approaching to be truly frightened. But the moment he realised the giants had taken notice of him, he began to shake. It wasn't dramatic but it was there, in his heart and in the deeps of his courage. Anyone able to look into his soul would see his fear.

Only ten yards from where he stood the central figure waved a hand, a languid gesture in keeping with their unhurried, strolling gait. The mighty beasts snorted, shook and bowed their heads, bellowing their displeasure. The sound startled man and horse alike. Gresse heard a shout and the thundering of hooves.

'Looks like we'll be walking back to the lodge then,' muttered a guardsman.

'The exercise will do us no end of good,' said Gresse. 'Face forward. Don't flinch.'

The machine halted and fell silent. The quiet was almost as shocking as the noise had been. Gresse could not hear a bird. But as the heat haze began to fade in the machine's wake, he had his closest glimpse yet of what was being done to his country. The accompanying anger did nothing to quell his dread.

The three figures approached. As Blackthorne had guessed, they were a good eight feet tall. Every stride ate up the space, the thud of their footfalls like tolling bells.

Those boots, their leggings and breastplates were all like leather but not. Apparently flexible yet burnished the way only metal could be. The designs upon the armour, if such it was, were as alien as anything the Calaian elves might dredge from their long and isolated history. A homage to ancient Gods perhaps. There were supplicating hands, spears of fire and great open maws wrought in chaotic fashion across the centre of each wide chest. And surrounding the images were either letters of a language he could not begin to fathom or angular scrollwork.

'They look like mathematical symbols,' he said.

'Beguiling, almost, my Lord,' said his captain.

The designs were picked out in a silver-coloured material that seemed to shimmer, even move, as the figures took each stride. It was not until the three of them stopped just five paces away that Gresse saw that his eyes had not deceived him. The silver settled to a gentle pulsing, only hurrying around those disturbing full-face helms as they looked down upon him.

Gresse could discern nothing about the figures inside. The narrow eye slits betrayed nought but shadow. More of the leather-like armour hung from the base of the helmets to cover the neck completely. The face plates themselves were carved with more of the symbols and with mouths open to scream. Of hands clawing for mercy. Livid images of pain.

'You are on the borders of my lands,' said Baron Gresse. 'I would know your intention before requesting you turn aside. You may not bring your machine any further.'

The figures did not respond at once. The three heads angled towards one another and moved as if they were conversing, yet without words. Gresse exchanged a glance with his captain, who shrugged his own uncertainty.

'I will have a response,' said Gresse at length.

The centremost figure turned back to him.

'My . . . apologies. Your language is seldom heard and less well understood.'

Gresse was startled. The words flowed like music, though slightly discordant. Symbols on the figure's clothing shone briefly. The figure cleared his throat and this time was beautifully in tune.

'That is better. We cannot accede to your request. Our route takes us one way only. If you stand on your lands as you say then we shall be walking across them. The lines of energy dictate such. But have no concern. We will take nothing that we do not need. We are simple foragers but we must collect or many will perish.'

'Collect what?' asked Gresse, transported so far by the gorgeous tones of the figure's voice that he found it hard to be angered by the rebuff.

'Material for our fight. Energy for our weapons and strength for our armour. Our foe grows more powerful and our need grows with it. If we are not to be defeated, we must bring fuel for our fires. Clear the path. Our time is precious.'

Gresse held up both hands, the spell of the glorious male voice broken.

'Whoa, whoa! I don't think so, forager. These are my lands and I decide who crosses them. And you will turn aside and you will not operate that machine in my country. You are destroying our lands and that cannot be allowed.'

The forager glanced back over his shoulder. Gresse thought he might have seen the ghost of a shrug.

'Damage is temporary. Your vegetation will regrow.'

Gresse gaped. '*Temporary?* You bastard.' He jabbed a finger at the devastation. '*People* lived out there. They won't regrow, will they?'

'People must learn to avoid the compass of the vydosphere. Until then, there will, unfortunately, be casualties.'

Gresse looked briefly at his captain. The soldier stared back, shaking his head, mirroring the baron's disbelief.

'And you think I'm just going to let you amble across my lands and swallow your temporary damage and unfortunate casualties, is that right?'

The forager straightened; Gresse hadn't realised he was leaning forward. The other two turned their heads and there was another silent exchange.

'We consider that you have no choice. We are Garonin. Stand aside. Our conversation is at an end.'

'Damn right,' said Gresse. 'Captain, let's cut these bastards down to size.'

Gresse heard the noise of the machine roaring back into life. He heard his captain order the attack. He even drew the sword one of Blackthorne's men had lent him. And the last things he remembered clearly were the sensations of swift airborne travel and of heavy impact.

'Take them down, take them down!' yelled Blackthorne at his mages.

The baron was already running towards Gresse, who had landed in a heap and rolled three times before coming to a stop. Action was all that prevented Blackthorne from refusing to believe what he had just seen. A brief conversation, plenty of finger pointing and, latterly, drawn swords. But never mind all that. Lines on the armour of the figures had blazed with light which had lashed out at Gresse and his men.

The invaders themselves didn't so much as move a muscle. Yet Gresse was hurled fully fifty yards back and he was the lucky one. Others who had rushed in more quickly were lying dismembered amongst the first row of vines. A few had survived the initial onslaught and were being ignored by their attackers while they screamed their agony clinging onto the stumps of hands, fought with boiling entrails or stared wide-eyed at terrible gashes. And all in the blink of an eye.

The invaders moved on. One stopped to brush what must have been gore from his boot and then all reassumed their long, casual stride, the machine following in their wake.

'Get messengers back to the lodge. Every mage to be ready. Every horseman saddled and awaiting a message to take out to the cities and towns.'

Blackthorne shouted his orders over his shoulder as he ran head-long down the slope, using vines to break his speed. Gresse was moving but it meant little. One leg was broken at the knee and jammed under his body at a sickening angle. There was crimson staining the dry earth. The enemy would roll right over him.

Every fear that Blackthorne had for Balaia surfaced once more. Every nightmare revisited him in those few moments while he slipped and slithered to his friend. And all that Gresse had said so recently hung in the air to taunt him.

The air flashed yellow. Blackthorne turned to see God's Eyes arcing high towards the enemy. Six of them, moving fast.

'Catch those, you bastards,' he said.

Blackthorne saw the trio tracking the skull-sized orbs of mana fire. They made no attempt to run and he got the impression they were merely curious about what was coming at them. They didn't break stride, they didn't flinch. The orbs struck them square on. Armour flared. Yellow light swept across the valley floor. An alien screech echoed out.

And when the light faded, Blackthorne could see the invaders lying motionless, burning brightly. Behind them, the machine and the animals that pulled it had stopped. Blackthorne jumped to his feet and punched the air.

'Die screaming, you fuckers!' he shouted, and cheers rose from the watching riders and mages.

At his feet, Gresse coughed. Blackthorne knelt to tend to him and found the older baron smiling.

'You still can't shake it off, can you?' Gresse said, voice sounding strong and sure.

'What, old friend?'

'That gutter language Hirad Coldheart taught you when he was living in the Balan Mountains all those years back.'

Blackthorne chuckled. 'He had a unique way with words, it's true. Effective if a little lacking in sophistication at times. Right. Think I'd better arrange a stretcher for you. That leg looks bad.'

'You should try knowing how it feels,' said Gresse.

'Lie still.'

'I hadn't thought to leap nimbly to my feet.'

Blackthorne stood and waved a rider to him. 'I need four men and I need a stretcher rigged up. There'll be plenty of material back at the lodge. Be quick. And send a mage. Baron Gresse needs his pain removed.'

'I do not need a mage, thank you very much.'

'Yes, you do, Gresse. Trust me on this. Go.'

'Yes, Baron.'

The rider turned and put his heels to his horse. The animal galloped away. Blackthorne sat on the dusty ground next to Gresse and looked down over the valley. The corpses of the invaders still burned. Behind them, the machine was quiet and the beasts were still, staring straight ahead. Some of his mages were making a slow and wary approach. One glanced in his direction and he nodded his permission for them to continue.

'I wonder who they were,' said Blackthorne.

'Garonin. Or I think that's what one of them said.'

'Well it's a name, but I was thinking a little more widely than that.'

Gresse drew in a pained breath.

'There'll be a mage here soon,' said Blackthorne.

'I'll try to contain my excitement,' said Gresse. 'So what do you think? From another dimension?'

'Probably. Good to see them folding under spell attack, though. It means we can fight them.'

'And win.'

'Easily.'

A smell of burned mana drifted across them. A moment later the valley was crowded with Garonin. Blackthorne shot to his feet, gaping. Fifty and more of them where a heartbeat before there had been none. Materialising as if dispelling a massed Beyen's Cloak spell. And these had not come merely to walk in front of the machine. As the beasts' roars split the air and they began to walk, Blackthorne could see what he assumed were weapons in the hands of most of the new invaders. They advanced.

'Gresse, I don't think we can wait for that stretcher.'

Chapter 7

The mournful calls of the ClawBound soared above the anxious rainforest, a companion to Auum's run north with his Tai towards Ysundeneth. The proud roar of the panthers, the guttural call of the elves combining to summon the nation to the Harkening. By day a clarion call to action. By night a haunting resonance that denied rest and demanded movement.

Every creature in the rainforest heard the song. For Tual's denizens, it was an alien sound that kept them in hides, burrows and nests; for the elves, a sign of mortal peril that none dare ignore.

From every corner of the mighty rainforest they came. Temples were left untended. Villages and towns deserted. Crops abandoned and fishing fleets drawn up onto riverbanks. All making the journey that had existed before only in legend and myth, lost in the ancient writings of elven history. Still, some had personal memories of the time before they would rather forget. All gathering at the huge natural amphitheatre that the elves called Ultan-in-Caeyin, where Gods are heard.

The last gathering here had taken place in the aftermath of the Elfsorrow which humans had unleashed on Calaius and which other humans had helped defeat. Auum had not been in attendance. This time it had to be different. Then it had been in celebration, now it was in fear of extermination.

Ultan-in-Caeyin was a gem unearthed not long after the founding of Ysundeneth on the northern coast of Calaius. A huge bowl of stone and grass banks on the edge of the rainforest, carved by the Gods for their words to be heard. Ringed by sheer cliffs, bordered by river and ocean, it had been embellished over the years. A vast stage stood at the northern end away from the entrance. Bridges and paths had been laid for people to walk the short distance from the city's western edge. Hundreds of brackets for torch and lantern had been hammered into the walls. Benching had been built in vast concentric arcs. Ultan-in-Caeyin could seat two hundred thousand comfortably.

Auum shuddered as he approached the wide entrance. Elves were streaming in and that was bad enough. But inside there were, he was told, upwards of thirty-five thousand already assembled. He stopped and stared at the masses inside. The gloom of evening was descending. Cook fires were being lit all across the bowl.

'Is there no other way to the stage?'

'Straight ahead is the only way,' said Ghaal.

Auum looked over at the stage, impossibly distant through the throng and blazing with light that taunted him. The walls of the Caeyin appeared to press in, sheer and impassable, pushing the crowd in, shoving them towards him. He backed up a pace.

'I don't like crowds,' he said.

Miirt exchanged glances with Ghaal.

'We will make passage for you,' she said.

Auum nodded his thanks. 'You are sure?'

'We were not born as you were,' she said.

'Tai, we move,' said Auum. 'Quickly.'

Elves outside the warrior castes stepped aside for he and his Tai to make their way to the stage. The faces that turned towards him were anxious but cleared on sight of him. He betrayed no fear, nodding at those who bowed their heads to him though he wanted no more than to close his eyes and have it all be over.

Word of his arrival spread like oil over sword steel and a hush descended on the Caeyin.

'Even when they are quiet, they make noise enough to shatter bark,' said Auum.

His Tai kept their silence, moving fluidly at his sides. He was glad of their attentions. Fine additions to the calling though none could ever truly replace those he had lost. He would forever mourn Evunn and Duele. At least their souls had made the journey to rest with the elders.

Rebraal was awaiting them on the stage. With a trembling hand Auum acknowledged the applause that broke out.

'Why do they applaud?' he asked, taking Rebraal's arm and leading him to a dark corner at the back of the stage.

'The great Auum is among them,' said Rebraal a broad smile on his face. 'Reluctantly. Why would they not?'

'None of them knows me.'

'There is nothing anyone hates more than unfounded modesty,' said Rebraal. 'Your reputation has no need of embellishment.'

Auum faced him. 'All my work, I do for Yniss. These people are Tual's people and Tual kneels before Yniss. That is enough.'

'The world has changed since you first ran in the rainforest,' said Rebraal. 'Then, people feared the TaiGethen because they did not understand your purpose or your methods. Now, while they are still wary of you, they revere you also. They love you. It is you who protects them from harm.'

'Not this time,' said Auum. 'That is why we are here. Shorth remains silent. Yniss cannot help us.'

'He will always watch over us.'

'Only if he is able.' Auum gazed out over the crowd from the shadows. It had become obvious to most that he had no intention of speaking and the hubbub of conversation was growing once more. 'So tell me, Lord of the Al-Arynaar, how soon can we leave Calaius?'

'I'm just . . .' began Rebraal, then he chuckled. 'All right, point taken. Preparations are going as well as they can. There is scepticism and resistance as you can imagine but we are getting through to most of the people who matter. Ships are assembling. We have pledges from three hundred and we hope for more every day.'

'That is nowhere near enough.'

'I cannot produce ocean going vessels out of thin air. We should give thanks for the huge trade we have developed with Balaia or we'd be in a worse state.'

'I know.' Auum nodded. He felt weary. Like a two-day fever at its height. 'You have the administrators of Ysundeneth working?'

'They have some of the Ynissul amongst them,' said Rebraal. 'They understand.'

'So few remain,' said Auum. 'Too many chose to die, thinking we were forever safe.'

'You didn't.'

Auum felt no satisfaction. 'Elves are never safe from harm. What is it, Rebraal?'

'What do you mean?'

'You are twitching away like a stranger bitten by a taipan. Speak your mind.'

'We're just running away. Can we really not beat them?' The words came in a rush when they started. 'We have lived here so long. We have beauty and we have peace. We have the rainforest. So much to lose.'

Auum shook his head, feeling every year he had breathed the air. 'They are too strong. Even for us, and we have worked so hard to keep ourselves hidden and to build our strengths. They are relentless. A menace without conscience. Without mercy.'

He closed his eyes against the memories.

'You faced them.' Rebraal breathed in sharply. 'Didn't you?'

Auum blinked and opened his eyes onto the young elf's steady gaze. 'And I ran. It is easy for you who were born here to believe this your home for all time. I've lived through too much history ever to get comfortable. I have watched too many friends die.'

'At least you have the blood to grant you all those years.'

'It is not the blessing you think it to be,' said Auum sharply.

'I'm sorry, Auum. I didn't mean that quite the way it came out.'

Auum nodded. 'I am certain you didn't. But the nation is in peril. Old prejudices never die, they merely hide.'

'You know Ilkar once said he almost wished he had never met a human much less befriended one. Hard to outlive those you love by so many hundreds of years, he said. It was the thing he feared the most.'

'Your brother was right about that, just as he was right about many things.'

'I can't feel him,' said Rebraal. 'Is he safe?'

Auum sighed and shook his head. 'We none of us can feel those we love. Last time it was the same. The dead were not safe. Many were lost to Shorth, never to be found again. I'm sorry.'

Expectant noise rippled across the crowd in the Caeyin. Robed elves hurried hither and thither across the stage. Auum trotted back out into the light. The TaiGethen arrived thus far assembled behind him.

'It's the priests,' said one.

'Early,' said Ghaal in Auum's ear.

'That cannot be good,' said Miirt.

A crescent of Al-Arynaar warriors and mages was advancing down the wide central aisle of the Caeyin. Behind them came seven separate groups of priests and attendants, each one guarded by two TaiGethen cells. At the rear, more Al-Arynaar. Auum could just see the silhouettes of ClawBound pairs at the entrance to the bowl. And at the head of the cliffs all around the Caeyin, more ClawBound appeared. Sentinels and messengers, waiting.

Auum spared the time to wish he were up there in glorious solitude rather than in front of a crowd that was swelling every moment.

'They are not all here,' said Ghaal. He pointed out into the midst of the approaching priests. 'Ryish is missing.'

'I expected it to be so,' said Auum. 'He would not leave his temple, not while the path to Shorth is obscured. We must assume he is lost.'

Quiet replaced expectancy. Out there, where the knowledge of why they had been summoned to the Harkening was incomplete, the nervousness was beginning to grow. For many, the significance of the priests' early arrival was not lost. And anyone who cared to look at the stage to see it filling with TaiGethen and Al-Arynaar would be forgetting the food they had thought to cook. The last time Auum had been in the presence of so many of the warrior castes, they had been about to sail for Balaia. So it would be again.

When they reached the stone apron in front of the stage, the Al-Arynaar fanned out to guard its periphery. The apron, a huge slab of granite laid by the Gods, was carved with the elven religious hierarchy, depicting its many glories. Each group of priests moved to pray by its God's symbols and images.

Yniss, father of them all; Tual, of the forest denizens; Gyal, of the rain; Beeth, of root and branch; Orra, of the earth's lifeblood; Cefu, of the canopy, Ix, god of mana. All were represented, leaving a hole at their centre where Ryish should have been standing.

Everyone dropped to their knees, fingers grasping the ground or palms raised to the sky, spread like branches or covering their faces. Each elf was drawn to a lesser god in addition to Yniss. Each elf prayed. Whispering and chanting grew in harmony, amplified by the rock walls of the Caeyin. Caressing the mind and soothing away ache, pain and fear. Auum shed a tear for the beauty of the moment and for the knowledge that precious few remained.

While the prayers continued, the high priests moved onto the stage. Each wore robes of a single, simple colour and carried the words that blessed them with their authority sewn onto their robes and written in the leather-bound volumes in their arms. Auum felt a hand on his shoulder and looked up.

'My Lord Auum, it is with gladness that I see you and with desolation that I know why.'

Lysael, High Priest of Yniss, had always been possessed of a beautiful voice. Beauty that spread to her face and the shape of her gentle hands.

'Yniss keep you, Lysael. I am relieved you are here.'

'Stand, Auum; you and your TaiGethen have no need to kneel before anyone, least of all the mere mouthpiece of a God.'

Auum stood and the two embraced. From the crowd he could hear cheering, and the chanting in the name of Yniss grew louder. Lysael kissed his forehead and stepped back. Her expression brought fresh tears to Auum's eyes.

'We cannot wait until the appointed day to perform this Harkening,' she said. 'Let the ClawBound sing now.'

'It will be done. And we'll talk later.'

Auum moved past her to the front and centre of the stage. Few probably noticed him. Most were still engaged in prayer, chant and song celebrating the arrival of their priests. All but ignored, Auum turned to face the stone at the back of the Caeyin, spread his arms wide, tipped back his head and called to the ClawBound.

'Jal-ea! Jal-ea! Jal-ea.'

On the second repetition, he held the 'a'. The note boomed around the bowl, flying up the walls and into the darkening sky. It stilled song and chant and reduced prayer to a whisper. A ripple fled across the crowd and the ClawBound sang the final call to the Harkening.

It had no words. From the mouths of the panthers came a circulating low growl that echoed and layered in melancholy, from the Bound elves a sound from the top of the throat that ran up and down a scale of high pitch, modulating and harmonising. It cut through the air. It would travel through roof and wall. It would traverse the harbour and penetrate the timbers of every ship. None within earshot who heard it would deny the call. They could not.

The ClawBound would sing until night was full. And then all the elves gathered at Ultan-in-Caeyin would hear their fate.

Denser was aware that the four of them were attracting considerable attention. In one respect, it was what he wanted. The citizens needed to see their rulers taking the short walk along The Thread up to the Mount of Xetesk in apparent calm. Yet there was no disguising the tension that pervaded the streets. It had deepened even in the short time he had been in The Raven's Rest.

The walk was uncomfortable. Hirad, naturally, was not helping in the slightest, and this stressful stroll was banishing any lingering doubts that he was who he affirmed.

'For the last time, will you get your finger out of that wound?' hissed Denser.

Hirad was grinning at the disgusted expressions on the faces of those for whom he had been staging his little demonstration. Again.

'Sorry, my Lord Xetesk-man.'

'And stop calling me that.'

'Age hasn't stopped you being grumpy, has it? Made it worse if anything.'

Hirad came to his shoulder. Denser glanced at Sol, who was walking slightly behind with Diera and fielding questions from those brave enough to approach him.

'Yes, we do have reports. And the man next to our Lord of the Mount does claim to be one of them and we are going to ascertain his truth or falsehood. There will be a full statement nailed to every notice board in the city by dawn tomorrow. Please, until then, there is no need for fear. Xetesk will protect you whatever the outcome.'

Denser gripped Hirad's arm. 'Don't you say a damned thing.'

'I'm hurt,' said Hirad. 'I remember being known as the soul of discretion.'

Denser upped his pace a little. 'Even for you, that is a poor joke. This is serious, Hirad. Let Sol do his job and we'll talk about something else.'

'All right. How by every God crying did two members of The Raven end up as Lord of the Mount and, unbelievably, king, respectively?'

'You know neither of us really wanted what happened after the demons were beaten,' said Denser.

He felt cold. It was always the same when the dark days resurfaced in his mind.

'I believe that of Sol. Not so sure about you,' said Hirad.

'I'm really disappointed you think that of me.'

'Oh come on, Denser. I may have spent my youth in the wilds of Rache and my best years trying not to die but I did pause to look around once in a while. And even I know that every Xeteskian mage aspires to the Mount. Why are you different?'

'I'm not. And yes, I did aspire to the Mount but not in the way it happened. Because I didn't want The Raven to be gone. But it has gone and we move on. And does not every man aspire to be king? To rule others?'

Hirad jerked a thumb at Sol. 'In his case, no. Seems to me you've been shut in the Mount for too long.'

'Seems to me you haven't been dead long enough.'

Denser saw Hirad flinch. So hard to believe it really was him behind the mask of a murdered merchant; so hard to argue it wasn't him having heard him speak of things none but Hirad would know. The heartbeat of The Raven, Sol always called him. He never had been good at tact, though.

'Sorry, Hirad.'

Hirad shrugged. A line of fresh blood leaked from his wound.

'It's just that you weren't here and you don't understand what happened in the aftermath of the demon war.'

'Being dead does take the edge off, doesn't it?'

Denser sighed and stopped walking. 'Whatever else you blame me for, don't blame me for surviving, all right? If you're bitter, fine, that's your choice. Me and Sol, we've had to get on because it's the only thing left to do. Not a day goes by that I don't wish you were still alive. And not a moment goes by that I don't want Erienne, my *wife* remember, to be beside me still. We're trying to build something worth the sacrifice you and the rest of The Raven's dead made that day. Wallowing in grief and bitterness won't do it. Remembering your friends and those you loved that would lay down their life for you, that is what is behind every breath I take.'

'Right, I get it,' said Hirad. 'Your wealth and position are things that you hate. A heavy burden you take on your shoulders for the good of us all. Well, we'll see what you're made of, won't we? Because what's coming at you is going to make the demons seem like irritating insects.'

Denser smiled. 'It's been a long decade and we have made great strides. Perhaps I should show you a few reasons why we shouldn't get too worried about this enemy right now.'

'Well my time dead hasn't dampened Xeteskian complacency at all, has it?'

'Let's keep this for inside four walls, shall we?' Sol's voice stayed Denser's next words. 'And can we move on? I've become tired of repeating myself. We need to compose a city wide announcement.'

'Yep, one that orders immediate evacuation,' said Hirad.

'Where to?' Denser spread his arms. 'Somewhere safer than within the walls of Balaia's most powerful city? I'm sure we'd all love to know where this mystical place is.'

'Denser . . .' began Sol.

'I don't know,' said Hirad. Tears had begun to fall down his cheeks. 'I just know we can't stay here and I want you to believe me before the pain inside gets too bad. Please, Denser, I don't want to be here but I know I have to help.'

Denser stared at Hirad and sucked his lip, feeling about as tall as the pebble by his foot.

'Let's get to the Mount, shall we?' he said.

There were a few people waiting at the gates of the college. All of them were plainly bodies of the recently deceased; and all of them were waiting for Denser and for Sol.

In a large meeting room in Denser's tower sat The Raven. Or rather, the souls who had once made up The Raven now unhappily ensconced in other bodies. What struck Denser immediately was that some of them had never even met each other though they had all been part of Balaia's most famous fighting team. What made him uncomfortable was that Sirendor Larn, who was currently seated next to Hirad, kept staring at him. He could understand the baleful expression. But mostly he just felt sad because this was an unwanted reunion for them.

The silence was stifling, adding to the already suffocating odours emanating from the assembled bodies that the opening of every window and balcony door had failed to address to any significant degree. While none of the bodies had ever been interred, each had brought with it the dirt of where it had fallen and in some cases the disease that had killed it. One of Denser's mages had already cast a number of cleansing spells.

'You know, it's depressing to realise that so many Xeteskians die alone and lost,' said Denser.

No one replied. The Raven were staring at one another, desperately trying to come to terms with their plight. The shadows on the walls from the steady light of lanterns picked out the true identity of each soul, but more than that, they all just knew too much to be any other than who they said they were. And, that done, they had lapsed into this confused quiet.

So much tragedy, so much irony too. Darrick the great cavalry general had found a body most unlikely to prove as competent in the saddle as he had been. Very tall and altogether too middle-aged. Died of a heart attack.

And Ren'erei too, lover of Ilkar, now sitting bewildered and scared, in pain and with nothing anyone could do about it, not in the short term. Her new body was that of a girl of about twelve. Pretty but for the sores across her face, evidence of the disease which had claimed her.

But no greater cruelty than poor Erienne in the body of a five-year-old girl. Erienne's daughter, *his* daughter, Lyanna had been five when she had died. And she was not here. And of The Raven, four were missing, most notably Thraun the shapechanger.

There were tears running down Ras's cheeks. The warrior, who had died on the same day Denser met The Raven at Taranspike Castle, was rocking back and forth, his arms folded tightly around his ribs. His body was that of a middle-aged man who had died of a cancer of the kidneys. The body was yellow and covered in dull brown spots. Ras's soul had made the body walk but that was about all.

'This man did not die alone,' said Ras eventually, his voice rasping out over a throat raw from coughing up the blood that still stained his once-white woollen shirt. 'As his soul fled, mine entered his body. He is lost forever and all I have done is cause such pain to his family, all there to comfort him into death. I don't understand why I'm here.'

Sirendor put a hand on his shoulder. 'It will come to you. It seems both you and I have been dead a long time. How fate plays her hand, eh?'

'We can ease the pain further,' said Denser. 'Fix you up so at least you can function.'

Denser felt Sirendor's gaze again and there was hate in it. He met it full on. Large bloodshot eyes stared out of a thickset face with chin, neck and cheeks hidden by a large growth of beard. What could be seen of the skin was sheet white. Blood matted the beard on his neck and dried onto a filthy brown shirt that reeked of damp. The slashed throat still oozed when he turned his head. It needed properly repairing before too long or he wouldn't be able to start his heart, much as Hirad couldn't just yet.

'I didn't mean it to be the way it was,' said Denser.

'That's comforting. One little cut of a poisoned blade. The wrong man moulders in the ground and the other rises to become Lord of the Mount.'

'I'm sorry, Sirendor. I don't know what else to say.'

'Your death saved Balaia from the Wytch Lords,' said Sol. 'You died a hero.'

'No, I didn't. A hero should know his death has meaning. I had no such knowledge. I died with a heart full of hate for him. And I have come back with it too.'

'And what of your time dead?' asked Hirad. 'Why did we not find you?'

Sirendor shrugged. 'There are corners of our resting places for us all, did you not know? I abided with many whose hearts were blackened at the moment of their passing. Together, we eased our suffering and knew the joy of death just as all of us surely have. But it seems the hate never really leaves our souls. Does it, Ras?'

Ras shook his head and his eyes locked on the boy across the table from him. Nine years old and dead of a waterborn illness that was still ravaging the poor tenements in the north-west of the city. He wore the loose-fitting nightshirt in which he had died; his hair was lank about his face and his lips were swollen as was the tongue in his head. He could not meet Ras's eyes.

'Nothing to say to me, Richmond?' asked Ras. 'You broke the first rule of fighting in line and I died. Nothing to say?'

Richmond shook his head.

'We were friends, weren't we?' continued Ras. 'All those years together even before The Raven. Nothing to say after what you did?'

The boy slammed his hands on the table and stood. His voice was shrill.

'I lived with it. Every day after, I lived with it. And when the Black Wing struck me down I was glad because the pain of the blow was nothing compared to that I carried with me. And I sought you out then. But I could not find you. Do not hate me, Ras. Don't make that the reason you were called back.'

The boy's chin was wobbling. He sat back down. Beside him, neither Ilkar nor Erienne offered any support.

'It gives me something to hang on to and that'll have to do for now,' said Ras.

'You know, we've only just sat down but I think we should break till morning. Give us all a chance to settle our emotions and make repairs to our bodies, those that need them,' said Ilkar.

People immediately began getting up to leave.

'That's just terrific,' said Hirad.

Denser could feel the beginnings of a smile on his face despite the tone of Hirad's voice. He caught Sol's eye and the big man winked. Hirad didn't notice.

'The Raven. Sitting round a table hating each other. Aeb, Erienne, anyone you want to point the finger at? No? Well, thank the Gods falling for that at least. For me, I'm here to *do* something. Help those I loved in life escape the menace that ripped our rest to shreds. I haven't come here to settle old scores. Anyone who does, leave now; you are not welcome. And though I love you, Sirendor, that means you too. Give it up. You tried to save Denser and you died. It still hurts. But it is not his fault. And whatever you think, you are a hero.

'Ras, you could start a fight with yourself if my memory serves and we need your aggression. Don't waste it.'

Hirad looked deep into each one of them.

'It is not hate that brought any of us back. But hate will undo us and cast our souls into the void. None of us wishes to be here but here we are, and any of us who turns, turns against the memory of everything The Raven became. Now I know that when some of you died we were just mercenaries and it was all about money.

'Well, money means nothing to a dead man, so what you do, you will do because you love those who stand with you. If anybody can't deal with that, step forward now. And I don't care if you look like a sick old man or a little boy or girl, I will drop you where you stand and send your soul screaming into the night. Whatever you take with you as you leave here now, take this:

'Dead or alive, when we stand together, we are The Raven.'

The ClawBound song was still resonating in the depths of the cliffs and out into the rainforest when Lysael began to speak. Before her, the elves crowded in. Ysundeneth had emptied. Children sat in the laps or on the shoulders of their parents, who sat or stood cheek to cheek with their families and neighbours. Tens of thousands of torches and lanterns set up a glittering picture, a firmament of elven-kind. Humans came too and this time were welcome. It concerned them in equal measure.

Auum could feel the awe from the crowd as they looked at the assembly on the stage. The stage itself was a gently sloping platform that swept back four hundred yards and measured more than a quarter of a mile across. It was lit by Keyel's Globes maintained by Al-Arynaar mages standing in the wings to either side. An arched timber roof painted with the colours of vibrant joy, a reminder of better times, projected the sound out over the bowl.

The stage floor was busy with the great and the rarely seen of Calaius. In addition to the seven high priests, a thousand Al-Arynaar stood as an honour guard. In front of them forty TaiGethen cells; and every Tai in every trio felt much as Auum did. Uneasy in the company of so many. Even a little nauseous.

'Friends, hear our words.'

Lysael's voice silenced the crowd completely. Expectancy, fear and pride swept over those present. A powerful mix, uplifting to the mass.

'A Harkening is called only in times of the most dire threat to all in the elven nation. Most of you would hope never to hear the call, whether Ynissul, Tuali, Gyalan or indeed human. There was no time to call Harkening when the Elfsorrow swept us. Now there is, but barely.'

There was a ripple through the crowd, quickly hushed. Lysael held up an ancient volume. The elves' most sacred text.

'The *Aryn Hiil* speaks of much that is central to the life of every elf in our nation. Of what made us, our purpose, where we came from and why. Hear me, my brothers, my sisters, my children. Hear the Words of the Earth.' She allowed herself the briefest smile. 'And forgive my translation. These are words not often spoken.

' "And from the air they came, as if spun into creation on the instant. With a voice that spoke friendship and a hand that spoke death. Some were joyous. The petty ire of elves forgotten. All faces turned to a mighty foe that cared not for battle yet garnered it with every pace.

' "Civilisation be trampled underfoot. Sucked in by the bellows of machines that bled the land dry. Yet proud are elves. And doughty. But for pain inflicted on our enemy, thrice back and more it came upon us. Oh that all should have taken up arms.

' "And so the greedy and the powerful clutched to their trappings and they died with them. And the weak and the young in dreadful numbers too high to count, the tears blurred eyes and minds.

' "Yet still we linger though not where we began. That place is lost in time and memory. The weak faced death, the strong searched for answers. And across the void they travelled and slammed the door against the faces of the enemy. Yet drifting across the emptiness, came the promise of destruction.

' "Even so, vigilance pales. Eyes turn and ears are distracted. When again the footfall is heard seek not battle. Seek instead Home. Because they are come and all you thought yours is dust and ashes though you still hold it in your hands.

' "They are come. Garonin." ' '

Auum felt the pages of his life turning. The entry in the *Aryn Hiil* was typically short but for those with memories long enough it unlocked all the pain, fear and despair. In the utter silence that followed Lysael's reading, Auum thought he could hear weeping mixed with the crackle of ten thousand torches and the nervous shuffling of infants.

Lysael waited a moment for her words to sink in. And when she spoke again, her voice was barely in check.

'Speaking words unchains the beast,' she said, her whisper carrying across the silence. 'There is no easy way. There is no way that can ensure success or even raise the odds above poor. But we have to leave and leave now. Shorth is silent. Our loved ones cannot be heard. In the Temple of Shorth, High Priest Ryish, witnessed by our own Auum and Rebraal, saw the passage of a soul denied and heard the poor victim speak the word. The Garonin are coming. They are already landed in the southern territories and they move north unstoppable. They will be on our seaboard in three days at most. We have no choice but to seek Home the only way we know how.'

Lysael raised her hands to quell the growing hubbub.

'Please, my friends, please. It is impossible to comprehend, I know, but we must or we will perish. There is little time but there will be questions. If you wish to speak, come forward to the stage. If you wish to prepare, go with our blessing. You will be summoned to the harbour and designated a vessel. Only bring what you can carry in your two arms. We sail north to Balaia in two days.

'Brothers, sisters.' The crowd quietened. 'We will survive and we will find Home. Deneth. We need you. All of you. Help the weak, the overburdened. Help any who need it. The *Aryn Hiil* speaks of times when we must put aside petty squabbles. This surely is one of those times. Trust in Yniss. Pray to Him. Pray to your chosen deity under Him. Trust us, his servants.'

Even among those assembled on stage, few had dry eyes. Lysael waited, her hands over her mouth or alternately in supplication to Yniss, praying for mercy. Praying for more time than she knew they had. Auum came to her shoulder, his Tai with him. He said nothing.

She acknowledged his presence. Together they waited while those with burning questions for all to hear came forward.

Auum saw their type. He had seen it before. The rich. Landowners. Merchants. Bankers. He sniffed. Among them, ordinary elves seeking order where there would be none. Questions to which there would be no answers. Few were leaving the Caeyin. To do so was to admit the unbelievable. He could see anger, frustration and, more than anything, the desire to hear it wasn't true.

'Questions will be asked. Answers shall be given. Speak in turn.'

Lysael gestured for the first elf to speak. Slender, narrow-faced and dressed in the sort of finery Auum shunned which wouldn't last an hour in the rainforest. Nor its wearer.

'Girales of Ysundeneth.' His voice, confident and already strident, rang out as clear as sky after rain. 'This is our home. We are stronger, more numerous than at any time in our history. We have no need to run. Surely there is another way?'

Auum acknowledged a fair question but shook his head when Lysael invited him to speak.

'I understand how hard this is to comprehend,' said Lysael. 'That anyone should announce on a moment that we must all leave our homes and our lives, our certainty, and head north into anything but certainty. But it remains the course we must take. There are enough writings. There are enough who were there and stood to fight the time before. And to fight is to die. To run is to live. Please, the next question.'

'Halis of Ysundeneth.' Fat like a human. Bulbous face. Loose clothing failing to hide a shameful body. And a voice that grumbled deep in the throat. He had probably never even entered the canopy. 'What I cannot leave behind is everything I own. A significant part of Ysundeneth. Houses, warehousing, the dockside marketplace. None of these can I transport by ship to Balaia. How will I be compensated? How will all my workers be paid if I have no business?'

'You will still be alive,' said Lysael. 'It is all anyone will have.'

'No, no, no, no.' Halis wagged a stubby finger. 'I have worked all my life to attain my position in the city. You will not take that from me with one sweep of the hand.'

'I offer no one anything but survival for now. Money, possessions, all will mean little. You have to understand, Halis, that we will all have to start again should we be lucky enough to live at all.'

'Preposterous. That I should be expected to simply abandon all

I have built. I will not do it without guarantees of future ownership in this fabled Home you speak of.'

Lysael was lost for words but there was enough support in the crowd for Halis's point of view. Auum moved smoothly in front of the high priest, stopping a hand's breadth from Halis's nose. The fat man barely saw him coming and raised his hands as if in defence.

'Then stay,' said Auum, never taking his eyes from Halis but speaking for the Caeyin. 'Be king of the city. Own it all. Count your riches. But know this. When the ships sail, there will be no escape from the Garonin. No deals to be done with them. No money to be made. They will move through here as easily as your hand brushes aside ears of corn in a field. And they will leave nothing behind. Not your buildings. Not your marketplace, not your flesh though you are possessed of enough of it. Any who stay will die. That is my promise.'

'You cannot know that,' said Halis, the stridency gone from his voice. 'Like Girales said, there has to be another way.'

Auum grabbed Halis by the lapels and jerked him forward.

'You know me. I am Auum, Lord of the TaiGethen. I faced them once before. More than two thousand years ago. In our former home, our beautiful, peerless former home. Now burned beyond recognition, repair or recovery. I fought them with every skill I possess and with the blessing of Yniss to guide me. I fought them with thousands at my left and right. Our numbers should have overwhelmed them then as should our passion and our determination to save our lands.

'But they did not. Tens of thousands died at their hands when they should have been journeying to their new home, far from these beasts. They died because people like you did not understand like you do not today. And I? When all was surely lost and all I could do was save as many as I could, I ran for my life. I ran because there was no other way to survive. We ended up here, sharing with the humans but at least we were *alive*. It is the same today, but today I will not let my people die in their thousands to serve such as you. Today we will run because tomorrow we must live. The elven race must endure.'

He let Halis go and turned to face the Caeyin.

'Any further questions?'

Chapter 8

Ilkar couldn't sleep. The skin in which he found himself kept him from comfort and his mind blazed with the pain of expulsion from his rest. Tonight, though, there was something more. Far beyond his subconscious, deep in his soul, that part of him forever tied to the elven nation bade him journey to stand with his brothers and sisters. He stood on the college walls and looked south, tasting the air.

The pull was distant. Distant enough to be denied. To go would be pointless. He would be too late. Yet still he rose from his bed in a servant's chamber beneath the tower of the Lord of the Mount and walked out into the quiet of Xetesk's night. He stared into the southern sky while his soul yearned to be lying beneath it.

There was an easing to his pain, just for a heartbeat. A knowledge that he had no need to travel. It should have made him glad but it did nothing but increase his desperation for them all. The elves would come to him. They were leaving Calaius. And that could mean only one thing.

'Looking for some company?'

Ilkar turned. For a moment he didn't recognise the man before him but then he put a name to the crooked smile he saw.

'Hello, Hirad. Insomnia got you too, has it?'

'I don't know about that but I can't sleep.'

'That was a joke, right?'

'You and your fancy words. How are you feeling?'

'Dreadful,' admitted Ilkar. 'This isn't much fun.'

'You know you don't look so good.' Hirad strolled up and patted Ilkar's cheek. 'You've looked better. When you had pointed ears.'

'I'll take that as a compliment. Fancy a stroll around the streets? We might even drop in for a drink at The Raven's Rest. I quite fancy staring at my picture and reminding myself how much better-looking I was than you.'

Hirad looked dubiously out over the walls and into the quiet streets. There was plenty of noise echoing around Xetesk. Plenty of light and smoke too.

'Bit of an atmosphere out there, don't you think?'

'Hmm. Not everyone is pleased to see the dead walking about.'

'I can't say I blame them,' said Hirad. 'I just wish they'd see we have no choice. Come on, let's go. Might get to the inn before closing time if we're lucky.'

'I think he might serve us after hours, Hirad.'

The two old friends in strangers' bodies trotted down the stairway to the courtyard and out onto the apron before the college. The Thread ran left and right past the gates. They turned right, heading down a gentle slope along the narrow winding road towards Sol's inn. The air was warm but carried a current of disquiet across the whole of the city. Three hundred and more dead had returned – figures were tricky to establish – and much of the living population had not taken to the events terribly well.

'What do you think they'll do?' asked Hirad.

The Thread was quiet. A few individuals and small groups wandered here and there and the cloak of the night meant no one could tell if they were living or dead unless they came good and close.

'You know what they'll do. They'll head out and try and fight.'

'It'll be carnage.'

'Will it?' Ilkar felt the pain in his body easing as they neared the inn. 'We had no defence but we had no magic and weapons either. Perhaps Xetesk will turn them aside.'

'You don't believe that. None of us do. We have all felt their power and it translates into something simply too big to handle.'

Ilkar nodded and sighed. 'You're right of course. But we have to hope, don't we?'

'What we have to do is get the returned dead and their loved ones away from here. This place is a target. West is the only sensible option. Beyond the Blackthornes and into the Heartlands of Wes.'

'Well, we're going to the right man to get that sorted out.' Ilkar shuddered. 'Damn but that felt strange. Do you—'

Bull's-eye lantern beams stabbed out from the left from one of the many side streets leading off The Thread. Temporarily disoriented, Hirad and Ilkar backed across the street to the right. Ilkar could just about see the shapes of men spilling into the street behind the lanterns. He shaded his eyes and immediately began casting to form the spell shape for a defensive wall. He heard Hirad drawing his sword.

'Get behind me, Ilkar,' he said. 'This smells very bad.'

The two of them had stopped retreating, leaving space to their left and behind, where their shadows on the buildings gave away their status.

'Want to run?' asked Ilkar.

'What do you think?'

'Just asking.'

Hirad squared up. Ilkar could still see nothing but shadows of men behind the lanterns. The street was suddenly deserted of casual strollers.

'Hirad Coldheart and Ilkar,' came a voice, strong and powerful, commanding. 'Members of The Raven deceased and you really should have stayed that way, don't you think?'

'You're welcome to come out and try sending me back,' said Hirad.

Ilkar shook his head. 'That's it, Hirad, work on defusing the situation.'

Hirad glanced over his shoulder. 'Just back me up.' But the merchant's face didn't inspire the same confidence that the old Hirad's had.

More people were pushing into the street and filtering around the lanterns. Ilkar counted twenty shapes. There didn't look to be too many weapons on display but this was a college of magic. There didn't have to be.

'I intend on doing just that,' said the voice, and the body from which it came moved in front of the lantern beams, which were hastily uncapped to shed a more general light. 'But I wanted you to see me first. And know why I am here.'

The face of the figure was still cast in shadow but he was tall, broad-shouldered and thick of limb. He wore chain armour and carried a two-handed blade. Ilkar cursed under his breath. He was bigger than Sol. Much younger too, maybe mid-twenties. It was hard to tell due to the half-helmet that covered his eyes and nose, leaving only his mouth and chin visible. There was an ugly slash across his throat that had been crudely sewn.

'All right, I'm impressed,' said Hirad. 'But clearly you're a returned soul too so you are aware we had no choice in the matter. What brought you back, though, I wonder?'

'You did.'

Ilkar frowned and saw Hirad pause, uncertain. The man moved a step closer.

'But you aren't Raven,' said Hirad.

The man scoffed. 'Hardly. I'm hurt you haven't made a better guess. Perhaps if that bitch who froze my face were with you she might work it out.'

Hirad straightened then pointed his sword at the man. Ilkar knew there was a sneer on his face by the set of his head.

'Selik? You returned because of me? I'm so touched.'

'And here to put many wrongs to rights.'

'Odd place for a Black Wing to show up,' said Hirad. 'You could lose your head in a place like this, you know.'

'It is I who will be wielding the killing blade this time, Coldheart. First over you, and then your mage friend.'

'Interesting choice of words for a man standing amongst the living population of Xetesk,' said Ilkar.

'Not all here are mages or mage lovers,' said Selik, and he moved forward again. 'These here want an end to the curse that is the allying of the college and the dead. This is magic of the very worst kind. And who better to help them achieve that?'

'We all want the same thing, surely,' said Ilkar. 'An end to the torment that puts our souls in unwilling bodies and a safe place in which to rest.'

'Dreams,' said Selik. 'I am happy enough. Happy that my time dead and wronged can now be cleansed from my soul by the blood of The Raven on my blade. Hold them.'

Men ran from either side of Selik. Ilkar, his spell prepared, cast and pushed his wall of mana to Hirad's left and into the crowd, pressing them back to the right-hand side of the street. Hirad took a pace back and slashed hard at the space Selik's lackeys were running into. Three of them pulled up short. Two, armed with broad blades, came on.

The street filled with the sounds of shouting and anger. The city guard would be here before long but they would not stop what was about to happen. While Ilkar edged left, taking in more of Selik's crowd but leaving the man himself free as Hirad would want, the two men attacked.

They came in left and right. A good strategy but with one error. Hirad ducked the high blow and blocked the low hard, pushing the man back. Then he was up and striking out at the first, his upward cut slicing through arm and glancing off his opponent's head, severing his ear. The man fell away, clutching at the side of his head. Hirad spun back, caught a blow from the second attacker on the hilt of his blade, straight-punched the man in the mouth and sliced back through his midriff, opening up a deep cut.

Hirad turned to face Selik.

'Body of a merchant, mind of a warrior,' he said. 'How about you?'

Selik said nothing. He moved very quickly, his blade coming around at waist height with frightening power. The old Hirad, the barbarian, would have been able to deflect the blow and riposte. But the merchant's body did not have the same strength. Hirad got his blade in the right place and avoided being cut in two but the force of the strike buckled his sword arm, jamming the edge of his blade against his body. He was sent sprawling to the dirt.

Ilkar began to move the mana wall but Selik was ahead of him. Hirad managed to turn onto his back but his arm was useless and the sword fell from his hands. He stared up into the face of the Black Wing. There was a smirk on Selik's face. He placed his blade on Hirad's throat.

'I hear the void calling you, Coldheart. Pleasant travels.'

Selik tensed to drive the blade home. There was a heavy thud. Selik's eyes rolled back in his head and he fell sideways, landing on the ground next to Hirad, blood seeping from the back of his skull. There stood Sol, cudgel in hands and a look on his face that would brook no opposition. He checked both Ilkar and Hirad were all right and helped Hirad to his feet before turning to Selik's people and the crowd of onlookers.

'Anyone else who wants to test my commitment to The Raven, feel free to go right ahead,' growled Sol.

Men and women were backing away from him as he spoke. City guards were elbowing their through the growing crowd. Sol collared the first of them and pointed down at Selik's prone form.

'He goes to the cells. And there he stays. He gets no treatment. If he survives till morning, he goes before the court. If he doesn't, then this body will be host to a less odious soul.'

'Yes, sir,' said the guard.

Sol addressed the crowd. 'These are my streets. You tell me you are my people. Act like it. There will be no summary justice dealt out by the living or the dead. If you have a grievance, you bring it to me or to my officers. That is the way it is and will stay. We are in a serious situation. The rumours of invasion will have reached all your ears. Transgressions will be dealt with swiftly. I need all of you to back your city and your college. We must stand together if we are to prevail.'

A pale-looking woman pushed to the front of the crowd and spoke into the silence that had followed Sol's words. She was no older than forty but had a haggard look about her that told of too many tears and too little sleep. She wore poor clothes but tried to make them appear smart with ribbons and ties. She stared at Ilkar and, before she uttered a word, he knew with a guilty cold feeling exactly what was coming.

'Then hear me speak, Sol of Balaia,' she said, her voice trembling. 'Tell me how should I feel and how should I react? There stands my son. The body of my son. Stolen by another soul. He treats the body as his own, yet it is not. He desecrates my son's memory by using his body though I know him to be dead because he does not know me.

'I want that body back and I want it now. To offer the respect my son deserves and to see him laid to rest in the right manner. This walking body insults me and it insults all my family and all of those taken by grief over the ones they have lost yet still see walking our streets. This cannot be right. It must be ended now.'

Ilkar felt the tension rise around them. Two of the city guard had begun to move the senseless Selik away, leaving four to stand in a loose ring around Sol. The crowd was still growing, albeit slowly given the hour of the night, but those present were four-square behind the poor woman. For himself, Ilkar could only nod and let his head fall forward a little to avoid her stricken gaze. He saw Sol move towards her.

'I am sorry for your loss and I will not claim to understand it,' he said, his voice gentle. The crowd fell quickly silent. 'How can a mother react when the son she knows is dead is seen to walk but it not be him? Your desire to want his body for respectful burial is natural and will not be denied any longer than it must be. But you must understand these are days the like of which we have never seen and we must all be patient, wary and have courage. People like you most of all.'

Sol reached out to touch her but she drew away.

'Your words mean nothing to me.'

'Will you hear me?' asked Ilkar.

'You even speak with his voice,' said the woman, tears falling down her cheeks. 'He was no virtuous lad but he doesn't deserve this, no one does.'

'No, he doesn't. But right now his soul is lost and that is far, far worse. Those of us returned, most of us, seek only to find a new resting place where we, and those like your poor son, can be at peace. Grieve for his soul but not for his body. The body is merely the vessel that your son used for his time alive. And if you can, rest easier knowing that his body, young, fit and wiry, is used now in an effort to save not just his soul, but yours too, everyone's.

'I don't know if that makes sense but I promise you I will take care of this body as if it were my own and will make every effort to leave it unsullied.'

'But where will that be?' asked the woman. 'Some distant battlefield? Some lonely corner of Balaia where I will never find him, never have the sight of him to close my mind on his life? What good is that to me?'

She turned back to Sol.

'This has to end, Sol of Balaia. I am but one of many who hurt this way and there is no comfort for us. We don't want the dead in the bodies of our loved ones. We want them gone. Leave us to fight our own battles. We do not need them. And we do not need you if you offer them sanctuary.'

Sol sagged visibly. 'My lady, all I want is to help you live through what is to come. You must try and understand where we find ourselves. Find it in your heart to trust me and the decisions that I make.'

But the woman shook her head. 'You are the mouthpiece of every ordinary Balaian, yet you are too close to the college, too close to the barons and too close to the elves. I have spoken but you have not listened. What more do we have to talk about?'

She turned away and was lost in the shadows. Angry faces glared at Sol, Ilkar and Hirad but no one said anything more. Ilkar put a hand on Sol's shoulder and Balaia's king turned an unhappy face to him.

'I'm failing them,' he said.

'No, you're not,' said Ilkar. 'They just have yet to see what we do.'

'I feel like a fraud,' said Sol.

'I'm the fraud. Standing here in her son's body. I feel for her, I really do. But what choice do we have?'

'Either to stand here and yak about it, or get inside and yak about it over a goblet of wine.'

Sol managed a smile. 'Well put, Hirad. Well put indeed. Come on. I've got some good stuff uncorked. Needs drinking with those I love.'

The evacuation fleet came in a night early. Throughout that night, quiet knocking on doors and silent escorting to the docks to take ship had worked well. Yet it was a slow process and with the morning came the inevitable anger and with it panic. Word spread quickly through those not destined to leave and tensions around the dock soared.

Ysundeneth was all but surrounded by flame and the clattering of the Garonin's vydospheres. Beyond the borders of the city, the rain-forest was part inferno, part charred dustscape. Out in the harbour, the forest of sails was slowly thinning out. The deep-water berths were full and every small craft had been pressed into service to ferry elves out to their only means of escape.

Forty thousand had come to hear the words uttered at the Caeyin, and all who desired it were offered passage and issued with papers. Yet twice that number now clogged the approaches to the docks or muddied the waters of the harbour in their own little boats, begging for passage. Ten thousand would be lucky. Thirty thousand would either take their chances in small craft or be abandoned to die.

Rebraal had said three hundred ships were guaranteed, and that was a number that would have been beyond imagining only ten years before. Yet, as Auum had predicted, it was nowhere near enough. Not even for the population of Ysundeneth alone, far less those who had journeyed from the rainforest.

Many thousands still waited to take ship and their path was being hampered by their less fortunate brothers and sisters. Standing in the harbour flag tower, Auum looked down on the growing and inevitable disaster. However much they had planned, it would still have come to this eventually. There had simply not been enough time to counter every threat. The Garonin, for all their ponderous advance, had left nowhere else to run.

Down on the harbour apron Al-Arynaar warriors were under serious pressure trying to keep the crowds from storming the dock-side. So far they had held the approaches while administrators searched for those holding transit papers. There had been scuffles and little else to this point but that would not continue.

'How long before we deploy mages?'

Auum turned to Rebraal. Ilkar's brother looked in little better shape than his long-dead sibling would have had he been dragged from the grave to stand here.

'How long since you've slept or eaten?'

'Long enough. But once we're away, I have plenty of time to rest, do I not?' Rebraal sighed. 'Do you feel guilty? Look at all those we are consigning to their deaths.'

'We have to focus on who we can save, not who we cannot,' said Auum, the nausea clogging his throat. 'One day we can weep. But it is not today.'

A surge of noise to their left signified the first concerted attempt to break through the Al-Arynaar. Forty warriors with mages behind held the line, just.

'We need to pre-empt,' said Rebraal.

'Agreed,' said Auum. 'But go carefully. Tint the walls. These people have enough pain to come. Best we do not add to it ourselves.'

Rebraal signalled the warning flag to be hoisted. Auum watched the black-cross-on-yellow standard climb the flagpole.

'It's going to get ugly,' said Rebraal.

'I know. Time we made ourselves known down there.'

Auum paused to watch the reaction. A short time after the flag was unfurled defensive castings were deployed on all four approaches to the harbour. Essentially walls of mana, the spells raised swirling yellow barriers in front of the increasingly desperate crowds, leaving small gaps to admit those with papers.

The howls intensified; simmering anger turned to spitting fury. Missiles were hurled at the walls, where they stuck before sliding harmlessly to the ground. Directly opposite the tower, the crowd had pulled back, leaving a couple of paces gap before the wall.

Auum frowned.

'Is—?' began Rebraal.

The crowd surged forward, crashing hard against the barrier. Auum saw the casting mages stagger under the weight. Their casting flickered then steadied. Auum was on the move.

'Someone's orchestrating that,' he said. 'Tai, we move.'

Ghaal and Miirt ran ahead, down the two flights of steps and out onto the harbour side, heading directly for the trouble. The apron was crowded, noisy and deeply unhappy. Crying children led by their parents. Angry shouts for speed and order. Al-Arynaar shepherding elves to their boats or directly aboard the docked ships. Confusion was rife. It was ever going to be this way.

Auum saw the elven wave roll back again. Rebraal was shouting for more mage support. The Al-Arynaar line stood back a pace and readied themselves. One or two refugees were still squeezing through the opening on production of papers. Many would never make it because their fellows had lost their courage.

'But can you blame them?' said Auum as they ran.

'I cannot,' said Miirt. 'What must we do?'

'Protect the chosen,' said Auum. 'That is Yniss's task for us this day.'

He felt both his Tai pause in their strides before nodding and eating up the last yards to stand in front of their Al-Arynaar comrades. Auum stood dead centre of the defence. Through the yellow tint he could see all he needed: a line of elves about ten rows back, clapping in time, generating noise, order and anger. The crowd ran against the wall again. The casting shivered violently. One mage cried out and crumpled. The other three still held.

'What's happening?' hissed Auum. 'Why is this casting so weak?'

Ghaal nodded his head towards the rising fires and the burgeoning heat closing in on the city. 'Garonin. They take too much mana from the air. Ix is weak today and our mages can find no consistency.'

The elves without had paused to see the effect of their work.

'End this futility,' shouted Auum into the moment's relative calm. 'Please. It cannot end well for any of us.'

'Not bad for you, TaiGethen!' came a shout. 'You get to live. We get to burn.'

'I know you, Halis. At the Caeyin you chose to stay, did you not? Despite my warnings. You had your chance. Another more worthy elf will travel in your place.'

Quiet had fallen and was spreading out across the harbour. Eyes and ears turned, sensing something.

'You have to offer us a way out.'

Auum straightened. 'All I can offer you are my prayers.'

Halis laughed. It was a short, bitter sound. 'And our souls will be trapped without rest much as our bodies are now. We will take ship and you will not stop us.'

Auum stared into the eyes of those in the front rank of the crowd. 'Yes, I will.'

'He cannot stop us all,' urged Halis.

Auum let his finger trail along the line of ten or so frightened, desperate elves.

'Who of you does not believe me? I have no desire to prove myself upon you. All the ships are full. You are putting your lives above those of your fellows. Do you really believe yourselves more worthy than those with papers whom you hold back? Yniss turns his head in shame from such conceit. It is you who should turn. Pray while you still have the time. Invest your energy in the survival of our race. Prepare your souls because we will free you to travel.

'Do not test me, for I will not fail.'

'Filthy Ynissul lies,' spat Halis. 'He claims more life yet how long has he already lived? We only have one chance to live. This is it. Push.'

The barrier shimmered for a moment and Auum heard Miirt curse under her breath. Seeing the spell weaken energised the crowd and Halis felt it, beginning his rhythmic clapping again.

'Tai, be ready,' said Auum. He pushed the regrets and the guilt from his mind.

'We need to get those with papers through these crowds,' said Ghaal.

'I know,' said Auum. 'We need the TaiGethen in the crowd, not fighting them. Damn these fools. I am ashamed to be an elf when I look upon them.'

Those near the front of the crowd could hear him. One or two had the decency to look guilty but none turned away. Like a spring tide, the crowd surged against the barrier once more. It guttered, wavering on the verge of settling for a moment, and then collapsed.

Ten wide, the crowd stumbled forward, some tripping, others leaping across the fallen. Death was behind them and it reduced their compassion to ashes. Auum's Tai stood before them, unflinching. The advance lost momentum. Auum could read the indecision in their faces. None would have faced TaiGethen before. Few, if any, would have seen them in action. Reputation stole the will from them, just for now.

Auum stared at the central figures in the front row, urged on by those standing safely behind. The truth was that a surge would roll over TaiGethen and Al-Arynaar warrior alike.

'Stand fast,' said Auum, pointing at one scared elf. 'Remember your words on crossing to adulthood.'

His Tai intoned: ' "Unto my race, I pledge my life. That my death should serve my people, such shall be my fate. Gladly accepted. Proudly travelled." '

'Then swap places, TaiGethen,' called a voice. 'Serve your people.'

'Gladly,' said Auum. 'And can I count on you to fight the Garonin street by street to allow the last ships to sail? Will you speak with the Lord of the Mount in Xetesk and describe our slim chance of survival? Will you finally lead the rest of our people to the west to talk with Tessaya, Lord of the Wesmen?

'Which of you will do this in the service of your race and hope to succeed?'

A momentary pause was followed by a ripple in the crowd. There was forward movement.

'Not another pace,' warned Auum.

He kept his arms by his sides; the jaqrui pouch on his belt was closed and his twin swords remained sheathed.

'We are many,' shouted a voice. 'And the ships won't wait. See the sails flying. To remain is to die.'

People burst forward. Fists were bunched. Crazed expressions replaced fear. Auum swayed inside a flailing blow and thumped the heel of his palm into an elven chest. The elf was propelled back into the crowd.

'Yniss forgive me,' he whispered.

Miirt dropped and swept the legs from another. She bounced back up to catch a punch in one hand and slam a fist into the chin of the same elf, knocking him senseless. Ghaal blocked a blow aside, paced forward and kicked out straight into the midriff of his opponent. The elf staggered back. Ghaal stepped in, both fists hammering out, taking down two more. Auum, next to him, and Miirt on Auum's right, moved up as one.

'We need that casting back,' called Auum. 'Tai, let us take the head from this beast. Arrowhead formation. Mind your flanks.'

Halis, his face contorted and reddened with his rage, was standing and shouting not more than ten yards away. Auum moved onto the offensive. He set himself a pace in front of his Tai, freeing his legs. One pace and he spun a kick into the temple of the elf in front of him. He twisted on his standing leg, reversed another kick into the chest of a second. He landed to face the next three. Auum punched the first square on the nose, splitting skin, The next he flattened with a reverse punch to the side of the head and the third pressed himself back into the crowd.

'Get out of my way,' hissed Auum.

All the impetus had gone from the surge. Twenty had been downed before the ordinary elf had time to draw breath. Some were unconscious. Any who moved were dragged aside by Al-Arynaar. The weight of the mass pressed against those at its head but none wanted to be next to face the TaiGethen, on whom not a blow had been landed.

A movement right and there was a scream. Auum glanced to see Miirt clutching the wrist of an elf. In his hand a blade dangled. Miirt continued to press. The wrist and two fingers broke. The blade fell.

'Next elf who shows a weapon dies here and now,' said Auum. 'I want Halis. Give him to me or I will come and get him.'

There was a gap of about two paces now between the Tai cell and the crowd. Halis was still calling for attack but the heart had left those of his foot soldiers who stood in the immediate path of his intended targets.

'I am not in the habit of repeating myself.'

A single arrow hissed from the crowd. Auum jerked his head to the side. The shaft whispered past his ear.

'The taipan is not quick enough to strike me from cover,' he said, his blades in his hands, his voice cold. 'For I do the work of Yniss and my time is not yet come to die. What makes you think you are faster than the deadliest of Tual's denizens?

'Bring Halis. Bring him now.'

'Spell ready. Casting on one.'

The words changed everything.

'Down,' said Auum.

The Tai dropped prone. Auum felt the spell come past him. It thudded into the crowd, flashed yellow and steadied. Auum rose to his feet and turned his back on the crowd, whose shouting had begun again in earnest.

'I want Tai cells to bring in those who are granted passage. I want archers here to fire on anyone who brings down the barrier. Leave Halis. His time is done.'

He turned back to the crowd and walked all the way to the barrier.

'And now I take my Tai and we will face the Garonin once more.

That is how I serve my race, giving you more time to face your fate like elves, not frightened humans.

'I am prepared still to lay down my life for you. And that is far more than you will ever deserve in this life or in the next. Tai, we move.'

Chapter 9

While much of Xetesk still struggled to recover ten years on from the wars that had all but seen the end of life on Balaia, the college itself had been restored to its opulent original state. The very centre of the college, the Circle Seven, six towers set around that of the Lord of the Mount, had escaped largely undamaged. But buildings of great age and importance had been severely battered or, in the case of the library, destroyed altogether.

'The shell is complete but inside the hollowness echoes for all we have lost,' said Denser.

'Very poetic.'

Ilkar did not turn from the balcony. They were stood at the tower's highest point. It was the morning after their abortive first meeting and some tempers had cooled considerably. Beyond the grand marble courtyard, on whose borders the other six mage towers stood, he could see library, Mana Bowl, long rooms, refectory, lecture theatres and the massed buildings of the college administration. All wrapped up in the college walls and all shining with recent paint and polished roof tiles.

Outside the college walls, repairs were still not complete on the city's own defences. Many buildings would never be rebuilt, their stone stripped for use elsewhere. There was poverty in parts of the city. Resentment too but no power with which to act. Smoke from open fires rose into the still sky. To the east, the horizon was obscured by mist.

Rich drapes hung in Denser's meeting room. Fine-spun rugs lay on the stone floor. Paintings and tapestries hung around the circular walls. Cut glass and gold-inlaid jugs sat on trays on the carved wooden table in the centre of the room around which The Raven sat. A bizarre gathering. The bodies of strangers with the shadows of lovers and friends.

'I wonder what the criteria are for making it back here,' said Ilkar

'We rather hoped you might be able to tell us that,' said Sol. He was sitting in between Hirad in his merchant's body and Erienne in her five-year old girl's.

'I'm working on it. The trouble is, this whole thing is so essentially *wrong* I can barely bring myself to believe what I am seeing and feeling. Indeed that I have the capacity to see and feel at all.'

Ilkar gazed down briefly at the body he inhabited. Its previous soul would never have seen the sort of finery on display in Denser's tower. Ilkar's soul, bursting into the air over Xetesk, drawn there by the presence and strength of Sol and Denser, had sensed the body immediately and he had reached it before others could take it for their own.

It had been lying sprawled in a narrow alley between the walls of two warehouses. From the attitude of the body, Ilkar had assumed the unfortunate youth had fallen while trying to jump between them. It had been an assumption confirmed by the broken neck, arms and ribs.

He had managed to heal the worst wounds but the pain of the fall was everywhere in the body. Still, it was young and strong, not yet twenty by his reckoning. Human though, and that was fundamentally unpleasant. Like putting on a suit of crawling insects.

'I have to say that I don't really understand that,' said Sol. 'I realise you are in strange bodies and that there is pain and confusion. But this is a second chance at life. Why is it so bad? Why does Hirad keep on saying he doesn't want to be here?"

All around the table Ilkar saw the reactions of the dead. And he saw their inability to put their thoughts into words. Hirad looked up at him.

'Go on, Ilks,' he said.

'All right. You see, the trouble is you are using assumptions based on the fact that you are still living. You assume that because of the manner of our deaths we must feel robbed of the life we expected and so would desire a return to finish what we started. Am I right?'

'Something like that,' said Sol.

'Well we don't. I haven't spent a moment regretting being dead. And that isn't a conscious choice; the thought just never occurs.'

'So what *is* it like being dead, then?' asked Denser. 'It seems you all find it hard to put into words.'

'Well that's because death doesn't conform to anything anyone living thinks it might be,' said Darrick, his new voice rich and full toned.

'Exactly,' said Ilkar. 'There is nothing to see, there is nothing to do in the way you would understand it. But the souls of those you love are always close and there is no risk that you will ever be separated from them. At least, there wasn't. Can you imagine the comfort that brings? We have memories; we communicate but not through speech. We drift, I suppose. Time does not exist. Every moment is both a lifetime and the tiniest spark.

'I know what you're thinking, Denser. It sounds terribly boring. Interminably so. And standing in this skin and breathing the air of Balaia, I can see why you'd think that. But it isn't. It's, well, bliss, I suppose you'd call it. Endless bliss.'

'Good job, Ilks,' said Hirad, and he was not alone in having a mist of tears in his eyes.

Denser was frowning. 'But you cannot see, hear, feel, taste or smell. There is no colour. There is no music. How can it be bliss?'

'That's exactly what Darrick was saying,' said Ren, her young voice chirpy and bright. 'You cannot apply the joys you experience as a living person to your existence after death. There is no comparison, barring the deepest feelings of love, friendship and intimacy.'

'You'll have to take our word for it,' said Hirad. 'It's not just enough, it's everything.'

'Coming from you, that is some statement,' said Sol. 'So how do we get you home? Presumably ridding ourselves of our latest enemy would be a good start.'

Silence inside the meeting room. The Raven dead could not look at him.

'Did Hirad not tell you?' said Ilkar, his voice quiet, the pain in his body intensifying. Heat was flooding him and the gale of the void threatened suddenly to sweep him away, such was the despair that surged over him. 'You cannot beat them.'

'He did say that but we are not bound to believe him,' said Denser.

'And even if you could, the land of the dead lies ruined. There is no going back.'

The words, like ice on Ilkar's tongue, rolled over the room.

'You're stuck here?' said Sol.

'Oh great,' muttered Diera. 'Mouldering Raven has-beens cluttering up my inn.'

'That would be the least of our concerns,' said Sol sharply.

Ilkar winced at the expression on Diera's face.

'He's right, Lady Unknown,' said Hirad. 'Our souls no longer have a place to rest.'

'So what?'

'So where do you think yours will go if you die?'

Diera put her head in her hands. 'You know, I've seen and heard a lot in my time. Being married to The Unknown Warrior and the first, albeit reluctant, king of Balaia means I can't get away from it. But this is too much. And I'm worried that I'm starting to believe you, like my daft husband and the Lord of the Mount do. So I'm going. Home. To open up.' She shot a glance at Sol. 'Let me know what hare-brained scheme you end up with. Meanwhile I'm going to spend some time with our boys.'

Diera got up to leave, ignoring the hand that Sol put out towards her. Hirad pushed himself from his chair and opened the door for her.

'It is us,' he said. 'Just look at our shadows and say you don't recognise them.'

Diera gazed at him. 'This is Xetesk, city of magic, home of the Dark College as was. You think this couldn't be some spell? Give me some credit, won't you?'

'Keep your boys close, Diera,' said Hirad. 'Be ready.'

'You know we named the youngest after the real Hirad Coldheart. There was a man we could all love. You? I don't know what you think you are.'

Hirad's face cracked into a huge grin when the door had closed.

'You've got a boy called Hirad, Unknown?'

Sol nodded, the beginnings of a smile on his careworn face. 'We have.'

'Hirad.' The barbarian's eyes sparkled. 'Not Ilkar, then. Or Sirendor, or Darrick. Hirad.'

'All right, Coldheart, we get it.' Ilkar felt his mood lift despite himself.

'Never mind, Ilks. Perhaps if they have a few more and are really scraping about for a name, yours might surface like a bloated corpse in Korina Bay.'

'Can we concentrate on what we are here to discuss?' said Ilkar. 'I don't know about you but every breath I take is shot full of needles, or so it feels. What happened to Hirad and me last night should also be concentrating our minds, don't you think?'

'It's the knowledge that my name will live on in a younger generation that I find so gratifying.'

'If we are to believe you, Hirad, there is to be no living on,' growled Sol.

Hirad sobered. 'We cannot let any of our names go to dust.'

'That is what I invited you all up here to avoid,' said Denser. 'And we have got nowhere fast. So why don't you, any of you, tell me what you know about whoever it is that is coming here to do whatever it is they're planning to do. Because I, for one, do not wish my soul to be casting around for a resting place when I die.'

'It's worse than that, my love,' said Erienne, the little girl's voice dripping with weary experience. 'We think that any souls unable to reach their birthplace are already lost in the void between dimensions, and that is an eternal screaming purgatory no one should have to suffer.'

'So talk to us,' said Sol.

'We can't tell you about their strengths, weaknesses, modes of attack and goals,' said Darrick. 'It doesn't work like that. Where we've come from there is nothing but certain knowledge and intense feeling. So all we know is, they have destroyed the dead dimension and they are here now and will do the same to Balaia. So everyone who wants to live and everyone who wants to die in peace has to leave because there is no point in trying to fight. This much we know.'

Denser kneaded the bridge of his nose, feeling a weight of frustration beginning to build.

'At the risk of repeating myself, go where?'

'I think that should be self-evident,' said Ilkar. 'Out of this dimension. Out of every known dimension, come to that.'

Denser threw up his hands. Sol held up a hand to still his protest.

'Even if that's possible, it doesn't help *you* much, does it? Where will you go?'

A short silence followed Sol's question. Hirad shrugged. Sirendor looked blank.

'We don't know,' said Ilkar. 'We hope to find another place to rest but we don't know. We aren't here for us. We're here for you, to try and save you. Stop you dying and being lost to the void. Believe me, you want to avoid that.'

'I'm not getting this,' said Denser. 'You've told us that the dead dimension is gone, but that to save us we should all leave for somewhere . . . else, right? So what happens when we die in this wonderful new home of ours? Where do our souls go?'

'We have to believe that a dimension beyond those we know will bring with it a new dimension for the dead,' said Ilkar. 'The theory is that the elves enjoy a different resting place now to that which they had in their home of millennia past.'

'*Theory.*'

'Yes, Denser, but it represents the only chance for all of us. The living and the dead.'

'And that is just plain ridiculous. Look . . .' Denser paused, seeing the expressions on all their faces. 'I really appreciate your passion and your belief but you're all a decade out of date. So much has happened here in the last ten years. So much strength has been built by so few but it is so solid. There is no more conflict here. Not with the Wesmen, not between colleges or barons. We can't afford it, the demons took so very many of us.

'We have worked together to make sure no one can threaten us again and we will not run away because our departed loved ones tell us we must on the basis of old information.'

'But it won't help you when you die!' shouted Hirad. 'Why aren't you listening to us?'

'Because I have to believe that if we defeat this enemy then your resting place, our resting place, will become, I don't know the right word . . . viable again. I don't see we have another choice,' said Denser, hanging on to his temper.

'We have just offered you one,' said Erienne quietly.

Denser's eyes pricked and he looked down at his wife. Now a five-year-old. He felt a surge of frustration. He sighed.

'But you don't know how to get us there,' he said gently, trying hard not to adopt a patronising tone. He reached out a hand to stroke her hair but pulled it back. 'I need to have proof or I have no option but to stand and fight. Evacuating the continent is not a realistic option.'

'How can you be getting this so wrong?' asked Erienne.

'At least tell us you're sending messengers to the colleges and Calaius,' said Darrick. 'Letting the powers know there is a threat.'

Denser smiled. 'And there you are, adding example to my argument. We are in constant contact with Lystern, Julatsa and Calaius.

We have delegates in the Wesman Heartlands and can speak with every baron and lord, and with the Mayor of Korina, at very short notice.'

'How?' asked Ilkar.

'I'll show you later. But right now I need you to trust that we have not been idle. We can and will repel this enemy. We have new spells and have enhanced those that already existed. Together, the Balaian people are strong. And you have our reluctant king to thank for all that.'

All eyes turned to Sol, whose face remained impassive. 'And yet I worry, Denser. Exaggeration has never been part of The Raven. This power, whoever it is, is strong enough to have destroyed the dead dimension, something the demons were unable to do. So while I share your confidence in our new-found strength, I think we must also plan for defeat.'

Ilkar nodded. 'At least that.'

Denser shrugged. 'But our main focus must be on repelling the enemy. Not running to our so far unnamed haven.'

'And we will face them as far from our cities as we can,' said Sol. 'We will identify their positions and we will go to meet them.'

Hirad sighed. 'I urge you not to. All you'll get is bloodshed, not enough of it theirs. And you will lose so many souls to the void.'

'You know it is something we have to do, don't you?' said Sol.

'I had hoped to persuade you otherwise.'

'We must attempt to secure our lands,' said Denser. 'Just to run is unthinkable, disastrous.'

'We must fight. We will not meekly surrender Balaia to anyone.'

'And, who knows, while you hold on to that belief, Unknown, perhaps there is a chance,' said Darrick. 'But we, the dead, do not see it, though we will stand by you.'

'Why?' asked Denser. 'If you believe it such a lost cause.'

'We don't have a choice,' said Erienne. 'Our souls were brought back here by the strength of our bonds to you in life. We cannot be parted from you by such a distance. The pain is too great and our souls would not be able to hang on to these bodies. Think about it, my love. What you intend involves us whether we like it or not. Don't force us to throw away what life we have.'

Ilkar pushed himself to his feet and walked back to the balcony window. The library caught his eye again and he felt a coldness enter his soul.

'You cannot have regained the power you had before the demons came,' he said. 'How much of the archive did you lose?'

The regret in Denser's eyes was answer in itself. 'Nearly everything. During the siege Dystran managed to salvage some texts but we have lost so much that was precious. Irreplaceable.'

'But, even so, you were more fortunate than Dordover,' said Ilkar.

Denser nodded. 'I can't ever see Dordover recovering as a college of magic. The Heart is gone and there are not enough surviving mages to construct a new one. But isn't it strange that, when all is said and done, Julatsa is the most complete college of the four?'

'You tell me; I've been dead almost fifteen years.'

'Lystern has its Heart and precious little else. Dordover has nothing but a library of lore that no one can use. Xetesk has lost two thousand years of teaching. Julatsa is almost untouched. The decision to abandon the college and run here worked in ways your fellow mages and elves could not possibly have imagined. The demons always meant to go back and consume the Heart after the battle here was done. They never made it. It makes Julatsa strong.'

'Only potentially, Denser. I can't imagine too many mages survived to begin the process of recruitment and training. You have numbers at least. But they won't do you any good.'

'So you all keep saying, and you'll excuse me if I don't immediately buy the opinion of people who have been dead for a good long time. We need to see this enemy for ourselves. Understand that I'm only just buying the idea that you can possibly be here at all.'

Ilkar nodded. 'Then do it quickly. Being dead was good. Being alive again really isn't.'

'And that's why Hirad has gone all emotional on me, is that it?'

'No, Denser, it's because he can feel something that he cannot explain.'

There was a knock at the door.

'Come,' said Denser.

A young messenger entered and bowed. 'Please, my Lord Denser, Master Haldryn of the Communion Globe sends his urgent wish for your attention. Calaius has fallen silent.'

Ilkar watched the colour drain from Denser's face.

'I take it that's not good, then.'

Denser shook his head.

'And what's a Communion Globe?' asked the elven mage.

Denser rubbed a hand across his forehead. 'Wait here, all of you. I'll be back as soon as I can.'

They all watched Denser go, following the messenger out of the door and away down the long spiral stairway. Ilkar took a seat next to Hirad and smiled, squeezing his old friend's healthy shoulder and regretting that he couldn't see the barbarian in his original body. For all the awful reasons they were here at all and not floating in the timeless sanctuary of the dead dimension, there was still pleasure to be derived from being among friends. Even the different faces and bodies could not detract from the sense of well-being.

'So what's eating the Lord of the Mount?' asked Hirad.

'Not sure, really. One of his toys is broken and he wanted to show it off to us, I think.'

'Oh, I see.'

As usual, it was plain that he didn't see at all. Ilkar looked over at Sol. The big man was studying the edge of the table, kneading the carved knotwork with his thumbs.

'It's not just a toy, is it, Unknown?'

Sol shook his head. 'It's the first line of defence against any invasion of Balaia or Calaius. It's the way we can talk over huge distances at any time. There are only two reasons for Calaius to fall silent. Deliberate cessation of the casting by the elves, and I dismiss that out of hand.'

'Or . . .'

'Or something overcame them so fast they had no chance to send a warning.'

'Go and have your fight if you must but you need to believe us, Unknown,' said Hirad. 'You need to worry about evacuating west right now. There is no time for doubt.'

Chapter 10

Pain where there had been comfort.

Fear where there had been calm.

Loneliness from love.

He would have screamed but he had no voice with which to do so. It had been so long, it seemed, since he had ascribed any living sensations to how he felt or what was happening to him. The pain soared, ripping at his being. Unstoppable, rising all the time, scaling heights he could never have conceived existed.

Tearing. Like he imagined it would be should his flesh be torn from his bones while he still lived. And he could not cling on. Could not save himself from being thrown into the teeth of the gale that carried him away from his resting place.

Flesh and blood. Bones and breath.

The trappings of the living. He had forgotten them and how they felt. Why should he be reminded of them now? Dimly, he had been aware that those around him had moved or were gone. He had felt fear through the mass but had not known what it meant. Still he didn't. Yet he was gone from where he had been content until now. But not adrift. There was something just beyond the borders of his awareness and slowly, slowly it resolved itself.

Direction.

He was *travelling*.

There was no reference. He could not see or feel his movement but there it was nonetheless. There was no scent to guide him, no light to show him a path. But there was something that dragged him onwards, that would not let him be lost to the chaos that surrounded him. And what coalesced from the confusion encasing him jolted through him with, he remembered, surprise.

It was *need*. That feeling of the heart reaching out to implore help, satisfy yearning and quench desire. To beg for attention. And to be reciprocated, meaning to love. All of this flooded through him and he thought that his speed, if he had one, increased. He had the sensation of flying headlong towards those that needed him the very most whether they were in trouble or just hoping without reason that he would return to them.

It was a feeling of the most basic kind. A necessity without which there was no life. And certainly no return to life. Because shortly before light blazed into the comforting darkness that had been his dead soul, that was what he was sure was coming.

He remembered nightmares from his living days when he was falling, falling. Always waking up just before he hit the ground. Yet though this was no nightmare, it was no less terrifying. The light was forming into vague shapes and he had the impression he was hurtling towards them at a speed he could not hope to arrest before he struck them.

There were many of them, grey and indistinct for the most part but surrounding a separate, familiar shape. And it was to this he was being dragged. Curious. The winds buffeting him were enough to blow him away like chaff in the wind but the draw to the shape was so strong. Like he was swimming down to an anchor.

In the next instant he was gasping in breath, opening his eyes and feeling the fear that had killed him. No, not him. The one who had inhabited this space before him. He lay on his back, barely daring to move. One at a time, he lifted his hands in front of his face, seeing strong, farmer's fingers, calloused and thick. He was not young or, rather, the body was not. Over forty but not yet in decline. The lungs heaved in the wonderful scents of grass and pine and the thick, heavy odours of animals.

He sat up, his soul clinging hard to the body, feeding energy into the heart to steady himself. The heart was tight, the muscles still in spasm. He could not afford to let the body die again. The winds would take him and he had nowhere else to go. He could not go back, that much he knew, and the knowledge sent pain through his new body. Pain of loss. Grief, he supposed, for all that was gone and could never be recovered.

The wolves surrounding him were all old but still he recognised them. Elders of the pack, his pack. He reached out a hand and nuzzled the nearest under the chin, feeling a delightful warmth. Sudden anxiety gripped him and he withdrew the hand.

'You have been waiting,' he said, though he knew they could not understand. 'This body. Waiting for me. You did this. How did you know?'

Words from his mouth. It seemed only a moment since he had spoken his last yet time had passed. Much time. He could see that in the whitening of lupine coats and he could feel it in the air around him.

The wolves, six of them, moved in to smell, lick and know him again. He could sense their relief but it was tinged with fear. Threat.

He stood. 'I am Thraun.'

His name echoed around the valley in which he found himself and the laughter that followed it from his mouth hid the pain of his return just for a moment. He stretched his new body, feeling strong muscle in his chest, arms and legs. The wolves had chosen well. Thraun bit his lip.

'I wonder who you were,' he said, looking down at himself, his rough woollen trousers and shirt. 'I wonder when you will be missed.'

Thraun scratched the back of his head. He was bald too. He looked down at the wolves, all of whom were stood utterly still, staring at him. Waiting.

'Something's not right.' He laughed again. But briefly. 'Something more than being back here at all, that is, and not having a blond ponytail. Bugger it, I wish you could talk. Where am I anyway?'

The valley was full of trees. Oak, ash and chestnut mainly. Pine too, of course. A very familiar landscape. He'd run here before but on four legs, not two. The valley rose to east and west, and if he wasn't mistaken this was Grethern Forest and he'd be able to see the castle and rooftops of Erskan if he climbed west. So he climbed.

The ground felt amazing beneath his feet, and despite the pain in his soul and the heat in his body he couldn't keep the smile from his face. Yet with every pace, that nag of something being seriously misplaced grew stronger. And every time he glanced back to see the wolves following him up the steep slope, whining quietly, his smile faltered a little more and his brow furrowed deeper.

He reached the top of the valley side and the edge of the forest. The sight of Erskan in the distance was satisfying but no more than that. He could hear a distant thumping sound, like a mighty machine battering metal on metal, echoing darkly. And to the north he was drawn to where he knew the towers of Xetesk lay.

'They are there,' he said. 'All of them.'

Thraun crouched by the wolves again, putting his arms around two of them and letting them all come close, to fire their breath into his face and give him comfort.

'I know I'm here to help you but I don't know how. Those I lost when I died are away to the north. They will know what to do. I have to find my friends. The Raven. Come with me. I will keep you from harm.'

The catacombs below the college of Xetesk had been extensively redeveloped in the decade since the demon wars. The Raven themselves had caused a good deal of damage there in their time and Denser had been keen to see them returned to their proper use. Research and archiving, rather than plotting and scheming. Parts of the one-time maze had been turned into a museum of the gory past of the Dark College and Denser had seen the catacombs signposted, properly lit, drained, ventilated and decorated.

Yet the odd bleak corner still remained, and he indulged one in particular. Knocking on the dark-timbered door of the suite of chambers hidden in a side passage near the old Soul Tank, now part of the museum, he always felt like a student sent to the master for some misdemeanour or other. It was an association the incumbents were keen to foster, leaving Denser having to remind himself every time he turned the handle that it was he who was Lord of the Mount.

'Enter.'

Denser pushed the door open onto a sprawling chamber clad entirely in oak and dominated by a huge fireplace in the left-hand wall. No fire burned within it and the chamber was cool. As always, tables across the back wall were covered in parchments, diagrams and equations. Books lined two walls on shelves which reached floor to ceiling.

A quartet of deep-upholstered chairs was set in a loose arc around the fireplace, its carved marble mantel and ornate candleholders. Above the mantel, a portrait of Dystran, former Lord of the Mount, gazed down benevolently upon those assembled in the chairs. At this moment, as with every other time Denser had been called down to the suite, those assembled were Dystran himself, demonstrating that no longer being lord of the college had not lessened his ego a great deal, and Vuldaroq, former Tower Lord of Dordover, now to all intents and purposes a dead college.

Both men looked up at him, adopting expressions of patronising sympathy, scrutinising him over their identical half-moon spectacles.

'Drives me mad,' muttered Denser. 'Am I to issue myself with a mild rebuke to save you the bother?'

'My dear boy, no. Come, sit by us. We have matters to discuss and decisions to make,' said Dystran, patting the arm of the chair next to him.

'*Boy?* Dystran, I am older than you.'

But he didn't look it. Denser sat and sucked his lip. Poor Dystran. A few wisps of white hair clung to his head. He was painfully thin and his hands trembled violently whenever the calming spell began to wear off. Even so, his bony digits shook a little and his voice was faint as if to speak any louder would be to court disaster.

And Vuldaroq was no better. Admittedly he was significantly older but Denser could still remember the truculent fat man who had hated The Raven as much as he hated Xetesk. Now he was reduced to a skeletal figure, blind in one eye and with a sagging right side to his face following a stroke four years previously.

That the two were the closest of friends was an unlooked-for blessing for them and an occasional pain in the backside for Denser.

'We have been noting the arrival of many, shall we say, old friends,' said Vuldaroq, wheezing as he spoke, his words a little slurred but wholly comprehensible.

'It's in danger of reaching epidemic proportions,' said Denser. 'How—?'

Dystran rang the little bell sitting on the arm of his chair.

'Tea?'

'Coffee,' said Denser.

'Ah. Still like to remind yourself of the tin pot of coffee on a Raven campfire, eh?'

'No, I just like it better than tea,' said Denser.

'And, speaking of which, we understand many of your former mercenary friends are on the Mount as we speak.'

Denser frowned. 'You're very well informed for men who never leave the catacombs for anything barring funerals.'

Dystran managed a shaky smile. 'Ah well, you know the way the Mount works. We must all have our sources, must we not?'

'So it seems.'

'And we understand that the Communion Globe on Calaius is currently not functioning,' said Vuldaroq.

Denser sucked in his cheeks and said nothing.

'Now, if you assume as we do that this is linked in some way to the problems afflicting the mana spectrum at present—'

'Wait,' said Denser sharply. 'That is not open research.'

'Oh Denser, all research is open to the Lord of the Mount,' said Dystran, patting Denser's wrist.

Denser moved his hand. 'Former.'

'Some will remain forever loyal,' said Dystran.

'You do remember it was me who gave explicit instructions that you were not to be killed, don't you?' Denser sighed. 'It has left you in a unique position and I rather hoped you might respect that. There are moments when I regret my leniency.'

Dystran laughed but it was brief and forced. 'There are times I do too, Denser.'

Denser nodded. 'Yes, I suppose there are. So tell me, what are your thoughts on all this?'

'You see?' said Dystran. 'Having the old lord about isn't all bad. If you're lucky, it'll become the done thing.'

'I think we've moved beyond assassination as a mode of ascension,' said Denser.

Dystran raised his eyebrows. 'Only a fool would truly believe that. And only a fool would see what is happening here and now as a serious threat.'

'Then I am a fool,' said Denser. 'I have dead souls reanimating fresh corpses all over the city, perhaps all over Balaia. I cannot talk to the elves even if I wanted to. I have massive mana dropouts to the east and getting closer, and I have reports that whatever it is that forced the dead out of their dimension is heading for the gates of Xetesk. How is this not a serious threat?'

Vuldaroq shook his head and exhaled loudly. Denser looked away and closed his eyes briefly.

'Something wrong, Denser?' asked the erstwhile Dordovan Tower Lord.

'Nothing that not being patronised won't fix.'

'Don't be so touchy. Instead, consider an alternative viewpoint.' Denser motioned for Vuldaroq to continue. 'Thank you. If there is one thing we learned from the demon invasion it was that the dead are far from the helpless onlookers we assumed. Not only do the Wesmen have direct access to their elders, the elves have a basic communication mode and was it not Ilkar who guided you to your destination all those years ago despite being dead?'

Denser shrugged. 'Yes. So what?'

'Open your eyes,' snapped Dystran, slapping the arm of his chair and dislodging the bell which fell into his lap. He was interrupted by a brief fit of coughing.

'You really believe they are here because something ripped open their own dimension? Something that powerful would not just be here by now, it would have destroyed us already. Think, my Lord of the Mount. This is not threat, it is opportunity. Find out what they really want. Find out why the mana spectrum is unstable. Xetesk thrives on harnessing fear, we always have.'

'You're saying I should dismiss the statements of my dead friends as lies?'

'We're saying treat anything a dead soul says with a little healthy scepticism. Every time one speaks, repeat to yourself, "Would I want to regain life if I were to die?"'

'Well of course I would. No one wants to die.'

'*Exactly*,' said Vuldaroq. 'And expect them therefore to come up with a solution to the problem they have so conveniently appeared to warn you about.'

'They already have,' said Denser and a frown crept on to his face. 'Are you saying . . . ?'

'Ha! I rest my case,' said Dystran, folding back into his chair, an expression of smug satisfaction on his pasty, thin face.

'Wait, wait, young Dystran,' said Vuldaroq, leaning further forward. 'What form does this solution take?'

Denser shrugged. 'Well, to be fair, this is where I have begun to lose it. They are convinced the enemy they say we face is too powerful and that we need to leave.'

Dystran gaped. Vuldaroq's smile was half knowing.

'Leave? And go where?' he asked

'Anywhere that isn't Balaia, apparently.'

'By which I suppose they mean south to Calaius, do they?'

'Oh no, that would be too easy. They want us to leave the dimension entirely.' Denser paused, sudden anxiety rippling through his mind. 'Look, I can see where this is going.'

'I should bloody well hope so,' said Vuldaroq. 'Bored dead people reappear in Balaia and announce the living should leave. I have no doubt you have been told their own dimension is damaged beyond repair or something like that.'

'Something like that,' said Denser. 'But hang on a moment. These people are my friends, my *wife*. I trust them. I love them. And they want to leave too. With us, I think.'

'So they say. And look who has come back so far,' said Dystran. 'That we know of. No simpletons. Of those who have announced themselves at our gates, or to you personally, every single one was a player before they died. The Raven. Styliann, my own predecessor, though his appearance was confusingly brief. Dear Gods burning and sorry you don't know this, but there is a man sitting in the Mana Bowl right now who claims to be Septern.'

'I did know that, and he is a fraud,' said Denser. 'He must be.'

'You are so certain?' said Dystran.

'I just don't see what point you're making. It isn't just powerful people. Ordinary Xeteskians are back too.'

'But they are not shouting, are they? And that's because they are merely pawns in this game. People of influence have returned. Drawn by something they clearly need. That, given what you have told us, appears to be a new home. Our home. And without us in it.' Dystran leaned right forward and his voice was a husky whisper. 'We don't know what being dead does to people, Denser. Even those we love. Don't trust any of them.'

'I may not agree with them, but I will never deem them liars. You are talking about the most loyal people ever to have walked Balaian soil,' said Denser. He pushed himself from his chair, unable to sit. He could feel his cheeks reddening. 'You are talking about the woman I love and over whom I still weep ten years on. You who sit here in your cave, too frightened to face the world a decade after we, The Raven, freed it from the shackles of the demons. You are not fit to empty their piss from a bucket.'

'And you will do your duty by your college!' Dystran's voice still held a surprising amount of power when he needed it. 'The Raven is gone. You are Lord of the Mount. Start thinking like him.'

A servant came in bearing a tray of tea and coffee and no doubt heard enough of the conversation to keep him in free ale for ten days.

Denser had to restrain himself from spitting on the tray on his way out.

'I only drink with friends.'

Chapter 11

Blackthorne had been chased by murderous enemies before but there was a bizarre quality to this one that was in danger of causing fatal complacency.

In the days since the Garonin had responded to Gresse's attack with such appalling violence, the survivors had moved ahead of them. But such was the slow pace of the enemy advance that Blackthorne and the partially recovered Gresse had been able to undertake considerable planning. And because the Garonin stopped at dusk, standing stock still as if frozen in time, and restarted at dawn, they could camp, rest, forage and track at leisure.

It was early morning on a misty but warming day. The thud of the Garonin machines was distant and they had become accustomed to it winding up with the morning songbirds. Blackthorne walked his horse alongside the open wagon in which Gresse sat a little reluctantly. Mages had healed the bone breaks but his distrust of magic was such that he refused the administration of Mother's Warmth to complete the healing process.

'It leaves me vulnerable. Out of control,' he grumbled.

'It leaves you asleep in your wagon for a day and fit to ride the next. Stubborn old goat.'

'The body recuperates at a given pace for a reason. No one has ever looked into the lasting effects of hurrying healing along with spells.'

'I'm not going to argue with you, Gresse,' said Blackthorne, rubbing at his mouth and beard to hide the smile. 'But you're grumpy because you cannot ride, yet you will not take the cure. It's up to you. Meanwhile, I thought you might not like to hear what our scouts are telling us.'

Gresse looked up at him and grimaced. 'That bad, is it?'

'We've riders on the ground and we all have ears. We've counted five of these machines. All of them travelling in straight lines, all of them driving people in front of them, leaving devastation in their wake. The devastation continues to expand as you feared, eating up the ground, killing everything. There's no escape. And all of their destinations are depressingly clear.'

'Let me guess. Korina, Xetesk, Julatsa, Lystern and Dordover. Key population centres.'

'Almost right,' said Blackthorne. 'But you have made one small error in your assumptions. It isn't populations and people they are after, necessarily. There is no machine headed for Dordover. It's going to Triverne Lake, to the site of the original college of magic.'

'Of course, silly me. No Heart in Dordover and not so many people either these days. You think they're after mana just like I do.'

'They are harvesting something, aren't they? And we've seen what the detonation clouds are run with. And the aftermath is very much like a mana fire. Stands to reason.'

'So it does. And as it happens, I agree with you completely. So presumably you have riders on their way to the target cities?'

'Of course.'

'Mages would be faster.'

'If they make it. Few will take the risk of flying such long distances. Hit a mana dropout and that's your lot. Too risky.'

Gresse was quiet for a moment. Blackthorne watched his old friend weighing up what he'd heard. He looked very old and sick this morning. His eyes had dulled since the run from the vineyards. Blackthorne wondered how long he could count on his wisdom and his enquiring mind.

'Stop looking at me like I'm about to die, Blackthorne. It's very off-putting.'

'Sorry. I'm sorry. It's just . . .'

'Well as a matter of fact I don't feel great but I am not yet on my last legs. Not on any legs right now as it happens. But it has given me time to think. Here's a question for you. Why didn't these machines appear right by what we assume are their targets? They seem to be able to appear anywhere they like so why this slow procession?'

'I don't know.' Blackthorne shook his head. 'I'll put it to the masses. See if anyone has anything bright to say.'

'No need.' There was a gleam in Gresse's eyes. 'I have a theory. Perhaps they need to attain a critical mass before attacking a college where the mana density is so great.'

Blackthorne felt genuine surprise. He took a sidelong look at Gresse before facing forward again.

'I see the cancer hasn't addled your brain just yet, then.'

'Improved it if anything,' said Gresse. 'Well, what do you think?'

'Plausible. Would you care to expand on your thoughts?'

Gresse sat up a little straighter. Blackthorne stepped closer to the wagon and rested a hand on its side.

'It's just observation, really. When we first saw the machine at the vineyards, it was big, yes, but looked, I don't know . . . deflated, if you see what I mean. And when the detonation clouds built up, the whole thing was rattling and wheezing fit to burst. Look at it now. That outer skin seems tighter, and when the clouds build, it all looks depressingly smooth and well-oiled, for want of a better expression. Still noisy as hell, but the noise of health not the rattle of death. The only thing I can liken it to is a horse. It needs breaking-in and running for a long time before it matures and understands what is asked of it. Before it can do everything for which it was born.

'What do you think?'

Blackthorne raised his eyebrows. 'I think I wish I'd been able to tell my riders that. It makes perfect sense to me. I'll talk to my mages and have them observe what they can both inside and outside the mana spectrum. The more we understand these things, the more we can report to Denser and Sol in Xetesk.'

'Bet you never thought you'd end up on a survey and research team, did you?' said Gresse.

Blackthorne chuckled. 'Not with a grumpy old sod like you, that's for sure. Is there room on that wagon for me? I feel like I deserve a rest. Feeling my age, you know.'

'You should try feeling mine.'

'All in good time, old friend. All in good time.'

Heryst, Lord Elder Mage of Lystern, had seen enemies come and go. Cheating death was a habit, so they said, and he thought it a good habit to adopt. But that was before the lost souls began lining up demanding access to the college, the city and their loved ones. All of them in other people's bodies. But what he had thought to be a distasteful charade had turned out to be the truth and a deep disquiet had settled on him.

Lystern was a poor city now. Perhaps in a dozen generations she would attain her former glory. Now, ruins and relics were all that remained alongside a fierce spirit among the people who had survived imprisonment by the demons and a feeling of close family among the handful who had kept the college from finally falling into demon hands.

Heryst would lament those who had died in that service. And it was their memories he would not see go to waste. The Heart had been saved and the college was beginning to recover. He looked with envy at the ease with which Xetesk appeared to have risen from the mire of the war, but at least he didn't have to fear them. The incumbent Lord of the Mount, a genuine hero of Balaia, was the first of his kind to eschew Xeteskian dominion for Balaian stability.

It gave him great heart for the future, but this morning he feared that future was about to be snuffed out. From the walls of the college he could look out south and east over the stinking city and see what was coming at them. He was told they were not numerous, indeed that a well-placed spell barrage would stop them. But those who told him these things had not spoken to his old mentor Kayvel, or to any of the other returned souls barracked in the college. He knew there were plenty in the city too. He wondered if they were saying the same things to their already nervous loved ones.

'How long before they are at your gates?'

Heryst was deep underneath the Heart of the college, where the mana ran so strongly and so true. He sat with a long-fingered hand on a silk panel linked to the Communion Globe by filaments of gold thread. He currently made up one of the six who kept the line of communication forever open. All six sat in low, comfortable chairs in order to preserve stamina. The panels were built into the left arms of the chairs, which circled the stand in which the Globe sat. The Globe itself was made from gold and steel and covered in fine cream silk. The combination channelled mana particularly well and the silk glowed with the base colour of the college magic. A green light bathed Heryst as the signal strengthened.

'Mid-afternoon at their current speed, my Lord Denser.'

'And you have not even managed to slow them?'

'Slowing them isn't the issue. Their pace is ponderous in the extreme. But they will not turn. They will not negotiate and they will not trade. They do not believe they have to.'

'What will you do? I can spare no one. We are mounting an attack on the enemy coming towards us, but like you the dead in our midst tell us we will fail. I refuse to believe that.'

'As do I,' said Heryst. 'We have precious little in the way of meaningful defence but what we do have will be unleashed the moment they set foot inside the city boundaries. They have been told this will happen. My conscience is clear.'

'Keep the Globe running,' said Denser. 'We can win if we work together. Anything you learn, anything we learn, we must exchange.'

'You have my word on that.'

'Good luck, Lord Heryst. The wishes of the whole of Xetesk are with you.'

'That means more than you know. I must go. The refugees are building up and I need to position my forces. We will speak later in the day.'

'I'm counting on it.'

The Communion Globe changed from vibrant green to a dull grey. Idling, the Communion teams called it. Heryst relaxed and removed his hand from the panel. Two others did the same, leaving three to maintain the casting at a low level. After a moment to gather himself, he stood.

'Whatever you hear and whatever you see in the coming days, we must keep this alive. I do not know if we can stop the enemy. All we know is that in their wake lies devastation and that they are coming right for us. Keep strong, you and the resting teams. Balaia needs you.'

Heryst moved to the heavy door of the chamber and knocked for it to be pulled open. Cool air washed in. The door was made from thick oak timbers and bound with iron. A dormant spell lay on the door, a WardLock ready to be activated by a command word from inside should anyone threaten the Globe. Heryst thought it likely they would need to use it soon enough.

Outside, the energy of the Heart warmed his body. It rested thirty feet above his head. A tall, cylindrical stone, similar to those in all the colleges in a chamber designed to circulate mana at high density. Without it, mages aligned to the college anywhere in the world would be unable to cast spells with any degree of certainty or success.

Heryst nodded to the guards and began to climb the long, gentle, circular stairway up to ground level. There were mirrors set along the outside wall every thirty feet or so, all of them ancient and tarnished, hung as a security measure by a high elder mage of generations past. He caught his reflection in one of them and rather wished he hadn't.

He admitted to being sixty but looked more like ninety. His once-proud head of hair was gone and he wore a skullcap to keep the chill away. His face was wrinkled and puffy, his nose and cheeks perennially red and veined. Heryst knew why but the shakes in the morning were only ever quelled by strong spirits.

The demons had taken so much. Maybe not his soul but the man he had been was lost forever. Sleep was a fleeting pleasure ruined by nightmares and food was taken merely to live. The joy of taste was a bitter memory.

Heryst sighed. His eyes were not still. The pupils performed a tiny, jerking dance and took the edge off his focus. He reached out a hand to the mirror and touched it with the tips of his skeletal fingers.

'I've been fooling you, haven't I? This isn't life; it is just a long decline to the grave,' he whispered. 'Perhaps defeat would be best for us all.'

Chapter 12

'I don't see this lot as being too much of a problem,' said Denser.

'No indeed,' said Sol. 'Hard to remember a time when I could count an enemy invasion force on the fingers of one hand. A well-placed Jalyr's Sun should do the trick.'

'You do realise it can't be that easy, don't you?' said Denser.

'Of course,' said Sol.

'Where do you think we should try and take them?'

Sol looked out over the gently rolling countryside that was so typical of inland Balaia. They were three days easy ride south-east of Xetesk on the southern borders of the Pontois Plains. The land north was beautiful and green, scattered with the purple flowers of heather. To the south the landscape was dominated by the great Grethern Forest, where Thraun used to run as a wolf. But to the east the ground was parched and dying, as if anticipating the disaster about to overcome it and reduce it still further. Its rolls and shallow dips hid the enemy for short periods, though their position could always be marked by the belching cloud, metallic thudding and occasional flash of mana fire that preceded a wash of heat.

The horizon was full of dust and the air tainted with an acrid burning scent that stuck in the throat. The enemy was transforming Balaia into a wasteland and their ambling pace told of a power mighty enough to have no need of urgency. It was clear even from this distance that they did not consider the soldiers and mages of Balaia any sort of threat.

The shock of seeing the enemy and their extraordinary machine had passed quickly enough. The moment's fear of the unknown had been washed away by relief that only three men walked in front of the machine which, it had been confirmed quickly, was drawing in mana, or rather whatever it was mana became after it had been ignited. It had made sense of the spreading dropouts in the mana spectrum. The huge, bulbous, metallic balloon being dragged on sled runners sent gouts of steam and smoke from multiple chimneys, while from within the thundering of metal parts hammering together occasionally drowned out all speech.

There was to have been a discussion about talking to the enemy. Seeing the spreading destruction left in their wake had strangled that thought at birth.

'I think as soon as we are ready we should attack. No sense in delay.'

They were standing with thirty mages and two hundred college guard, having ridden to their forward camp late the previous evening. The returned Raven, unable to ride horses because no horse would take a dead man on its back, had joined them this morning.

'I thought all you dead folk liked to stick together,' said Denser 'I'm surprised no more of you came. Solidarity and all that.'

'They can't, as I am tired of explaining,' said Hirad. 'Not unless their loved ones are standing here too. And add to that, they're bloody scared of this enemy. Just like me.'

'But I thought the whole was greater than the sum, if you get me,' said Denser.

'And that is why they congregate close together in Xetesk for the most part. But they, like we, have other compulsions,' said Ilkar.

'You've felt it, Unknown,' said Hirad. 'Don't pretend you haven't. Or you, Xetesk-man. The weight of souls around you. They need something to hang on to. Alone they just get blown away one by one. But together there is strength.'

Ilkar nodded. 'In our own dimension we congregated because the more that are in one place, the greater the bliss and comfort. Now we congregate if we are not to fade. Not all of them have purpose beyond survival, and for them the dual support of being by their loved ones and in a mass is safe. But for us it's different. For us to survive, we need a purpose and we need someone living to show us the way. We're beginning to think that, for better or worse, that's you, Unknown, and you, Denser.'

'I'm not with you,' said Sol.

'You two are what binds us all, that's what we think,' said Erienne, her young frame dwarfed by that of Sol. 'We can't prove it, but what we do know is that now we're back, the further we are from you, the more it hurts.'

'So you're saying you want to help us in this fight? I thought you said we couldn't beat them,' said Sol.

Hirad hefted the sword in his hand. 'Yeah, but you have to try, don't you?'

'You're talking about revenge,' said Sol.

'Bloody right. Now we're here, it seems rude not to. I still don't want you to fight, but if you are that determined, we will stand with you.'

Sol smiled, a little familiar warmth from standing with The Raven seeping into his bones.

'Well, fair enough, but this isn't a Raven fight, it's Xetesk's. We're casting. There won't be anything left for you to confront.'

Hirad's eyes widened. 'That'll give you a bit of an itchy sword hand, won't it?'

Sol laughed. 'I'm over fifty. I use the cudgel on unruly drunks but I don't pick up my sword any more.'

'But—'

'Hirad, this isn't going to be like the old days. Gods drowning, if I walk too far the arthritis in my hip puts me in a chair for two days. That body you're wearing gives you twenty years on me. At least.'

'So what's that on your back, then?'

Sol's two-handed blade was sitting in its snap-clip fastenings, hilt over his right shoulder like always. He shrugged.

'You know how cautious I am, Hirad.'

Hirad nodded. 'Whatever you want to believe. But when the fight begins, I still want you on my left-hand side, arthritic hip or not.'

'I'll bear it in mind.'

'Good. So when are you casting?'

'About as soon as you stop jabbering, Coldheart,' said Denser. 'Just watch what a Jalyr's Sun can do.'

Ilkar and Erienne blinked in unison.

'A what?' asked Erienne.

'That'll be the new name for a FireGlobe,' said Denser. 'First successfully tested by Jalyr in the Xetesk long rooms seventy-odd years ago, as you no doubt recall from your history.'

The little girl's face pouted beautifully, and Sol had to suppress a laugh.

'Why have you renamed it?' she asked.

'We renamed pretty much every offensive spell,' said Denser. 'And a few others.'

'Why?' asked Ilkar. 'What was wrong with the old names? Never left me in any doubt what the effect was meant to be.'

Denser spread his hands. 'Well, it was felt, when we eventually got round a table – the three colleges, the elves, barons and Wesmen – that certain spell names were overly aggressive and gave a negative impression of mages. And they had no style either, some of them. No imagination.'

Ilkar's eyes sparkled. 'You're joking, right? You sat round a table and discussed spell names with the Wesmen. Was Tessaya there?'

'He's not joking,' said Sol. 'And yes, he was there. Still going strong too, our lord of the united tribes. Made some good suggestions on the names too.'

'Didn't you have more important things to discuss?' asked Erienne. 'Like how to get the birth rate up and repopulate the place. How you were going to rebuild the country. Tiny trifles like that? Seems to me you're trying to reinvent mages into some outdated romantic ideal. Bit stupid, really.'

'Say what you think, my love,' said Denser. 'I hate it when you vacillate.'

Erienne smiled, the gaps in her teeth augmenting her air of innocence. 'So go on, then, what did you call HellFire?'

'Could I point out that we have an enemy advancing on us? Slowly, I admit, but advancing.' Darrick hadn't taken his eyes from them. 'You're going to miss the best place to cast this spell if you don't get on with it. If they get another half a mile closer, you'll have lost the slope for any infantry advance and your watchers back there on the hill will be feeling a little close to the action. I presume they are to run if it all goes wrong?'

'Bloody soldiers,' grumbled Ilkar. 'Always have to be so practical.'

'We're in danger of losing focus,' said Darrick. 'And that would surely be catastrophic.'

Sol nodded. 'He's right of course. Thank you, General. Let's get the mage team preparing. They need space and a little peace. Any of The Raven who want to stand with me, I'd be honoured.'

'I wouldn't stand anywhere else,' said Hirad.

He moved to Sol's right-hand side and Sol felt a tingle through his entire body, even though the sight of their borrowed bodies made him sad. He had to stop himself reaching for his sword. Sirendor came to stand on Hirad's right, the place Thraun had filled after Sirendor's death. Ras came to Sol's left, standing next to Aeb, once a huge warrior from the disbanded Protector calling, now in the body of a street fighter, short, squat and powerful.

In the old days Ras would have taken position with Richmond but his nine-year-old's body could not handle a sword and he was standing frustrated behind the mage line. Darrick completed the line to Sol's left. Erienne and Ilkar were with Denser while the Lord of the Mount issued his instructions to the casting team.

'Gods falling, we'd better get this spell right,' muttered Sol.

The air became taut. Mana poured into the spell construct as it expanded. Sol couldn't see mana, only a mage could tune into that spectrum of light, but he knew well enough what he would see if he could. Long hours with Denser drawing him diagrams had seen to that.

A circle, widening every moment and with lines criss-crossing it like hundreds of spokes on a cartwheel, to keep it under control. The shape would be a deep, pulsing blue, the colour of Xeteskian magic. Once the circle had reached the required size, more power would be fed into it. The lattice of lines would bow out above and below, like the inflation of a pig's bladder for a child's game. The lines would glow brightly. They would strain and then they would hold.

The spell was almost ready to cast. Denser, his eyes closed, his body linked to the construct but not a part of it, spoke final words of encouragement to his mages. Their faces were red and sweating. They were all blowing hard, concentrating everything they had on keeping the shape steady.

Denser opened his eyes and smiled. He looked out over the enemy, still half a mile distant. The concentration of mana had caught their attention. Heads that had been looking down now gazed directly at the group of mages, whose spell, invisible to the naked eye, would be bobbing just in front of them, awaiting release on Denser's command.

As if in response, a resonance built up in the air. A cloud quickly formed above the machine. It was shot through with lightning spears of colour. Yellow, green, orange and blue clashing and exploding. Another wave of heat pulsed out. Fire raged briefly in the wake of the machine and more of the Balaian landscape was turned to dust and ash.

'I've seen enough,' said Sol.

'Me too,' said Denser. He turned to Erienne and smiled. 'Cleansing Flame.'

'What?'

'HellFire, my love,' he said. 'It's now called Cleansing Flame.'

And accompanying her delightful child's laughter, Denser inclined his head and the Jalyr's Sun was released.

Barely fifteen feet from the ground, the deep blue sphere, flashing with white and blue light deep in its core, sailed out from the casting team. It was vast. Forty yards in diameter at best guess.

'You really mean business, don't you?' breathed Hirad.

'People really shouldn't take bits of my country away without asking, should they?' said Denser.

The sphere crackled with barely suppressed power. It increased in speed as it approached the enemy, and veered sharply up right in front of them. Their eyes followed it. The beasts pulling the machine ignored it completely. A curt nod from Denser and the sun set on the invaders.

The sphere dropped like a stone, impacting the ground and the enemy, bulging at its base before exploding in a deluge of blue fire. A hot wind rushed out, forcing Sol to turn his head briefly. The sound of the detonation rattled overhead, a thunderclap in a clear sky.

In its midst the invaders had been obliterated. Sol could see nothing of the three who had been walking in front of the beasts, nothing at all. One of the two beasts had let out a brief wail but now both huge corpses burned blue, the flame eating them to ashes faster than the eye could see. Grass, bush and tree had been scorched in an instant. Through the clouds of smoke all that could be seen was the machine, glowing red in the heat, its seams turning white.

The sound of metal straining and rivets popping echoed across the land. The shell of the machine was expanding. Sol put his hand up to his eyes to protect them from the fierce heat the Jalyr's Sun had caused. He could see masts buckling and melting, funnels falling and the links of chains turning to drips of molten metal. A metallic screeching and grinding scattered the watching mounted guard. Everywhere men and women clamped their hands over their ears.

Steam and an oily smoke erupted from bursting seams and through the torn openings of funnels. The blue fire continued to gorge on the metal, eating quickly through the shell. A dull thud was felt through the ground. In the side of the machine a dent had appeared, as if smashed there by the fist of a giant. The next instant it bulged back out with an agonised tearing sound.

'Down!' yelled Sol. 'Shields. Shields!'

He dropped to the ground, dragging Hirad with him. He put his face to the dirt and covered his head with his hands, praying everyone was following his lead. The machine exploded. A scream was torn from Sol's lips, lost in the teeth of the detonation that roared overhead, filling the sky.

He dared a look. Ash and dust were a thick, choking cloud. Ripped metal sheets whistled overhead. Others sailed high into the sky, turning and spinning. The air was hot, painful in the lungs. The blue of the mana fire was gone, replaced by the orange and yellow of burning wood and glowing metal. All around him pieces of the machine were beginning to fall to the earth, slapping onto the ground and into defenceless bodies.

'HardShields up,' said Ilkar and Erienne together.

More debris drummed onto the outside of their dual shield, harmless now, bouncing or sliding to the ground around The Raven. Sol could hear other shields being cast. He could hear the screams of the wounded too. They would have to wait just for a moment. He rose to his feet and brushed himself down, giving Hirad a helping hand when he was done.

Denser lay where he was for a moment before rolling onto his back and spitting dust from his mouth.

'HardShield,' he said, getting gingerly to his feet. 'I think you'll find you mean Orsyn's Cocoon.'

Ilkar just laughed. 'Call it what you like, Denser.'

The air had stilled and Sol turned back to the devastation the Xeteskian spell had wrought. Small fires burned all over the ground and the base of the machine flickered with dozens of flames.

'We need to see to the wounded.' Denser was behind him, talking still.

'Agreed,' said Erienne. 'A somewhat unexpected result, wasn't it?'

'Indeed,' said Denser. 'I hope no one is too badly hurt. Something wrong, Sol?'

Sol didn't reply. He began walking towards the husk of the machine. Unless his eyes were deceiving him, burning parts and charred debris were disappearing, plucked by an unseen hand. So were the bodies of the beasts.

'This can't be good.'

The wreckage of the machine blinked out of existence, leaving baked earth beneath it and runner marks as the only evidence it had been there at all. Sol stopped and began to back away. At the edge of his hearing there was a whine like the distant buzzing of bees.

Fifty men stood before him, no more than a hundred yards away.

Big men. Eight feet tall and more. Armoured from head to toe. Another fifty. Then another hundred. Another harvesting machine appeared behind them. Sol was rooted to the spot. He could hear Hirad shouting from just a few paces behind him but could do nothing but stand and stare.

Every one of the enemy had something in his hands. Not a sword nor a spear but surely a weapon of some kind. They raised the weapons and pointed them at Sol, at The Raven, at the whole Xeteskian force. And they began to march.

The Unknown swallowed.

'Oh shit.'

Chapter 13

The south walls of the college rocked once and simply crumbled. Heryst, standing on the wide raised courtyard of Lystern's tower had not even seen what had hit it. It hardly mattered.

The enemy had reached the city boundaries and not even paused for breath. Terrified people ran before them. The few who stood up to them had been trampled underfoot, rendered to dust. A swathe of destruction two hundred yards wide and expanding angled directly towards the college gates. Buildings had rippled and fallen. He'd seen streams and teardrops of pure white light streaking out from the approaching attackers.

Mages had dropped spell after spell on them. And all it seemed to do was bring more of them to the fight. Twenty armoured soldiers walked lazily over the rubble they'd created. In their wake came the machine his mages told him was sucking the mana from the air. The Heart of the college was next.

College guard and mages streamed into the lower courtyard below him. City folk were running in the opposite direction, fleeing north, heading out of the city.

'Volley!' he yelled into the tumult, unsure if anyone could hear him to relay his message. 'Volley!'

In truth, his orders were immaterial. Order existed but barely. Archers, the precious few he had, were firing at will. A truly pointless exercise it seemed with shafts bouncing off armour wherever they hit. But still they tried.

The noise seemed to intensify with the heat belched out by the machine. Another cloud was forming above it, crackling with energy, shot through with green light, draining away the power of Lystern, college of magic. Heryst fought the urge to cry, to turn and run from his utter helplessness. He was surrounded by his leading mages and every one of them looked to him for direction.

'Bastards,' he said. 'Give them everything you've got. Pour fire and ice on them. Take them down. They can't reinforce forever.'

Mages began casting and Heryst did too. A wildness gripped him and he found he did not care if what he did stopped them or not. He just wanted some of them to die at his hand. Heryst had always been an accurate and efficient mage. His casting was sure and quick; IceBlades were his favourite attack.

He targeted the centre of the enemy line, brought his hands together palms up and sides touching, and blew gently along the line of his fingers. The casting fled away, multiple flechettes of ice, flat, needle-pointed and with razor-sharp edges, flying to their mark. Heryst kept his hands steady. In the smoke and dust the enemy would not even see them coming.

Moments later they struck, snipping through armour and biting deep, pushing and burrowing before the heat of the target body rendered them useless. The enemy howled in pain. Blood spurted and streamed from countless wounds in his chest and head. He dropped his weapon and put his hands to his helmet. He fell to his knees and pitched forward.

More spells poured in from the upper and lower courtyards. More ice and fire, deluging their foe. Three more were cut down, two bodies burning where they lay. Lystern gathered a little confidence. Heryst prepared to cast again. Once more his preparation was smooth.

The enemy continued to advance, curious light chasing itself across their armour, illuminating what looked like runes or figures. Heryst chose his target and cast. The Blades struck the enemy's armour, which flared blinding white in response. Heryst shut his eyes reflexively, opening them again to see the armour of every invader beginning to pulse.

In moments the figures were obscured by the glare coming from the lettering covering their bodies. Tongues of light lashed out on the crest of a wave of force. The tower of Lystern rocked on its foundations. Below Heryst, men and women were screaming. He had never seen such carnage. Heads, limbs and body parts littered the ground where just a heartbeat before sixty and more mages and archers had been standing. Some had survived the onslaught but the enemy turned on them. White light like teardrops poured from the complex rods they carried, tearing into the helpless wounded, blowing them apart.

'No!' screamed Heryst.

'Time to go, my Lord,' said Kayvel, returned from the dead and still standing by him though his new body was hardly more healthy than the one in which he had died.

'We must fight.'

'We cannot, Heryst. It is as I told you. They are too strong. Cut the head from one beast and ten more appear.'

All the energy, all the strength and belief flowed from Heryst and he sagged, letting the sound of the machine and the dying cries of his own people wash over him. From the upper courtyard mages still cast. One section of the courtyard wall exploded inwards. More died. It was a procession.

'Then what can we do?'

'The only thing that is left. Get to the Communion Globe and warn the others. Tell them to run.'

Heryst nodded, direction giving him something to cling on to for just a while longer. He ran from the courtyard shouting to his people to run, to save themselves in any way they could. The rumble of falling masonry was loud in his ears. The stonework shook beneath his feet. The tower of Lystern was coming down.

Heryst took the long spiral staircase two steps at a time. Everyone he met he ordered away from the college. Down beneath the still-beating Heart he went to the chamber of the Communion Globe. Outside the door two frightened-looking guards remained at their posts.

'There is no hope,' said Heryst. 'Go. Save yourselves if you can. Do not fight. Run north.'

'My Lord, we are sworn—'

'I release you from all such bonds. Go. Please.'

He opened the door, stepped inside and closed it behind him. Peace descended. All he could feel was the rumble of the approaching machine and all he could hear the distant crump of collapsing stone. Not long now.

'Xetesk. I must speak to Xetesk.' Heryst half-threw the nearest mage from his chair. 'Enact the ward. Lock that door.'

He sat down and placed his hand on the silk.

*

Sharyr had retired from the research and casting of dimensional magics after the demon wars. The fact was, he couldn't stand casting at all after it was over. His hands weren't steady, his mind wasn't sharp and he had simply had enough. But when Denser asked him to be master of the Xeteskian Communion Globe, he had felt it was a job he could safely accept. Not difficult and yet commanding great respect among the colleges and even the elves.

Since the failure of the Globe on Calaius, Sharyr had spent much time in the chamber, set away from prying eyes, deep in the catacombs. Rumour had it that not even Dystran knew where it was but Sharyr didn't believe that for a moment.

They had not raised a whimper from the elves.

Sharyr was not an old man, though like every veteran of those terrible days he surely felt like one. He'd managed to keep his hair, an achievement of which he was proud. But still the nightmares plagued his sleep and tripped up his bladder. One day he was certain it would all fade away. One day.

He sat in one of the six low chairs with his hand on the silk, on call just in case he should be needed to help channel messages through to Denser out in the field. Just like his last conversation with Heryst over in Lystern. The enemy would be at their gates now. But their Globe was still active and stable. In Xetesk they could feel it.

'What if the Calaian Globe isn't actually down but the focus of the spell has shifted for some reason,' he said as the thought occurred. 'We assume a certain shape to their construct, and it is that we cannot find. What if we should be looking for a slightly altered shape. We should think what the construct might look like if it was, you know, just ever so slightly tuned out or something.'

'Master Sharyr. It's Lystern,' said a voice from across the Globe.

'I'm here,' said Sharyr.

He settled more deeply into the chair, flattened his palm against the silk and fed his own Communion structure into the Globe where it joined with the other five to amplify and solidify the contact with Lystern.

'I am Master Sharyr and this is Xetesk.'

What came back when the contact was open sounded like screams and rock falls. Nothing should penetrate the sanctity of the Globe chambers.

'Lystern, speak.'

'They are at the doors. They're at the damned doors,' shrieked a voice consumed by terror.

'Heryst? My Lord Heryst, is that you?' Sharyr's heart was pounding. He could feel the anxiety of his team adding to a rippling in the construct. 'Steady. Steady.'

'Sharyr, listen to me.' A second voice. Calmer. This was Heryst. 'The enemy have breached the college. The tower is coming down around us. They—'

A massive crash sounded. Sharyr pressed his hand to the silk to stop himself jerking it away to hold over his ear. He winced as the report fed through the Globe. At least one of his team lost the casting.

'Get yourself back in,' he hissed. 'Steady it. Come on. Breathe.'

'Dear Gods above. The Heart. Stop them.'

More sounds of destruction. Sharyr heard a scream, cut off abruptly. The Communion flickered and steadied.

'Heryst. Can you hear me?'

Sobbing from Lystern. Screams and explosions. It had to be happening right outside the chamber. Or within.

'It's gone,' managed Heryst, his voice tight and whispering. 'They've ripped it right out of its cradle. Dear Gods burning, we are finished.'

'What, Heryst, what?' But he knew.

'The Heart, Sharyr. Taken and consumed. Listen to me. Run. Do not fight them. You cannot possibly win. Tell Denser. Call off his attack. Save lives, it's the only—'

A cracking of timbers.

'They're here. They're inside,' hissed Heryst.

'Who?' urged Sharyr. 'Who is inside? What are they?'

A strangled cry and the Globe flickered.

'Where are they?' demanded an alien voice that bounced in Sharyr's skull. It was strangely melodic but this did not disguise either the power or the menace.

'Who?' Heryst's voice was cracked and desperate.

'Those who light the way. Those who will seek the path to us.'

'I don't know what you mean,' said Heryst. 'Please, you have what you want. Spare my people.'

Sharyr heard the sound of something cracking. Bone and cartilage. The alien voice said something else but he couldn't pick it up. The voice of another of the Lysternan Globe team began to speak. Something fell, something heavy.

The Communion Globe was silent, reducing to a dull grey.

'Heryst? Heryst, can you hear me? Any of you?'

Sharyr kept his hand on the silk still, praying for the contact to be re-established. Futile. All he could hear was the hard breathing of his team.

'They've gone,' said one. 'They've gone.'

'Did anyone catch what the other voice said?' asked Sharyr, his cracked voice echoing painfully in the Communion chamber.

'I believe so, but it hardly matters,' said the mage to his right. 'Garonin, or something.'

'Everything matters right now. Go and look up that word. Any clue as to who they are could help. I've got a feeling I heard it before when we were researching dimensional alignment. Those texts weren't in the library; they're still down here in my old workshops.'

'As you wish, Master Sharyr.'

'And the rest of us, let us not be next,' said Sharyr. 'Let's get this construct back steady. We have to get hold of Lord Denser.'

'Unknown! Get down!'

The impact in Sol's back sent him sprawling to the scorched ground. The earth vibrated beneath him with the force of multiple explosions. He heard screams and rolled onto his back. His scabbard dug in painfully. Hirad and Ras were both above him, looking towards the enemy.

'What di—?'

'Down!'

Hirad again. The barbarian in a merchant's body flung himself on top of Sol. There was a distinct clicking sound like the unlatching of many doors. An arc of white pulses in the shape of teardrops fled over Sol's head and slammed into helpless mages, soldiers and mounted guards.

Defensive shield castings collapsed under the onslaught, flaring deep blue as they failed. Light ripped through bodies, obliterating people, punching holes in torsos and tearing horses apart.

'It's going to be a slaughter,' said Hirad.

'No, it isn't,' said Sol. He pushed Hirad off him, got to his feet and snapped his sword from its clasps. 'Let's get to it.'

'Raven!' roared Hirad. 'Raven, with me!'

Sol was ahead of him, charging towards the slowly advancing line of enemies. They were huge, all of them tall and powerfully built. Covered from head to toe in armour that seemed to glisten in the sunlight. Numerals and lettering woven into breastplates and leg guards shone.

'Get amongst them,' he called over his shoulder. 'They can't shoot at you if you're inside their guard.'

More fire spat from enemy weapons. Sol felt the heat as a teardrop fizzed past his shoulder. There was no time to check how far behind the rest of The Raven or the Xeteskian guard were. He ducked his head as more fire whipped about his ears. He felt the pain begin to flare in his damaged hip and whispered an apology to his wife and sons.

'What do you think you're doing, old man?' he muttered.

Sol brought his sword to ready and hoped he remembered how to use it. There was not a flicker from his target. The enemy were well spread out, marching forward carefully. Detonation followed detonation but Sol dared not look behind to see what was happening.

The man in front of him had turned his weapon. Sol ducked reflexively. A teardrop smashed into his blade, shearing the top clean off above his head. His hands rang with the vibration of the impact. Sol swung the remainder of his blade through two-handed. It thudded hard into the midriff of the enemy just beneath his arms. Sol's momentum carried him straight on, barging the man off his feet.

Sol landed on top, snatched a knife from his belt and jammed it under the chin strap of the enemy's helmet. The scream of death was a keening wail. Blood pumped from the wound briefly and the man lay still. Sol rolled away, coming to his feet in time to see Hirad and Ras enter the fray. A few paces behind them came the rest of The Raven, mages behind warriors, magical shields in place for what good they would do. He knew it was them behind the masks of their borrowed faces but still he worried. They looked so *ordinary*.

The Xeteskian mage team had been largely annihilated. Four still stood of the thirty who had cast. They were casting again. God's Eyes of blue fire sailed over Sol's head to crash into the ranks of the enemy.

'Form up, Raven!' ordered Sol. 'Dead or alive, get your memories working.'

The Raven surged across the open space. As one, the enemy stopped moving. Hirad buried his blade to the hilt in the neck of his victim, having to angle high to reach his target. Ras sliced through a leg guard and his opponent fell. The front rank of the enemy dropped to one knee; the second rank remained standing.

Sol frowned and squared up to his next target. His two-handed blade was useless. No balance and no bludgeoning point. He discarded it and drew a second knife. Many eyes had turned towards him and The Raven coming up fast in support.

'Shield covering you,' said Ilkar. 'We have projectile and spell covering. Those teardrops are mana based.'

Sol relaxed just a little. The Raven took their positions. Angled chevron. Just like the old days. Well, almost. They advanced. In front of them the enemy, still widely spaced, checked their weapons, made small adjustments and brought them back to bear. Still Xeteskian spells dropped in their midst but now a white flaring told of their impotence.

'Hit them hard, Raven,' said Sol. 'Let's go.'

The Raven ran in. Every enemy weapon fired. The front rank spewed teardrops. Others launched projectiles that trailed smoke in lazy arcs. Multiple impacts shivered into Ilkar's shield. Sol heard him grunt with the effort of maintaining it. But behind no such strength prevailed. Explosions ripped the Xeteskian guard apart. Volley after volley landed in their midst. And each detonation sent red-hot fragments of metal in all directions. Flesh was flayed from bones. Skulls imploded. Limbs shredded or torn from bodies entirely. Souls shrieked as they were cast into the void.

Sol heard a drumming sound. Metal shards were raining against the projectile shield. Erienne gasped, a terribly frail sound from her young mouth. The shield flared the intense brown of the One magic casting, the ancient original magic discipline reborn in her daughter, Lyanna, and that had passed to her on Lyanna's death. The Raven halted. The fire on them intensified.

'Ilkar?' called Sol.

'Holding. Just. Move on. Be quick.'

'Pick your targets,' said Sol. 'Get inside those weapons. Fight dirty.'

'Just the way I like it,' said Hirad.

White light, metal, heat and fire washed over the shields which Ilkar and Erienne clung on to. The attention of the enemy was on them. Huge figures turned and moved in.

'Keep it steady, Raven!' called Hirad.

Sol could see the eye slit of his target's helmet. The armour was beguiling. Cool light swam through the runes and symbols. But inside the helmet the eyes were shadowed and dark. The enemy brought his weapon to bear. He fired. White teardrops flattened against Ilkar's shield. Sol grunted a smile. He stepped in close, grabbed the man's shoulder and drove his blade up into his neck. The enemy reared back, blood spewing out. Sol's blade was all but ripped from his hand.

Two more filled the gap. Hirad was next to him. The young body he inhabited was fast, the soul inside adding skill to speed. He ducked a flailing weapon and slipped his sword into the gap between leg and torso armour. His target collapsed forward, Hirad shovelling him sideways.

A figure flew into the fight on Hirad's right. It was a moment before Sol realised it was Sirendor. Simultaneously, the squat power of Aeb barrelled forward to Sol's left. He brought down an enemy, arms around his waist, his body slamming into the surprised man, toppling him backwards. The two turned over, Aeb's fists smashing again and again up into his opponent's face. The enemy managed to bring his weapon round. He fired from close range. Inside the shield Aeb had no protection. His body juddered, smoked and blew apart, raining gore across The Raven's line.

A second man inside the shield turned his weapon on Ras. The Raven warrior jumped and sliced his blade at the enemy helmet. The dull clang reverberated inside the shield. The man did not flinch. He fired. Ras's head disintegrated and his body flopped to the ground.

'God's drowning!' spat Hirad.

He ducked a flailing blow and came up to block the return and hack down with his sword on the man's arm. His strike bit but did not pierce the armour. Sol wiped blood from his face. The enemy had seen the way to victory. They came on.

'Back up!' he shouted. 'We've got to back up. We can't let them inside the shield.'

The enemy ate up the ground. The Raven retreated. Every weapon appeared trained on them. Projectiles trailing smoke fell on them in their dozens.

'Turn and run,' ordered Sol. 'Go, go, go.'

The decade of inactivity, the lack of familiarity with new bodies and simply being dead told. Sol spun round, the pain in his hip shooting agony into his lower back. He stumbled. Hirad reached out a hand to support him but the barbarian's body was not the one his memories knew. Sol brought them both down, clattering straight into Ilkar, who pitched to the dirt.

'Shield down, shield down!'

White teardrops tore into them. Ren lost her entire right leg, screaming as her soul was torn from her body. Darrick had charged at the enemy line, drawing fire all the way. His body jerked, smoked and was torn through with burning holes, falling unrecognisable to the ground. Denser paused to cast but Sirendor dragged him away.

'No time, come on.'

Sol tried to get to his feet but his leg wouldn't support him. He stumbled again. And then Erienne screamed. The cry of a little girl in agony. And in the midst of hearing Hirad shout for them all to run, Sol saw her staring at her arms while they blistered and burned, the flames reaching up to her head and engulfing her hair and face.

'No, no!' It was Denser, but Sirendor wouldn't let him go. 'Not again, please, not again.'

Sol began to crawl towards her. She was lying writhing on the scorched earth, beating at the flames which encased her. The others of The Raven downed were already gone. So brief a return, snuffed out so easily.

A foot came down on his back. He turned his body to grab at it and another pressed into his neck. Weapons pointed at his head and chest. He lay still. All he could see were the helmets of three of the enemy ringed by smoke and fire. He heard the screams of the few survivors as they were hunted down and obliterated. He fancied he could still hear Hirad but it had to be wishful thinking.

'Sorry, Hirad. Why didn't I listen?' he whispered.

'You.' The voice belonged to one of the helmeted figures. The voice of a God. 'You are the key.'

Sol frowned. A thundering, guttural roar told him the new machine had begun its work.

'We will fight to the last man and woman. Your losses will be beyond contemplation.'

'Not any more.' Sol wasn't sure, but he thought the man laughed. 'Come.'

'I—'

It wasn't an invitation. A hand reached down to grip him and Balaia ceased to exist.

Chapter 14

Auum waited until the *Calaian Sun* had reached deep waters before shedding his tears. The greedy and the disbelievers had burned in their paper castles surrounded by their brief empires just as he had said they would. Clamouring and crying on the docksides as the last ships sailed.

He should not have been desolate for them but he was. Desolate for what they had become. More human than elf in their last moments. Hanging on to material things when the elven nation was reverting to that which it had been for long periods of its history. Back to the life of which the most ancient writings spoke. As nomads. Akin to the Arakhe, the demons, in more respects than they would care to admit.

And just like the Arakhe, the elves were chased from dimension to dimension, their enemy relentless in pursuit of the prize which each elf carried and each temple and city harboured in great density. Mana.

Auum had watched the glorious spires and proud houses of Ysundeneth consumed by flame. Scorched by the heat of mana fire. He had seen the clouds rise above the vydospheres and had known the hungry machines sucked in the very life of Calaius with each belching breath. He grieved for the city. And he grieved for every elf who died trying to keep the Garonin back for long enough that the fortunate few should escape.

But he grieved for the rainforest infinitely more. Not its temples. Though they were beautiful and ancient, they could be rebuilt and rededicated. But for all of Tual's denizens, innocent victims of a war of millennia that simply brushed them aside. The rainforest was gone. His home for over three thousand years. The place where he had thought he might choose to step across to his rest when his work was finally done.

It might recover. Eventually. There was little more tenacious than the root and branch over which Beeth presided, after all. But would Tual's denizens return? Those not immolated would have been pushed south into the desert lands or north and east into the sea. So many species would be gone forever. Just like the elves. Forced to adapt and move on, otherwise to perish.

Auum stood in the stern of the vessel. Five days on, the tears had long dried up but the cloud was still visible above ruined Calaius. Behind him Captain Jevin kept a steady hand on the tiller as he had done for as long as Auum had known him. A sea captain without peer and a braver elf Auum had yet to meet bar those of the TaiGethen themselves.

'It will get no better for the want of staring at it,' said Jevin.

Auum turned to see Jevin's broad back.

'We killed our own to save ourselves. There can be no greater crime.'

Auum's memories came flooding back. The flames hemming them in as Ysundeneth burned. The desperation to make it aboard ship. The pleading, the threats and the promises. And finally the spells deployed to force order and the TaiGethen attacking those demanding passage when they had originally chosen to stay.

'Think on who you saved, not who had to die. It is the way of elves.'

'I cannot forget so easily,' said Auum. 'Every drop of blood is on my conscience.'

'Who said anything about forgetting? We're a long time alive, some of us, and our memories come with us all the way. But for now focus on what you have, not what you have lost.'

'You sound like me,' said Auum, coming to his side.

Jevin smiled at him. 'Well, you talk a good deal of sense. Most of the time. And I make it my mission to listen to elves who kill with your efficiency.'

'And what do we have, Captain?'

'Look about you, Lord Auum. The sea is full of elven sails pushed hard by the devil wind the Garonin have caused with their fire. Almost three hundred, and all will make landfall before night.'

'But do you know how few of the elven population of Calaius that represents?'

Jevin's smile faded a touch. 'Less than ten per cent, I am sure.'

'Less than five, my friend, even though every vessel is over-burdened. I should be happy, I know. It is more than we took from the fires of the Garonin before. But we must also pray for the souls of all those who perished. For all that we achieved, we only saved forty thousand of our people. Every other soul is trapped and restless until we can find a new home.'

Jevin nodded and turned back to the wheel for a moment. Auum looked out over the crowded deck at the desperate and desolate, the bemused and the stricken. The confidence of millennia swept away in a few days.

'You have many problems ahead before that time comes,' said Jevin, inclining his head at the civilians.

'The Garonin at our backs, an army of the displaced to move and feed, and Yniss only knows what state Balaia will be in. We have to assume they are also under attack.'

'You'll be lucky to find a college standing,' said Jevin.

'Yet we must hope Julatsa's Heart beats for long enough to see us safely to the Wesmen and away.'

'And you. Still determined to go through with your plan, then?'

'Two men still live who I regard as highly as any TaiGethen elf. I will not leave them behind. The bulk of the civilians will travel to the west with Rebraal to appeal to the Charanacks. They have no mana, surely their path to the spirits is clear, and if it is, it might provide our means of escape.'

'And if it doesn't?'

'Then the elven race dies on Balaia.'

Jevin blew out his cheeks and nodded his head. 'Anyone else would sound overdramatic. You just scare me.'

'Remain scared, it is a wise state of mind.'

Mages were flying back to the fleet. Dark specks against the cloud-strewn sky, flying against the wind. Auum felt his heart rate increase. News was at hand. He watched the trio approach. Jevin ordered a red burgee raised atop the main mast to guide them in. Rebraal had chosen well. All appeared unhurried and in control of their castings after several hours away although they had probably been unable to land.

But as they drew near he could make out the distress on their faces ever more clearly. He prayed to Yniss that it was simply exhaustion but he knew otherwise. The trio circled the *Calaian Sun* and landed on the wheel deck.

Everyone on board was looking at them. Every elf on deck had risen and there was a concerted bunching towards the stern. Auum didn't blame them. The first mate asked for calm and assured them that information would be given to all. It did little to quell the thirst for knowledge.

'I hardly need to ask, do I?'

Dila'heth shook her head and wiped dust from her face.

'They are there, my Lord Auum. Yniss preserve me, you can see the clouds from here if you look for long enough. It is no mirage.'

'Is Gyernath secure?' asked Jevin. 'Can we still land there?'

'Yes, but it will do us little good other than to disembark the ClawBound we need to scout north. The Garonin will have pressed into Xetesk before you can make it on foot, Lord Auum. You will need to find another route to Xetesk.'

'And the colleges?' Auum was sure more bad news was on the way.

'Lystern is gone. Xetesk and Julatsa will be under direct attack in a little over ten days. Other vydospheres are headed to Korina and to Triverne Inlet, meaning even the site of the One college will not be spared. Balaia is dying. Consumed by the fires of the Garonin and soon to be dust and ash.'

Auum put his head in his hands. He heard a collective groan from the assembled crowd behind him on deck.

'Are we already too late?' he asked.

Dila'heth shrugged. 'It is hard to be sure of anything. I do not want to give you false hope.'

'Did you land? Is there any good news?'

Dila laughed and exchanged glances with her two fellow mages.

'The Balaians are fighting, we saw evidence of that. But they are compromised just like us. Some of their dead are returned. Their messages carry no hope of victory and speak only of running, but they do not know where. They have no idea who to turn to.'

Auum nodded. 'Then they shall turn to us.'

The survivors of the massacre barely stopped running until they reached the questionable sanctuary of Xetesk. The enemy had stopped moving once the defenders had fled. Scouts reported them actually turning away from their path, heading further north with their machine.

Inside Xetesk, confusion obscured all else. Refugees, living and previously dead, were flooding into the city from Erskan, Black-thorne, Pontois and Denebre. All told the same story. Unstoppable advance, total devastation. No quarter given, no hostages taken. Nothing left but ashes and dust, the stumps of trees and naked rock.

The authorities, shorn of Denser and Sol, had struggled to cope. As many as possible had been directed to parks and waste grounds and given what food and shelter could be found. Others received charity in private dwellings and yet more had been fleeced by unscrupulous landlords and inn owners. The city was creaking.

The arrival of the Lord of the Mount, dishevelled and riding with just a handful of those with whom he had set out, only deepened the disquiet. Tensions had been rising steadily between the living and the dead. Violence was breaking out. Divisions were deepening and the advance of the enemy added fear to the mix. Denser's ears rang with problems, none of which he was immediately willing to face.

In the relative peace and quiet of the Mount, Denser poured a jug of water over his head and let the icy liquid soak down over his shirt and trousers. He handed the jug back to his apprentice, who refilled it from the butt in the corner of the bedchamber. He upended this second jug too, hearing the water splash over the stone floor and force life into his bones and muscles.

'Thank you, Brynar. You can go. Find me some food; I'll be down to the main chambers shortly.'

'Yes, my Lord Denser,' said Brynar, a keen young mage, bright and determined. 'Baron Blackthorne, Sharyr and Lord Dystran all request urgent audience. As does Mayor Haved.'

'And I will see them as soon as I can, assure them of that. First I must rid myself of this dust and stench.'

'My Lord Denser?'

'Yes.'

'It is good to see you back safe.'

Denser nodded and suddenly he was clinging hard to his emotions. 'I can scarce believe it myself. Off you go.'

The door closed behind Brynar and Denser sank down onto his haunches and let the sobs roll over him, his tears mingling with the water that dripped from his face and hair. His body shook. He clamped his hands to his thighs, rocking back and forth.

The pounding flame and the incessant white teardrops. Her hair alight, surrounding her face while she screamed. The fire engulfing her hands at which she stared until the heat blinded her and suffocated her. Fingers clawing at the ground while she died. The tearing agony as her soul was lost to the void.

Worse than before. Ark had saved her soul from the demons the first time. Nothing could save her now, and even in his death Denser would not be near her. Not ever again. Denser let images of her face, her first face, settle in front of his eyes. He reached out but they distorted like reflections on windblown water.

Denser sat while the water chilled his body, making him shiver and interrupting his despair. He raised his head and wiped his face with his hands. He drew in a huge pained breath and coughed violently. So brief, returned life.

'Get up, Denser,' he said to himself. 'Wallow later. Do something. Do *something*.'

He pushed himself to his feet. And, while he dried himself and found a change of clothes, he thought. He cleared his mind of his visions as far as he could and thought back over all that had happened out there on the battlefield and all that the dead had said in the days before.

And when he was done, he found that there was only one question that really mattered. Had his mind been playing tricks and, if not, what in all the hells had happened to Sol?

Denser studied himself in the mirror. A little greyer than the last time he had looked. And plainly exhausted too, but rest would have to wait. He placed a fresh skullcap on his head and made his way down the spiral stair of his upper tower to where Brynar would have left his food for him.

He opened the door to find he would not be eating alone.

'Bloody hell, what's brought you up out of your hole? And who let you in without asking me?'

'My Lord Denser, it is customary to extend the hand of friendship to those with your best interests at heart,' said Dystran.

The old Lord of the Mount chose not to stand, and instead remained seated on one of the leather-upholstered chairs in Denser's dining chamber.

'I see you've already helped yourself to most of my lunch. Don't they feed you down in the catacombs? Too many rats and grubs, is it?'

Denser stalked into the room and slammed the door shut behind him. He rang the communication bell, poured himself a large goblet of wine and sat opposite Dystran, whose eyes were sparkling from his prematurely aged face. Mischief and conspiracy, no doubt. Dystran waved a hand impatiently.

'Oh, Denser, do shut up. There is more and better food in this tower's kitchens than in entire quarters of our once-great city.'

Denser looked past Dystran to the grand fireplace, above which a portrait of the man in his younger days looked down. It was one of a set depicting the last eight Lords of the Mount in what could loosely be termed relaxed attitudes. Dystran was smiling.

'And one day your picture will hang above the fireplace and mine will be consigned to the corner by the old broken window over there.'

'I think not,' said Denser. 'I have told the committee that deals with such things, whatever it's called—'

'Heritage and History.'

'Yep, them. That the most relaxed painting of me they'll get is when I'm dead.'

Dystran laughed hard. 'Very good, Denser. Very good indeed. I'm glad your sense of humour remains intact.'

'It has been some time since I made that remark,' said Denser. 'Now tell me what you want. I have much to do.'

'Indeed. One of the few survivors, I understand. Even King Sol is missing and, we presume, lost.' Dystran's attempt at a sympathetic expression was poor, more resembling a smirk. 'No doubt the last few days have been . . . difficult for you.'

Denser gaped.

'*Difficult?* I have witnessed a massacre. I have seen my best field mage teams obliterated. I have seen my guards dismembered, literally, right before my eyes. I have seen The Raven dead torn to pieces . . . and I have seen my wife, my wonderful wife, burn. Gone in moments. And I was helpless and so I ran. I ran, Dystran. Like a scared child behind the legs of its mother, hoping the monster wasn't real. But it is real. And it is coming this way. So yes, you could say things have been just a little tricky.'

He grabbed Dystran's plate from him and shoved over to him the thin remains on the serving dish instead.

'And I come back here to find my city in chaos. The dead are bunching together towards the east gates because too many of my people think they are a curse on the living or whatever. Refugees are sleeping on every street corner and in every doorway and I have no way to feed or house them all. And profiteering appears rife. Such are the mercies of our wonderful city folk, eh?'

'The problems within the city can wait a while. There is more to your massacre than you think,' said Dystran.

Denser spoke through a mouthful of meat. 'Meaning.'

'Meaning you need to ask more questions of those here to help you and lean less upon the dead you choose to trust. The solution is plain to see but you have allowed old loves and loyalties to obscure it. You have witnessed a massacre, yes. But you have also witnessed the path to defeating this enemy.'

Denser scratched at his head under his skullcap. A pain was growing behind his eyes.

'It's an interesting version of events, I'll grant you that. My own battlefield mathematics reckons we lost about two hundred, maybe more, once the wounded are brought back or not. Whereas the enemy lost one machine, a couple of animals and, what, twenty men? All of whom were replaced by ten times that number as quickly as you can snap your fingers. If this is the path to victory, then damn right it is obscured from me.

'You know, I've had a really trying day on top of about ten really trying days. I don't think I want to hear your befuddled reasoning if it's all the same to you.' Denser stood. 'And if the words "you can't trust the dead" are in anyway allied to your theory, I suggest you go and speak it to the deepest stone in the catacombs because I already don't believe it. They warned me this enemy was too powerful. I should have listened.'

Dystran remained in his chair and eyed Denser coolly. His hands were trembling but not with the effects of his nightmares. Not this time.

'Then you are more stupid and obstinate than even I had imagined. And you will consign us all to death. I should warn you that Lords of the Mount holding the reins of inevitable disaster are often thrown from their runaway wagons.'

Denser felt a cold breeze across his entire body. A smile played on his mouth and he pointed a finger at Dystran.

'You're threatening me,' he said. 'I really don't believe it.'

'No,' said Dystran. 'I really am your friend and ally. One of the few that remains, I suspect, within or without the Circle Seven. I will take my leave now; my appetite has diminished considerably since you came in. But I will say this. Ask yourself why it is that the enemy is not currently heading directly for Xetesk. There is a man here who knows why. I believe him at any rate. A most trustworthy man. And you might want to speak to your Communion Globe master too. He has a name for this enemy. Amongst other things.'

Dystran stood and walked to the door. He paused there for dramatic effect.

'Your dead want you to run. They spread dissension among those who will listen in Xetesk, and some have taken heed and departed. The dead do not wish for you to see. The enemy creates a barren wilderness where nought but a floating soul could possibly find joy with its fellows. I see glory for Xetesk and I want to be standing before the man who will finally deliver it to us.'

'Get out,' said Denser, ringing the communication bell.

'I am yours to call.' Dystran smiled. 'When you need me.'

Brynar entered before the door was fully closed.

'You summoned me, Lord Denser.'

'Bring me Sharyr. And Barons Blackthorne and Gresse. And someone who can tell me how far the surviving Raven dead are from the gates.'

'Yes, my Lord.'

'And, Brynar?'

'Yes, my Lord?'

'Dystran is not to leave the catacomb chambers he scurries about in with Vuldaroq. Neither is anyone to have access to him without my express permission. His cook, his bed-maker and his arse-wiper can live with him until I say otherwise. Am I clear?'

Brynar nodded. He was chewing his bottom lip.

'It is time, young apprentice, that people understood who is really in charge on the Mount of Xetesk.'

'That's you, isn't it?'

Denser gave a wry smile in defiance of his heavy heart.

'Go to the top of the class.'

Chapter 15

Sol was seated. Not uncomfortably though he could not move his arms or legs to any great degree. Looking down he could see no ties or chains binding him yet the chair sucked his body into place, it seemed. He could recall little from the moment the Garonin had spoken to him and Balaia had vanished. A vague sensation of movement was all. And now he was here, wherever 'here' was. Sol looked about him.

His first thought was that he recognised this place, yet that was plainly ridiculous. It had no memorable features whatever bar the fact, he supposed, that it was completely featureless. The ground, if such it was, ran away endlessly. He could see no walls. Everything about him was the same pale ivory in colour. Even the chair on which he sat, though that at least had solidity. He'd have clung to it had he not been secured to it.

Dark motes wandered across Sol's vision. He blinked but they remained. It was a while before he realised that they were not dust in the air close to his eyes but figures moving in front of him. Distance was impossible to gauge and the figures were all faint, shimmering as if only partially there. Some were tiny and he assumed them far from him but it could be a trick of the even, gentle light.

Sol felt no fear. He was beyond that particular emotion. The enemy had not killed him and so they wanted him alive, temporarily at least. Curiosity, then, that was what drove him. And frustration. He wondered how long he would be made to wait.

Not long.

Figures resolved from the emptiness. Three of them, walking slowly towards him. They wore no armour and appeared the epitome of three friends out for a stroll. Long robes covered their huge, powerful bodies. Hands the size of Sol's head hung from thick wrists. Their heads were large and covered in bone ridges. Their eyes were bulging and black. They had no noses, but slits in the centre of their faces opened and closed in what he assumed to be a breathing action. And when they opened their mouths, he could see no teeth. They reminded Sol of a lesser strain of demon but it was plain enough that they had infinitely more power than those dangerous creatures.

The three came to within a few feet and towered above him where he sat. They fell silent, the melodious tones of their voices echoing away into the vast space, bouncing from whatever it was that formed this place. They studied Sol, their gazes so intent he turned his head away until a force he could not resist turned it back.

'You have achieved that of which few are capable.'

The words flowed like music about Sol's head. He fancied he could see symbols flashing to brief life in the air in front of his eyes. Sol did not answer. In truth he took a while to realise he was being addressed.

'Speak. You are worthy.'

How words sounding so beautiful could issue from mouths so ugly was a mystery. Sol stared up at each one of them.

'I will stand as an equal,' he said, his own voice sounded harsh in comparison, like fingernails scraped on metal.

He heard a ripple as of water over pebbles.

'But you are not equal. We are Garonin.'

'Then I will say nothing. You want my information, I presume. I demand your respect.'

'If you did not have that, you would not be here.'

Sol felt as if they were talking in concert. Their voices flowed over one another.

'I will stand,' he said.

And he stood, the chair no longer able to bind him. It faded away and now the four of them were truly alone in a barren land.

'You learn quickly. That is . . . advantageous.'

'To who?'

Sol was only half talking to them. He was trying to hide his amazement at what had just happened. The simple act of standing. Impossible moments ago. Achieved through what? Belief? Will-power?

'To all of us.'

Sol focused back on the Garonin. He gazed up at their faces. Ugly they might have been but there was no malice in them. There was nothing in the dark orbs of their eyes. Nothing in the set of their jaws that Sol could read.

'Why have you brought me here? Where *is* here?'

What probably passed for a smile appeared fleetingly on all three faces.

'People are drawn to you,' said one. 'Why is that?'

'I—' Sol paused. 'I'm not sure what you're getting at.'

'We want you to bring all the people to you. To make it an easier passing for them. We have no wish to inflict unnecessary suffering.'

'You could have bloody fooled me. Last thing I remember seeing was one of my dearest friends dying in a wreath of flame.'

'We will take what we need. The mode we employ is the only variable.'

'And what is it you're taking? Mana, we presume.'

There was a shrug. A very human gesture.

'If that is what you call it. The element your world possesses in such abundance is useful when combusted. We have need of considerable quantities.'

Sol scratched his neck under his chin. He hadn't shaved in days and the stubble was beginning to itch. Something didn't ring true here. They had no need of any negotiation, surely. Still, an opening was an opening.

'Let me tell you what I understand,' said Sol. 'I understand we've caused you a problem you didn't anticipate. That'll be the achievement you talk about. The destruction of your machine, perhaps. And while I accept you are far more powerful than we are, no one has infinite men and resources to fight. Eventually you reach breaking point. And I think we are delaying you, and you cannot afford that.

'How am I doing so far?' Sol smiled up at their hesitation. 'Pretty well, eh?'

The three Garonin turned their heads to one another, conversing without words.

'You must see that you cannot beat us,' said one eventually.

It was Sol's turn to shrug. 'I see that we have not yet perfected a way to defeat you.' A thought occurred. 'And in any event opinion is split as to whether we should be attacking you at all. There are those recently returned to us who believe we should run.'

'There is nowhere to run. Nowhere you have the means to go.'

The reply was just a little too quickly spoken.

'You fear us, don't you?' said Sol

'Preposterous.'

'You fear what we might become, where we might end up. You

even fear that what we do now is enough to cause you serious damage. You say you need some element that is created from burning mana. Why?'

'We all have those we fear. Be assured that you are not among them.'

Yet they paused and spoke again, came to another agreement though it was clearly not unanimous.

'Verrian. That is what we call the element you term . . . mana. Its combustion yields vydos, an element central to the construction of our weapons, armour and projectiles. Without it, our enemies would roll over us as simply as we roll over you. That is our situation. We fight a war that claims the lives of countless millions. We must be victorious. You will not stand in our way.'

Sol raised his eyebrows. His heart was beating hard in his chest.

'So you need something we possess. So there is a negotiation to be had here.'

'No!' It was the first hard sound any of their voices had made. Sol flinched. 'We take from the weak; we do not negotiate.'

'We lie down for no one,' said Sol.

'We appeal to your sensitivity as a ruler of men. To die in fear is needless. Die in sleep. Die painlessly. This we can guarantee. But die you must, to provide us with what we need.'

'I cannot. I will not ask my people to close their eyes and be slaughtered,' said Sol. 'You must understand that. We fight to defend our lands. That is our right. Our duty.'

The merest hints of light appeared in the eyes of the Garonin. A transitory tightening of their faces.

'People come to you. Trust you,' said one. 'Your living . . . and your dead.'

'How do you know that?'

'We see all that passes through this place.'

'What?'

But they would not elucidate.

'You will tell your people to lay down their arms and die with dignity.'

The tone was more strident now.

'I will do no such thing. I don't even understand why you want us dead. If it is the mana you want, take it. But leave us alive. We know where you are headed. The Hearts of our colleges are thick with mana. Why must we die for you to take them?'

'Every soul possesses verrian. We will take what we must.'

'Then you must fight for it,' said Sol. ' We will not surrender and become extinct to satisfy your desire for simplicity.'

'Then do it knowing an acquiescent soul holds more verrian than one in torment. That your chosen way of death can help others to live, to win their battles.'

Sol stared at them open-mouthed.

'You have one fucked-up morality, my enemy.'

'We will take what we must.'

'And you will pay for it in your blood every step of the way.'

'Destruction in agony, death in peace. It is your choice.'

Again the flashing in the eyes, the hardness of tone. But this time Sol was ready for it. He jabbed a finger into the chest of the centre Garonin, feeling great solidity beneath the robe.

'You have made a huge mistake bringing me here. You reveal your fears and you attempt desperate, ridiculous bargains to cover for them. No deal. No surrender. I repeat: your blood on our lands every step of the way. Unless you guarantee the lives of every man and elf in my world. What is it to be?'

'We do not need to make bargains with the weak.'

'Then our business is concluded. And now I will return to my people. Those I love and will protect with every mote of my strength.'

'No. You will not.'

'You think you can stop me? Then you underestimate just how quickly I learn and what I understand about this place.'

'You cannot hope to go against our wishes, human. You have neither the wit nor the means.'

The three of them stared at him and he heard that sound again, water over pebbles. Laughter. Sol's head cleared and he felt a satisfying coolness in his body. Releasing himself from the chair had been merely the first step. He held his hands in front of him, imagined his old two-handed blade, its weight, its every nick, its pommel and grip. And there it was in his grasp, as real as the breath in his lungs. Sol was moving before the Garonin had registered their surprise. The blade moved easily, as if wielded by his younger self.

Sol punched the blade straight forward, piercing the middle enemy's stomach. He dragged it clear and swung it up and left, catching the second Garonin's right shoulder and hurling him from his feet. Sol squared up to the third, in whose hands a weapon now lay.

But there was fear in his face and a tremble in his arms. Sol brought his blade back to a cocked position under his chin and buried it in his enemy's chest.

Sol stood over the man as his blood soaked into the ground, leaving no trace. They locked eyes.

'Two things. One, I have learned enough to defeat you here. Second, it is rude to laugh.' He let his blade go and it had disappeared before it hit the ground. He felt terribly tired. 'And now I will go home.'

Sol pictured Balaia. He pictured The Raven's Rest and he pictured the empty place beside Diera's body in their bed.

And the next thing he knew was Diera screaming into his face where he lay.

Sol grabbed her arms and dragged her close to him. She was incoherent, a quaking shuddering through her body. Her face was wild, terrified. He tried to calm her but his own terror was beginning to bite. Delayed, kept under control while he had been gone from Balaia but now given licence.

'Diera. Stop. Stop. Please.'

Sol was choking up. His throat was tight and the tears were welling in his eyes. Diera's fists were balled and she was thumping them into his chest. He was still dressed in the bloodstained clothes he had been wearing on the battlefield. Even down to his boots.

'How can you be here!' she screamed. 'How can you just appear like that?'

The dark was complete. It was night in Xetesk. Outside, there was quiet. In The Raven's Rest peace was shattered. Sol could hear his boys crying, frightened by the explosion of noise from their mother. One of them was already banging on the door to the bedroom.

'It's all right, boys,' said Sol. 'Go back to bed. Just nightmares.'

'Of course it's not bloody all right,' Diera shouted into his face. 'Their father has been missing for three days. Dead for all we knew. And then you appear in the blink of a cat's eyes. They lost their father and I my husband. How can you be here?'

Sol pushed her away, held her at arm's length.

'Three days?'

Diera sagged in his arms. The door to their bedroom opened and in the gloom he could make out both Jonas and young Hirad, standing fearful in the frame. Hirad was crying and clutching a small soft toy to his mouth.

'When did you get back?' asked Jonas.

'Just now,' said Sol quietly. 'Look, I'll come to see you in a little while, all right?'

'Why is mother shouting?' asked Hirad, mumbling through the toy.

'I'm sorry, darling,' said Diera. 'Your father gave me a shock. It's nothing. Go back to bed. We'll see you before you know it.'

The two boys hesitated. Diera pulled her arms from Sol's grip and went to them, hugging both of them to her.

'Everything's all right, I promise.'

'But my friends say an enemy is coming. That we'll have to run and that there are dead people everywhere and they are helping the enemy,' said Jonas.

'That is a lie,' said Sol sharply. 'You tell your friends in the morning that the dead are here to help us. I know they scare you but they mean you no harm. We will keep you safe. Nothing will happen to you. I will not let it.'

'See?' said Diera brightly. 'Your father will protect you. Now run along. We'll come and tuck you in. Go on now.'

She shooed them away and closed the door, turning an angry, pale face on Sol.

'Tell me it is going to get better. Explain to me what I do with our children. Make me understand what just happened. This is too much for me, Sol. You know that, don't you?'

Sol nodded. 'Just tell me one thing. Did anyone say how far the enemy are from Xetesk right now?'

'They are not heading this way at all at present, so Denser said when relating your heroics. Stupid old man that you are. If and when they turn, we will have four days, maybe five. How is your hip, anyway?'

'A little stiff.' Sol smiled.

Diera did not respond in kind. She came and sat on the side of the bed. She gestured at him, his clothes, and she shook her head.

'Where have you been?'

Sol swung his legs over the side of the bed to sit next to her and brushed dust and dirt from the sheet. The blood of the Garonin was still wet on his clothes and would stain.

'Sorry about that.'

Diera shrugged. 'Doesn't really matter now, does it?'

'I suppose not.' Sol leaned forward. 'I don't know where they took me. The enemy, that is. I hope Denser and the college can help me with that. Somewhere beyond our dimension . . . any dimension come to that. But there was familiarity there that I can't explain.'

'Why didn't they just kill you?'

'They wanted to make me agree to passive genocide, if you can believe it. But I made them see that we would fight them to the last man.'

Diera smiled at last. 'The mighty King Sol. Still fighting the good fight though this enemy is by all accounts too powerful to defeat even if we had a dozen colleges and a million soldiers.'

'Who told you that?'

'Hirad. Old Hirad, that is.'

'Survived, did he? That's good.' Sol felt a little warmth for the first time since he had returned. 'And you believe him to be the soul of Hirad in another body now, do you?'

The nod was fractional. 'The weight of evidence suggests that he might be telling the truth. His shadow completely freaks me out. Why does that happen?'

'Because the soul remembers the body it once inhabited, I suppose. It just goes to show that whatever skin you're in, you're still the same.'

Diera chuckled. 'And you can stop your lectures on the nature of man right there. And how did the enemy respond?'

'Garonin, that's what they call themselves. They didn't believe me. Showing them resulted in the three of them dying.'

'Back to the old methods of negotiation, is it?'

'You have been my wife for too long. Is my face really that revealing?' Sol shook his head. 'They made me angry. Wanted to stop me getting back to you. I can't have that, can I?'

Diera stroked his face. 'You never could. Lucky for me you always make it, isn't it?'

'I tell you one thing though. They mean to drain us of every drop of mana we possess and they will not stop until they get it. They are too powerful here on Balaia. We can't turn them away forever. And that means for you, for ordinary Xeteskians, it is time to leave.'

'And go where? If they are determined to kill us all, then nowhere is safe.'

'We'll find an escape,' said Sol. 'Things the Garonin said to me, mistakes they made. This isn't over, not by a long way. The dead will help us.'

Diera threw her arms around his neck and they clutched each other tight.

'Why does it always have to be you?' she said, her face buried in his shoulder.

'I'm just lucky, I suppose.'

She broke away and punched his arm. 'Bastard. What happens now?'

'Well, we get a few hours more sleep. Then I go to the Mount and we work out how to turn the Garonin away once more and where to run in the time that gives us. As for you, my love, I mean what I say. Take the boys. Take anyone else who believes enough to go with you. Head west. Find Tessaya. He knows you. The Wesmen will guard you until I get to you again.'

Diera nodded and sighed. 'All right. But you know Jonas is already talking about Beshara. He's not stupid. If we have to run, why not to a place where dragons will guard us?'

Sol blinked. Beshara. Realm of the dragons and inextricably linked to Balaia by the mental connections between Kaan brood dragons and selected human mages. And Jonas was a Dragonene. The Dragonene of Sha-Kaan, leader of his brood.

'How can I have been so stupid?'

Chapter 16

Sha-Kaan soared back into the clear blue heavens above Beshara and looked down at the devastation below. A line of seven vydospheres travelled the plains of Dormar, driving towards the steaming forests of Teras. His forests. Home of the Kaan.

The vydospheres spanned a huge swathe of the once-beautiful plains. Flush with Flamegrass, dense with life and the dwellings of the Vestare, human servants of the Kaan and all of Beshara's multiple broods of dragon. The war-torn world had known peace for many cycles and now this threatened to destroy all that had been built.

Behind the vydospheres, Dormar was a wasteland, worse than the ancient blasted lands of the Keol. The Garonin had already visited destruction upon the homelands of the Naik, the Skoor and even the ocean-going Veret. Now, closing on the lands of the largest brood, they were meeting significant resistance. Sha-Kaan could still see the wilderness expanding, the fires burning, spreading and consuming on a wider and wider arc.

Away to the south, the smoking ruins of an eighth vydosphere littered the ground, sparking fire here and there as it slowly disappeared. From the funnels of the others belched smoke and ash while above them the ground was occasionally obscured by the clouds formed as mana was burned for collection.

Sha-Kaan roared his flight to him. Thirty dragons, climbing hard into the sky, beyond the range of the tracers of white fire and the looping, smoking explosive projectiles. The Garonin had flooded the plain with men and weapons. They crushed Flamegrass underfoot, powdered the homes of the Vestare in their path and rendered all that was living to pale dust.

Yet they were still vulnerable. Six flights of dragons were in the air above them, awaiting the order to strike. Others from allied broods were on the way. The sky was filling with the massive shapes of dragons and the deafening noise of their calls and barks.

Sha-Kaan twisted his long, slender neck to check the damage to his one-hundred-and-twenty-foot-long body. Russet gold scales, some warped with age, others blistered by the heat of enemy weapons. Those blackened by the lick of dragon fire were trophies earned in forgotten conflicts.

He snapped his wings to their fullest width and executed a long, graceful turn, bringing him round behind the centre of the Garonin advance.

'Hold your shape. Breathe only on my command. Do not break, do not falter. Escape at best speed and angle.' Sha-Kaan's pulsed orders were greeted with thoughts of acknowledgment, determination and assurances of victory. 'Kaan. Dive.'

Sha-Kaan's bark was a shattering cry that echoed over the clanking, thundering noise of the Garonin invaders and their machines. In their harnesses, the dim-witted hanfeer tossed their heads and shuddered. The dragons dived. Wings tucked in tight, necks stretched out, the wind whistling over the mounds of their bodies. Their tails stabilised their lightning descent.

Sha-Kaan led them screaming towards the ruined plains. He snapped his wings out to brake and turn barely a hundred yards from the ground. He swept up to the horizontal, dipped even closer to the dust, and forged in. Garonin weapons were trained. They fired. A hundred teardrop streams of white light rattled out.

Heat blossomed on Sha-Kaan's body. Scales were burned and ripped from his belly, from his back and flanks. To his left, a Kaan was struck square in the muzzle. The dragon roared agony. The head, engulfed in fire, was torn apart and the body dropped to the ground to impact the dust and roll over and over. Sha-Kaan ignored the pain in his body and the tears in his wings as fire drops clipped them. He urged his dragons to hold and they did. Up and to the right another was caught in a crossfire of six weapons. The vast body exploded under the pressure of the impacts. Flesh filled the sky, knocked dragons aside. A wing spiralled down, folding in on itself and colliding with another Kaan below it. The dragon lost his bearings and, temporarily blinded, ploughed into the plains.

Sha-Kaan opened his mouth and felt the flame ducts swell. He swept through the line of Garonin soldiers. His jaws beheaded one, his claws dropped and tore up four more, breaking them and casting them aside. Around him his Kaan exulted. Sha-Kaan tasted blood in his mouth and sniffed more revenge.

He focused on the rear of the vydosphere. Huge before him, a billowing metal shell, vibrating as it built to another combustion. He let the fuel from his flame ducts enter his mouth. Through his nostrils, he inhaled the air of his land.

'Breathe.'

Twenty mouths disgorged super-heated flame. The dragon flight split around the body of the vydosphere, pouring flame across its surface. Funnels collapsed. Antennae shrivelled and melted. The skin darkened, blistered and bubbled. Sha-Kaan breathed again, coming over the spine of the machine. His flame ate into the vydosphere. Rivets popped and plates buckled. The whole skin heaved.

Sha-Kaan crested the apex of the vydosphere. In their harnesses, the hanfeer were burning, screaming impotent rage. One had fallen sideways. The other still tried to move forward.

'Clear, my Kaan. We are done.'

The vydosphere gouted smoke and steam through torn plating. Huge areas of the skin were sucked inwards. Sha-Kaan did not look round to see the explosion. He used the wave of force to drive him over the ground at even greater speed and into the forward lines of Garonin already engaged in fighting the dragons clouding the air above them.

Sha-Kaan dropped until his claws were brushing the ground. He opened them and scooped enemies into each before angling his wings and beating away high into the sky. Safe in the heavens once more, he snaked his head down to his claw and brought one of the writhing, struggling figures to his eye. He set his wings to a lazy glide.

'All will go the same way,' he said. 'Take your machines and leave our lands.'

'We will take what we must,' said the Garonin. 'You will not stop us.'

'Wrong,' growled Sha-Kaan. 'Beshara will not fall to you.'

'Even you are vulnerable and we know how to hurt you.'

'You will not find them.'

The Garonin laughed. 'You are mistaken, Great Kaan. We already have.'

Sha-Kaan closed his left claws and let the blood flow over them. His other claws he opened, letting his victim drop.

'Puny foe.'

But there was anxiety in his mind. He needed to know they were lying. He flew to the upper skies and sought the mind of his Dragonene while the battle raged on below him.

Jonas was awake when Sol looked in to see him that morning. Or rather he was vaguely conscious. Sol hurried to his bedside and knelt by him, smoothing the hair from his face and putting a hand on his sweating brow. Jonas's eyes were moving rapidly below fluttering eyelashes. The rest of his body was utterly still.

'Diera!' he called. 'Jonas is speaking with Sha-Kaan. He'll need you. Hirad, go and get dressed and washed. Wait in our bedroom.'

'But I want—'

'Hirad, please. Be a good boy.'

Diera appeared in the bedroom doorway and held out her hand.

'Come on, Hirad. Let's find a game. I'll be back, Sol.'

Sol nodded and turned back to Jonas.

'Jonas, can you hear me? I'm here right by you.'

'Fire . . .' mumbled Jonas, a line of dribble coming from the corner of his mouth. 'Burned scales. White fire. Ahh!'

The gasp was accompanied by an opening of his eyes. He stared about him for a moment before settling on Sol. His face cleared a little and a hand moved to grip his father's arm.

'Are you seeing or relaying?' asked Sol.

'Seeing,' whispered Jonas. His bottom lip trembled. 'The enemy are there. Garonin. The dragons are fighting. I think they are losing.'

'Jonas, it's important. I have to know if we can escape to Beshara. Can I speak to Sha-Kaan? Will you channel for me?'

Jonas frowned and his teeth grabbed at his upper lip. 'Father.'

'I know I'm asking you to endure pain. Believe me, I wouldn't ask unless I thought we had no other choice. I need answers and I don't think you can ask the questions, even if I'm here. I need to hear Sha-Kaan. Jonas?'

Jonas's eyes had closed but his mouth had curved up into a smile.

'The Great Kaan says you had better be careful with me or . . .'

Sol laughed. 'Or he'll crush me like a twig, I know.'

The room filled with a new presence. A smell of oil and wood and the weight of great age and power. Jonas's mouth hung open. He breathed deeply but otherwise was completely still.

'Sol. It is good to feel you though the times are our darkest yet.'

'As ever, your presence honours me.'

'We can dispense with that. Your family gives so much that the

Kaan value. You have questions. I have questions. Jonas is strong but he still cannot support this for long. He is young yet.'

'Then ask, Great Kaan.'

'Jonas relates that you are attacked. Is it the Garonin?'

'They destroy everything in their path and leave an expanding disaster behind them. We have hurt them but I do not think we can stop them. I have to know. Can we escape to Beshara? Can you protect us?'

There was a heavy silence. Sol could feel Sha-Kaan's concern in the air. He could all but taste the tension.

'No. They would combine forces and we could not repel them. The damage they have caused is extensive but I believe we can turn them if they do not reinforce. But not if we lose Balaia. Not if I lose Jonas.'

'You will not lose him. Not while I still draw breath,' said Sol. 'But we are on the verge of losing Balaia already. Only Julatsa and Xetesk still stand and both are weak.'

'You have questions. You need another way to fight.'

'Yes. Sha-Kaan, I was taken by the Garonin. They wanted to negotiate a peaceful end to our existence. They took me to a place beyond anything I have known and yet it was familiar. Something they said made me wonder. They said they saw all that passed through the place. I got the impression it was outside everything else, every other dimension but perhaps a route to each one. Something like that. And I travelled from there by force of will to appear back here. This is vague, I know, but you are a dimensional traveller. Do you know of this place?'

'It is impossible,' breathed Sha-Kaan, and for the first time in their long association Sol heard awe and fear in the great dragon's voice.

Sol's heart sank. 'What is?'

'I know of where you speak,' said Sha-Kaan, his voice rumbling but quiet, his tone reverential. 'In your language we would describe it as the top of the world. It is not a place any should be able to travel to by choice.'

'But it is a place we can fight them, I'm certain of that.'

'That may be so but there are two things you should know. If indeed you were there and the Garonin can travel there at will, they are more powerful than even I imagined. And for them to have taken you there speaks even more highly of their abilities as travellers and more dangerously of their capacity to rape any dimension they discover. Because from all the lore I know, only the soul free of the body may travel there, and even then only to pass through on the journey to ultimate rest.'

Sol felt another door close on their chances. Diera laid a hand on his shoulder. He covered it with one of his own and squeezed.

'Diera,' said Sha-Kaan. 'Your son bears up well.'

'He looks weak,' she said. 'But it is good to hear you.'

'We have little good news. Sol, should you wish to pursue this path, speak with me again. But tell me. Jonas said the dead have returned. No doubt pursued by the Garonin into Balaia through the top of the world. Who has returned? Only the strong bonded souls?'

Sol relaxed a little. 'So it seems. Much of The Raven though we have already lost many of them again. Hirad is here.'

'Ahhh. I would love to feel his mind again.'

'I'm sure it can be arranged. He has not changed.'

The Great Kaan chuckled. Pictures vibrated on the walls.

'Is Septern returned? His soul would desire it and his ego would bring him back, I am sure.'

'There is a man in Xetesk claiming to be him,' said Sol.

'Then speak to him of where you were taken. He knows much he did not commit to parchment. Jonas is unsteady. I must tend to his mind and return him to you.'

'We will speak again, Great Kaan.'

'Remain strong. We will fight, you must fight too. If you should flee, do not leave us in the dark.'

'Never.'

Sha-Kaan's presence left the room. Jonas was still for a moment before screwing up his face and opening his eyes.

'Mama!'

Sol left them to their embrace.

Hirad had been clutching at his stomach while the pain threatened to swamp him and the wind threatened to tear his soul from its anchorage and cast him into the void. Neither Ilkar not Sirendor was in any better shape. Yet abruptly the pain had eased, returned to what Ilkar would describe as a manageable level. He blew out his cheeks and straightened in his chair. To his left and right he could see the other two were feeling the same. Across the table Denser paused in his reading and looked at the three of them.

'What just happened?' he asked. 'Something good, I'm hoping.'

Hirad could not keep the smile from his face.

'He's back. I told you he wasn't dead. I told you.'

'What?' Denser was gaping. Hirad knew how he felt. 'Where?'

'Close. Right now that's all I care about.'

Denser smiled. 'That is good news. We need him on the streets.'

Hirad nodded. News of the losses of Xeteskian mages and soldiers had spread quickly through the city. The confidence the departing force had inspired had dispersed like dust on the breeze with the returning stragglers. The populace was nervous and the returned dead were beginning to have a serious impact. People were leaving.

'And what do you expect him to be saying?' asked Ilkar. 'I'd have thought he'd be showing the way to the west, not trying to shore up morale.'

'There is no need for this panic reaction,' said Denser.

It was dawn now and a pale light was streaming through the window of the dining chamber, where an early breakfast had been laid and ignored by all but the Lord of the Mount.

'Where does that opinion come from? The catacombs? The destruction of one machine shouldn't give us rash confidence about saving Balaia,' said Ilkar. 'You heard Sharyr. They just rolled into Lystern and rolled out with the Heart. We are down to two functioning colleges and Julatsa is likely to fall within days. You know where that leaves us.'

'Yes, with Xetesk still standing and not even under threat because we turned them away.'

'But that is not victory,' said Sirendor. 'It is delay at best. Don't revise what you know you saw out there. It was slaughter. And your mage team that broke the machine? All dead.'

'And your second salvo of spells was useless because they learned how to defend against them,' added Ilkar. 'Come on, Denser. You know it as well as we do. We cannot win here.'

Denser's face reddened and the bread in his hand remained halfway to his mouth.

'No? I'm looking at facts, not suppositions. We now have proof that Gresse's theory holds water. Those machines are initially incapable of sucking in the mana density from an attractor as big as a Heart. They have to reach a critical mass first. That means if we time our attacks well, we can keep them at bay indefinitely.'

'Your logic is seriously flawed,' said Ilkar.

'I'd have put it differently,' said Hirad.

'That's why I jumped in before you. We can do without your version of tact right now.'

'Please explain the errors of Xetesk to me, my dead friend,' said Denser.

'Enough sarcasm, Denser, we're talking about the lives of everyone here. And the deaths of everyone too. We cannot afford any errors, don't you see that?' Ilkar cleared his throat. 'Isn't it obvious how they will react to another machine or two being destroyed? They'll just appear here with everything they've got and level this place.'

'Why haven't they done that already?' asked Denser. 'Where's your logic for that?'

'They want to achieve their aims with minimal manpower,' said Sirendor. 'Just as we would. I have no doubt they have the capacity to do whatever they want but why commit it until necessary?'

'I'll tell you why. It's because they can't,' said Denser. He pushed a scorched parchment across the table. 'Sharyr found this. It refers to these Garonin and talks about an unending conflict beyond the boundaries of our known dimensions. Unending. And this was written by Septern. That's well over three hundred years ago. All we have to do is chip away and we will turn them for good. They'll give up and go somewhere easier to exploit.'

Hirad closed his eyes. 'How can you read this so wrong? Denser, you're a Raven man. You know Lystern is gone. You know Calaius has gone the same way. That leaves plenty of enemy to focus on Xetesk. We have to concentrate on finding an escape, not on futile defence.'

'Ah, and there's the rub, isn't it?' Denser leaned back in his chair and picked up his coffee mug. He cradled it in his hands. 'Neither my mage teams nor you have any idea where we might escape to. I mean, you have come back here – and I love you for it – to tell us to run, but you cannot tell us where. You say nowhere on Balaia is safe but you cannot supply a single ship, so to speak, to transport us to sanctuary. What is this desire to head for the west? What will it gain us?'

Hirad sighed. 'All right. Admittedly, we don't know. But we are drawn there. The Wesmen will be able to help us. I know this sounds flaky but their paths to the dead are different from ours. We think they can open the door to a new home. But we can't prove it.'

'Right. And until you can, my streets will remain unsettled by your divisive presence and your scaremongering, and my efforts will necessarily have to be focused on defending my people. Keeping them from running to an uncertain future when they should be standing and fighting. If I do not, I am derelict in my duty, am I not? Do you really feel I have a choice?'

Hirad shook his head and stood. 'You believe them, don't you? You believe the word that we are here to chase the living away and have this place for ourselves. Be straight. Do you think the Garonin are here at our behest? Is that what you actually believe?'

'Gods drowning, of course I don't. Bloody hell, Hirad, I have locked Dystran up in his rooms precisely because I don't believe that rubbish.'

'But you still visit him, don't you?' said Hirad, feeling his skin getting hot. 'You still hear what he says.'

'Who I visit and what I ask and listen to is my business and not yours, all right? And yes, I do listen to him because he is smart despite his unfortunate views in some areas. And one thing we do agree on is that we don't know what more good you can really do. The dead as a whole, that is.'

Hirad reached across the table and hauled Denser from his chair by the collars of his shirt.

'I'll tell you what we can do. We can stop you from signing away the lives and deaths of everyone who ever came from Balaia. We can help you find a place where we can all start again.'

Hirad's breath fired into his face. Denser's face deepened into a scowl.

'You will unhand me, Hirad. Right now.'

Hirad did not.

'You have to listen to him, Denser,' said Ilkar, coming to his feet also. 'There is only one way to delay the Garonin and give us the time and chance to find a way out of here. Surrender the Heart. Do a deal.'

Denser stiffened. 'Surrender the Heart of Xetesk? Never.'

'Then they will take it from you,' said Ilkar.

'That you could utter such . . . heresy, here in this tower,' said Denser, his face blazing with his rage. 'I am the Lord of the Mount and you will release me, Hirad. Perhaps Dystran was right. Guards!'

The door opened but it was not guards who entered, it was Sol.

'Fantastic,' he said. 'This is the face of unity, is it? Gods drowning, Hirad, put him down. And all of you calm down. I could hear you half way down The Thread.'

Hirad shoved Denser back into his chair.

'I want—'

'Denser, shut up. We're in big trouble but there might just, just be a way out. We need to talk to Septern. I presume you've verified it is him by now. And first you need to hear an old friend.'

Sol pushed open the door. Hirad sat back in his chair, unable to believe his eyes.

Standing in the doorway was Auum.

Chapter 17

Auum stared at the humans, the living and the dead, as they bickered their way towards catastrophe. At first it had been fascinating. The legendary mage Septern had spoken at length about the history of his dimensional discoveries but had not been allowed to discuss what he was here to discuss. Hirad Coldheart, whose shadow adorned the wall to Auum's left, had brought to the table all the raging belief that had at first irritated but now endeared him to Auum and indeed all the elves. And Ilkar had spoken carefully and tactfully about what had happened to the dead of Balaia. Yet still they fought, and in the middle Denser appeared not to know who to believe.

Auum himself had remained silent, answering only direct questions thus far, and there had been few enough of them. He had been content to rest a little, eat a little and drink a good amount of water. The mages who had carried him and his Tai from the ship and all the way north to Xetesk on flickering Freedom Wings were exhausted and sleeping. He had no time for that. Not yet.

'I'm not going to repeat myself again,' said Denser. 'No one else is leaving because there is nowhere to go. Here we stand and here we fight. As for you and your dead, Hirad, you do what you like.'

'That is a shameful statement,' said Hirad. 'We exist in pain every heartbeat yet we endure it because we desire only to help the living survive and so secure ourselves a new place of rest. Or we hope that. The fact is, we have no certainty whatever about the outcome. We're here because of those we love. I had counted you among those people. Perhaps I was mistaken.'

'But you have no answers!' Denser was practically screaming in his frustration. 'Your best gambits so far are: give them the Heart and hope they stop, or get us all to the west and some mythical Wesmen-organised escape route. You are talking about the end of magic on Balaia at the very least and an abandonment of our home dimension at the ridiculous worst.'

'We are talking about a return to a more natural state of magic,' said Ilkar. 'And is that not better than certain extinction?'

'I will not relinquish our only true chance of beating these bastards, Ilkar.'

'No, what you won't relinquish is Xetesk's power over Balaia. And it'll do you no good because they will simply come in here and take it. They make the demons look like a bunch of apple scrumpers. Why won't you understand that?'

Denser was on his feet again and Ilkar stood opposite him. Both jabbed fingers and puffed out chests. Auum watched Ilkar with discomfort, the elf's words coming from a youthful human mouth.

'You fear that, don't you, Ilkar? Xetesk being the only magical power remaining on Balaia. It's pathetic.'

'I'm dead, in case you hadn't noticed. I couldn't care less who is left and who isn't so long as it means I can return to my rest. But you, you and your Circle Seven and that bastard snake Dystran, you desire dominion, don't you? And that should scare us all. Because you'll sacrifice the lot of us pursuing this folly. But you have to listen to what everyone bar your inner circle of power-mongers tells you: we have to run.'

'Where, damn you, where? What do I advise my people? Follow these dead west but I don't know where or why? Dear Gods falling, please throw me a scrap here.'

'I know where,' said Auum.

For a moment the noise of the argument continued but Auum's voice had a way of leaching through even the most sewn-down of ears. One by one, they turned to him. He waited until he had the attention of them all.

'And so do the Wesmen.'

'You could have said so before,' said Hirad. 'Told you, Denser.'

'But then, like all of you, I would have been speaking before I was truly ready,' said Auum. He was staring at Denser. 'I will speak without interruption.'

Denser spread his hands. 'Help yourself.'

'Then sit, all of you, and hear me because time runs short and your complaining brings all of our deaths closer. Denser, you are wrong. The Garonin are unstoppable but they are escapable. Their resources are stretched but this dimension is so dense with mana that they will pour what they must into it to gain it all. And they will come back time and again when the density builds. This world is no longer viable for man or elf.

'Ilkar, you are wrong too. They will not stop after gaining the Hearts. The mana held in the soul of each man living and in each dead soul is too much to ignore. This is still a populous country. They will annihilate everyone while collecting their verrian. You should have read the lore of the Ynissul more closely while you still lived.'

Auum gestured at Septern. 'And you, great mage returned, you have many of the answers but your memories are flawed. You have been dead too long. But even you are aware of the cost to some of our survival, as are all of the dead around this table though they hesitate to admit what they truly need. I see it in your eyes. In a moment you shall speak of Ulandeneth but first I shall say this:

'Any who wish to escape the Garonin, and that is the only way to survive them, have two choices. The first and infinitely prefer-able, though terribly dangerous, is to travel west to the Charanacks, the Wesmen. They and their Shamen can open the first door. It is dangerous because such a concentration of souls will attract the Garonin and you will be beset.

'The second choice is to try and hold the fastnesses of Julatsa, Xetesk and Korina for long enough to allow those who travel the first door to find the new home and open escape routes there for all remaining souls in this dimension. However, the Garonin are already too close and will overwhelm your cities within days. Far too quickly in any event for the corridors to be opened.'

Sol raised a hand. 'Auum, if I may speak before you call on Septern?'

Auum nodded.

'Thank you. One point of interest you raise is the concentration of souls. Surely if we break up those concentrations, we deflect Garonin interest or certainly dilute their attack front by spreading ourselves more thinly.'

Auum smiled. 'That may be so but it merely delays the inevitable. The Garonin means of travel and detection of mana will bring them to their quarry in time.'

'But surely worth a try,' said Denser, staring squarely at Hirad. 'Anyone who wants to run and hide in the Blackthorne Mountains and the Wesman Heartlands can do so. That will draw attention from those dedicated to the service and defence of Xetesk and Balaia.'

'I may be dead, Denser, but I'm still quicker than you, all right?' said Hirad.

'Spare me, Hirad.'

'You are betraying The Raven.'

'I am trying to save my people,' said Denser.

'We are your people.'

'Were.'

'Enough,' said Sol, resting a restraining hand on Hirad's bunched arm. 'Auum.'

'You demonstrate further ignorance, Denser,' said Auum.

Denser shook his head and sighed. 'I will beat myself later. What is it this time?'

'None of the dead around this table have the luxury of running to hide. Do they, Septern? Do they, Hirad, Ilkar?'

'What is he talking about?' asked Denser.

'Ulandeneth,' said Septern. 'It is the place through which all souls are said to pass on their way to birth, and on their way to death. It is the only place that links every dimension in every dimensional cluster. If we are to escape the Garonin, those tasked with opening the corridors must travel there to seek the new home. I searched for it all my life. I found so many places and all spoke of it. But I never found Ulandeneth. That is the elven term by the way. The Soul Home. There are many others but it is perhaps the one that sits most easily on the tongue.'

'Can we go back a bit?' asked Denser. 'Dimensional clusters?'

Septern nodded at Sharyr, another so-far-silent presence. 'Go on. I like your explanation of it. You'd have made a fine student of mine, you know.'

Sharyr blushed. 'When Sol described how the dragons were under attack, it led me to thinking. The demons have been destroyed, so we understand from souls claiming to have escaped them. The dead dimension has also been torn apart; Balaia is under attack; every place that we know, simultaneously invaded. To me, it means that the Garonin found them all at once.'

Sharyr crabbed his hand. 'Imagine this to be Ulandeneth. It sits at the top of everything. It's the hub of all life, like this tower is the hub of Xeteskian magic. Then imagine lines coming out of Ulandeneth, countless lines probably and each one leading to a cluster of dimensions.

'What I think is that each cluster is self-contained. It has a place for the dead and a number, probably variable, of places for various living species. It's a way of organising the vastness of creation, if you like. If you are able to travel dimensions, even in a limited sense like dragons and demons can, it is because you can sense some of the lines that lead between dimensions. And when you die, you are channelled back up to Ulandeneth and then down to your particular place of rest.'

'You're sure there is a place for the dead in each cluster, are you?' asked Denser.

'It's just a theory,' said Sharyr. 'Nothing is certain.'

'And Auum, you cannot confirm absolutely that your dead travelled to a different place in your former home than they do now, am I right?'

Auum inclined his head.

Denser glared briefly at Ilkar. 'Go on, Sharyr.'

'Thank you. Now because for every soul there is no pause, the transit through Ulandeneth is brief indeed. Rumours of seeing light, sensing others around you, helping hands, fleeting fear just as you die . . . all these things make sense if you believe in Ulandeneth. It provides for them all. And it is a safe haven. The only trouble is, it appears the Garonin have learned how to stop there.

'And not only that, they have begun to detect the lines that lead out to other dimensional clusters. I think they do this by following the souls of the dead because, as we know, the barrier between the dead and the living dimensions is actually very thin. It is a short step from communicating with the dead across the barrier to crossing it physically. All the Garonin had to do was rip open the dead dimension and then follow the dead to whichever home was theirs.

'Simple, really.'

Sharyr leaned back and took a long draught of water from a goblet held in a slightly shaking hand.

'Yeah,' said Hirad. 'Really, really basic stuff. I just soak up dimensional theory, I do.'

Denser was considering all that Sharyr had said. 'So, in effect, you could argue that the dead have brought all this trouble on us.'

Ilkar's shoulders sagged. 'Oh dear Gods falling, is that really the way your mind has started to work?'

'Stands to reason. If you don't come back, the Garonin don't follow you,' said Denser.

'You really don't see what a prat you're making of yourself, do you?' said Sirendor. 'And to think I died to save you and they all spoke so highly of you. We didn't have a damn choice, Denser. It wasn't like we could drift in the void and decide whether to return here or whether to carry on drifting. If we felt the pull of Balaia, that's where we went. I hate all this apportioning of blame shit. We're in trouble. Let's deal with it if we can, all right?'

'I can't help feeling that a solution is near but that a couple of crucial pieces are being left out, possibly deliberately,' said Sol. 'Because at the moment it is clear that the most sensible thing to do is to head west, get the Shamen to open the door and people like Hirad and the rest of The Raven dead go through and we wait for them to open the door to our new home while we fight off the Garonin if we can. So, where are the snags and why do I feel I am going to be directly affected?'

There was silence for the first time since the meeting convened. Auum studied them all. None of the dead could face Sol. Denser looked perplexed now as well as angry and Sharyr, who had done his part, seemed lost in his own thoughts.

'Anyone?' Sol spread his hands. 'Hirad, you're looking embarrassed. What are you hiding?'

'I'm so sorry, Unknown. When I came back, I did not know it would lead to this.'

'To what? Come on, I've got an inn to run. Special ale to offer the Garonin when they come a-knocking.'

'We're here because we were attracted to your soul. You're the reason we made it across the void. You and Denser, to be accurate, but you mainly. Fortunately. Anyway, without you we are just a loose collection of souls again. Without cohesion or direction. We'll be lost.'

'Fine, so I'll take you to the doorway myself before I wave goodbye. So what?'

'Don't make me say it, Unknown, please.'

'I'm afraid I must insist,' said Sol.

Hirad swallowed. 'We need you with us all the way, Unknown. To Ulandeneth and beyond. The Garonin know your influence. Why do you think they took you? This cannot be done without you.'

'Terrific,' said Sol. 'Fucking terrific. And how do I travel there with you alive?'

'You do not,' said Auum. 'If my memory serves, the ritual to open the door to Ulandeneth requires the sacrifice of a man of free will because the soul must be pure in order to seek and to lead.'

'I see,' said Sol. 'Does anyone here want to volunteer how I explain my imminent and voluntary demise to my wife?'

Chapter 18

'I should have beaten you with the cudgel while I had the chance,' said Sol.

'I'm sorry, Unknown. Truly. We all are.'

Denser had largely cleared the room. Sharyr and Septern had returned to the catacombs. Auum had gone to rest. The Raven, such as they were, were alone in the dining chamber.

'Why did I let you in and listen to you?'

'Because it's me!' Hirad spread his arms and smiled.

'It certainly was bloody you. Mayhem from beyond the grave. Who else could it be?'

Sol slumped into an armchair. His body felt strange, like he was in the grip of a fever. He wanted to be furious. He wanted to shout and scream at them about the injustice of it all. That he had a wife and children and had sworn to protect them.

'And that's just it, though, isn't it?' he said.

'Sorry, Unknown?' said Sirendor. 'I didn't quite catch that.'

'Just thinking aloud. Denser, pour some wine, would you? And let's all sit. Like we used to do in the back room of The Rookery all those years ago.'

He waited until they had all taken seats by the cold fireplace. Hirad's feet were on the low table in front of them. Sirendor and Ilkar both leaned forward, forearms resting on their thighs. Denser sat upright, tense and uncomfortable. And Sol, well he sprawled like he always had.

'Remember when we first met Denser? How we all felt it was a long, hard and probably fatal journey ahead even before we heard he was after Dawnthief? And how when he talked to us in the back room that sinking feeling took over for a while before we decided we just had to face what was coming? Sorry, Sirendor, I know you don't.'

'But you were there,' said Hirad helpfully. 'We put your body on the banquet table and covered it with a cloth.'

'I am thus reassured,' said Sirendor. 'I trust I looked my best.'

'Well there wasn't much blood or anything, except what you coughed up when you were dying.'

'Can we leave this until later?' said Sol.

'Sorry,' said Hirad.

'Me too,' said Sirendor.

'You've ruined my moment,' said Sol. 'Forget it.'

'No,' said Hirad. 'Go on.'

Denser leaned forward. 'I do not believe you are seriously entertaining this prospect.'

'Why wouldn't I?'

'Because it is preposterous and the ultimate act of selfishness on the part of the dead to demand you kill yourself to save them.'

'But if it is the only way to save the Balaian people? My people?'

'*If*. Yes. If.' Denser sipped at his wine. 'And I say what I am about to say with due deference to all the quite unbelievable things I've seen and places I've been with The Raven. Isn't this just a little bit far-fetched?'

'You're joking, right?' asked Hirad. 'A load of dead people walking about and Calaius evacuated and destroyed being normal business, I suppose?'

'No, Hirad, I'm not joking.' Denser pulled his skullcap off his head and rubbed a hand through his close-cropped grey hair. 'Look, I'm not playing down the threat we face. I'm not pretending the situation isn't desperate. But you're expecting Sol, The Unknown Warrior and King of Balaia, might I remind you, to follow you into the Wesman Heartlands and commit suicide to open a gate to somewhere so you can head somewhere else and open a gate back? It's madness.'

'It's the only possible solution,' said Ilkar.

'It quite clearly is not,' said Denser.

'Your solution will lead to our annihilation,' said Hirad sharply.

'Big word, barbarian. Who taught you that one?'

Sol was out of his chair and between them before a blow could be landed. He felt a perverse sense of comfort and satisfaction.

'That's what I was thinking about. Real Rookery debate.' He allowed the smile to leave his face. 'Now sit down, both of you.'

Denser threw up his hands and sat heavily. 'It wouldn't be so bad,

Sol, but they are offering you no choice, no alternative. This is blind faith at best. It was never the way we did things.'

'Oh, you misunderstand,' said Sol. 'It was always the way we did things. The Raven's way was trust even in the face of ridicule. Nothing has changed bar the fact that there is no chance I will survive versus a very slim chance.'

'But isn't that it? We always believed that somehow we would escape and survive.'

'I'm not sure that's true either,' said Sol. 'I had no thought that we would survive the demons. I was certain we'd be trapped there, weren't you?'

'But there was always the tiniest chance,' said Denser.

'All right, you've made your point. Now I want to speak. It is me after all who is being asked to die in this rather inglorious manner.'

'Could be Denser,' said Ilkar, his eyes twinkling. 'Any man of free will can make the sacrifice.'

Denser scoffed. 'I don't think so.'

'Neither did I,' said Hirad.

'The thing is, Denser,' said Sol, beginning loudly before letting his voice drop a little. 'The thing is, that there was never really any hope of surviving this one, was there? And so any chance to save Balaia's living and dead must be taken. However small and however far-fetched it may appear.

'When we were at our best, it was in pretending that the only option open was in any case the best one and that others would present themselves if needed. But we never had choice, not really. There was never the option to stand aside and let someone else do it because there was no one else. And it is the same now.

'I am king, you are right. And as king I am responsible for all the people of Balaia. Right now they are being slaughtered, and I don't see that we can defend against this enemy. That means we have to go elsewhere to live. It's something you have to learn, Denser. Sometimes you cannot win. And you have to choose the next best option. In this case, survival.'

Denser slapped his hands on the table. 'But you won't survive, Sol. Win or lose, you'll already be dead.'

'But if by my death others live, that is enough. If I can save my wife and sons by this action I will do it in a heartbeat, don't you see that? Wouldn't you do the same?'

Denser's shoulders sagged. 'Well, yes. But I'd have to believe. Do you believe?'

'When The Raven assure me that something must be done, I believe them. When that assertion is backed up by Auum, I believe them even more. But when I've been to the place where we must go, where we can fight the Garonin if we must, there is no room for doubt in my heart.'

'Yes. You've been there. And come back. Alive. Why not again?'

'Because the Garonin are not going to take me there again.' Sol finally sat down again. 'Denser, if I face the Garonin here again, I will die. If I am to fight them and help my people live, I need to take the chance to even the odds.

'It just makes perfect sense. In Ulandeneth you can do anything you believe you can, I'm certain of it. And who else to travel with but those in whom I believe the most. The Raven. I wish you'd come but I understand if you feel you can't. Decision's made, my dear friend and Lord of the Mount. I will do this thing and we will prevail.

'Denser. Denser, look at me. Thank you. I respect your objections. Gods drowning, I love you for your caution and your pragmatism. But the time for both has passed. And I need you to support us in what we are about to do. You may be Lord of the Mount now but you are still Raven. In spirit it may be but we need you with us. What say you?'

Denser studied his wine goblet and sucked his bottom lip. When he looked up, he was shaking his head.

'I cannot,' he said. 'I cannot because you are my friend and I think you're making a colossal error. And because you are king and first warrior, and your people need you to stand with them, not disappear off to converse with Wesman Shamen. And because your head is turned by the thought of fighting with The Raven one more time. Only it won't be how you remember. How does a soul fight, do you think? I'm sorry, Sol, but I can do nothing but repeat my strong objections. I can't let you do this.'

'Can't?' said Hirad. 'Exactly how are you going to stop him?'

Denser said nothing. He sipped at his wine and stared out of the window.

The Raven quartet descended the long spiral stairway in silence. They found nothing to say as they walked across the floor of the tower complex and out into the warm of the morning sun.

'Fancy a walk, anyone?' asked Ilkar.

'Not if it's like the last one we took,' said Hirad. 'How is dear Selik, by the way?'

'Raging in his cell. We're wondering whether to put him out of his misery and let another soul take the body.'

'Pointless now, I should think,' said Ilkar. 'No one else is going to make it here now. The void will have taken them all. We just can't hang on to anything without a body and the dead dimension is utterly destroyed. We can feel it. Let him rot.'

'I'll put your opinion to the Circle Seven,' said Sol. 'Look, I really need to go and talk to my wife and children. Stop by later, why don't you? Pick up the pieces of my teeth perhaps.'

'She'll understand, Unknown,' said Hirad.

'Don't be stupid, Hirad. She will neither understand nor accept it. And neither should she.' Sol tried a smile but it didn't come off. 'See you later. Don't drift too far; I know how much it hurts.'

Ilkar, Sirendor and Hirad watched him go before a shrug from the latter and a point towards the eastern quarter of the city sent them on their way. Just beyond the apron outside the gates of the college Ilkar saw, through the passing hubbub of a nervous day on The Thread, three figures detach themselves from the shadows ahead. He touched Hirad's arm.

'Seen them,' said Hirad.

The three old friends carried on walking across the stone of the apron and made their way across The Thread itself. The figures were waiting for them, watching. There was no point avoiding them. And no need. Hirad took his hand from his sword hilt.

'I thought you'd gone for a lie-down,' he said.

'There are more pressing matters,' said Auum. Ghaal and Miirt stood close behind him. 'This city is on the verge of tearing itself apart.'

Ilkar felt the hairs on the back of his neck stand up. Not a pleasant experience in this body. 'What's going on?'

'Come.'

Auum didn't wait to see if they were with him. He spun on his heel and trotted away into a wealthy residential area of Xetesk. Much of it was empty of its usual occupants. All senior mages and administrators had been closeted in the college for many days now. It gave the area an eerie feel.

An angry shout rang out close by. Abruptly, Auum and his Tai broke into a run, leaving the Raven trio trailing in their wake. Ilkar recognised the tenor of the shouting. Violence hung in the air. Breaking out into a square bordered by tall houses and centred by a fenced garden, Ilkar saw a handful of figures in pursuit of something or someone with Auum's Tai hard on their heels, eating up the distance between them.

Ilkar, running a few paces behind Hirad, couldn't quite see the head of the chase through the trees and hedges bordering the garden. He heard a scream and the sounds of combat. He upped his pace. Ahead of him, Hirad and Sirendor drew their swords. Ilkar began to prepare a HardShield, or whatever it was Denser called it these days.

A mob of Xeteskians was attacking at least one poor unfortunate. Ilkar was in time to see Auum fly into the aggressors two-footed and at head height. One of them took the force full on the side of his skull. Auum dropped in amongst them. Ghaal and Miirt splitting left and right behind him.

The TaiGethen's leader blurred. He flat-palmed a second in the chest, sending him sprawling. A third had his legs taken from under him, and before a fourth could react, Auum had bounced back to his feet and round-housed his target in the temple. He finished his move standing astride the single victim, both short swords drawn and ready.

Ghaal and Miirt pulled others away but in truth they had lost all desire for a fight. Hirad and Sirendor trotted into the circle of angry locals and Ilkar joined them. It was the safest place he could think of.

'Ilkar, see what you can do,' said Auum, nodding down at the prone form.

Ilkar knelt by the woman. Blood from repeated blows matted her head. Her arms were held up to shield her face and she had drawn herself into the foetal position. She was not breathing. Ilkar shook his head and stood. Auum looked up at the attackers. All of them just normal citizens of Xetesk. They held clubs, knives, axes and shovels. There were about twenty of them standing. Three others moved on the ground, groggy and moaning. The fourth was still and by the set of his head would remain so.

'This is how you treat those who return among you, love having guided them here,' said Auum.

'Leave us to our business, elf,' said one, a young man, face fired with rage and carrying an axe in a way that suggested he knew how to use it.

'Which would be what, exactly?' asked Hirad. 'Beating innocent people to death?'

The young man pointed at Hirad. 'Only your sort. Dead men. Time you all went back where you came from. You've brought bad luck to Balaia.'

'Simpleton,' muttered Ilkar.

'We brought you a message, idiot,' said Hirad. 'Pity you weren't listening.'

'You've stolen bodies. Now you sleep in our houses and eat our food. You have brought war to our doorsteps.'

Ilkar rubbed his forehead, already tired despite the time of the day. He made to speak but Auum got there first.

'You will disperse and take this body with you to be returned to her loved ones. Now you have rendered her unrecognisable, I am sure her family will be delighted by your efforts.'

'This is our city. You do not tell us what to do.'

Auum stepped up to the young man, who immediately brought his axe to the ready in front of him. Auum planted both of his swords in the dirt by him.

'Then mete out your justice. Strike me down if that is your will. I am unarmed.'

The man swallowed, confused. His lower teeth rubbed on his top lip.

'You are of the living. Our fight is not with you.'

'But I side with the dead. Strike one and you strike at me.'

Silence had fallen around the group. Somewhere a bell was ringing and there was the sound of running feet approaching from the south, across the gardens.

'You will trick me if I try to strike you,' said the man.

'No.' Auum's head shook fractionally. 'I will kill you.'

Hirad cleared his throat. 'Aren't you getting this? He's giving you a chance to back away and leave. I strongly suggest you take it.'

'I—'

But the youngster did not get a chance to speak further. Auum broke the grip on the man's axe, moved inside his guard and had placed a finger on his lips before he blinked. Auum's other hand held a blade to his eye. The axe clattered to the ground.

'Not another word,' he said quietly. 'Take her and your fallen friend and go.'

A tear spilled down the man's cheek as he nodded.

Auum stepped back and away, leaving a path to the dead woman. He watched as the two bodies were lifted up by a few of the mob and carried away.

'I see what you mean,' said Ilkar. 'What do you intend to do? What's down here?'

'Allies. Many of the dead too.' Auum began walking again, sheathing his blades as he went. 'We need to get them away from here. Out of the city and to the west. Now. Tonight.'

'But they can't stray that far from their loved ones. You know that,' said Hirad.

'Some of them are here too. The rest we must find and persuade to our cause.'

'Denser is not going to like this,' said Ilkar.

'If I have my way, he won't even know about it.' Auum stopped and turned to them. 'Will you help me?'

'What do you need us to do?' asked Hirad.

Auum smiled and walked on. 'Keep Denser busy. Keep his eyes from the north and south gates. We'll move them out those two ways a few at a time as often as we can.'

'No problem,' said Hirad. 'And who are these allies so we don't hit the wrong people?'

Auum chuckled. 'The two old barons. Seems they don't much like the way Xetesk leans either. They are very useful. Money still turns heads on Balaia, even now when disaster comes.'

'Good for them,' said Sirendor.

Auum stopped once more and the humour had gone from his face.

'I respect Lord Denser more than any other living human mage. But his mind is wrong. You can see it in his eyes. He will not be turned from his action. Look to your friends and see they escape, and look to Denser for he may betray you yet though he means you no harm. Someone has poisoned his thoughts and this will bring only death to any who stand with him. I have seen it before. Only those who run will live.'

Chapter 19

Sol did not go home immediately. Sitting there in Denser's tower, brave words were easy. Out here on The Thread, just a few hundred yards from his family, they sounded so hollow. So he walked while he gathered his thoughts. And he did many of the things that Denser wanted him to do.

He spoke to his people. He spread calm and confidence though he felt none himself. He answered the questions of the fearful and calmed the anxieties of the desperate. He reminded any who would listen of the help the dead were bringing. Of the strength they added to the defence of Xetesk and the belief they brought to the beleaguered and the weary.

Words. Easy. And all the while his wife was organising the day in the inn. Almost normal but for the fact that nothing was normal here any more. Trade was stuttering. The prices of food and drink were rising sharply. Only the caravans coming through Understone Pass from the west still arrived every day. It was not only word that was scarce from Korina, Blackthorne, Gyernath and any other place he cared to name.

How comforting it would be to get lost in the affairs of state. To sit with Denser and organise messengers and scouts. To plan rationing and discuss defensive tactics. He envied Denser. Right now the Lord of the Mount would be heading to a meeting with Septern where the peerless genius was going to impart his knowledge on building a ward grid to protect the city.

'But you have to stop running, old man,' he said to himself.

Sol sighed and turned around. He walked back along a couple of side streets and back onto The Thread. The college and its great ornate gates, open to all comers, was just to his right. He paused a moment to look at it. Imposing walls fifty feet high and with the Circle Seven Towers visible as they were from every point of the city, fingers of power thrusting into the sky. Foreboding and awe-inspiring.

'But they won't save you, Denser. Not this time.'

Glancing to his left, he could see the sign of The Raven's Rest swaying gently in the breeze that seemed forever to be blowing up Xetesk's main street. The Thread ran from the north to the south gates. As colourful a street as any in Balaia. Packed with history, filled with the dark times of the old college, which were only just washing away in the face of the new Xetesk. A place of which they could all be proud.

'And soon to be so much rubble.'

Sol chided himself. The king muttering to himself as he tried to avoid going home to his wife. No better than the midnight drunks he ejected from his inn every closing time.

He took a deep breath, calmed himself and strode down The Thread, nodding and smiling at all he passed though there was only anxiety on the streets. There was an ugly undercurrent too and he felt eyes on him, not all of which were friendly.

Sol walked down the alleyway to the side of the inn and opened the gate to the yard. In the stables to his left Jonas was grooming his horse. The other two mares were turned out into the small paddock at the back of the inn. There were the clattering sounds of work going on in the kitchens and someone was whistling tunelessly to the accompaniment of a sweeping broom.

'Jonas, how are you feeling?'

Jonas turned a beaming face on Sol and ran over. Sol hugged him and ruffled his hair. He was going to be every bit as big and powerful as his father. Sol hoped he got his hair from his mother's side.

'I'm fine, Father. Did you tell them what Sha-Kaan said? What are we going to do? He's in danger, Father, I can feel it. Despite what he says. We have to help him. What's going to happen?'

Sol fought the urge to crush his son to him and burst into tears. A wound opened in his heart and the ache was unbearable.

'Everything will be all right, Jonas. I promise.'

Jonas pulled back and looked up at Sol, his head cocked to one side and his eyebrows raised.

'I'm thirteen, Father, I'm not stupid. That doesn't mean anything. Only little Hirad would be satisfied with that sort of answer. What are you going to do? It hurts in here.' Jonas placed his hand on his chest. 'The Kaan are fading.'

'What do you mean?' Sol crouched down and took Jonas's arms. 'Fading how?'

'Their link to Balaia, to me and all the Dragonene. The melde. It's weakening. I can feel it.'

'Then you aren't fine, are you? Why didn't you say this before?'

'I didn't know before, Father. Or I wasn't sure what I was feeling.'

'And I'm fifty-one and I'm not stupid either. Tell me what happened.'

Sol stared into Jonas's eyes. The young man was frightened beneath the bravado, and to see it in him was a sword to the soul.

'It was the last fleeting thought Sha-Kaan gave me. The melde is attacked directly. Dragons resting in their Klenes have been killed where they lie. Inter-dimensional space is filled with enemies. What happens if they kill Sha-Kaan, Father?'

'They won't. He's too smart and too powerful. But this is big information for our fight to come. Why didn't you tell someone?'

'Because I was waiting for you to come home. Don't be angry with me.'

Sol pulled Jonas into another embrace. 'All right, son. You've done the right thing.'

'What happens now?'

'We get you sorted out. I'll speak to Denser. There will be others in your situation after all.'

'What about the enemy? What about what you told them?'

Sol stood. 'That'll have to wait.'

Jonas followed Sol into the inn. The kitchens were a-buzz with activity but there was none of the usual humour in the voices he heard. Diera was wiping down tables in the bar, and when she turned to see who it was, her face turned his heart to dust.

'What's up?' he asked. 'Somebody die?'

Diera threw her cloth into the pail. Water slopped onto the floor. 'You, apparently.'

'Wait outside, Jonas.'

'What does she—?'

'Jonas!' Sol caught himself. 'Please, son, just for a moment.'

'All right.'

Sol waited until Jonas had closed the door behind him.

'Denser's been here, has he? Doesn't waste much time, I'll give him that.'

Diera turned her back on him. 'Yes, he has. At least there's someone in this ridiculous city who still has a steady head on their shoulders.'

Sol moved towards her. She wrapped her arms around herself and stiffened.

'I need you to understand why there is no choice for me.'

He reached out a hand.

'Don't touch me, Sol.' She rounded on him. 'And I understand perfectly well, thank you. Your dead friends want you to join their merry band of lost souls, and you're too stupid and blinded by your wonderful Raven past to see you're being sold serpents for firewood.'

'I can hear Denser in everything you say, Diera. So let me speak. Do you really think I'd be doing this if I felt there was any other choice? It's a long shot, granted, but we are truly desperate. Denser has no answers and the Garonin will tear this city down stone by stone. Come with me to the west. I can protect you all the way and you can be first to follow me to our new home.'

'Follow you? You'll be dead, damn you! What good is that to me?'

'There is no other way to save you and the boys.'

Sol hadn't seen her arms tense and he felt the full force of the slap across his face. The sound ricocheted about the bar and Diera was screaming at him.

'How dare you say that to me. Your death does not save us, it damns us. What will I say to the boys when nothing comes of it? That their father threw his life away after people long dead but still more important to him? You can't do this to me, you can't. I can't do this without you. It isn't life without you.'

Sol resisted the urge to reach out to her again. She stood tall and resolute despite her words. He chest was heaving and her cheeks were damp but she would not crumble.

'What will you tell them if, by my actions, countless thousands are saved?' he asked quietly. 'What then? Would that be throwing my life away?'

Diera put a hand to his face and stroked the red mark she had made.

'No, of course it wouldn't, my darling. But you don't do this any more. It's all just a memory. You have to listen to Denser, to reason. The place to stand and fight is here. Chasing heroic deeds won't work. Look at me. At Jonas and at little Hirad. Can you really bear to know you have seen us all for the last time? Can you die knowing you are depriving your children of the father they worship? Can your sacrifice really be worth such loss?'

'What I cannot do is follow a path in which I do not believe and have that cause your deaths. This isn't about being a hero, Diera. It never has been. It's about doing the right thing. The only thing.'

'Oh dear me, they really have done a number on you, haven't they?'

Sol spun round. Denser had appeared from nowhere and was walking the last couple of paces to the front door.

'What the fuck are you doing here?' demanded Sol.

'Determining the state of mind of my king,' said Denser. His hand rested on the door bolt. 'And I don't like what I hear.'

'I don't have to explain myself to anyone who eavesdrops from behind a cloaking spell.' Sol turned to Diera, sure she had knowledge of Denser's presence, but the look on her face told him otherwise. 'I suggest you leave, my Lord of the Mount.'

Denser nodded. 'I will, Sol. And I'm sorry, I really am.'

He opened the door, stood back and began to cast. Six men were running in. Big men.

'What the—'

Diera screamed Sol's name. No time to think. Sol picked up a chair and threw it at Denser. It caught him around the waist and knocked him into the wall just below the painting of Hirad, disrupting his casting preparation. Sol strode towards the six, reached above his head and grabbed the cudgel from the beam mounts on his way past.

'Come on then, boys. Let's see you take an old man, eh?'

The college heavies fanned out, shoving tables and chairs aside to give themselves clear space. Sol moved into the centre of the room and tapped the end of the cudgel on the timber floor of the inn. To his left, Denser was getting back to his feet.

'Diera, keep on poking that bastard; don't let him get a spell off.'

'With pleasure.'

'Who's first? You?' Sol pointed his cudgel at a squat man with a barrel torso. Pasty skin, flabby arms and a thick powerful neck.

The man grunted but didn't move forward. Sol cursed under his breath. He knew what was coming. They rushed him as one. Two dived forward, aiming to grapple his legs. The other four went for his upper body. Sol jumped, bringing his legs up under him. He swung the cudgel, feeling a satisfying thud as it connected with a long-haired skull.

He landed on top of one of the divers, forcing the air from his lungs. He brought the cudgel round again, meeting the gut of a third man. Below him the diver moved, sending Sol off balance. He fell backwards, already beginning to turn before he hit the floor. He thrashed the cudgel above his head, missing this time.

Someone was on his legs and he kicked out hard, feeling his boots pummel soft flesh. But the arms clung on. Three others dived on top of him. Sol dropped the cudgel and smashed his left then right fist into the face of the closest heavy. The man's nose and lips burst, showering blood everywhere. Sol took a punch to the stomach. And another. Someone else was on his legs now and he couldn't move them.

He heard the splash of water, plenty of water. Denser swore. Sol managed a smile. He cocked his fists again but this time his shoulders were forced back onto the ground and his arms pinned by his sides. Sol bucked and twisted under the weight of the men on top of him. He glared up at the nearest, who set his fist above Sol's face.

'Don't make me, Sol. Relax. Relax.'

Sol let the tension flow out of his body. The college men did not let up their pressure and they would not. He was beaten. For now.

'Stand him up,' said Denser. 'And one of you get Diera off me, please?'

A slap of hand on face. Another expletive from the Lord of the Mount.

'Don't any of you so much as lay a hand on her,' growled Sol. 'Diera, it's all right. It's over.'

Sol allowed himself to be hauled to his feet. He pushed the college men away and tried to shake off restraining hands. Diera retreated towards the bar. He saw her hand go over the counter but he shook his head and she withdrew it. He let his eyes play over the six in front of him. One had blood pouring from the side of his face where the cudgel had struck him. Another was resting on a table, hands on his belly. A third stared balefully at him while the blood continued to run from his nose and mouth.

'Don't worry, you were ugly already,' said Sol.

'Don't push your luck, my King,' slurred the man.

Sol turned his head to stare at Denser. The Lord of the Mount was soaked through.

'And you.' Sol spat on the ground. 'You have betrayed me, Xetesk, Balaia and most of all The Raven. I no longer know you.'

Denser stalked in to stand a few feet away.

'I am doing what is right for our city and our country. You will not be allowed to fragment our defence by running off on your fool's errand. No one is leaving Balaia. No one needs to. I know what Auum and those foolish old men are planning even if you don't, and they will be stopped. We have the power and the strength to beat these Garonin. Xetesk will prevail.'

'You will all die and I will laugh in your faces,' said Sol.

'Lystern has fallen. Julatsa is under attack. Dordover is long gone. And that leaves Xetesk as the one power on this continent. Do you think I or any mage of my college would pass up the opportunity for us to take up our natural position as rulers of Balaia?'

Sol felt numb. He stared at Denser and searched his eyes.

'What's happened to you, Denser? All that we've done in the last ten years. Does it really mean that little to you? The deaths of your friends?'

'Until the Garonin came, it meant everything. But it's all been washed away now and I cannot have dissension. There is a single purpose, and it is the protection of this city and its college. You need to spend some time alone thinking about that and about why you should be protecting the living, not seeing them into the hands of the dead and a fool's march west.'

Sol shook his head. 'I would rather protect the dead than the living like you.'

'Right,' said Denser. 'Time for you to rest. We don't want a scene when we return up The Thread, now do we?'

Denser began to cast, Sol's eyes burning into him the whole time. And when the spell was done and the hands laid on him, Sol slipped quickly into unconsciousness, his head falling to one side and his eyes flickering closed. But not so quickly that he didn't see the door to the yard, which had been open a crack, closing quietly.

Above the mage college of Julatsa a dense, dark cloud exploded and evaporated. Rebraal stood with his primary mage, Dila'heth, five miles from the city yet still they could feel the heat and the vibrations through the ground. Their horses, bought from a farmer on the coast of Triverne Inlet, grazed nearby, showing little sign of nervousness.

Julatsa sat like a pearl on flat open ground below them. Even from this distance the elves could see the dust of the Garonin approach, the flash of spells and the damage the city had already taken. At its centre the college still stood proud. Banners from her masts fluttered and a constant stream of spells fled out from her walls, tower and other high places.

'The Garonin are in the city,' said Dila. 'It will soon be over.'

Rebraal turned to her. 'I am sorry, Dila. Tual will give you strength. Ix will not desert you nor your brothers and sisters.'

Dila'heth fell to her knees.

'Tual help us,' said Rebraal. He crouched by her. 'Dila?'

She was not looking at him but past him. Down across the plain the sky was dark. A cloud wider and deeper than any they had seen before was building over the centre of the city. It was spiralling slowly and its core was dense with the yellow of Julatsan magic.

Dila retched and groaned. Rebraal put an arm about her shoulders and held her to him, feeling her trembling and gasping for breath as if her chest was constricted. The cloud was spinning and growing. The cracks of lightning sent echoes across the plain. Spells still flew from the college but nothing would save them now. A stillness fell, emanating from the centre of the cloud. The pressure built, pressing on Rebraal's ears like he had dived too far underwater. Dila was shuddering in his arms. He could feel her tears splash on his fingers and the low moan she uttered was strangling his heart.

Wider and wider the cloud spread. Faster and faster it turned. Yellow light shimmered all around and flashed dangerously within it. The stillness became a hum and the ground began to shake. Just a slight quiver through his feet but there all the same.

Rebraal saw buildings rocking. He saw slates fall and walls begin to collapse. From the west gates, people were running. Tiny dark shapes on the pale grass of the plain. The hum rattled the teeth in his jaws. Dila put her hands to her head and scratched at her skull. Her voice became a keening wail.

The cloud detonated.

A blinding yellow light flashed across the plain. Thick black smoke chased it away. The sound wave rolled out. Buildings shivered and fell. The tower of Julatsa exploded outwards. Stone was catapulted high into the sky, huge boulders turning lazy arcs to smash down on the city and the college. A massive column of yellow light streamed up, turning to smoke and haze before shutting off with the finality of a prison door slamming.

The force of the explosion swept out. Grass was flattened, trees bent, snapped, were uprooted or swayed back, scattering their leaves.

Heat washed over the elven force. Rebraal turned himself and Dila away. The wave knocked them down. He breathed in hot air and choked out a cough.

Struggling to breathe for a moment, Rebraal dragged himself and Dila'heth to their feet. Across the plain was a sight that he could not take in and one that would remain with him until death closed his eyes the final time.

Half of the city was gone. Levelled. Dust was rising and billowing. Only the western edge of Julatsa remained, while beyond it the escaping Julatsans could be seen still running, protected at the last by the stone of their homes.

In the midst of the devastation he could hear exultant voices raised to the sky. In his arms Dila was reduced to wracking sobs, the centre of her life stolen away. He rocked her there for a while until she had calmed. She pulled away from him a little.

'Nothing left for us here now,' she said, her voice empty. 'We should get back to the ships. Time is against us.'

Ilkar pulled himself upright and leaned back in the deep armchair. The nausea passed but the gulf in his body remained. He met the barbarian's even gaze and could see the old Hirad shining through the unfamiliar face he now wore.

'It's over,' he said, feeling a strange sense of relief. 'Only Xetesk left now. And I think that should worry us.'

Hirad stretched over from his chair and patted Ilkar's knee. 'Well it would if it weren't for the fact that the Garonin are going to roll over here in a few days too. How are you feeling?'

'Like I've been robbed. I can't touch anything that is mine, if you see what I mean. The house is empty and will never be refilled.'

He smiled but was aware how hollow it must look. Hirad rubbed a hand over his chin.

'So is that it? End of you as a mage?'

'Well, some would argue that happened when the Elfsorrow killed me.'

'You know what I mean.'

'Yep, sorry. And no, it isn't the end, but you have to understand the mechanics of spell casting.'

Hirad's face fell. 'Must I?'

Ilkar laughed. 'Gods drowning, I'm glad you're with me. This is the most depressing day in the life of any Julatsan mage but at least I can console myself that I am not you.'

'Mechanics,' said Hirad.

'Look, until the Garonin take every bit of mana, then any mage can still cast, sort of. What a Heart does is concentrate and feed out mana. It brings consistency to the mana density and each college's Heart balances the others. Or used to. Now, if I try and cast, I'll find it hard to drag enough mana in to construct my casting. It'll take a whole lot more effort too and the outcome will be less certain.'

'So, more difficult, more tiring and more dangerous to cast.'

'Nothing gets past you, does it, Hirad?'

'Fu—'

The door to the frugal student chambers that the two of them were sharing with Sirendor opened with some vigour. Denser stood in the doorway. Dystran was at his back and a cluster of other men could be seen in the corridor outside.

'Come in,' said Hirad. 'Oh, I see you already have.'

Ilkar stood slowly, a crawling sensation in his gut. 'What's going on?'

His tone was picked up by Hirad, who tensed and let a hand drop to his sword hilt. Denser walked in and let the room fill behind him. Ilkar nodded at Dystran and counted the number of guards with him. Too many.

'Ilkar, I am deeply sorry about what has happened to Julatsa. We were tracking the battle by Communion Globe but of course there was little we could do.'

'Any idea how many escaped?' Ilkar raised his eyebrows. 'Or who in particular?'

Denser shrugged. 'They had begun an evacuation when it was clear all was lost, but who actually got out is anyone's guess.'

'Pheone?' Ilkar didn't really want to utter the name of his former lover, now High Mage of Julatsa, lest it damn her.

'Like Heryst she was in the Globe chamber until very late on. Heryst did not try to run, we know that. As for Pheone . . . I'm sorry, I think you have to assume the worst.'

'The good news keeps on pouring in, doesn't it?' muttered Hirad.

'It does rather,' said Denser. Ilkar saw him shift uncomfortably and redden a little at the neck. 'And that's kind of why I'm here. Why we're here. There's been a change of plan.'

'Oh?' Ilkar did not like the way Dystran was smiling.

'With Julatsa fallen it rests with Xetesk to rise to the challenge as the last bastion of power on Balaia, the last chance to save our country for all who survive the Garonin. We cannot countenance desertion. So many people in far-flung parts of the country will be untouched by the enemy but will feel the effects of their passing. For the greater good of Balaia, for her people and for the continuation of magic, Xetesk must and will survive. No one is going to the Wesmen. Here we stand and here we fight. I am closing the gates to the city.'

'Have you completely taken leave of your senses?' asked Ilkar, disbelieving what he had just heard for a moment. 'I mean, no doubt you are about to deliver that same great leader speech to the masses or something, but this is me. This is Hirad and Sirendor. You know you can talk to us person to person. We're friends, remember? And we all agree we need a way out of here should you fail. Right?'

Denser shook his head. 'Wrong. We will not fail. We have the means and we have the ability. Xetesk will stand and will rule the new Balaia.'

Hirad's mouth hung open. It was almost comical. Ilkar cleared his throat and rubbed his face.

'I know you aren't wild about our escape plan but you can't just put a stop to it. It doesn't make any sense. What does The Unknown have to say about this?'

Denser looked at the ceiling. 'Our king is currently indisposed.'

Hirad exploded across the room. Two of Denser's guards got to him. Just. He jabbed a finger between them as they pushed him back away from their Lord of the Mount.

'Fucking idiot. Fucking betrayer. You'll kill everyone. Are you blind? I am coming for you, Denser. You can't do this.'

'Shut up, Hirad,' said Denser. 'I can and I will. I am Lord of the Mount of Xetesk. This is my duty.'

Ilkar had his hands on his mouth. He felt detached. Like he was watching a play or something.

'You stand on the brink of annihilation and yet still you dream of power and dominion,' he breathed. 'I will not help you do this. No dead will help you do this.'

'That's not strictly speaking true but we anticipated such a reponse. We know what drives the dead. We know what you desire for yourselves and for those who brought you back. Did you really think I wouldn't get wind of your little plan to sneak my people out of my city?'

'You have no right—'

'Don't talk to me about rights, Sirendor. This is my city. I cannot, I will not have the dead poisoning the minds of my people any longer. There is fighting in the streets, there is tension where there needs to be calm preparation and there is divisiveness where there must be unity. But you can still help me. Your friend Auum has conveniently collected nearly every one of the dead in a single place. You will join them but you will not leave there. And when the Garonin breach the walls of the city, you will have your chance for revenge while we continue laying our plans for victory. Every moment will count. Fight hard.'

Ilkar sat back down. 'You bastard.'

'What?' asked Hirad, still restrained by the college guardsmen.

'You heard what Auum said. About splitting the density of souls to fragment the Garonin invasion force. That bastard wants to use us as a decoy.'

Hirad's face greyed. 'You traitorous little fuck.'

'That's enough, Hirad,' said Denser. 'I have to save those who can be saved. You are dead. It is already too late for you.'

'Have you listened to nothing?' Hirad's lunge forced his guards back a pace. 'There is nowhere for the dead to go. Nowhere for the living who die to go. You are betraying everyone. For fleeting power. You were a man I loved and trusted. A Raven man. What happened to you?'

'Goodbye, Hirad. Ilkar, I wish you well. And Hirad, don't make it hard, eh? You will leave the college right now or your soul will fly to the void.'

Chapter 20

'It really is the only way,' said Dystran.

'Then why do I feel like I am the lowest form of life in this city?' said Denser.

'Feeling sorry for yourself won't help you.'

'It seems a good place to start, all right?'

Denser walked out onto the highest balcony of his tower. It afforded him unsurpassed views of his college, his city and beyond. It showed him the few remaining dead scattered about his city being rounded up and escorted to their desolate quarter of Xetesk. Easy enough to do. For the ones that weren't displaying the manner of their deaths like a badge, all that was needed was to shine a lantern on them and their shadow gave them away. No hiding place. No exceptions. Well, one.

'But you can feel the tension lifting, can't you?'

And he could. It was quite something. With his guards erecting barricades across all exits from the area of parkland and abandoned homes in which the dead were effectively corralled, the living were regaining control of their city. Already, they were beginning to gather in the college courtyard, on the apron outside the college's south gate and anywhere on the approaches. Denser was due to address them from the tower.

Denser turned. The exception, Septern, was at his shoulder. On the table behind them the master mage had overlaid a ward grid on a map of the city. It was a true work of art both aesthetically and technically.

'You had to do something,' added Dystran. 'The dead were dividing us just by their presence and the more dangerous souls were sowing rotten seed. Feel the mood of the city when our defence is organised. Think of the support when you remind them that hundreds and hundreds of mouths to be fed are gone. Never underestimate the greed of the individual desperate to survive.'

'I certainly won't do that,' said Denser.

Out in the city his mages were laying wards in locations matching Septern's exact specifications. Beyond the gates the horizon was obscured from north to south by the Garonin's expanding cloud of dust and burned mana. Korina was the only other major city still standing and was not as yet under concerted threat; it was as though the capital was being left until last.

What Denser really needed to know was when the new Garonin machine would achieve its critical mass and head back towards Xetesk. He had scouts tracking it and mages ready to fly in with any news. So far though, the Garonin were content to amble along in a seemingly random pattern about four days out. It was a hiatus that would not last for long.

More dead were moving along The Thread. Hirad, Ilkar and Sirendor were with them. He had acquiesced and let them say their goodbyes to Diera and her boys but had refused them leave to see Sol. At least they were causing no trouble. He bit his lip and swallowed a lump in his throat.

'They were fine people when they were alive,' said Dystran. 'But something changed in them when they died. The manner of their deaths, the places they died. Something. They *are* different. Not The Raven you remember. Don't be beguiled into remembering what you saw as your friends. They stopped being that the day they died.'

'What do you think, Septern?'

'If death changed me, then I do not remember my old life. But I care not for loyalties and guilt. Both are wastes of effort. I only care whether my grid will work. Let me take you through it.'

Denser moved to the table. Septern was right. And he was different from every other dead person that Denser had met. Completely consumed by himself and what he could do for magic on Balaia. Just like the stories about him when he was alive. And Hirad *had* been different from his old self, hadn't he? The old Hirad would have wanted to fight to the bitter end. Save his country and all that. It was not and never had been his way to run from his enemies.

'I'd better be right about this,' Denser said.

'I beg your pardon?' asked Septern.

'Nothing. Let's look at your plan.'

The three men leaned over the map and its overlay. The city was picked out building by building, street by street. On top Septern had indicated the position of every ward, and had added a symbol as code for its exact construction, direction, exclusions and power. Each ward was connected to others by lines either dotted or solid. He had drawn arrows to indicate things like mana flow, energy spill and trigger direction.

'The beauty of this is its simplicity and its perfect logic. As with all my finest creations.'

Denser smiled at him. 'You haven't lost your modesty, I see.'

'What use have I for modesty? I suspect I still am the greatest mage ever to walk any dimension in this or any other cluster. And cut off in my prime too. Betrayed by my own students, agents of the Wytch Lords would you believe?'

'Yes, but we got the Wytch Lords,' said Denser. 'I cast Dawnthief to destroy them.'

Septern choked on his next words and pulled back from the map. He grabbed Denser's shoulders and turned him round.

'You *cast* it? What were you, crazed? That spell was never intended to actually be used. It was a theoretical demonstration.' Septern spluttered a little more then waved a dismissive hand. 'But clearly you got it wrong or else none of us would be here, would we? This place would be a vacuum.'

Denser bridled. 'I didn't get it wrong, thank you very much. I adapted it. Luckily you left enough room in the lore for Dawnthief to be cast at less than its complete power using an altered structure. So it destroyed the Wytch Lords and left us, well, nearly intact.'

'Nearly?'

'There were . . . consequences. Side effects.'

Septern shook his head. His eyes were twinkling and there was a smile on his face. 'Fascinating. So tell me. What did it feel like to actually cast?'

'Painful, if I remember rightly. I stopped breathing for a while, I know that.'

Septern looked crestfallen. 'Not engorged with power or elated or something like that?'

'Possibly, but the pain blotted it all out.'

Dystran cleared his throat. 'Much as I would love to hear more, can it wait until later? We need this working and understood or the Garonin will do to us what Dawnthief didn't.'

Septern chuckled. 'It is turning into quite a day. We must dine together, Denser.'

'I think that is a very good idea. So. The grid.'

'Yes. Now, when I was constructing the grid for my own house, a somewhat smaller task I admit though the principles are the same, I was concerned to build outer deterrents followed by inner cells designed to kill everything that ignored the first warnings.

'Here I've dispensed with the deterrents as I think they will be of little value. I've concentrated on feeder cell formation and causing maximum damage when a given ward is tripped.'

Denser may not have felt elation when he cast Dawnthief, nor when he was throwing his old friends out of the college to face the Garonin. But he felt it now, listening to the man whose genius remained, as he had guessed, unsurpassed.

'So, to illustrate. Take this cell here.' Septern circled a group of about fifty wards positioned by one of the outer grain stores and covering some of the south-eastern streets leading onto The Thread. 'Now, all the wards will be active when the enemy move into the area but only one has a physical trigger. This one here.'

He pointed at a central ward at the head of the grain store where the Garonin would have to pass if they were to access any of the surrounding streets.

'When this ward is triggered it dominoes mana through every second ward in this cell and they all go off simultaneously. HellFire, FireGlobe, FlameOrb, EarthHammer. I don't know your fancy new names and I care less about them. The area is deluged in flame and levelled by earth movements in less time than it takes me to drain a glass of wine.

'But that's not all. Because we expect the Garonin to be determined and adaptable, we can expect them to come through the same area again, assuming the danger has passed. So the triggering of the first set of wards also passes mana to the other half. The trigger ward becomes this one here and the process begins again.

'And that's not all either. The fact of a detonation of a set of wards feeds mana back up through the chain to the adjacent cells, bringing them to a ready state. The point of that is that we leave as little mana floating about as possible, making it very hard for the wards to be detected. Dormant wards last for ages if they are set correctly.

'And the final thing is this. Right here, above the gates of the college, is your master ward. Master switch, if you like. The whole system lies dormant until this ward is completed. Once it is, the mana circuit is active and we sit back and watch the Garonin getting destroyed while we manage our mana stamina for any close combat.'

The twinkle remained in Septern's eyes. 'Good, eh?'

It was a while before Denser could speak. He stared at the map, the cells and the connectivity and could do nothing but shake his head.

'Good? It's genius.'

'That's all I ever deliver.'

'This would have saved us a whole lot of bother when the demons came knocking,' said Dystran.

'Yes, but it will level the city,' said Denser.

'Which is no more than the Garonin will do anyway,' said Dystran.

'Thank you, Septern. That is truly amazing.'

'I can do nothing but agree with you,' said the master mage.

'Can we bring all the population within the college walls?' asked Dystran.

'I have designated safe areas to the west as well,' said Septern. 'Plenty enough for those who remain.'

'And the dead? They are going to be right in the middle of the grid. Murdering them wasn't in my plans,' said Denser.

Septern waved a hand to quieten him.

'If you look more closely, you'll see that I have excluded their area from the main grid but left a defensive line on their borders. Your guards will not need to stand there once the grid is activated. And, in addition, we can expect any Garonin stumbling into the dead's area to be damaged and demoralised. Easier to fight. A positive outcome, wouldn't you agree?'

Denser nodded, feeling just slightly less guilty at his actions.

'Yes, thank you. Though I'm not sure my former friends will feel the same.'

There was a knock on the door. After a brief pause, Brynar entered.

'You, my young mage, have just missed a master class,' said Denser.

'But don't worry,' added Septern. 'I'll be walking the grid with Sharyr later, checking the accuracy of today's work. Why don't you attend me?'

Brynar looked at Denser, who inclined his head.

'It would be an honour, my Lord Septern,' he blustered.

'Then it is settled,' said Septern.

'Brynar, you have something to report? No doubt our king is still ranting about dragons?'

Denser chuckled at his own cleverness. Something about Septern and his effortless genius was infectious and energising.

'Yes, my Lord Denser. He is adamant that he must speak to you because he says the entire melde is in crisis, and should it fail, we will be yet further weakened.'

'I see. And what have you told him?'

'That you will see him as soon as you are able. As soon as the city defence is complete. He said that wasn't good enough.'

Denser chuckled. 'I'm sure he did.'

'But he was a little more cheerful when I left,' said Brynar brightly. 'His son had come to see him.'

Denser went cold and clammy. 'You didn't let him in, did you?'

Brynar's face had paled. 'W– well yes. He's thirteen years old. What harm can he do.'

'Idiot!' stormed Denser, his mind tripping over a thousand things as he ran for the door and sprinted down the stairs yelling for guards to follow him.

'What have I done?' asked Brynar.

'You have much to learn, youngster,' said Dystran. 'Jonas may only be thirteen but he is also Dragonene to the Great Kaan.'

Brynar mouthed the word before speaking. 'That matters, doesn't it.'

'Just a bit,' said Dystran. 'Just a bit.'

At least Denser had seen fit to provide him with comfortable accommodation for his incarceration: a bedroom and living area with decent furniture and even a fireplace. The decoration was somewhat austere but that was the way of many of the catacombs beneath Xetesk's tower complex. Since his abduction Sol had ignored the food brought to him and had found no time to sit. He had preferred to pace between the rock walls of his limited domain.

His last conversation with Jonas nagged at him and his anger flared ever more brightly every time his demands to speak to Denser about the dragons were rebuffed. He cared little right now about the Garonin, travelling to the west or the dead. His boy was at risk and he was impotent to do anything about it.

The door to Sol's rooms was unlocked and opened. Sol ceased his pacing and turned to glare but his frown turned to a smile.

'Jonas!'

Sol ran to his son and hauled him into an embrace. Jonas hugged him back.

'Are you all right, Father?' he asked.

'Never mind me, how are you? Anything more from Sha-Kaan?'

Sol glanced back to the door. Two guards stood in the doorway, watching.

'No. I feel fine, really.'

Sol put an arm around Jonas's shoulder and both turned away from the guards and walked towards the armchairs and sofa.

'I have to get out of here quickly,' said Sol quietly.

'It's why I'm here, Father.'

'Those guards won't move so they'll see a doorway appear. Whatever happens, don't break contact. Go with me when I talk to you. I'll divert their attention somehow, all right? Sit here.'

There was a chair with its back to the door. Jonas sat on it and Sol took the one at right angles to him.

'So, how's your mother?'

Jonas shrugged. 'Angry and panicking. Lord Denser has closed the gates of the city and forbidden any of the living to leave. The dead have been herded to the eastern parks and the mage quarter.'

'What?' Sol's eyes widened. 'Dear Gods falling, he really has lost his mind. This is madness. When did it happen, all this?'

'Straight after they took you away. He's speaking to the city in an hour or two, I think.'

'Really?' Sol stopped himself saying more. He raised his eyebrows to Jonas, who nodded and settled back into his chair. 'A drink, Jonas? I'm afraid the cellar isn't well stocked. Water?'

'Thank you, Father,' said Jonas, voice a little distant.

Sol smiled, pressed his shoulder and stood up. Standing beneath a mirror near the door was a table carrying drink and food. Sol walked towards it, nodding at the guards and making sure he was interfering with any sight of Jonas beginning his contact with Sha-Kaan.

'Thank you for letting me see my son,' he said, pitching his volume just a little high. 'It means a lot that I can calm him myself. Perhaps you'd like to remind Lord Denser he needs to speak with me if we are not to get into even more precarious a position very soon?'

One of the guards shrugged. 'I'll mention it to Brynar, I suppose.'

Sol filled two goblets with water, picked them up and sauntered towards the door. The two guards straightened a little and hands dropped to sword hilts.

'You think I'm going to make a break for it? Old man, dodgy hip, son in a chair by the fire? Come on, relax. I'm merely offering you some water.'

'You should come no closer,' said a guard, sweating under his helmet, his expression anxious and embarrassed, as it had been ever since Sol had been here.

'Fine. Be thirsty.' Sol stopped moving.

From behind him Jonas emitted a brief moan of pain as he made contact with Sha-Kaan.

'What's that?'

'Toothache,' said Sol. 'Funny thing, isn't it? About me being in here rather than in a cell.'

'Why?'

The question dripped suspicion. Both guards were looking past Sol, or trying to as his powerful upper body was in the way.

'Well it's the door, isn't it?' he said. He stepped forward and threw the goblets at the guards, who brought their arms up reflexively. 'It opens the wrong way.'

Sol dived for the door and slammed it in their faces. He sat with his back to it and jammed his hands and feet as hard as he could onto the stone floor, bracing himself for the inevitable.

'Jonas, as quick as you like,' he said.

There were shouts outside the door. He felt the first impact against it. The door opened maybe an inch before his weight shut it once more. He had little time.

Next, a double impact. One high, one low. Sol was shovelled across the stone a good way. Hands came around the frame. Sol put his shoulder to the door and forced it back hard. There was a pained cry and he heard his name being taken repeatedly in vain.

'Jonas . . .'

A thin white line had appeared in the air above Jonas's chair. It described a horizontal about eight feet long before beginning to draw down both sides to form an opening into Sha-Kaan's Klene, his corridor and resting place within the healing streams of inter-dimensional space.

Sol heard a flurry of conversation outside the door and, echoing down the corridor, the unmistakeable sound of Denser's voice. Sol braced himself for another impact but there was quiet instead.

'That can't be good.'

The door shattered, its timbers cracking and bursting inwards. Sol was hurled across the floor, rolling and tumbling. Pain flared in his lower back and he felt the warm slick of blood at his waist. He came to a halt and tried to stand. The pain in his back intensified and he stopped, having to be satisfied with a stoop.

In the doorway stood the guards and a mage. They had taken a pace but stopped. None of them was looking at Sol but beyond him. There was the sharp smell of wood and oil. Sol craned his neck. Sha-Kaan's golden-scaled head was thrusting from the opening to the Klene. Inside the chamber it looked massive. It was as tall as a man on its own, suggesting the enormity that could not be seen beyond the portal. A bone ridge ran from between Sha-Kaan's eyes and away down his body. That mouth opened lazily, revealing twin rows of fangs and molars.

'Lie down, Sol, you're in my way,' he rumbled.

Sol gladly complied, the pain in his back easing. Jonas was standing next to Sha-Kaan's head, one hand resting on that portion of his neck that was visible.

'Damn you, Sol, don't do this.'

'I have friends in all sorts of places, Denser.'

'You will not obstruct our departure,' said Sha-Kaan.

'Xetesk and Balaia need their king,' said Denser.

'Locked up in the catacombs. I don't think so,' said Sol. 'What they need is a way out. What you're building is a mass grave.'

Sol shuffled away from Sha-Kaan's line of sight and got gingerly to his feet. The blood was flowing fast from the wound in his back and soaking into his breeches. He felt a little light-headed.

'You will come back,' said Denser. 'Need I remind you that your wife and younger son are still here.'

'Need I remind you that if one hair of either head is so much as breathed upon, I will rip your fucking head off.' Sol glanced at Jonas. 'Apologies for my language.'

Jonas shrugged. 'We need to go.'

Sol nodded and moved to the portal. Denser stayed the hand of one of his guards with a shake of the head and a knowing look.

'One last chance for redemption, Denser. Come with us. We are stronger with you.'

'Sorry, Sol. Xetesk is where true strength lies. I think I'll stay where I'm likely to stay alive.'

'If you remember one thing, remember this,' said Sol. 'The Raven never get it wrong.'

Sol and Jonas stepped past Sha-Kaan's head, the dragon withdrew it into the Klene and the portal snapped shut.

Chapter 21

With Jonas anchoring the Balaian end of the Klene, it was a stable, secure edifice. With him standing inside when the link to Balaia was broken, it became as a loose end of rope flailing in the gale of inter-dimensional space. Sha-Kaan did his best to moderate the buffeting but, with the Klene only tethered in Beshara, it was a bumpy ride.

'I have to find safe purchase quickly or return to Beshara,' said Sha-Kaan. 'We are vulnerable this way.'

'Who can you feel?' asked Jonas.

Sol and Jonas were each being held in one of Sha-Kaan's front claws. The great dragon was being as gentle as he could but with each violent shift of the Klene, the claws tightened reflexively. Sol could focus on nothing. The pain in his back was immense and the shuddering and shaking of the Klene made him nauseous.

'Old friends,' said Sha-Kaan, and the wistful quality of his voice brought a smile to Sol's lips. 'The great Septern and Hirad Coldheart. So long dead it is both pleasure and pain to feel their minds once more.'

'Go for Hirad,' said Sol. 'He'll have Ilkar with him. We can work out what we need to do.'

'I will see what I can do,' rumbled Sha-Kaan. 'His mind is not as tuned as once it was.'

Even through his pain, Sol had to suppress a laugh. 'Hirad, tuned? When did that ever happen?'

'He had more ability about him than you know,' chided Sha-Kaan.

'I miss Hirad's talents every day,' said Sol.

The Klene bounced once before ceasing its random movement. Sol breathed deeply, his stomach settling, his eyes able to focus.

'I have him,' said Sha-Kaan.

The Klene was smaller than Sol remembered. Still grand with its huge fireplaces, Kaan crests, mural-painted walls and oppressive heat but somehow lessened.

'What happened to all the drapery and antechambers?' asked Sol.

'We are not as strong as once we were,' said Sha-Kaan. 'We can no longer afford such excess.'

Sol caught Jonas's eye and saw the sadness there.

'I am a very old dragon,' continued Sha-Kaan. 'It is inevitable.'

Sha-Kaan released the pair of them and Sol felt at the wound in his back.

'Jonas, come and help your father, would you? Tell me what you can see.'

Sol pulled up his shirt at the back. Jonas took in a sharp breath.

'You need attention, Father. That must hurt.'

'What is it?'

'Splinters of wood. Some quite big, really. Do you want me to—?'

Sol felt a touch on his back and winced.

'No, no. Don't move them. I've lost enough blood as it is. Dammit.'

Sol moved onto his hands and knees. The pain eased a little. He crawled across to the wall of the Klene and lay down on his side.

'Hardly the heroic arrival I'd envisaged,' he muttered.

The main door to the Klene swung back. Fresh air flooded in. Sha-Kaan rumbled happily to himself and shifted forward a little way. Four figures appeared in the doorway, silhouetted against the light. Others were clustering outside. There was a hubbub of voices. Sol managed a smile when he saw Hirad's face. It might have been the face of a dead merchant but the joy in the eyes and the display of every rotting tooth in his mouth was the old Hirad, pure and simple.

'Sha-Kaan,' Hirad said. 'Now here's something worth coming back to life for.'

He walked in and placed a hand on the tip of Sha-Kaan's muzzle. Ilkar, Sirendor and Auum were just behind him. If Sha-Kaan was perturbed by the sight of his old Dragonene, he did not show it. The great dragon pushed forward fractionally, dumped Hirad on the seat of his breeches and laughed, a huge guttural sound more akin to a building falling than anything else.

'Very funny, Sha,' said Hirad, standing again.

'It is good to feel you again,' said Sha-Kaan. 'The body is substandard, frail human, but your soul is every bit as strong. Well met.'

'What are you doing here? The Garonin after you too, are they?'

'They are failing to beat us on Beshara. But not here. You need help.' Sha-Kaan inclined his head fractionally in Sol's direction. 'And your king needs attention now.'

Sol waved weakly. 'Good to see you lot. Ilkar, a little help?'

Ilkar trotted over, leaving Hirad talking to Sha-Kaan.

'The best help you can give us is torching Denser. Bastard traitor is going to kill us all,' Hirad was saying.

'Killing him will not solve your problem,' said Sha-Kaan. 'My Dragonene reaching a new safe dimension will. That will secure the future for us all. That is where we must focus our efforts.'

Sol tried to raise himself to speak but his head was too foggy. Ilkar's hand on his shoulder was enough to stop him trying further.

'Don't move, Unknown, you're a bit of a mess.'

'Will he be all right?' asked Jonas.

Sol nodded. Ilkar didn't.

'Ilkar is a fine healer. Watch and learn,' said Sol. He caught Ilkar's expression. 'What's up? A quick bit of wood extraction and some Healing Hands should do the trick. Easy for you.'

'You don't know, do you?'

'Know what?'

'Julatsa has fallen. The Garonin have taken the Heart. Nothing I try is easy any more.'

Sol sighed and moved a hand to squeeze Ilkar's forearm. 'It all starts to make sense, doesn't it? Sorry, Ilkar. But we knew it was coming, didn't we?'

'I feel empty, Unknown,' said Ilkar. 'Hollow. And the void wind is stronger now. I'm not sure how much longer I can cling on to this body.'

'Try and keep strong,' said Sol. 'Look, I'll be fine. Just bandage me up or something.'

Ilkar's expression turned to one of slighted hurt. 'I may have lost my college but I think I can do a little better than *bandages*, Unknown. Now try and relax and don't say anything. I need to concentrate.'

Sol winked at him and settled down onto his front to give Ilkar room to work.

'Sha-Kaan, we need to get the dead that Denser rounded up away from here. All Xetesk's returned dead. Hundreds of them. Just outside the walls of the city is far enough. They have to be close enough to feel the souls of those who brought them back. Can you do it?'

Sha-Kaan grumbled in his throat. 'Travel without the beacon of a Dragonene is difficult. Tiring.'

'We can't leave them. They're trapped in the city and right in the path of the Garonin.'

'I will not know when I have travelled far enough,' said Sha-Kaan.

'Oh you will,' said Hirad. 'Because every one of them will start to scream when the pain in their souls grows unbearable. Then it's time to stop.'

Sha-Kaan considered for a moment. 'Bring them inside.'

Hirad ran to the door. Sol could hear him shouting for the dead to come in, not to be afraid. The latter would be difficult for them.

'And afterwards. After I have ferried them to safety. What must we do?' asked Sha-Kaan.

'Find a Wesman Shaman able to perform the ritual of opening,' said Ilkar.

Sol coughed. 'No.'

'What did I just say?' said Ilkar. 'Hold still and shut up. This is delicate, all right? Jonas, can you give me a hand? I need you to staunch the blood while I cast.'

'Hold on,' said Sol. 'Hirad. I'm not leaving my wife and son in Xetesk to die.'

'There's no time, Unknown; you know that.'

Sol tensed. 'Then we have to make time. I'm not sacrificing my life until I know my family will be safe.'

'What are you talking about, Father?'

Sol closed his eyes, cursing himself for a fool.

'Father?'

'Do you trust me, Jonas?'

'I love you, Father. I won't let you die.'

Sol blinked back his tears. 'Trust me now. Help me. Be brave and be strong. We have a lot of work to do.'

Jonas nodded but there was confusion in his face. 'Tell me what to do.'

Hirad was walking back into the Klene. The dead were following him, albeit rather reluctantly.

'Sol.' It was Auum.

'Yes, my friend.'

'I will find your wife and son. I will see them to safety. Don't go back to the inn. Come east. Seek me.'

Sol nodded, wincing as Ilkar probed his injury a little roughly.

'I am in your debt.'

Auum bowed. 'Any debt was repaid a very long time ago.'

The TaiGethen leader turned and trotted out of the Klene, hurrying the last of the dead inside, where they stood in fear, crowding as far from Sha-Kaan as they could. Behind them the Klene door clunked shut.

'Hang on,' said Hirad. 'We're going for a little ride.'

'Now is the time of our greatest peril.'

Denser's voice boomed out from the top of his tower. The Intonation spells turned every flat surface into an amplifier for his words. His voice carried out over the college, across the apron and into the wider city beyond. He was a just a speck from Diera's vantage point just inside the college gates. She hadn't wanted to hear him but knew she had to. Young Hirad, holding her hand tight, was at her side, and she hadn't missed the positioning of three college guards nearby. Life with Sol had taught her many and varied things.

The crowd that had gathered after the entire college guard had walked every street, summoning the population to hear their Lord, was easily fifteen thousand strong, probably twenty thousand. Perhaps eight thousand were Xeteskian born and bred, survivors of the demon invasion and utterly loyal. The rest were refugees and migrants, curious and anxious.

'But it is also the time of our greatest opportunity. Any of you who have come to our great city for protection will know first hand how dangerous and deadly our foe is. But their advance will break against the walls of Xetesk. We are prepared and we are strong. We will defeat them.

'And from the ashes Balaia will grow again. Stronger and better than ever before. Under the leadership of Xetesk as the lone college of magic, there will be an end to magical conflict. There will be stability and there will be order. There will be growing wealth for all those who work with us.

'We don't want to rule this great country. We want to lead you forward to a brighter future where you can make every choice yourself. But for that to happen, I need your trust. And I make you this promise. Xetesk will protect you in the days to come. We will keep you safe and we will keep you from becoming hungry or thirsty. And when the battle is done, we further pledge to reward you for all that you do for Xetesk.

'And now I ask you, Xetesk, my brothers and sisters, are you with us?'

Diera had to admit the roar of approval was impressive. Hirad cheered too. She kept her mouth firmly closed.

'Please, my people, enough,' said Denser, and his voice cast a shroud over the noise. 'Our time is short before the Garonin are at our gates. We must all pull together. Next follows instruction on how you can help and where you must go when the general alarm sounds. Listen closely because your lives truly are at stake.'

Diera felt movement around her and she clutched Hirad in front of her. Gentle hands touched her arms.

'My lady Diera, here is no longer safe for the wife and son of The Unknown Warrior.' An elf stood in front of her. He seemed to have appeared from nowhere. 'I am Auum. Do you remember me?'

Relief cascaded through Diera's body. 'Yes, of course I do. Sol said you were in the city. Surely you are a divisive element under the new terms pushed under my door. Haven't they arrested you?'

Auum raised his eyebrows. 'They have tried. Come with us; we will keep you safe.'

They began to make their way back through the crowd to the gates of the college. Guards tracked them all the way. And others. Mages planted in the crowd. Auum's hand moved minutely. His Tai disappeared.

'Where are we going?'

'Somewhere quiet,' said Auum.

'Sol will come back for me. I need to wait at the inn.'

'No. The college is watching your home. Trust me. Your husband knows where to find you.'

Auum led her quickly through the crowds massed around the gates and across the apron. Diera could see others moving in the periphery of her vision.

'We're being followed,' she said.

'Yes.'

Auum headed for one of the east-facing alleys that snaked away from The Thread. Home to tenements and warehousing mainly, they were a quiet, narrow maze where only the unwary would tread after dark, even this close to the college itself. Auum upped his pace. Once inside the alley, the noise of the crowd diminished. Another voice was speaking from the tower. Diera caught snatches of it and didn't much care for what she was hearing.

'What's going to happen to the city?'

'Denser thinks to raze it to the ground in an effort to stop the unstoppable,' said Auum. 'Stand over there, under that overhang.'

Diera led Hirad to where she was directed. Despite the bright sunlight, the alley was gloomy and frightening. Buildings leaned across it from both sides. The ground was mainly mud with weeds and tufts of grass here and there. The overhang sheltered a pair of doors on runners that let into a warehouse. Diera backed into the shadows and pulled Hirad close to her. The little boy was too scared to utter a sound and clung on to her arms, digging his fingers into her flesh.

'It'll be all right,' she said, though it looked anything but.

Auum had stopped about ten yards from the entrance to the alley and had turned to face it. Diera heard careful footsteps. One by one, eight men appeared. Six guards and behind them two mages in skullcaps and long dark robes. Old Xetesk garb. She shuddered.

'You have one chance to turn and go,' said Auum. 'You will not be harmed.'

'A lone elf is in no position to make bargains,' said one of the guards. He signalled behind him. 'Cast at will.'

'You are mistaken,' said Auum. 'A TaiGethen is never alone.'

Two shapes dropped from the rooftops at the end of the alley. A blur of movement and both mages crumpled. Auum moved, his speed truly startling. The guard in front of him had no time even to raise his sword to his waist. Auum's blade flickered in the mottled gloom and he buried it to the hilt in the guard's neck. Diera covered Hirad's eyes.

'Every guard is to be valued and respected,' came the voice from the tower. 'No violence against them can be tolerated. Every mage is one who might just save your life.'

Auum had not paused. He dragged his blade clear, dropped and swept the legs from under another guard. A second blade was in his other hand. He rose and stabbed down. The guard's cry was cut off. He jerked and was still. Auum was still rising. He twisted in the air and kicked out straight, catapulting a third guard backwards.

His Tai's blades whispered. The guard was dead before he hit the ground.

Three remained. Their confidence was gone. Two of them dropped their swords and held out their hands.

'No prisoners,' said Auum.

His Tai brought each man down. Blades bit into throats. Blood surged out over the ground. One more. He clutched his blade in both hands and faced Auum. The elf nodded and brought his blades to the ready. The guard struck forward. Auum was not there. One of his blades knocked aside the powerful thrust. The other swept through the back of the man's neck from close quarters. He fell without a sound.

Diera mouthed silently. She had seen fighting before. She had seen Sol kill four men in a similar alley in the port town of Arlen years ago. That had been shocking in its brutality. But the speed of the violence she had just witnessed was terrifying. Sol had said the TaiGethen were the fastest he had ever seen. He had not done them justice.

'I am sorry you had to see that but I could not have you any further from us. Enemies are all around.' Auum cleaned and sheathed his blades. 'Ghaal, Miirt. Ahead. Bring the cleaner team to clear this alley.'

'Why did you have to do that? They had surrendered to you. That's murder.'

Auum's face bore no guilt.

'We cannot risk discovery.'

'What are you talking about?'

'Come,' he said. 'Trust me.'

Auum trotted away down the alley. Diera shuddered as she turned her back on the bodies and followed him. Hirad seemed happy to run. It relieved the tension in both of them. The base of the alley opened out into a small square. Gated and fenced gardens were at its centre and it was ringed by the houses of the wealthy, all shuttered and dark. Shapes moved on the roofs. Like cats only much bigger.

Auum crossed the cobbled street and into the gardens. Diera followed him. Through the trees was an ornamental lawn. She stumbled to a stop and once again clutched Hirad to her. The boy had started to cry and tried to crawl up her body. There were wolves. Lots of them. And a man in their centre with his hand ruffling the fur of a pair of them like they were nothing more than pet dogs. The man smiled at her.

'Diera,' he said.

'Thraun?' she said, fear turning to hope. 'Is that you?'

'Back and running with the pack.'

Chapter 22

It felt like slipping into the most exquisite tailored clothes. The enemy were on his doorstep, his oldest friends presumably wanted him dead and the fate of Balaia rested squarely on his shoulders. And it felt now as if not a single stitch were out of place. Birthright, Dystran had just called it.

'Destiny,' said Brynar, who had been given a chance to redeem himself.

The word didn't matter too much. The three of them clinked their cut crystal glasses, full of the finest Blackthorne red from the cellars, and drank.

'You know the most amazing thing of all is the energy I feel. I really can do all that I have promised. I can rule here and make Xetesk a power to rival any other in any dimension, known or not. Birthright? More like reborn.'

'But to be complete, to truly own Xetesk and by definition now, Balaia, to have the unwavering loyalty of the Circle Seven for long enough, there is one more thing you must do,' said Dystran.

'And what is that?' asked Denser, mind bright with opportunity and hazy with authority. Damn it if he didn't feel a little drunk.

Dystran indicated the three huge and ancient leather- and brass-bound books he had brought with him from the catacombs.

'You have always been something of a rebel. Accommodated by such lords as Styliann because of your rather unique aptitude for Dawnthief. But the time has come, my Lord Denser, to write your name indelibly into the lore of this college. You must take the "y" into your name. Let it speak for the power you wield as it has done throughout the generations of our great college. Become a true Lord of Xetesk.'

He patted the book. Denser felt a frisson of discomfort. Ever since he could remember, he'd fought against this. Seen himself more as a fighter against the system. For a moment it was difficult to admit he now *was* the system.

'It is not a big change,' continued Dystran.

'Wrong. It changes me forever.'

'Surely that has already happened,' said Dystran.

Denser considered briefly and then nodded. Dystran opened the book to display a double spread of pages. On the left-hand page, wrapped in ornate decoration, was his own name and beneath it those of the Circle Seven and other named mages and officers of influence or particular bravery or commendation. The page opposite was blank. Brynar had inked a pen and he gave it to Denser. Dystran turned the book to face him and held the page flat.

Denser bent to write then let the pen hover. He closed his eyes and fought his doubt. So many years about to be washed away. So much youthful anger and righteous thought. And it had brought him full circle. He suspected that Styliann, Nyer, Laryon – all of those who had nurtured and schooled him – had known all along. Presumably it was why they had tolerated him at all.

Denser put the pen to the heavy parchment and wrote in careful, Xeteskian lore script:

D-e-n-s-y-r

He leaned back when it was done and looked. Fitting. Entirely fitting.

'You are so named,' said Dystran. 'I, Dystran . . .'

'And I, Brynar.'

'. . . witness the taking of "y by the mage Denser, who shall now be remembered in perpetuity through the lore of our college.' Dystran took the book back and blotted Denser's work expertly. 'The scribes will do the rest. I think a full ceremony is out of the question until we are safe from the Garonin. Do you agree?'

Densyr nodded. 'I do.'

'And what are my Lord's next wishes?' asked Brynar.

Densyr looked out on a quiet Xeteskian evening. His people scurried about, doing his bidding, securing his city and seeking out the few dissenters.

'Where are we with our – ahem – high-profile handful of rebels?'

Densyr had taken the news that the dead had departed en masse inside a dragon's Klene with some relief. He didn't much care where they had gone though he presumed it would not be far from the city. But what it did mean was that the blood of the dead, and more importantly The Raven, was no longer on his hands. And it might still deflect a portion of the enemy's attention from the college.

'We are yet to find where they are hiding this time,' said Brynar. 'General Suarav is confident they are scattered about the city.'

'That is no basis for confidence and you can tell Suarav from me that I believe he is wrong. Blackthorne, Gresse, our TaiGethen friends . . . scattered, no. They are together and plotting something stupid, I have no doubt. I want them caught and incarcerated. Killed if they resist. They are taking precious resource from the city's defence. Tell me you still have Diera and young Hirad under close observation?'

Brynar paused just a little too long. Densyr sighed.

'My last report is of her in conversation with Auum of the Tai-Gethen. They were followed from the college but I have had no reports since.'

'Terrific,' said Densyr. 'And you know why that is? It's because anyone who followed them is undoubtedly dead. Did no one listen to me when I said the TaiGethen were dangerous? This isn't steep-stairs dangerous. This is get-slaughtered-in-a-heartbeat-unless-you-are-unbelievably-careful dangerous. Am I clear?

'And so Auum has Diera too. All I need now is Sol to come riding in on a white charger and my day will be complete.'

'Um . . .' began Brynar.

'You're about to tell me that's already happened?'

'No, but there were other reports following your speech and the instructions from General Suarav. Guards have reported people saying that there are wolves and panthers in the city.'

'I beg your pardon?'

'Wol—'

'I heard you. Go away. Dystran go with him. He clearly needs an older, wiser head to help him.'

'Of course, my Lord Densyr,' said Dystran. 'Do you have any other requirements?'

'I trust you, Dystran. Do what you consider needs doing. And send me Septern. I feel in need of good news. At least he won't let me down.'

Densyr watched the two mages leave. The door closed behind them. He stood up, drained his glass and refilled it. He stood over the Book of Names. It held the name of every Lord of the Mount since the sundering. And now it held his. Living up to this was not going to be easy.

Densyr took his glass and walked out onto his balcony. Panthers. That meant ClawBound were loose. Not good. And wolves. Wolves just had to mean that Thraun was back and had found Diera too. Their bond would certainly be strong enough after all their shared time on Herendeneth. The years when Thraun was lost to himself.

Panthers or wolves. He found himself wondering which would be better and quicker at tearing out his throat. He was still itching at his neck when the door opened to admit Septern.

The Klene was being buffeted again by the void of inter-dimensional space. The dead had been left outside the walls of the city, no more than a mile distant, and asked to trust that The Raven could deliver their loved ones to them soon. The Raven, returning to Xetesk, had no idea how they were to make good on their promise.

Sha-Kaan's and Jonas's minds were locked together while the dragon sought Diera through him. All The Raven quartet could do was hang on and hope purchase was found soon. Sha-Kaan would be unable to make absolute connection with Diera so their landing was going to be hit and miss but it was better than nothing.

Sol, hanging on to one of Sha-Kaan's forelimbs, couldn't take his eyes off Jonas. His back throbbed and occasionally sent shooting pains throughout his body but Ilkar had done enough to give him some movement and had staunched the bleeding.

Jonas looked so terribly small where he lay in the crook of Sha-Kaan's other forelimb. He was not conscious though he burbled and cried out from time to time. His face was pale and sweating and his breathing was too shallow and fast.

'How long can he keep this up?' asked Sol.

'I will not let him suffer harm,' said Sha-Kaan, opening one of his huge blue eyes, its centre a flat black slit. 'He is strong. In his father's image.'

'And how's it going?' asked Hirad. 'This is making me feel seasick.'

He and Sirendor had secured themselves to Sha-Kaan's left rear claws with belts. Hirad was clutching the claw in both arms too. Sirendor appeared to be asleep, though how he was able to do that was beyond Sol. The Klene thumped again, like a ship on a down swell.

'Frail human,' rumbled Sha-Kaan. 'We can sense Diera. We know she is calm and safe. But the city is not so large that I can open the Klene anywhere and expect to find her. If we are wrong by five per cent, we might find ourselves inside the college. Patience, my old friend. It will not be long.'

Sol smiled to himself. How gentle the great dragon was and how terrifying he had been when first they had encountered him. A lot of years ago now. But he had changed from the haughty king of his brood and user of man into something so rich and deep. Jonas loved him. Hirad did too. Sol could understand why, and a pang of jealousy crept into his heart for that which he could never fully know himself.

The Klene thumped again. Sol imagined it as a tail behind a behemoth, swishing this way and that, searching for a comfortable place to coil. And again. Sha-Kaan's eye flicked open once more, and this time his pupil was narrow to the point of invisibility. A sound reverberated through the Klene like a distant impact. A second was much closer.

'We are discovered,' said Sha-Kaan. 'Prepare to—'

To Sha-Kaan's right a section of the Klene crashed inwards. One of the huge fireplaces disappeared into fragments. A howling wind tore into the chamber, grabbing and sucking.

'Hold on!' shouted Sha-Kaan above the din of the gale.

The dragon's neck twisted and his head darted towards the hole, which was as big as a house. Loose debris was being dragged out of the hole, through which Sol could see nothing but a roiling brown mass shot with pale flecks like snow. Sha-Kaan opened his mouth and discharged a searing tongue of flame into the void. The sound of screams was surely a figment of Sol's imagination.

What wasn't his imagination was the increase in the power of the wind in the Klene, nor the voracious nature of the hole in its side. The ragged edge was growing by the heartbeat. Sol saw pieces being torn away and sucked into the void. And Sha-Kaan was beginning to slide himself.

'How do we stop this?' yelled Sol, but the noise was far too great to be heard.

Like the scything of a mighty claw, a rent was dragged in the left-hand wall of the Klene. The wind of the void was all-consuming. It roared from side to side. It tore the mantels from the walls, ash from the grates and the Kaan crest from above the Great Kaan.

Down on the ground, Ilkar, Hirad and Sirendor were hanging on desperately to Sha-Kaan's claws even while the dragon was being dragged slowly across the floor to the larger hole. Sha-Kaan's head spun and he looked first at Jonas before twisting down to Sol.

'We must make purchase on Balaia. Then I can fight.'

'Anywhere,' said Sol.

The Klene rattled as if some ancient God had picked it up and shaken it. Sol's grasp was broken. Jonas, poor unconscious Jonas, was thrown like a rag doll into the teeth of the wind and sucked helplessly towards the gaping, expanding opening. Sha-Kaan roared.

'Jonas!' Sol cried and tried to steady himself.

Pressed against the floor, he found a little purchase. Above him, Sha-Kaan's neck writhed and twisted as he fought to keep Jonas from being drawn into the void. But it was as if the wind had fingers and they plucked the boy away from him.

Sha-Kaan moved to place his bulk against the hole. A second rent appeared in the opposite wall. And a third. Sol saw the flash of metal beyond, just for a beat. Jonas had woken and was screaming for help. There was blood on his face. Sol didn't pause. He sprang from the floor, diving upwards.

The wind caught him and propelled him further up. Jonas flashed by. Sol reached out a hand and grasped his son's leg. Their combined weight brought them both down to the stone floor, hard. Sol landed back first, Jonas square on top of him, winding him. His wound flared pain.

'It's all right, son. It's all right, I've got you.' The stone floor shuddered. Slabs rippled and bucked. 'Oh no.'

Sol turned his head where he lay. Sha-Kaan was moving across the floor towards them. Of Hirad, Sirendor and Ilkar, there was no sign. The Great Kaan's head snaked out, mouth agape. A thundering crash reverberated through the Klene. The wind strengthened yet more. And Sol, with Jonas clinging to him, was sliding feet first along the floor.

'Hang on!'

About ten yards ahead of them much of the floor had gone. They picked up speed. Sol tried to dig in his feet but there was no grip to be had on the polished stone. A shadow whipped overhead. Sha-Kaan's head and neck arced past and thrust into the hole. Flame gorged out. He withdrew.

Sol's slide was unstoppable. His back bumped over broken stone at the edge of the hole. He flailed with one hand and gripped briefly but the gale was too strong.

'Close your eyes, Jonas. It'll be over soon.'

Sol felt hot breath firing over his shoulder. His vision filled with scale and fangs and he was airborne once again. He grabbed Jonas even closer to him as they swung wildly in the air. Sha-Kaan's neck withdrew to the formal 's' shape and he reared high. Sol felt the bone of the dragon's fangs scrape his shoulders and upper right arm. Sha-Kaan held him as lightly as he could.

Through the smashed floor of the Klene, in the midst of the maelstrom, Sol could make out indistinct shapes.

'What now?' he yelled.

'Now we land,' said Jonas, and he'd be damned if the boy wasn't actually smiling.

Abruptly, the Klene stopped its juddering and the wind lost much of its power. Sol could still hear the roar as the chaos passed by the openings the Garonin had torn in the fabric of the Klene but the sucking and grabbing strength had ebbed almost to nothing.

Sha-Kaan moved swiftly, placing Jonas and Sol on the ground.

'Beware,' he said. 'They are outside.'

Sol became acutely aware that he had neither armour nor weapons. He backed away to a safer section of wall, keeping Jonas behind him.

'Where are the others?' he asked, imagining them being pulled helplessly into eternal night.

'They chose a safer place to be,' said Sha-Kaan, glancing back over his body.

And there they were. All three of them. Unclasping their arms from the very tip of Sha-Kaan's tail. Hirad stood and brushed himself down; Ilkar was rolling his shoulders and Sirendor flexing his legs. All looked battered and bruised. But still here.

Without warning, Sha-Kaan turned his head and breathed fire into the gaping hole in the floor. Flame boiled around its edges, smoke billowed. This time Sol did hear the screams above the roaring of the wind.

'You must leave now,' said Sha-Kaan.

'We need to stay and fight with you,' said Hirad.

'No. They cannot hurt me. In a blink I will be back on Beshara.'

The door began to open inwards, revealing a night-time scene.

'Where are we?' asked Sirendor.

'We're about to find out,' said Hirad.

Sol walked towards the door, the others following him.

'Jonas,' said Sha-Kaan.

'Yes, Sha.'

'Your mother is quite close. Go. I will be here when you need me again.'

Jonas smiled. Sol put an arm about his shoulder, as much for support for himself as comfort for his son. His back, shoulder, arm and legs were all protesting.

'I must warn you of one thing,' said Sha-Kaan. Sol turned. The dragon was not looking at them but tracking something beyond the Klene. 'They are closer than you think. And they move faster than you know. Good luck, my friends.'

The Raven and Jonas walked out into a mercifully quiet night in Xetesk.

Chapter 23

Auum haunted the empty streets by the east gates of Xetesk. Miirt and Ghaal ran the rooftops above him. A ClawBound pair sat in the shadows on the gates themselves, sampling the air and looking back at the college or out over the open ground to where the clouds were gathering.

Sol and Hirad were here somewhere, he could sense it. Diera's mumblings had been mere confirmation. The ClawBound had chosen the hiding place in the small park well. The bordering houses belonged exclusively to the mage elite and all of them were ensconced full time in the college. The odd servant had been in residence but none now remained at large to cause any trouble. It was amazing how good a jailor a single wolf could be. No bars had been necessary.

Auum heard footsteps. He faded into the shadows and indicated to Ghaal and Miirt that an intruder was approaching. A man appeared from an intersection of the narrow, winding artisans' quarter. He turned right and towards Auum. The TaiGethen withdrew further into his chosen doorway and ceased all movement. He watched.

The man was dressed in plain shirt and trousers and wore a light cloak about his shoulders. He was of average height, with short dark hair. He appeared unhurried. However, his actions marked him out as a man not merely out for a stroll. He was criss-crossing the street, crouching occasionally and laying his hands on blank stone or timber. Each time he did so, he uttered words of incantation.

Auum waited and watched. There was little point in doing anything else. The man, clearly a mage, moved closer. He crouched to attend to a spell not five feet from Auum, crabbed two paces to his left and saw Auum's boots.

'Ah,' he said.

He tried to leap out of the way but Auum's hand was already around his neck, pushing his head back and lifting him upright.

'Ah, indeed,' said Auum. 'Do not attempt to cast. Do not attempt to cry out, or I will kill you.'

'What do you want? Why are you here? We thought . . .'

'Speak. Thought what?'

'Thought . . . you were hiding elsewhere.'

'Then I have disappointed you. What are you doing here?'

'Just walking. These are the streets where I was born,' said the mage brightly.

'And where you will die if you lie to me again. You were studying trap spells – wards you call them. Why?'

The mage's brightness had deserted him and he had begun to shake. He put his hands to Auum's to try and shift his grip. It was like trying to crush stone.

'Please, you're hurting me.'

Auum cocked his head. 'I know. What of it?'

'I'll tell you if you let me go.'

Auum shrugged and released his grip. The mage turned to bolt and collided with Miirt's fist. He doubled over, coughing and retching, dropping to his knees.

'Speak,' said Auum.

'It's nothing,' gasped the mage, wrapping his arms around his stomach. 'We have to test the segments of the defensive grid. Check the linkage. Can't afford any errors.'

Auum looked up at his Tai. Both shook their heads.

'We do not believe you. Try harder.'

'It's true, I swear.'

'Kill him,' said Auum.

A short blade flashed in Ghaal's hand. He dragged back the mage's head and struck down, stopping a hair's breadth from breaking the skin. The mage fouled himself and held up his hands.

'Please no,' he said, wheezing and crying. 'Sorry, sorry. I'm sorry.'

'Speak.'

'Septern changed the exclusions of the wards. We hoped you were still in the grid somewhere. Needed to trap you here. Anything larger than a dog will trip them when they go active. I was checking to see the exclusion formula had filtered down to the periphery. Please, I'm telling the truth.'

'Yes.' Auum took a step back, happy to be away from the stench of excrement and urine. 'When will the grid be active?'

'When all the mages have reported back to the college.'

'You will not be reporting back,' said Auum.

'Please!' The mage held out his hands in supplication. 'I told you the truth. Please.'

'You will come with us. We have a place where you can clean yourself.'

'Yes, yes of course. Thank you.'

Auum's nose wrinkled at the pathetic gratitude. 'You may be of some use to us yet.'

'I'm hoping you recognise this place,' said Hirad.

They'd walked out into an area of scrubland that bordered the blank faces of warehouses. The scrub was littered with pieces of stone and broken timber. A quick scout of the immediate area had told them that the college was to their north. Directly opposite the warehouses, more buildings rose about a half a mile away, and the city walls loomed a further mile or so distant.

Sol was sitting with his back to a wall while the pain in various parts of his body settled. He'd fussed over Jonas's scrapes and cuts until the boy had pushed him away with a comment about his age and ability to look after himself. Sol felt tired and at a loss.

'I'm too old for all this racing about,' he said.

'Well you should die and pick yourself a younger body,' said Hirad. 'It does wonders, you know. Anyway. Where are we, exactly?'

'South-east corner of the city. Not too far from the east gates. This used to be a pretty rich area until the demons came. It never got rebuilt and all people did was steal the stone and wood to repair elsewhere. I think Denser wanted it to be some form of remembrance park or something. As you can see, dreams are yet to become reality.'

'We ride around here quite a lot,' said Jonas.

'Didn't I tell you not to because of the risk of injuring your horse on all this loose stone? Full of holes, this place.'

Jonas shrugged. 'Probably. Anyway, we're lucky we didn't appear in the middle of the college or somewhere like that, aren't we? At least I can tell you every way out of here that takes us away from most patrol routes.'

'Yes, but where are we going?' asked Ilkar. 'Back to where the dead were? Auum won't have stayed there.'

'Yes, but he said he'd be in the eastern quarter somewhere,' said Sol.

'Diera's relatively close to here, so Sha-Kaan said.' Sirendor was walking in small circles, scanning the Xeteskian night.

Sol nodded. 'I have no doubt at all that Denser would use her as a hostage if he had to. So if she's calm and safe as we are told, that means she's away from him and we can assume Auum has been as good as his word yet again. The question is, where would he hide her and himself?'

'Some place with trees. With high-sided buildings and plenty of routes in and out,' said Hirad. 'When I was running with the Tai-Gethen back on Calaius, he used to keep going on about keeping every option available for as long as possible and having height on any enemy. Easy in the rainforest, not quite so easy here because he doesn't know it so well. How's Xetesk off for parks?'

'Well, there are a good number of squares with gardens. There's the old Park of Remembrance but that's just lawns and grazing these days. Jonas?'

'There are three or four squares a short ride from here,' said Jonas. 'The park is way over the other side of the city and it's too open if Auum wants what Hirad says he does.'

'Can you take us to these squares?'

'With my eyes shut, Father.'

Sol stood up slowly and grimaced at the state of his body.

'That won't be necessary. Lead on. Hirad, up front with him just in case you remember some of your Tai training on markers and tracks.'

'Fat chance,' said Ilkar. 'He has trouble walking and breathing at the same time most days.'

'Can we keep it quiet?' asked Sol. 'We're not welcome here.'

Jonas led them to a wide street that ran away in the direction of the east gates. Every house, every tenement and business, was shuttered and quiet. No lights could be seen, no noise could be heard close by.

'This place has been evacuated,' said Sirendor quietly.

Sol nodded. 'I presume Septern's ward grid has been laid by now. No doubt Denser was planning to squeeze the entire population into the western side of the city beyond the college. I hope he's right about which gate the Garonin come through. He's taking a big gamble.'

'It won't make a damned bit of difference,' said Hirad. 'It's not a gamble, Unknown, it's a guaranteed defeat.'

'I want everyone to stop right now.' Ilkar's voice brooked no dissent.

'What's up, Ilks?'

'Well, I don't want to alarm anyone, but if we're about to walk into a ward grid, our chances of walking out of it again are slim in the extreme, wouldn't you say?'

'The elf in man's clothing has a point,' said Hirad.

'But you go right on walking, Hirad. Test my theory, why don't you?'

'Touchy, touchy.'

'Focus,' hissed Sol. 'Ilkar, what I know is that Septern was intending to tune out anything man-sized. He was also going on about leaving the grid dormant until the Garonin got here. Something about maintaining cohesion of wards and retaining mana stamina; does that make sense?'

'Kind of. And easy enough if you're a genius, like him. Put it this way. If he hasn't done the things you said he was talking about, every step could be our last.'

'Can't you detect them as we approach them?' asked Sirendor.

Ilkar's face was glum. 'Not now. That kind of fine work is denied me. Our turn to gamble. How big was this grid going to be, anyway?'

'The whole eastern half of the city if we had time,' said Sol.

Ilkar whistled. 'Now that is something I'd like to see.'

Hirad began walking. 'Well, if the Garonin get here before we're done, you're going to get your wish. Come on, Raven, and sons of Raven, let's get out of here.'

'Hirad, be careful.'

'How?' asked Hirad over his shoulder. 'If I can't see it, how can I avoid it?'

Jonas fell into step with him, and at an indication from the boy the two of them turned left. Sol spread his hands and began to follow. They'd turned into a wide residential street that led towards the eastern grain store. Ten yards along it, Ilkar gasped.

'Whoa,' he said, dropping to his haunches and blowing hard. 'That is not good.'

'Jonas, Hirad. Stop moving. Ilkar? Talk to me.'

Sol's eyes darted left, right and up. Nothing out of the ordinary.

'Something . . .' Ilkar closed his eyes and reached out with his hands. 'Something.'

'What?' Sol thought he heard a whisper on the wind. A sound from his distant past.

'There's—' began Ilkar.

'How interesting,' said a voice from above their heads. 'Even without a college Heart, a Julatsan may still feel a construct should it contain enough power, I see.'

Two figures descended slowly into view, hovering thirty-odd feet away. Denser and Septern.

'I wondered how long it would be before you came back here to get your wife and completely bugger things up, Sol. Did you really think a dragon opening a second Klene corridor in one day could go unnoticed in my city?'

'I will do what I came here to do, Denser, and that includes beating you to a bloody pulp. One punch for every time I considered you my trusted friend. That's a lot of punches.'

'A couple of points, if I may. First of all, no, you won't lay a finger on me, and I'll tell you why in a moment. Secondly, and it's a small thing, but I have, um, adjusted my name. Just to aid the record keeping of the college, you know.'

Sol felt a rush of sadness, the end of possibility. A closing-down on the potential for redemption.

'You've taken the "y", haven't you?'

'Yes. So it's Densyr, not Denser.'

'Makes no difference to me,' growled Hirad. 'You're still a traitor to The Raven and Balaia and you will die for it.'

Densyr chuckled. 'How I have missed your idle threats, Hirad. Now, as Ilkar will be able to tell you when he gets his breath back, you have walked into the middle of a cell of explosive fire-based ward constructs which, as luck would have it, Septern was able to make active when we spotted you. These wards, like all of them across the city, have been tuned to include moving shapes of your size, but I'll leave it to you to decide whether to believe that or not. I don't really have the time to care.

'Should you stay exactly in the positions you are, you will come to no harm. Not until the Garonin blunder into them in a day or so, anyway. I'm sorry it has come to this and I truly don't want to kill any of you. So the choice remains yours. To try and get out of your current predicament or to come voluntarily into custody and let me decide your fates when the battle is won.

'I'll leave you for a few hours to make up your minds. I trust I don't need to demonstrate what happens when a ward is triggered?'

'Not for my benefit,' said Ilkar.

'Good. Until later then.'

Septern and Densyr rose quickly into the night and were lost, missing much of Hirad's colourful volley of abuse.

'Do you mind?' said Sol. 'My son is standing next to you.'

'It isn't like I haven't heard all those words before,' said Jonas.

'But perhaps not strung together with such alacrity and with the multiple repetition of certain choice terms, eh?'

'So do we believe that bastard?' asked Sirendor, who was standing next to Ilkar.

'Ilkar?' asked Sol.

Ilkar, who had recovered from the shock of the surge of mana all about them, scratched at his chin.

'I think testing if he's bluffing would be incredibly stupid.'

'Can't we just throw something at one of them?' asked Hirad.

'Must I repeat myself? You haven't studied Septern. There are very interesting passages and witness testimonies discussing his death, and more than one talks about wards triggering other wards in chain reactions. Big chain reactions. Throw one stone, bring down the whole street, that sort of thing. What I need is a little quiet and I'll see if I can divine any wards, triggers or linkage lines.'

'I thought you said you couldn't do that any more,' said Hirad.

'Got a better idea?'

'Nope.'

'Then shut up.'

Diera came to, lying on her back with her head cushioned by a cloak. The images she'd seen, so real and so terrifying, began to fade, and the relief of waking from a dream washed over her.

'Welcome back,' said a voice.

She turned her head. Baron Blackthorne was kneeling by her. His kindly face wore lines of worry.

'What happened?' she asked. 'Where's Hirad?'

'He's safe. Thraun is showing him not to be scared of wolves. As for you, well you were complaining of a headache, and the next we knew, you'd collapsed. You muttered some strange things about dragons and your son. You said they were coming. You said that over and over. Who did you mean?'

Diera shook her head. 'Can you help me up?'

Blackthorne supported her to a sitting position and waited while her blood settled and the faintness passed.

'I don't remember too much. It was just a dream. Jonas and Sha-Kaan being attacked somehow. There was wind and darkness. It's nothing. Just a mother worrying about her son.'

'I don't think so. Neither does Auum. He is out there now, looking for Jonas and Sol. You said they'd come for you. We believe they have.'

'Based on a dream?'

'And elves know the perspicacity of dreams.'

Diera hugged her knees. 'I hope they're right.'

'And let's hope they get to them before the guards do. Altogether too many roaming the city right now.'

'Will they find us here? The guard that is?'

'Eventually,' said Blackthorne. 'But we'll be ready for them.'

'I don't really understand what we're doing here. Shouldn't we be going west?'

'Auum has high ideals and I share them until my courage falters.' Blackthorne chuckled at his own joke. 'He aims to break the college hold and get people away from here before it's too late.'

'He doesn't have much time and very few here to help him. What can he do?'

'He is waiting for an opportunity to present itself.'

'And will it?'

'When the battle starts.' Blackthorne raised his eyebrows.

'But surely that will cut things too fine.' Diera searched her memory. 'Sol wanted everyone away days ago. You know what he's planning to do, don't you?'

'Rumour has it that there is some thought we can escape to a new home. Seems a distant prospect to me. But I know that staying here is folly. I've seen this enemy, and a few spells set about the city will not stop them.'

There was a brief commotion at the gates to the garden. Auum barked an order and ran in. Diera had never seen worry on his face before. Blackthorne stood.

'Auum?'

'We have a problem.'

Away to the south and east of the city, a ClawBound panther called out. It was a disquieting sound. Auum listened to it and his frown deepened.

'Two problems.'

Chapter 24

The awful truth about the fate of Julatsa had dampened hope three days before. The fleet had been sailing out of sight of the north Balaian coast and there had been no encounters nor indeed any sightings whatever of the Garonin. The ships were scattered over a wide area, attempting to diminish the density of souls for the enemy to sense. There had been an uneasy quiet across the whole fleet. It felt like the absence of belief.

And now, approaching Wesman territory at North Bay, with the hard grey peaks of Sunara's Teeth dominating the near horizon, trepidation reigned. Mage reconnaissance had revealed no evidence of Garonin activity but neither had it revealed any sign of the Wesmen.

Rebraal was not unduly concerned by that. This desolate, dangerous coast had been largely abandoned since the storms of the Night Child had swept away the bay's lonely fishing village over fifteen years ago. They were a superstitious race, the Wesmen, and Sunara's Teeth were cursed.

'I'll drop anchor half a mile from the shore,' said Jevin. 'Well before we get snagged in the currents close in.'

He and Rebraal were standing in the prow of the *Calaian Sun*, staring at the coastline and searching for any sign, good or bad.

'Let's hope your plan works. I feel nervous at the thought of three hundred ships crowding in here, even in rotation.'

'We've had plenty of time to plan,' said Jevin. 'Weather conditions and tides are both in our favour to begin right now. Have faith.'

'It's still going to take three days to disembark. We're exposed the whole of that time.'

'I do not rule the tides. It's the best I can do.'

'Forgive me. I'm not being critical. I'm just . . . well.'

Jevin nodded and slapped Rebraal on his back.

'So are we all, Rebraal.'

'Indeed.'

Rebraal looked back to the beach and wished it four miles long rather than the four hundred yards afforded them. North Bay was a funnel trap for the unwary sailor, an invitingly broad shelter that narrowed quickly into rock-strewn shallows around which the water eddied and surged, denying escape for ocean-going vessels that strayed too close to the shore. Multiple wrecks beneath the waves only added to the risks.

Three TaiGethen cells had already landed to scout the immediate area and secure the path away from the beach. One cell waited on the beach. The other two would be looking for shelter and cover. They would not find a great deal of either outside the lee of the mountains.

The *Calaian Sun* was leading the first twenty ships into the landing area. The decks were crowded with evacuees, who had now been joined by all of the TaiGethen and Al-Arynaar warriors. Half their mages too. It had been a risky transfer. Jevin kept a tight grip on the ship's progress from his forward position. Topsails hung from two masts, giving a speed of little more than one knot. Periodically, Jevin would hold out his right or left arm to direct the helm to starboard or port. He would also display a number of fingers to indicate the degree of turn he desired.

The flagship of the elven exodus slipped into the wind shadow of Sunara's Teeth, which ringed the entire bay and glowered down on all who sailed within their compass. Immediately, the topsails flapped. Here the eddies in the water and the currents that drove them played havoc with the handling of the vessel.

Jevin held up two fists to signal steady as she goes. Any desultory conversation died in throats. People lined the rails, staring down, looking for disaster to loom up at them. Plumb lines in the water spoke their depth. The beach crawled closer.

'That'll do, I think.' Jevin began striding back towards the wheel deck. 'Helm, bring her up into the wind. Bosun, make our masts naked. Stand by, anchor. On my order. Signals, fly the all stop. This is as far in as we dare go. Oars, ready the boats. Rebraal, get your people organised. I want out of this bay in two hours or I'll not get another squadron in before the tide moves against us.'

Rebraal nodded. The ship had exploded into activity. Al-Arynaar and TaiGethen assembled by their boats. Refugees were herded this way and that as crew set about their tasks. Blocks and tackles were set up to winch out cargo. Nets were filled with crates and barrels.

In the hold of the *Calaian Sun* was the statue of Yniss that bound the elves to life on Balaia. He would not be coming ashore. When Jevin's work with the refugees was done the captain was to perform one last task. To scuttle his ship and send the statue to the bottom of the ocean, far from the destructive hands of the Garonin. Jevin had expressed his intent to see Yniss all the way down.

'Anchor away,' called Jevin to an accompanying rattle of chain.

Rebraal checked his armour and weapons. He stood before his warriors and the TaiGethen. To their left another ship had dropped anchor about fifty yards away. ClawBound crowded the deck. Panthers growled. Bound elves sniffed the air.

'They, like us, desire the ground beneath their feet,' he said. 'My brothers and sisters, now we reach the most dangerous part of our flight. The lands of the Wesmen are open. Our souls are a beacon for the Garonin, bound as they are with the mana that suffuses each one of us.

'Yet we must not rush. Our people depend upon us. They must be supported at every point. Our camps must be sound and our direction clear. We must neither pause nor falter. You all have your tasks. Contact with the Wesmen at the earliest opportunity is vital. Warning of attack equally so.

'My friends, we hold in our hands the fate of the elven race. Yniss cannot help us. We must help ourselves. To your boats.'

Four longboats were lowered to the sea. Elves swarmed down rope and net. Cargo followed for forward and aft stowage. Oars were readied. Rebraal felt Jevin come to his side.

'Good luck out there,' said the captain.

'Yniss blesses you, Master Jevin,' said Rebraal. 'Your path to the ancients is assured.'

'Only if you succeed.'

Rebraal turned to find Jevin smiling at him.

'And we will.'

'See that you do,' said Jevin. 'I might have had the wander in me as a sailor but I like to think my soul will find eternal rest. No pressure.'

Rebraal and Jevin clasped arms. 'You should wander the northern oceans a little. How many are coming with you?'

'Twenty assuming no others change their minds. And we intend to. Who knows what sights there are to see?'

Rebraal climbed down into his longboat, and when he looked back to the ship's rail Jevin had already turned away. He could hear the captain barking orders. The longboat pulled smoothly from the ship and sped into the shore at North Bay. Up in the sky, the cloud was heavy and grey. Rain was coming, perhaps a storm. Rebraal, his heart a little heavy, looked forward. There was no sense in looking anywhere else.

'You cannot let them kill my son,' said Diera. 'Please. You have to do something.'

'He is no immediate danger. None of them are,' said Auum. He turned to Miirt. 'Get our prisoner back here now. I don't care how bad he smells.'

'No danger? You've just told me your panther has seen them and that they are plainly trapped. You told me that Densyr knows exactly where they are. How does this represent no danger?'

'I think it is a relative term,' said Baron Gresse. He was lying flat out on the grass, his leg surely agony yet he retained a morbid cheer. 'In any event it appears action is imminent, and if that means damage to the wielders of magic, I count myself satisfied.'

'Bloody right it's a relative term,' said Diera. 'We're talking about my family.'

Auum stared at her for a moment. He was unsure what he saw and felt a frisson of nerves.

'Were you joking?' he asked.

'Kind of,' she said. 'It's what I'd call executioner's humour. At least it got your attention. What are you going to do about my husband and son?'

'We have another problem,' said Auum.

'That isn't an answer. What of it?'

Auum paused again, gauging her mood and likely responses to what he wanted to tell her.

'The two are connected,' said Auum carefully.

Down on the ground Gresse was chuckling away to himself. And patting the ankle of Blackthorne, who was standing by him and failing to get him to be quiet.

'Are you drunk or something?' asked Blackthorne. 'We are in

serious trouble here, Gresse. Laughter isn't the answer. Not this time.'

'Oh but it is, my dear Baron Blackthorne. Besides, whichever way this goes, I am soon to die. And is not the confusion of a male over a female always the most magnificent thing to watch. Even the great Auum squirms.'

'I am not trying to confuse him, Baron Gresse,' said Diera.

'You never do, my dear, you never do.'

'Patronising bastard,' she said. 'Go on, Auum, unless you're too nervous to speak to me. What are we going to do? My family are in trouble and I will not stand by and wait for them to die. Do you understand me?'

'We are all in similar trouble,' said Auum.

'I beg your pardon?'

'We have information that makes staying here impossible. It also makes leaving here extremely difficult.'

Auum felt the pressure of a dozen pairs of eyes on him. The two barons and their small retinues, Diera of course, and also Thraun, who had remained in earshot. Of his eight wolves, four were by him. Of the others, there was no sign. Auum feared for them.

'Difficult how, exactly?' asked Gresse.

Auum respected the old baron though their paths had barely crossed. Anyone who had survived the demon invasion, remaining free the whole time, was clearly worthy.

'The ward grid, when it is activated, will not exclude human or elf. Neither will it exclude wolves and panthers.'

'But we're right in the middle of it, aren't we?' said Diera.

Auum nodded. 'There are spells covering much of this area.'

'We're camping in a trap,' said Blackthorne.

'Well, there's one way out of it,' said Gresse, and he gestured at the rooftops. 'Those who can't fly will just have to climb and jump, won't they?'

Auum nodded again and Gresse smiled at him, understanding very clearly what it meant.

'There is one other possibility,' said Auum.

'Well there needs to be. Certain among our party of young rebels are not merely old and riddled with cancer, they also can't walk.' Blackthorne was glaring at Gresse. 'I told you to stay behind.'

'Right. To bring down the system from within. Not really my style,

Blackthorne. Don't worry about me. I'll keep the place warm for you.'

'I think when the God's Eyes start firing you'll find it warm enough,' said Blackthorne. 'Stupid old man. I bet you thought this might happen. I'm not leaving you.'

Gresse stuck two fingers in his mouth and made a retching sound.

'Spare me the bleeding hero stuff, Blackthorne. I'm sure I can make myself a nuisance.'

'It's got nothing to do with that. I have hauled your wretched carcass from your own vineyards. You owe me.'

Gresse laughed out loud and clapped his hands. 'Good for you.'

'I'm sorry, I'm not finding this at all funny,' said Diera.

'When you get to our age, Diera, you are forced to see the funny side of most things.'

'Well, right now, getting to your age seems a distant prospect, doesn't it? And what about my son? He's five years old. He deserves the concentrated effort of every one of us, don't you think?'

Gresse reached out a hand, which Diera, a little reluctantly, took in both of hers.

'Yes, he does, my lady,' he said quietly. 'And he shall get it. I'm sorry if I offended you.'

Diera shook her head. 'No, it's not that. It's just, you know . . . all of you. You're used to this. You've grown up with fighting and death and blood. I married someone who has too, but I've seen so little because he won't let me see it. So I'm scared. And I'm terrified for my boys. Auum, please?'

For a third time, Auum nodded.

'Miirt. Bring him.'

The mage was brought forward. Dressed in breeches and shirt both several sizes too big, he cut a ridiculous figure. He was deathly pale and the sight of the wolves caused him to jam his feet into the soft grass. Miirt's hand in the small of his back kept him moving.

'Name?' asked Auum.

'Brynar,' said the mage. Young and scared. Good. And there was more.

'You are apprentice to Densyr, aren't you?'

'And you are Auum.'

'Neither of us wishes to die this night. Help us and we will not cause you harm. You know where you are?'

'Hespyrin Square.'

'Then you know that when the ward grid is activated, we are in a poor position.'

'We'll all die,' said Brynar. 'There are thirty wards in these gardens alone. And they will trigger the collapse of every building on the four sides.'

'So, we are in agreement,' said Auum. 'I need options. Did Septern plan safe routes through the grid?'

Brynar shook his head. 'The Garonin would probably divine them. Too risky. It's complete blanket coverage.'

'Second. When will the grid be activated?''

'When all the mages return to the college, as I said. But not necessarily at that instant. Don't get your hopes up, though. Any of us over an hour late will be assumed lost, probably to you as it happens, and therefore the grid will not be delayed.'

'And how late are you, young man?' asked Blackthorne.

'I am well beyond my time already. I was late when I met Auum.' Brynar shuddered.

The howl of a wolf sounded to the east. It was picked up by those in the park and joined by the granite growl of the ClawBound panther. Thraun calmed his pack as best he could but the four were on their feet, pacing and sounding anxiety deep in their chests.

Auum was still for a moment. He sniffed the air. Tension and magic, which was no surprise. But the agitation of the wolves and the guttural tone of the panther's call were not to be ignored.

'Thraun?' he asked.

'They've heard something. I don't know what. I can't sense anything.'

'Well, let's not hang about,' said Blackthorne, and then he raised his voice. 'Everyone. Prepare to leave. Gresse, you are going on a stretcher and I will drag you up the sides of buildings as and when I have to . . . I'm sorry, I didn't catch that. What did you say?'

'I said, you are a stubborn old goat and you have the beard to prove it.'

'Ungrateful wretch.'

Auum shook his head and turned back to Brynar. The young mage stared all around him, blinking and swallowing hard.

'It is real,' said Auum.

The wolves howled again, their voices rising quickly to a whine high in the throat. All four gathered in front of Thraun, staring up at him and backing towards the west.

'Something's coming,' said Thraun.

There was a pressure in the air that hadn't been there a few moments ago. And Auum could hear a low throbbing sound on the periphery of his hearing. He exchanged glances with his Tai. They felt it too.

'Quickly. Tell me. What is the trigger radius of a ward in this grid? Are we safe on the rooftops?'

'Until someone triggers a cell of wards that brings the building down in a ball of flame around your feet,' said Brynar. 'I can't over-estimate the trouble we are all in.'

'Then I am glad you are sharing that trouble with us.' Auum stared at Brynar, looking for malice and trickery. The mage could not hold his gaze for long. 'Do not think to walk us to our deaths. I will know your thoughts.'

'If it's any consolation, I think the Mount has got this all wrong. We should be heading west.'

'Then you should have made your voice heard a little more clearly, shouldn't you?' said Gresse.

'Why do you think I was dispatched to check on the ward grid, my Lord Gresse?'

'It matters little to me,' said Auum. 'I do not trust you. My Tai do not trust you and nor do the ClawBound. I would have you understand that.'

Brynar nodded. 'Not that we really need to head west. Septern told me he knew all about the Wesman ritual. He just doesn't believe it'll work.'

Auum pulled up short. 'Are you sure?'

'Yes. He likes a drink and he likes to talk. Put the two together and all sorts comes out. Have I said something wrong?'

'Does Densyr know about this?' asked Auum.

'Not as far as I'm aware. Septern told Sharyr about it and Sharyr told me. I have told no one until now.'

'That changes everything.' Auum waved his Tai to him. 'Miirt. Contact the ClawBound. Ghaal. Run with Thraun. We need his wolves alive. I want a route to the college. Quickly. I'll see you on top.'

'You can get to the rooftops through most of the houses on this square. I'll show you if you like,' said Brynar.

'Go,' said Auum. 'Tai, we move.'

Miirt grabbed his arm. 'Look.'

Up on the rooftops immediately to their left, the ClawBound elf was standing and staring away to the east and high up into the sky. While Auum watched, the elf's panther joined him and he laid a hand atop its head. The physical contact worried Auum more than anything he had seen this night that was bleeding away to a pale dawn in the eastern sky. The gesture was only ever for mutual comfort in the face of fear. And the ClawBound feared almost nothing.

The throbbing sound intensified, grew louder. The wolves were beyond control now, running this way and that, desperate for Thraun to move. Down on the ground Blackthorne was feeding Gresse some form of drug against his pain. Two of the larger men stood ready. The old baron was to be chaired away. Diera held young Hirad close. Auum came to her side.

Up in the eastern sky, the clouds were heavy and grey. It was the same grim picture all the way to the sunrise horizon. Auum fancied he could see movement within. Something that showed itself where the cloud was a little thinner. Whatever it was, the noise it emitted was rattling the teeth in Auum's jaws and sending low vibrations through his body.

A silver shape descended through the clouds. Gently, serenely. It was bulbous, like a worn waterskin, stretched and bumpy, destined to leak. And huge. The size of a ship. Auum stared up at it. What else could any of them do? Below it, lights shone from what looked like windows and other lights played out over the city still swaddled in the last throes of night.

'Vydosphere,' he breathed.

'What?' Diera next to him could barely hear him for the growing drone.

'Garonin.' Auum's heart pounded in his chest. 'We have to get to the college before it does or we are all lost.'

Diera shook her head. 'What about Sol and Jonas?'

'We will rescue them,' he said, though he had no idea how that might now be achieved.

A beam of intense light stabbed down from the vydosphere. Somewhere near the east gates there was a detonation followed quickly by a dozen others. Orange, blue and yellow fire flared into the night sky. There was a rumble and the ground shifted beneath their feet. The sound of falling buildings echoed across the city to them. Brynar gasped.

'The wards,' he said. 'They're triggering the wards.'

Blackthorne swore under his breath.

'Run,' said Auum and he raised his voice. 'Run now.'

Chapter 25

Densyr ran to his east-facing balcony, Dystran and Septern to either side of him. Flame was leaping into the dawn sky, licking at the thick cloud cover above. He could see lights in the sky and blinked before realising that the dark shape he thought he had seen disappearing up into the clouds was a mere trick of the half-light.

'Where is that?' he asked.

'It is the single active cell right by the east gates. Within the boundaries of the city,' said Septern. 'So far the gates themselves are untouched.'

'How can you tell from here?'

'Because the colour of the main ward spell is a deep, vibrant green over the gates. I've colour-coded most cells to give us more accurate information.'

'But if the gate hasn't gone down, then surely the Garonin are not inside,' said Dystran.

'Which means that some stray idiot has probably blundered into them,' said Densyr, feeling a clash of emotions.

'I told you it was a risky strategy,' said Septern. 'Now those wards are gone and only half the cell is left. It weakens us there. What damage could a few elves do anyway?'

'More than you would ever believe,' said Dystran.

Densyr raised his eyebrows.

'What now?' asked Septern.

'It's dawn, near as dammit,' said Densyr. 'I want mages in the sky to the east. Keep them high and reporting back on a regular basis. Are all our testers accounted for?'

Dystran shook his head. 'Three are still out there. Including Brynar.'

Densyr clacked his tongue. 'How long do we dare wait before we activate the whole grid? They'll be coming, you know. I can feel it.'

'Can you hear something?' asked Septern. The dead mage put a hand to his chest and breathed in a shuddering lungful. 'I don't feel quite right.'

'Sit down, take some water,' said Densyr. 'And whatever you do, don't die again before you've activated the grid.'

'It's like a weight pressing hard on my soul,' said Septern, gripping the rail of the balcony and blowing hard. 'Can you not feel it?'

Densyr shook his head. 'But I can hear something. It's faint. A droning noise, like those appalling death dirges people took to singing after the demons left.'

'It's like a Wesman chant,' agreed Dystran. 'But it's everywhere.'

'The wind is howling,' said Septern. 'Something comes.'

Densyr caught him before he fell. He and Dystran helped Septern to a chair and sat him in it. The ancient genius was still breathing, his eyelids fluttering.

'Can you activate the grid?' asked Dystran.

'In theory,' said Densyr.

'Good. Then let us make Septern comfortable and get busy. We could do with seeing more of the dead. I wonder if it is affecting them all.'

The flat tone of a thousand horns sounded. Crystal disintegrated and windows blew in, showering glass in every direction. Densyr ducked his head and put up his hands, feeling shards rip across his skin.

'Dear Gods drowning, what was that?' he spat.

Densyr ran for the balcony again. He could hear people screaming and shouting all across the college. He stared up into the sky to the east and saw all his plans for the folly they surely were.

Auum whispered up the stairs behind Brynar. Diera followed him, carrying young Hirad. The young mage had a good turn of pace but he was noisy. Fortunately, they had no need of secrecy. Four flights and Brynar pushed open a door to the roof of the house. It was like another world. Half a dozen chairs and a table sat on a manicured lawn. They were surrounded by all manner of decorative pots in which a host of brightly coloured flowers demanded attention. The sweet scents were beautiful.

Diera put Hirad down for a moment while Auum ran to the edge of the building to assess their route. She gazed over the rooftops. Everywhere was colour and light, and she found herself wondering why they hadn't thought of a roof garden at the inn.

'Silly woman, does it really matter?' she muttered.

'Why are we up here, Mama?' asked Hirad.

'It's not safe on the ground, darling. So we're going over the roofs. What an adventure!'

'Where's Father?'

'We're going to get him now.'

And how she wished he was standing by her right now. She felt desperately scared. Auum and his Tai were so strong and quick and full of confidence but she was not. Did they really expect her to leap across the chasms between houses? It couldn't be done.

Behind her, elves and men spilled onto the roof carrying sheets. They set to tying them together. Someone had even found a length of rope. An irritable voice below told her that Gresse was approaching, carried by two others and arguing all the way.

Up in the sky, the machine had retreated back into the clouds and there was some small respite from the droning noise that had hurt Hirad's ears. But she didn't imagine it would be gone for long. She drew her son back close to her as the wolves leapt out of the doorway, following Thraun. Soon a line of elves and wolves plus the returned shapechanger were standing on the edge, looking out. Auum was pointing. Brynar was shaking his head. Miirt took a pace back and leapt the gap, landing easily on the other side. Diera spread her arms. 'I can't do that,' she said.

She took Hirad by the hand and trotted to the edge. Auum made a space for her.

'I will carry your son on my back,' he said.

The gap was about ten feet where roofs overhung the street below. Beyond, there was a clear run to the next square.

'But I can't jump that gap.'

'We will not let you fall,' said Auum.

'What about Baron Gresse?'

Auum's face was impassive. 'He knows where his journey ends.'

'The grid around us is not yet active,' said Brynar. 'They could take their chances on the ground.'

'That is for him to decide. Ghaal, Miirt. Back over here. Help Diera.'

Across the city, the flat horn tone washed out from above and the machine descended once more through the clouds. It hung above the east gate for a moment and then began a slow move west. Lines fell from its sides to the ground and the rooftops. Garonin slid down the lines, advancing the moment their feet found purchase.

Brynar drew in a huge gasping breath. 'That's the grid active.'

'It will do them no good,' said Thraun. 'The Garonin can target the wards from a distance.'

'Don't be so sure,' said Brynar. 'Septern's linkage is quite brilliant. Some wards lie dormant until others are triggered. They will not find them all.'

Garonin were moving across the rooftops towards them. Black-armoured and -helmeted, weapons in their hands, they appeared to simply step across the largest of gaps, their armour flaring briefly white as they did.

'Yniss preserve us, I have put you in greater danger,' said Auum. 'Give me Hirad.'

Diera crouched by her son. 'Hang on to Auum, darling. I'll be right behind you.'

'No, Mama. I want to stay with you.'

Diera kissed Hirad's cheek and wiped away a tear. 'It'll be all right. Fun. Auum is going to teach you how to fly.'

Hirad looked at her suspiciously. 'Really?'

'Really. Now go with him.'

Hirad let go of her. Diera stood. Auum inclined his head and took her hand.

'Trust me. Come, Hirad. Jump up on my back.'

He crouched and the little boy threw his arms around Auum's neck. The TaiGethen put his arms under Hirad's legs and held him piggyback-style. Diera breathed deeply. Miirt and Ghaal had returned over the terrifying gap.

'We'll all do this together,' said Auum.

He bounced Hirad on his back and walked back a few paces. Diera, with the Tai either side of her, let them take an arm each.

'Don't think about it,' said Ghaal. 'Just run as fast as you can. We'll do the rest.'

Diera's heart was pounding. 'I don't think I can do this.'

'Don't think at all,' repeated Ghaal. 'Do.'

Garonin were closing. Diera could see them only three streets away. She gathered her tattered courage.

'All right,' she said.

'Go,' said Auum.

They ran for the edge. Diera's scream built on her lips, and as she planted her foot and felt the TaiGethen pull on her arms, she let it have full voice. She cycled her legs in thin air and closed her eyes momentarily. An endless heartbeat later she felt another rooftop beneath her. She stumbled but the Tai did not let her fall. Diera opened her eyes and looked back and then into Hirad's beaming face. Auum crouched to let him down.

'Run to the far end. Join the ClawBound. Tai, we fight.'

And in no time the elves had jumped the gap again and were running back along the rooftops, straight at the Garonin.

The pain in Hirad's chest caused by the arrival of the vydosphere made his head swim. He and Sirendor were seated together, holding each other upright. The Unknown and Jonas were standing, arguing, and Ilkar, bless him, was still trying to find a safe way out of their prison despite the crushing weight he must surely be feeling.

'The door will trigger any ward near it,' said Sol. 'We cannot take that risk.'

'Then what do we do, Father? Sit and wait for Densyr to come back and kill us? I'm prepared to take the chance.'

'And we will if we must. But not yet. Let Ilkar do what he can first.'

Away to the east, they could see the Garonin machine hanging in the air. They had heard explosions and Ilkar had felt a massive flood of mana as the whole ward grid activated.

'Even if we do get out of here, there is nowhere to run,' said Jonas. 'There will be wards everywhere, won't there?'

'He's right, Unknown,' said Hirad, gasping for breath. 'Ilkar?'

'Wait,' said Ilkar. 'I'm just . . .'

Ilkar's face tautened visibly, like his skin was being stretched over too much bone. Where his hands were in contact with the ground, it seemed to shimmer slightly, obscuring his fingers.

'Ilkar?' The Unknown began moving towards him. 'Ilkar.'

'Gods . . . burning.'

Hirad struggled to his feet, bringing Sirendor with him. The pressure inside his body was growing steadily more intense. The pair of them began to move towards Ilkar.

'Talk to us, Ilks,' said Hirad.

'Help . . . me . . . trapped.'

'Trapped how?' asked The Unknown.

'Does it matter? We have to move him, don't we?' said Hirad. 'We have to break him away from there or his soul will be torn out.'

'And set off a ward or ten? Think, Hirad.'

'You know that's never been my strong point.'

Hirad pushed Sirendor away from him and began to run at Ilkar.

'Hirad, no!' shouted The Unknown.

'My advice would be to duck,' said Hirad.

He had planned to dive at Ilkar, to knock him carefully aside from his entrapment, but the pain in his chest flared throughout his body. He stumbled once, lost his footing completely and fell into the returned mage, barging him from his feet and taking them both into the wall of a building and then into a heap on the ground.

The ward Ilkar had been probing triggered. Flame seared across the street at an angle of forty-five degrees from the ground and on a line five yards wide. The blaze clipped the back of Hirad's boot and his entire foot was engulfed in mana fire. He dragged his foot clear, hooked the heel into a crack in the stonework of the building and pulled. Hard. Heat grew incredibly fast inside the boot. The leather smouldered and began to melt. He pulled harder, crying out as his toes started to cook.

Mana fire chewed through the laces and tongue. The boot released and he yanked his foot out, gasping as he did so. Still the flames rushed out of the ward. Their power magnified in the narrow street, reflecting from the walls opposite before channelling upwards into the dawn air. Hirad could hear Jonas crying and through the flame could see The Unknown covering him as best he could. Clothing and hair were smouldering and skin would be blistering.

The spell shut off.

Cold air rushed to fill the gap and it tasted so sweet. Slowly, they stirred, barely daring to move. Ilkar's body shivered beneath Hirad's and the barbarian rolled away to let him sit up and breathe. The elf in human skin nodded his thanks and winced at the sight of Hirad's foot.

'It doesn't feel so good.'

'I'll see what I can do.'

Hirad heard footsteps. He turned in time to be hauled from the ground by his lapels. The Unknown's face pushed in to his.

'I told you to think, you idiot! You could have killed us all.'

'I had to save him, Unknown. I had to try.'

'You had to wait, you bastard. Look at us now. As if being here wasn't enough, we all look like we fell asleep in the sun for five days. Look at my son.' The Unknown spun him so he could see. 'Look at him.'

'I'm sorry,' said Hirad. 'I didn't—'

'No, you never damn well do, do you?'

Sol thrust Hirad away, winding him against a wall. He put down his foot to steady himself and the pain tore a cry from his lips.

'Burned, is it?' asked Sol.

'It's a little tender,' said Hirad.

'Good. It'll remind you what an idiot you are.'

'I saved him, didn't I?' Hirad spread his arms. 'What were you going to do? Stand there and watch the life getting sucked out of him? Because that's what it looked like was happening. At least I did something.'

The Unknown bunched a fist, thought for a moment and then let it drop.

'You just don't get it, do you? Dead for ten years and you still have no more sense than when you fell. Septern's grid is interlinked in ways that even he probably barely understands. You could have set off five, ten, twenty more wards, all in this small space. What then, eh? Who was going to head west and kill himself to save the living and the dead then?'

'Sorry, Ilkar, but if you had died before we came up with a plan, that was just going to be tough.'

Ilkar nodded. 'Yeah. Yeah, I understand.'

Hirad felt heat in his face but it was from inside him. 'Right. I see. So you're ungrateful too, are you?'

'No, Hirad. I just see the bigger picture.'

'I'll tell you the big fucking picture,' said Hirad, voice rising in volume all the time. 'We're trapped in this dusty little street, Xetesk at one end and the Garonin at the other. And neither you nor the Unknown has the first clue how to get out, do you? What happened to you anyway?'

Hirad's last thought took all the anger from him.

'I thought you'd never ask.'

'I got sidetracked.' Hirad rubbed his hands across his face and tried to ignore the burning throb in his foot. He gave the Unknown a light punch on the shoulder. 'Sorry, big man.'

The Unknown nodded. 'I know. And as usual you were luckier than a fox born in a chicken run.'

'Sorry, Jonas.'

'It's all right, Hirad. Do I really look all red and blotchy?'

The Raven quartet all nodded simultaneously.

'Look what's happened to my clothes. Mama's going to *kill* me.'

The Unknown ruffled his hair. 'I think she'll forgive you just this once. So, Ilkar, is it the usual news or do you have something good to tell us for a change?'

'Good, I think. Look, the whole ward grid has gone active. Septern has done some very clever things with how mana is channelled between groups of wards. Some of the energy from an exploding trap goes to activate other so-far-dormant groups, that sort of thing. Don't say it, Hirad. If you can't understand me, assume I'm talking to someone else, all right?'

'If you insist.'

'I do. The point I'm getting to is this. The whole system is clearly linked all the way back to Xetesk and draws its mana direct from the Heart, because that way no mage has to expend mana stamina. All very clever so far. But the Garonin have found a way to tap into it. They are drawing off huge amounts of mana, direct from the Heart. Septern's whole grid is like one big feed pipe to them. Hirad was right: I was literally having the life sucked out of me. Every mote of mana I possessed, dragged out kicking and screaming all the way.'

The Unknown laughed but there was little satisfaction in it. 'Poor Densyr. He refuses to listen to what is coming. How unprepared he is.'

'So the good news is, the Garonin can drag off mana as fast as they want in the short term and so don't need to attack the college directly,' said Sirendor. 'But there's an obvious problem, isn't there?'

'Top marks,' said Ilkar. 'At any moment Septern and Densyr might close down the grid.'

'And that is bad for us how?' asked Hirad.

'Well, they have two choices. Either shut down the grid nice and gently, rendering every ward inert. Or send a massive pulse through it and set the lot of them off.'

'Ah.'

'And from the Garonin point of view, someone will have shut off their flow of mana. What do you think they'll do about that?'

'Ah.'

'We have got to get out of here,' said The Unknown. 'Ilkar, where are the wards around us?'

'There are nine that I can divine, spread relatively evenly.'

'Anything in front of that door, for instance?'

'I'm afraid so,' said Ilkar. 'I don't know what exactly, but it'll either be very hot, very cold or make the walls fall on us.'

'We're going to have to take a chance,' said The Unknown.

'Oh, all right if it's you, eh?'

'Shut up, Hirad. Ilkar, do you have it in you to put up an Ilkar's Defence?'

'A what?'

'Or maybe an Ilkar's Heal My Foot spell?'

'Hirad.' The Unknown glared at him. 'You'll have to wait. Ruminate on why you got burned or something. Sorry, Ilkar, that's the new name for a ForceCone.'

'Very flattering, I'm sure. Look, I know where you're going with this. Are you sure? I can't guarantee the Cone will stand up to much.'

'I can't think of a better idea. Can you?' Ilkar shook his head. 'Then let's get started.'

Chapter 26

Auum led his Tai back across the rooftops, across a fifteen-foot gap to the next line of houses, along five pitched roofs and into the lee of a huge chimney stack at the east end of the square. Here the smoke from the cook fires of every dwelling in the tenement house was released to the sky. He wasn't sure if the Garonin had seen them coming but he was sure they had hit the roofs and ground looking for him and his kind.

'Ghaal, what can you see?'

The Tai peered slowly out around the edge of the stack.

'They have stopped about two hundred and fifty yards from us. Something's happening. Perhaps they aren't after us after all. On the ground they have stopped too, as if they've formed a perimeter at the edge of where they cleared the wards earlier.'

Auum joined him, Miirt went the other way.

'The vydosphere is collecting,' she said.

And so it was. The cloud was darkening slowly above the malevolent shape hanging in the sky, which had begun a lazy spiral. Funnels were belching out smoke and the metal rods across its bulk were fizzing and crackling with energy as the reaction built to detonation.

'Where is it getting the mana from?' asked Ghaal.

'It doesn't matter.' Auum was sizing up the distance to the enemy. 'We can strike here. They are unprepared.'

'They will follow if we do.'

'So much the better. We need to bring them further into the grid and away from the others. We can do both if we're quick.'

Ghaal was smiling. 'Like a decoy run in the rainforest.'

'With the rooftops as our canopy,' said Miirt.

'Are we one on this?' asked Auum. 'Draw them to the south if you can.'

'Yniss will guide us,' said his Tai.

'Split and run hard, my warriors. Keep low and loose. Tai, we move.'

Auum hurdled wall, low chimney and alleyway. He sprinted on a long gentle curve, his angle and the presentation of his body making it hard for any projectile weapon to take certain aim. Seventy yards into the run, the Garonin began to fire, the entire front line of over seventy enemy soldiers carving up the dawn with their white teardrops.

Tile and flowerpot exploded by him as he ran. He saw Ghaal turn, dive and forward-roll while energy bit into a loft window where he had been standing momentarily. He came up low and ran behind a decorative wall. The fire followed him but when the smoke and debris cleared, he was long gone.

Auum had time to acknowledge his Tai's skill before he approached a wide avenue. Thirty feet wide at a guess. He needed speed. The wind was already behind him. Garonin weapons tracked him. In his wake the tiles of a pitched roof shattered and melted. He leaned forward, gathering pace, stepped onto the building's edge and launched himself head first, arms tight by his sides, body axle-straight. The white tears flooded his vision. He felt heat as they ripped by underneath him and he angled his body to allow a stream to pass by his left-hand side.

Auum brought his arms in front of him, took the impact of landing on his right shoulder and turned into the direction of motion, coming to a stop on his haunches. The Garonin were just over the next roof apex. He could hear their footsteps as they advanced on his position. Beads of fire still swept into the sky, chasing Ghaal and Miirt. Auum unclipped his pouch of jaqrui throwing crescents, plucking one out and taking a short blade in his right hand. He moved diagonally up the slate-covered roof, heading for a cluster of chimneys at the centre of the building.

The Garonin felt no need for the same stealth, their tramping feet giving away the position of each of six soldiers. Auum put a mental picture of them in the forefront of his mind. He switched his blade and jaqrui around.

'Yniss, spare my soul to do your work as dawn lightens tomorrow. Tual, guide my hand to smite my enemies. Shorth, hear my prayer; I commend my soul to you should I fall. Seek for me a path to my resting place. This I ask in the names of the great Gods of the Ynissul. Hear me, my masters. I am Auum, your servant.'

Auum reached the cluster of chimneys, stepped to the right and threw the jaqrui round-armed. The blade whipped across the roof-top, taking a Garonin under the chin guard and burying itself in his neck. He jerked backwards and fell, his weapon firing wildly into the sky. Auum dived back behind the chimney stack. He grabbed another jaqrui. Masonry and tile blew apart above his head under the wilting fire of the Garonin.

Auum ran left. He threw again. The holes in the body of the jaqrui caused it to make a keening, unearthly sound as it travelled straight and true. The target Garonin raised his weapon reflexively in defence. The blade sheared deep into the weapon, which exploded in the Garonin's hands, taking off his arms at the elbows, ripping deep holes in his chest and forcing upwards to shatter his jaw.

Metal shards whistled as they flew. Auum flattened himself against the roof. The four remaining Garonin had turned their backs against any impact. Armour flared white. Auum was up and running left. He dragged his second short blade out with his right hand.

He leapt and spun in the air, his blades flashing left to right in quick succession buoyed by the power of his turn and the pace of his body. The first slashed deep into the helmet of his target, the second, adjusted lower, whipped through his throat, ripping free and carrying blood and gore with it.

Auum landed facing right. The remaining three were moving towards him. They could not see Miirt sprinting up behind them and the fire from their fellows nearer the vydosphere was tracking Ghaal.

He heard the howl of a jaqrui. The blade flickered past his left shoulder and embedded in the arm of the leftmost enemy. The soldier jerked back, but steadied and fired. Auum glanced back to see Ghaal duck and roll under the stream of white tears.

Auum rose and ran. He came under fire from the other two. He dived left, rolling and rising, the roof at his feet obliterated. He dropped a blade, reached for a jaqrui and threw. The Garonin ducked it, his head moving to track it just for a moment. More than enough. Auum picked up his blade, ran four paces and launched himself two-footed at the Garonin's midriff. He caught the soldier square on. The enemy doubled over, and as he fell, Auum's blades jabbed up under both his arms.

Auum shovelled the body aside and came to a crouch. Miirt had leapt up and backhanded her blade through the back of a Garonin neck. Ghaal had jumped and struck the other in the eye slit. Blood was running down the side of the roof, staining the red tiles a dark shade of crimson.

'Yniss saves us for greater deeds,' said Auum.

He turned to the vydosphere. More Garonin were advancing. Fifty-plus breaking from the main force. Above them, the sky darkened by degrees and the pace of the cloud spin increased.

'Breathe the air, my warriors. And let us run like the jaguars are on our scent.'

The Tai cell touched hands briefly, stowed weapons and ran south, exhorting Tual to guard their every move. Behind them not every Garonin turned to follow. Auum watched eight carrying on forward.

'The Ravensoul worries them,' he muttered. 'I hope it is strong enough to turn them aside.'

Baron Gresse settled into his chair on the rooftop garden of one of Xetesk's premier mages, it didn't matter which, to watch his last, glorious Balaian dawn. The house was well stocked and he had one of his servants find him some fresh leaf tea, a plate of bread and cold meat and some fresh fruit. The table was laid properly, with white cloth, napkins and crystal glasses. Wine would follow the tea. A little early perhaps, but when one was short of time, early was not in the lexicon.

Blackthorne reappeared from the house.

'It's mine,' he said. 'One of my finest vintages too. A pity to let it go to waste.'

Gresse had dismissed his servant but his and Blackthorne's retinues were still loitering at the far end of the garden, unwilling to desert their lords.

'Then join me, old friend. And take a look at this spectacular, if unfortunately unique, sunrise.'

'There's still time to get away from here,' said Blackthorne. 'We can enjoy this under a new sun.'

Gresse indicated over his left shoulder. Eight Garonin soldiers were making their languid way across the rooftops.

'No, there isn't, Blackthorne. And I'm tired of running. Tired of being hauled about like some chattel. I am a baron of Balaia. And that is how I will die. Better than straining to reach some foreign shore and having the cancer claim me anyway.

'What are we running for, you and me? Are you really going to build another Blackthorne Castle? Do you have the energy? All those you protected have been swept away by these bastards. Just like my people. I'm going down with this ship and I'm looking forward to it.'

Blackthorne looked away towards the Garonin heading directly towards them and then to those making their steady way towards the college.

'Go!' he shouted to the servants still waiting at the end of the garden. 'We'll be along presently.'

Not one of their men moved. Instead, a show of hands resulted in them returning to the barons and forming a ring around them at a deferential distance. Blackthorne nodded his respect and thanks, pulled out a chair and sat down.

'You know, you are absolutely right.'

'It's a common complaint.'

'Can I pour you some more tea?'

'I think wine more appropriate now.'

'Good man.'

Blackthorne produced a corkscrew from his pocket and set to work. He drew the cork expertly and sniffed the end, nodding approvingly. He handed the cork to Gresse while he poured each of them a mouthful to taste. The two barons sniffed, sipped, rolled and swallowed.

'A red to satisfy the desire for a full body, a head of blackcurrant and an aftertaste of dark plum,' said Gresse. 'Outstanding. We should have ordered the steak.'

A servant stepped in, took the bottle from Blackthorne and poured each of them a full glass with a remarkably steady hand. The sounds of the enemy approaching were growing louder.

'A little late for steak. Even for something blue.'

Gresse shifted his legs on their footstool. 'Do you remember that time when we brokered that agreement with the Wesmen for a supply of each vintage?'

'Interesting negotiations. I'm not sure they were ready for the concept of laying down a wine for a decade.'

'Who was that idiot who insisted on broaching a bottle of the thirty-eight vintage?'

Blackthorne chuckled. A detonation sounded away to the east. He paused while the echoes faded. 'Riasu. Almost choked on it. Nothing so sharp and unpleasant as a young wine.'

'As I recall, he was keen to have us both divided in two,' said Gresse. 'Remember what you said about trusting the vintage?'

Blackthorne laughed out loud this time. He held up a finger and wagged it as he spoke. ' "Patience is the province of the civilised man. A fine wine is the fruit of that patience just as it is proof of the wisdom of its owner. However, if you are not completely satisfied when you come to open the first bottle in ten years' time, I promise to provide you with a full refund. Just bring the shipment back to the castle and I'll authorise payment on the instant." I recall it as if it was yesterday.'

'Lucky that envoy of Tessaya was listening in, I'd say.'

'They were good days, Gresse.'

'Damn it but they were, Blackthorne.'

The two barons clinked their glasses and drank deeply.

The footsteps drew ever closer. Gresse ignored the thudding steps, the drone of the machine and the calls of wolves. When you put your mind to it, it was quite easy.

'We have company,' said Blackthorne. 'I'm proud to have called you my friend, Baron Gresse.'

'And you likewise, Baron Blackthorne. Good hunting in the forests of your fathers.'

'I'll send you an invitation should I ever find them.'

Gresse turned to see the eight huge figures looming over them and the men who had refused to leave their sides.

'Join us, the red is a quite superb vintage. Oh. I see.'

'One cannot simply turn it off,' snapped Septern. 'Not without taking down the whole eastern side of the city.'

'Do you see anyone who cares if that happens?' Densyr pointed out towards the Garonin machine and the malevolent shapes of soldiers bounding over his rooftops. 'It is only enemies out there. Take down every wall if you like. I don't care. But do it quickly. Meanwhile, our enemies are sucking the life out of the Heart of Xetesk. It is an unsustainable loss. They are killing us from a distance.'

'And your friends? The Raven?'

Densyr bit his lip.

'Casualties of war,' he said, the words ash in his mouth.

'Yet they represent the best alternative should we fail to hold the city.'

'We will not fail,' said Densyr. 'We cannot.'

Septern held his gaze for a moment and then nodded. 'Very well.'

'Are you sure you're all right?'

Septern was pale, even for a dead man.

'Whatever it is the Garonin are doing, it affects the souls of the dead or, rather, the mana surrounding them. The call to the void is strong and painful to resist. But don't worry; I won't let you down.'

Densyr let his eye wander out over his city once more. Way to the east, not far from the gate and in the shadow of the machine, he could see a fight going on. Garonin weapons were firing. At who? he wondered. It had to be Auum and his TaiGethen. A shame the elf had taken the wrong path. He would have been a useful ally today.

'How long will it take you?' asked Densyr.

'That is hard to quantify right now. I need to understand the nature of the mana flow and the volume being dragged through the grid. There will inevitably be some risk attached to the shutdown procedure.'

Densyr's eyes narrowed and he felt a chill anxiety in his gut.

'Risk?'

'Well, simply put, if I snap off the flow, two things happen. First, as I said, every ward will trigger because there is no longer a circuit, and hence no way to channel the mana away safely. But second, there will be far more mana in the grid than it was intended to support because of the Garonin action. There could be feedback.'

'Feedback?'

Densyr's anxiety had coalesced to dread.

'Into the Heart. That's why I have to know the level of the depletion. Because enough mana feeding back into the Heart all at once could, theoretically, destroy it.'

'Theoretically?'

'Well this has never been tested, as you can imagine . . .'

'Stop blustering. What is your view? And let's say for the sake of argument that the Garonin are dragging away half of the Heart's power at any one time.'

Septern shrugged. 'Theory would become practical reality.'

*

Ilkar had concentrated like he never had before and yet forming the shape of the spell had still been torturous. The pain in his chest was a constant drain on his concentration and the howling of the void echoed around his head. Yet here it was. An Ilkar's Defence construct. Conical, formed of a lattice of yellow lines of mana, tightly bound. Slightly modulating but nothing serious, and rotating a little quickly. It would have to do.

With eyes and mind tuned to the mana spectrum, Ilkar could see the ward in front of the door through which The Unknown wanted to go. FlameOrbs would fly from it when it was triggered, he could see that now. On a spread that would cover a hundred men in flesh-dissolving mana fire. Best not to think about it.

'Are you ready, Ilks? The Garonin will be tapping us on the shoulder if we wait much longer,' said Hirad.

'I'm not sure why I bothered,' said Ilkar. 'I completely forgot that all you have to do is open your big fat mouth and the FlameOrbs will get sucked right in. Idiot. And yes, I'm ready.'

Ilkar nailed his concentration back down to the spell. He made sure he was standing square in front of the door. He checked again that the spell diameter would cover the spread of the ward. He took a deep breath.

'Tuck in behind Ilkar, Jonas,' said The Unknown. 'Sirendor, behind me.'

Ilkar glanced over his shoulder. Hirad winked at him.

'You could have chosen a wider body,' said Hirad. 'You're a bit weedy for us all to cower behind.'

'You know that in all the years I was dead, all I ever dreamed about was being an elven shield for your filthy carcass.'

Hirad laughed. 'I knew you always loved me best.'

'All right,' said Ilkar. 'On the count of three. I'll cast and move the spell to the door. Everything else, I leave to your imaginations. One, two, three . . .'

Ilkar cast. The Defence hung in the air in front of him. Solid, shot through with yellow, rotating gently about its axis. He pushed out his arms slowly. The conical shape lengthened, the flat circle expanded to take in the door and then the entirety of the wall of the building. He could see the pulsing of the ward as the Julatsan casting neared it.

'Be ready,' he said, voice distant with effort.

'For what?' asked Hirad.

'To sweep me into an ash bucket if this goes wrong.'

Ilkar crabbed his hands to better grip the spell and thrust it against door and wall. The ward triggered. Blinding blue light flashed across the surface of the Defence. Ilkar leaned his weight against his spell while the FlameOrbs, or whatever fancy name they had these days, formed and crashed into it again and again.

He shuddered. Nausea gripped him. The spell shimmered. Ilkar grunted defiance and forced more strength into the head of his casting. The Defence steadied again. Blue light rippled across its surface, fizzed into the ground and slapped back against the building. Fire leaked around the edges of the spell and lashed at the air and the ground at Ilkar's feet. Sweat dripped into his eyes.

Ilkar could see the end coming. The effort of dragging in so much unfocused mana told eventually. There was not enough flow to keep the construct steady for long. The sides of the cone wobbled. The lattice unpicked from front to back. Another orb slammed into the cone and the spell collapsed.

'Down!' yelled Ilkar.

He angled his hands up. The final orb deflected off the remnants of his spell and arced away into the dawn sky. He followed its lazy movement up until it reached its zenith and began to fall back down.

'This is not good,' he said.

The Unknown had seen it too. 'Up! Up! Get inside. Move it, Raven.'

He picked up Jonas by the back of his collar and charged through the wrecked entrance of the building. Sirendor and Hirad were scrambling to their feet, the barbarian cursing at the pain from his burned foot. But still he stopped to grab Ilkar and help the tired mage up.

The orb fell to the ground on the right-hand side of the street. Hirad and Ilkar dived inside the house, rolling away from the opening and heading for the stairs up which The Unknown was already running. The orb splattered across wall and street, triggering wards all around it.

Flame lashed inside the building, reducing broken timbers to ash and engulfing the stairs in fire. Ilkar dived headlong onto the landing from the top step. A whoosh of heat behind him and a crackling of paint on the walls told him how close he had been to incineration.

The ground heaved beneath them. Great rending sounds of stone on stone, rock smashing into rock and the splintering of wood sounded far too close. Ilkar came back to his feet and grabbed Hirad's arm, helping him along. The others were ahead, stampeding up another stairway towards the roof. A massive column of stone broke through the floor and carved its way up through the bedrooms on Ilkar's right.

'EarthHammer!' he shouted into the tumult but no one could possibly hear him.

Plaster dust and debris filled the air. The house rocked. Detonations of more columns of stone breaking upwards could be heard surrounding them. Hirad made the stairs and took them three at a time, wounded foot almost forgotten in his desperation to escape. Ilkar was right on his heels, pushing him faster.

Light poured in from above. A great swathe of the roof slipped and fell into the street, showering shattered tiles down on the fleeing Raven. Up ahead, Ilkar saw The Unknown battering down a door with his feet and running into clear sky. The front wall of the house cracked along a jagged horizontal, the upper portion teetering and falling outwards, dragging roof and beam with it.

Ilkar gave Hirad a mighty shove and rolled out of the top door after him. Hands grabbed him, almost lifting him from his feet and running him towards the shuddering building's edge. He cried out as he left the ground, cycled his legs and landed on the other side in a heap. He turned to watch Hirad make the jump. The barbarian's poor foot gave way beneath him. He didn't have the height to clear the balustrade. His hands grabbed at guttering and he disappeared from view.

Behind him, the house crumbled to the ground, sending up clouds of dust that glowed in the blue flame of Xeteskian wards. As the sound of the collapse rolled away, Ilkar could hear Hirad swearing. The Unknown ran to the building's edge and hauled the barbarian to safety

Ilkar felt someone's gaze on him. He looked round. A man was standing by him, four wolves at his feet. He recognised those hands as the ones that had helped him escape. Others were there too. A woman and a boy who would bring joy to The Unknown's heart and, oddly, Brynar, Densyr's apprentice.

The man with the wolves was smiling. The sun on him projected his shadow onto the wall of a dormer window behind him. It was of a tall, powerful man with hair tied in a long ponytail at his back. Ilkar felt a comforting warmth.

'Hello, Thraun,' he said. 'Glad you happened by when you did.'

Chapter 27

Auum led his Tai to the city walls. Leaping and climbing, rolling and dodging, they had easily kept ahead of the Garonin sent to chase them down. Yet the vydosphere had not changed its course. Indeed, it had not moved, and Auum worried what that might mean. Threads of comfort sprang from the knowledge that despite all their might, the Garonin were still prey to feelings of revenge. It was the reason they were chased and the reason the Ravensoul was sought.

The enemy knew that harm could be done to them. Men could be lost, perhaps enough to affect their battles elsewhere. This deflected their attention only minutely, but minutely could be enough to buy the time they so desperately needed.

Once on the walls, the TaiGethen ran free, putting real distance between them and their pursuers. Auum tore around the battlements and through abandoned watchtowers. He scaled the outer sides of the south gates and dropped onto the roof of the gatehouse. Only here did he pause. He climbed onto the crenellations.

From here he could see across the city to the walls of the college. The towers within stood proud and he could make out a solitary figure on the uppermost balcony of the central edifice. Auum whispered a short prayer to Shorth. He let his eye wander to the east, to the deserted streets of Xetesk bathed in a watery sunlight.

Auum could pick out figures running across rooftops. In amongst them, he could make out the bulk of Sol and the flashing shapes of wolves. And he could see the Garonin advancing too. In the skies above, the vydosphere sucked up its fuel. The clouds still darkened and the swirl still gained pace. He wondered briefly when Densyr would realise the appalling mistake he had made.

'Auum.'

It was Ghaal. He was perched on the crenellations looking out over the west of the city. Auum followed his gaze and his heart fell into his boots. When you saw one, suddenly, thousands were

revealed. People. Ordinary Xeteskians with their faith in a college
that would inevitably fail them.

'Cattle awaiting slaughter,' said Ghaal.

'Enjoying the dawn of their last day in this or any other life,' said
Miirt.

'And we will free them when we can,' said Auum. 'Now, my
friends, it is time to break into the college.'

'Can it be done?' asked Ghaal, he and Miirt jumping back onto the
roof.

Auum put a hand on each of their shoulders. 'With Yniss to guide
us, we must believe it so. Tai, we pray.'

Densyr had been staring straight at where he had left The Raven
when it happened. He watched the single blue orb fly skywards and
did not even consider why it had travelled in that direction, so
consumed was he with watching it fall to the earth. No time to get
Septern to deactivate the cell. Time only to pray the wards would not
trigger.

A prayer that went unanswered.

Ten wards. He knew the number so very bloody well though it was
impossible to count them going off individually, such was the force
and speed of the multiple detonations. Flames lashed from both sides
of the narrow street on shallow angles, incinerating everything taller
than a house cat. God's Eyes pounded the enclosed area and Earth-
Hammers shoved their fingers of stone high into the sky, ripping
apart buildings and standing as insulting gestures in his mind. He
was stricken with a sudden regret.

Last night, he had been so cocksure that leaving them trapped was
the best way to neutralise them until he decided to free them. So sure
that they would not attempt an escape. Ilkar might have been shorn
of his college's Heart but he was no fool and would be able to detect
active wards given the amount of time he had.

'What did you do, my old friends?' whispered Densyr. 'Why did
you try to outwit the master? I'm sorry. I'm so sorry it had to end like
this.'

Densyr took one last look at the dust cloud that covered the scene
of their deaths and closed the balcony shutters on his crime. In his
deep armchair by the fire, Septern was studying the ward lattice. The
sheen of sweat on his face didn't encourage Densyr's confidence.

He sank into the chair opposite and sipped at the tea his servants had left them. All the way down the line, he'd made the right decisions. He was certain of it. What the dead had told him really did make no sense. There was no other home. No escape route. Just like every time before, Balaia had to stand up and fight for herself. And win. Just like every other time.

Maybe he had been a little heavy-handed with those he once counted as close friends and allies. But decisions had to be made and some people always had their noses put out of joint. Not everyone would ever be happy. And at least his people, the Xeteskian people, knew he was doing all this for them.

Should it have worried him that Auum claimed to have seen all this before? Surely not. If indeed he was thousands of years old as he claimed, things move on. The elves had had no magic back then, no defence. Densyr had the might of Xetesk and the unexpected advantage of Septern. Balaia had to survive, and for that to happen, Xetesk had to remain strong. The right decisions still had to be made.

Even if it meant his friends had to die.

'Septern, can you hear me?'

'Of course,' said Septern, his voice clear enough though a little strained.

'You needn't concern yourself with The Raven now.'

'I know. I felt it. Saw it. Doesn't feel so much like casualties of war now, does it?'

'No,' whispered Densyr. 'Tell me what you can do.'

'The news isn't too good.'

Densyr's heart skipped a beat. 'What do you mean?'

'The enemy is cleverer than I thought.'

'Smarter than you?'

'Let's not give them too much credit. The problem lies in shutting off the mana flow.'

'Not doing so isn't an option I'm prepared to entertain.'

'I know, Densyr. But the risk to the Heart is greater than I thought. It is possible that they intend us to shut off the flow, triggering an explosion in the Heart. Mana will be pumped up into the atmosphere . . .'

'To be collected by the machine hanging up there for just that purpose, if it can collect mana that way.'

'Precisely.'

'But you can stop that, Septern, can't you?'

Septern's face held the first element of doubt Densyr had seen.

'Probably,' he said.

'Probably isn't good enough.' Densyr leaned forward in his chair. 'You know the stakes here. We cannot fail. Not now.'

'Now your friends are dead.'

'Indeed.' Densyr pressed his lips together. 'And anything you do, do quickly. We don't have much time.'

'I shall attempt the cell-by-cell closedown. That way, I can isolate surges in mana being fed back and dissipate them through harmless areas of the grid.'

'If you say so. And what if it begins to go wrong?'

'A mage can always act as a buffer if necessary,' said Septern.

'Get going.'

'They know what we intend, I'm certain of it,' said Sol. 'Brynar. Hirad needs attention. Ilkar, Sirendor. Assess the next jump and the bridge the ClawBound has left. Thraun, let's see if we can't find ourselves a better route than the one we already have. But don't go far. Quickly. The enemy are closing.'

He stood with Diera and his boys. All four of them in a huddle and he at least realising that it could be their last. The Garonin still came on. He had counted eight of them. Moving carefully over the rooftops, no doubt aware of the capacity of the TaiGethen and hopefully unaware of their current whereabouts.

The rooftop to which they had jumped from the collapsing building was a work in progress. They were standing amidst the debris of a building site. Half-built walls, piles of stone, sand and barrels of water. Pots of whitewash, brushes, trowels and even a couple of straw hats. A block and tackle had been hanging from the near edge of the building but the ClawBound elf had stripped it for its rope. Every tool of the trade was scattered about, evidence of a hurried evacuation or perhaps merely a poorly run site.

'Why do you say that?' asked Diera.

'Because while the bulk of them stand and guard their machine, these eight are heading right for us. Raven, I want an ambush plan. Here or at the next intersection.'

Sol looked after the ClawBound, who was still creating a path to the college gates. He had laid ropes and even knotted sheets where he could and left markers for jump points, so Thraun had reported. The Garonin were less than a hundred yards away now and would soon be in weapons range. Sol pulled away from his family.

'Time to move. Brynar, how are you doing?'

'Hirad is all right to walk now.'

'Good. Freedom's Wings for you again if you don't mind. Brynar.'

'Yes, my King .'

'Not "king", just Sol. And thank you for not abandoning my family.'

Brynar shrugged. 'What sort of man would I be? Besides, Auum made it clear the fate I would face if I ran.'

'I'll bet he did.'

A short incantation and gossamer wings appeared at Brynar's back. He held out his arms and Diera placed young Hirad in them. It was several hundred yards to the apron in front of the college gates. They had to traverse another four intersections and get across the heavily trapped open space.

'I could take him all the way,' said Brynar.

Sol paused on the verge of agreeing. 'But they wouldn't let you leave. We need you.'

'Keep out of sight of the college as long as you can,' said Brynar. 'I'll open the postern gate for you.'

'There isn't a postern gate any more,' said Sol.

Brynar raised his eyebrows. 'Trust me on this.'

Sol nodded. 'Diera?'

'Gods drowning, yes, take him inside the walls. All right, Hirad? You go with Brynar to the college and he'll keep you safe.'

'Yes, Mama.'

'I'll be there very soon.'

'Go, Brynar,' said Sol. 'And thank you.'

Brynar took to the air, skimming low over the rooftops. Sol watched him, a lump in his throat.

'We need to get out of here,' said Sirendor.

Sol glanced back at the Garonin and shook his head. 'No. I've had an idea. The next roof is too open. Pretty garden but too open. Plenty of places to hide here.'

'Good thought,' said Sirendor. 'The Garonin will have to drop out of sight of us before they reach the adjacent block.'

'Good,' said Sol. 'Diera, Jonas. Time to go.'

'Father . . .'

'Don't argue with me, Jonas. We don't have the time.'

Sol stooped to pick up a shovel. It was a satisfying weight in his hands.

'The rest of you, I suggest you pick up your choice of implement. I will stand centre to make sure they know where to come.'

'Sol . . .'

'Diera, it's all right. This is what I do. Did.'

'Remember you aren't thirty any more.'

'Just take Jonas and run. And be careful on the ropes. Raven, hide where you can back me in a hurry. I know we wouldn't normally lower ourselves to such tactics but today I make an exception for any underhand attack from the rear without warning. All these Garonin have to go down. You all know the attack signal.'

Ilkar took no weapon but hid himself on a narrow ledge behind a wall that was to hold a dormer window. Sol heard him begin to mutter as he attempted to draw mana from the chaos around him. Sirendor picked up a crowbar, hefted it in one hand and picked up a cement trowel in the other. He moved forward of Sol and crouched by a group of three barrels.

Hirad picked up a pickaxe, smiled and lay flat behind a stack of wooden beams to Sol's right, pulling a canvas sheet over his body. Thraun had not yet returned but Sol was in no doubt that the dead shapechanger was keeping an eye on them. He looked forward to a few wolves entering the fight.

The Garonin, just as Sirendor had said, had dropped briefly out of sight, forced to take a slightly different path due to the collapse of the building through which The Raven had escaped. Sol could hear them though, their heavy footsteps like metal sheets clanging together, the impact of their jump landings echoing against the surrounding blank, deserted buildings.

'I hope my hip stands up to this,' he muttered.

'I think you'll find it's your head they'll be aiming at,' came a voice from beneath the canvas.

'Thank you, Hirad. Here they come.'

Sol tensed. The risks of his strategy became depressingly apparent and his words to Diera sounded awfully hollow. Eight giant soldiers in full body armour landed on the roof in a semicircle around him and began to close, their weapons trained exactly as Hirad had said.

Sol hefted the shovel, patting the shaft into his open left palm. The Garonin closed, stopping only when they could almost reach out and touch him. Weapons dropped very slightly. Diera and Jonas were way too close but getting more distant with every passing moment.

'Fascinating weapons,' he said. 'You must show me round one.'

'Sol,' said a voice full of beguiling melody. 'How disappointing. You stand alone. All your subjects have deserted you.'

Sol shifted his feet, taken aback. 'You. You're joking with me? I killed you.'

'Not so. Some among you are fascinating and worthy of some small investigation to further our knowledge of your world. You are one such. No other has demonstrated understanding and belief. No other has been able to leave our domain by an act of self-will.'

'*Your* domain? I've heard from several reliable sources that it is no one's domain but a transit to everywhere. A place you have infiltrated and where you can be beaten.'

Sol considered he might have shown too much of his hand.

'The risk of such an eventuality is small. But we do not deal in small, we deal in nil. And so your journey ends here, Sol. As it will for all your people in this city, your other major population centres and for those you think are escaping beyond your western mountain range.'

Sol's face must have betrayed him. One of the Garonin cocked his head.

'Did you think we were not aware of those running west? Elves mostly. We concede that your people are brave and resourceful. We concede that we underestimated you and have been forced to move our vydospheres into the air, an inefficient use of vydos that we cannot afford but one that conserves our equipment.'

'So why are you talking to me? If you intend to wipe us out, why bother to tell me all about it? Seems a waste of time.'

'Not for us. Respect is a ritual.'

'But all rituals are finite, aren't they?'

Sol tapped the blade of the shovel on the ground, once, twice, three times.

'It is time,' said the concerted voices of the Garonin.

'Yes.' Sol ceased tapping the shovel. 'Time for you to meet The Raven.'

Chapter 28

Sol was fast. Even at fifty-one, he was the better of most men half his age. The shovel blade whipped up and forward, Sol darting in a step simultaneously. The cutting edge struck under the chin of the centremost Garonin. Sol felt it bite into flesh. Blood poured down the shovel's muddy face.

The Garonin reacted quickly. Weapons snapped up to ready. They spaced themselves for clear shots at Sol, who dived into the midst of them, bowling the stricken Garonin over. He pulled the shovel clear of his victim and rolled onto his back with the blade covering his face.

A Garonin soldier readied to fire. He jerked violently. Blood flew from his mouth and he slumped forward onto his knees revealing Sirendor behind him, bloodied cement trowel in hand. He did not pause. The crowbar in his other hand swung across the back of an enemy skull. The soldier's head rocked forward but he did not drop, turning instead to backhand Sirendor across the face with his weapon. Sirendor tumbled back into the barrels, scattering them.

At the same time, Hirad leapt up from his hiding place and planted his pickaxe straight through the midriff of his nearest enemy, driving the man backwards from his feet. His weapon fired. Hirad screamed in agony.

'Keep down.'

It was Ilkar. Winter's Touch flew from his open palms. A howling, super-cooled blast of air that struck the Garonin square on. Two turned their backs, taking the force of the freeze on their armour on which the runes flared white. Two were caught in the helmet, burning cold drilling into their eyes, freezing them blind in moments. Weapons dropped from hands to clutch at faces and claw inside eye slits.

A weapon sounded close by Sol's head. The half-built wall disintegrated into a shower of stone shard and cement dust.

Sol scrambled to his feet, thrashing the shovel blade in front of him, clattering it into the legs of one of the two Garonin still facing him. The enemy fell. Sol moved to finish him. A blow caught him on the side of the head, sending him spinning. He rolled into a pile of sand.

Sol spat grit from his mouth. He looked up into the darkening sky. The cloud framed the helmet of a Garonin soldier and his cruel weapon. Sol held his gaze. The weapon was raised. A black shape flew from left to right. Howls split the dawn. The Garonin's fire flashed past Sol's shoulder, kicking up sand.

Sol sat up. The ClawBound had arrived. The panther was ripping the throat from one enemy, the elf had enveloped another. Wolves streamed in. A solitary Garonin weapon traced teardrops through the air. One of the animals fell, soundlessly. The other three feasted in revenge.

From behind him Sol heard the thump of metal on leather. Again and again. He climbed painfully to his feet. Back, arms, legs and now the side of his head. Everything was bruised. He put a hand to the hinge of his jaw. It came away wet. Sirendor straightened up from behind the tumble of barrels. His nose was bent across his face and blood covered his lips and neck. His crowbar too was covered in blood, hair and gore.

'Never take a fallen man with a crowbar as beaten,' he said.

'Hirad,' said Sol, starting to run across the roof.

He jumped the bodies of the fallen Garonin, those that had not already faded back to whence they came, and dropped to his knees by the barbarian in his merchant's body. That body was broken. White tears had blasted through his right shoulder and all the way down his body to the hip. Clothing had been burned away and the flesh was smoking and cauterised. Hirad still clung on to the pickaxe handle, his face buried in the Garonin armour.

Sol rocked back onto his haunches. 'Damn it,' he breathed.

Sirendor placed a hand on his shoulder and crouched by him. 'Don't despair, not just yet. He's still with us. Just.'

'What does it matter? He will never survive a journey to the west like this. His soul will be lost. We can't stop it.'

Sol's mind filled with visions of Hirad's outstretched grasping hands disappearing into the murk of the void, his mouth open in an eternal scream.

'Not west. College.'

Sol looked up into the eyes of the ClawBound elf. Blood dripped from the ends of the sharpened nails on his long fingers. His black and white halved painted face was impassive and his voice, as with them all, was hoarse and unused to speech.

'What do you mean?' Sol searched the roof for Ilkar. 'Sirendor, find our mage, would you? Assuming he's alive behind that pile of broken stone, I need him to do whatever he can for poor Hirad.'

'Thraun. Speak.'

The ClawBound elf pointed to where the shapechanger was kneeling by his downed wolf. Sol nodded and dragged himself away from Hirad. The barbarian's soul could barely be breathing and Sol feared to move him lest he do more harm than good. Sirendor had made his way over to the shattered half wall and was kneeling behind it, already talking.

Sol made his aching way to Thraun.

'I'm sorry,' he said.

Thraun nodded. 'They brought me back, you know? My soul had no direction when the Garonin ripped our resting place apart. They called for me. They needed my help. They knew something was wrong. And here they are, dying one by one. Three remain here. Four are lost in the city somewhere.'

'We'll save the rest. But tell me. Why does our ClawBound friend say we no longer need to go to the Wesmen? I'm presuming you know what we intend to do.'

'I have spoken to Auum about it. The mage, Brynar. He is sure Septern knows the ritual of opening but is reluctant to perform it. Auum feels that he can persuade him.'

Sol felt as if a door to hope had just been edged open. 'And I thought he was taking young Hirad into Xetesk purely to keep him safe. My mind is clearly not sharp. Thank you, my friend. Get ready to go.'

He straightened up and looked east. The black cloud swirling around the Garonin machine was growing deeper and spreading across the city. Dark blue light flashed within it. Ominous signals. So far, Xetesk appeared powerless to stop the drain on its Heart. But Sol could feel the pressure building. Densyr had already proved himself prone to desperate decisions and he would not allow this situation to continue.

The enemy soldiers were beginning to fan out along the rooftops of eastern Xetesk. They were readying for something. Sol had to assume it was the final assault.

'Sirendor, have you—'

'Yes, he has,' said Ilkar. 'Didn't anyone hear me calling?'

'Sorry,' sad Sol.

'Clinging on by my bloody, literally bloody, fingernails for ages.'

'And still alive,' said Sol. 'Which is more than we'll be able to say for Hirad unless you can do something fast.'

'I know, I know.' Ilkar knelt by the prone Raven warrior and studied his wounds briefly. He shook his head. 'This is way beyond me, Unknown. He needs powerful focused magic. Only one place to get that.'

'Then it's fortunate that all our answers are within,' said Sol. 'The only question that remains is, how in all the hells do I get him to the college gates without killing him.'

A shattering, rippling detonation ripped the momentary calm apart. The foundations of Xetesk shuddered. Sol turned east to see flames and dust in the sky on an arc that stretched almost from south to north gates. The east gatehouse had gone. Buildings lining the walls were falling. Fists of stone ground their way into the sky. And up above them the machine wobbled and the detonation cloud above it flashed a dangerous white.

Moments later, another line of wards exploded and the next concentric ring of buildings was demolished under the force of Orbs, walls of blue fire and the Hammers deep in the earth. The rumble did not die away. More quickly than the second ring, the third triggered.

Massive mana energy burst into the sky, far more than Septern would have planned. Garonin soldiers were consumed in the roar of flame and the collapse of buildings. The machine rose higher into the air, the cloud moving up with it. there was huge energy within it. Unstable. The drone intensified and the flat tone of horns sounded over and over.

'This is not controlled,' said Ilkar.

'Yep. And heading our way. Oh, Densyr, what have you done?'

'Help me,' gasped Septern.

'What the hell have you done?' shouted Densyr. Once again, the balcony doors were open and this time they showed the crumbling of Xetesk. 'The outer wards are collapsing. The stream is heading this way.'

'Polarity. Reversed,' managed Septern. 'No control. Please.'

Densyr tore his eyes from the ruination of the city.

'Inside out, I said.' He sat down next to Septern and put a hand over the great mage's clawed fingers where they grasped at the arm of his chair. 'Must I do everything myself? I . . . Oh dear Gods drowning.'

Densyr had tuned into the mana spectrum, and saw the disaster rolling towards them with the speed of a tidal wave being forced up a narrowing channel. Flares in the grid described wards triggering with ridiculous power. Every line on the complex lattice was throbbing with barely controlled mana energy. The loose ends of the unpicked grid flailed in the chaotic maelstrom of unsuppressed mana, sending bursts of fire into the sky.

Densyr could see the shape of the Garonin machine and its cloud, depicted by the dense, dark roiling blue that seemed to hang over the entire spectrum. The blue deepened with every detonation, and the spinning of the cloud intensified. They were causing this, he knew, but couldn't see how. All he could see was a chain reaction with an inevitable conclusion.

'We have to break the cycle,' said Densyr.

'I have not the strength,' said Septern. 'The flow of mana is too great.'

'Then let me help you. Tell me what to do.'

Densyr had lent his strength to Septern and the mage's voice steadied but remained full of panic.

'Have to block the feedback. Break the linkage and place your mind in front of the Heart. Deflect the pulses away.'

'You're asking me to render myself helpless in front of this assault.'

'Not helpless,' gasped Septern. 'Hero.'

Into Densyr's eyes sprang unforeseen tears. He closed them and entered Septern's failing construct.

Sol, with Hirad slipping ever nearer towards death in his arms, ran headlong at the next intersection. His hip protested, his back was bleeding again and his arms screamed for relief. But behind them the rattle of explosion and demolition grew louder, the space between each set of wards firing grew shorter and the surge and shake beneath their feet grew more violent.

Already, the dust clogged their lungs and threatened their vision ahead. Loose roof tiles slipped and crashed underfoot. Balustrades wobbled. Every landing point was a shuddering accident waiting to happen.

'Hang on, Hirad,' said Sol. 'That soul of yours has never given up on anything. Don't you dare start now.'

Sirendor hit the edge of the building and leapt into space, circling his arms and coming down for a slithered landing on the sloping tiles across the alleyway. He turned as soon as he'd stopped and stood a little to the left of Thraun.

'Six feet maximum,' he called. 'We're ready.'

'Sorry for the jolt, Hirad. Over soon.'

Sol ran harder and faster, the dead weight of Hirad a terrible drain on balance and strength. He leaned his body forward, caught the very edge of the building and pushed off with everything he had. He tried to work his body a little more upright as he flew but time was so short. He was falling fast. Too fast.

Sol sought forward with his left leg and prayed. His foot snagged the edge of the building's balustrade. Sirendor snaked out an arm and gripped his collar. Thraun's arms took the weight of Hirad. Sol blew out his cheeks, steadied and stepped off the balustrade.

'Next up, not so easy,' said Thraun.

Sol looked behind them. The Garonin were in temporary disarray. Up in the sky, the machine was being forced higher and higher as the mana energy blasted upwards. Of the soldiers on the ground, there was nothing. Not a sign. A small mercy. A quicker, surer death was stampeding towards them.

'We have to try. Go, go.'

Thraun carried Hirad. His younger body was stout in the arm and chest and Sol was blowing badly. They ran up the slope of the roof, over the apex and slid down the other side. The air was full of the sound of explosions and the cloying drab of dust and smoke. Heat billowed around them as intense as dragon fire.

The next roof was flat and held an ornamental garden and fish pond. The carp in the pond all floated belly up. The water was steaming. The Raven tore across it, shadowed by wolves running along the roofs of adjacent buildings. Another flat roof ended in a gap of twelve feet.

'No way,' said Ilkar. 'Don't even attempt it.'

'What do you expect me to do, leave him here to burn?' Sol beckoned Thraun over and held out his arms to receive his old friend.

'No,' snapped Ilkar. 'I don't know. But this is suicide. I mean, we need you to commit suicide but not here and not now.'

'So bloody comforting,' muttered Sol.

Explosions blew apart the roof of the building they had just left. All three ducked reflexively as splinters of stone rattled the tiles at their backs.

'We can't stay here,' said Thraun. 'I will jump.'

'You won't make it. None of us can make it.' Ilkar looked around desperately. 'We have to risk the ground.'

'We won't get ten yards. The wards go from here to the apron.' Sol's fists clenched in frustration. 'Which way did the ClawBound go? And my wife and son?'

Thraun gestured away across the street. 'Easy. ClawBound jumps. Ropes are fixed. People cross. ClawBound retrieves ropes.'

'And never mind the stragglers,' said Ilkar.

'Well they got that bit right,' said Sol. His sigh was lost in another detonation. Smoke billowed up from the alley they'd crossed. 'Hirad's last chance. Any ideas.'

There was nothing. The street was too wide to jump, the ground was covered in traps none of them could see and they had no rope, no focused mage and now no hope at all.

'Drop him and go,' barked a voice from directly above their heads.

'Brynar. What are you doing here?' asked Sol.

'My bit,' he said. 'Hurry. Get down to the street and run. I'll take Hirad.'

'The street?'

'Trust me, Sol. The wards are triggering out to in. I've been into the spectrum to see what Densyr is doing. Nothing is active ahead—' Detonations, very close. A whoosh of flame and a grinding of stone. 'It's all behind you. Run. Please.'

'Bless you, Brynar. Thraun, put Hirad down.'

'How do we get down?' Panic edged Ilkar's voice.

There was a skylight in the roof. Sol jumped straight through it, covering his face. He landed on timbers about eight feet below.

'Come on!'

The building shook to its foundations. Sol saw Ilkar at the shattered skylight, Thraun shadowing him. He turned and ran to a wide stair that led down to a second level. He leaned against the wall with the building shaking enough to cast ornaments from their stands, shudder a table across the floor below him and bring down plaster-work in lumps.

'Up the bloody stairs, down the bloody stairs. Make up your mind, Unknown,' grumbled Ilkar, stamping down the stairs behind him and overtaking him on the way to the final flight.

'Where are you going?'

'Ahead of you. If Brynar is wrong, best it's a dead elf that catches it rather than a live king we want to make into a dead king later on.'

Sol found a smile on his face as he hurdled a low table. He felt a spear of pain through his old hip wound and took the last stairs one at a time. Thraun was right behind him, his wolves anxious to be outside.

'And for a moment I thought your action truly selfless.'

Ilkar pulled open the front door on a scene of dust and crumbling stonework not thirty yards to their left.

'Wrong word. I put the "elf" in self*ish*, old friend.'

'That is a joke worth dying to avoid,' said Sol.

The Raven and the three wolves ran from the door, taking a hard right turn away from the arcs of wards that were reducing Xetesk to rubble. Above them, Sol saw the shape of Brynar rise into the sky, struggling under the weight of his charge.

The heat from the countless fires raging in their wake washed over them in waves. Sol coughed, a spasm fled down his back and into his hip. He stumbled into a wall and would have fallen but for Thraun's grasp on his arm. Sol could see the stone apron that sat in front of the college gates. It looked distant.

He set off after Ilkar. Thraun's wolves were already way ahead, giving some comfort that Brynar had been right about the wards. But still, with every step, the thought of tripping something instantly fatal played on the mind. Behind him the noise of detonation and collapse was deafening. It rang straight through his head and set his feet vibrating in his boots.

Sol counted the paces he ran between each new set of explosions. Blue auras flashed in his vision and stark shadows played on the walls ahead and to the sides of him. Eight paces. It kept his feet one in front of the other if nothing else. A leaden fatigue was beginning to settle on him. The pain in his back was soaring with every jarring step he took. His hip protested. He was losing ground to the rest of them.

'Stupid old man,' he said to himself.

Six paces. The jolt through the ground took his balance and sent him sprawling. Sol turned onto his back and saw the house they'd descended through disappear, consumed by mana fire, stonework reduced to shards by God's Eyes and EarthHammer.

Too close. Way too close. He scrambled back to his feet and pushed himself on. He was limping badly, the pain shooting into his jaw and up into his skull. Four paces. The wave of heat scorched the back of his head and his clothes began to smoulder gently.

Sol ran out of the street and into the open of the apron. Two paces. The last buildings bordering the apron teetered as EarthHammers thrust through them. Sol gave himself one last push. He was gasping for breath, could barely put his right leg down and his lower back was losing blood way too fast.

The detonations were right behind him. The borders of the stone apron exploded under the pressure of a Jalyr's Sun that formed and burst at ground level. Sol felt the heat and the fire in the moments before the wind plucked him from his feet and hurled him across the apron. He landed, slid and thumped into the walls of the college.

The last ward arc had triggered and the sound of detonations rolled away across the city. The reverberations carried on and on. As an encore, weakened buildings tumbled, strewing stone, timber and tile.

Sol rolled onto his front. He didn't even have the energy to look and see if he was on fire. He didn't think so but he could smell his own flesh.

'Dramatic. I'll give you that,' said Ilkar from somewhere nearby.

Sol turned his head. There was a gap in the wall. Ilkar, Thraun and Brynar stood in it, the latter looking very anxious and casting repeated glances behind him.

'Everyone's looking over the walls at the moment, but it won't last long.'

'Can someone help me up?' asked Sol. 'Presumably, we've been seen.'

'Yes, but not all the way into the postern gate,' said Brynar. 'Please hurry.'

'How's Hirad?'

'Alive, Sol, but that's about it,' said Thraun.

'Well then, let's make this count.'

Sol, helped by Ilkar, climbed slowly and painfully to his feet. He took one last look east. Obscured by dust and fire, the city was gone.

The only question was how long it would take for the Garonin to regroup and attack the college itself.

'Come on, Raven. A day standing with you and death seems a blessing.'

Chapter 29

The panic spread through the western side of the city almost as fast as the explosions from the east. Auum, Miirt and Ghaal ran hard through the periphery of the populous zone, ignoring the shouts of guards and patrols, knowing that in the maze of narrow, deprived alleys, little could be done to stop them.

At the outset the population of Xetesk had crowded onto the streets in huge expectation. The first set of wards had been greeted with cheering. The second set as well. But very quickly the mood had darkened. This was a city of magic. Plenty enough knew that the repetition and speed of the triggering of wards was not what was intended. Either a massive invasion force was pushing through the kill zone or something had gone badly wrong.

By the time the TaiGethen had steered back towards the walls of the college, ordinary folk and a good number wearing the livery of the college guard were making their hurried way to the west gates and out onto open ground. Auum only hoped they weren't too late. The Garonin were creatures of habit and marched in straight lines everywhere they went, but even they would eventually realise that another path existed. And then stopping the exodus, to herd, corral and massacre the people, would be relatively simple.

Auum led his Tai into the lee of the western walls of the college. The explosives display to the east had turned every head. The barrier before them was some fifty feet high, dark and imposing. But Ghaal merely smiled.

'Smooth walls and beautifully repeated stonework,' he said. 'Old concrete and moss. My trusted friends.'

He reached up with both hands, set his feet into a crack at about hip level and began to climb, his brother and sister following his every move.

*

Densyr was weeping with the effort. He could easily imagine himself standing between two forces desperate to pull apart and release the power contained within while he held on to each one with every mote of strength that he had. And he wouldn't be able to hold on forever.

He could feel Septern with him. The master mage was weak but his mind still clung on, and would do for as long as his soul could do the same in his borrowed body. Septern's grid had come under extraordinary pressure but some sections remained undamaged by their efforts to pull the plug on the Garonin attempt to drag mana direct from Xetesk's Heart.

Densyr, his own heart flailing and his temples pounding, relaxed enough to be able to look about him in the mana spectrum. The Heart had returned to something like normal balance. The hourglass shape of mana encasing the Heart was no longer distorted like a glass-blower's nightmare. There were wild pulses within it but the depletion had been halted, with Densyr acting as the door wedged firmly into the frame.

Still, the remains of the grid, particularly at its periphery, were a disaster waiting to happen. What had been a tightly bound structure built on lines of energy criss-crossing in arcs, horizontals and verticals to join each and every ward together, had become a fractured mess.

Loose lines whipped and spat with the remnants of mana within them seeking a place to earth themselves. The entire security of the arc lines was gone, ripped to shreds by the feedback of mana along the grid itself. Eighty per cent of the wards had detonated when they had been torn asunder. Densyr shuddered to think what had happened to the eastern side of his city. The remaining parts of the grid were all active, and that was some relief should the Garonin still pursue their plan to march east to west without deviation.

Unfortunately, it seemed to Densyr that he would be unable to abandon his position. The grid was so unstable that to remove himself, and probably Septern too, from their buffering duties would allow the flailing mana lines to reconnect to the Heart so closing the circuit once more and feeding back the remaining mana. It might only be twenty per cent active, but there was enough power there to do serious damage. Destruction? Only Septern could tell.

'Did we win?' asked Septern.

Through the haze of the mana spectrum Densyr could see him slumped in his chair, eyelids fluttering.

'That depends on your point of view.'

'Where are the enemy?'

'I can see no sign of them in the spectrum. But that means little, I suspect. We've surely given them a bloody nose and pause for thought.'

Septern chuckled. 'And now you want me to work out a way to unpick the rest of the grid safely.'

'It isn't that I don't enjoy standing between these two unruly forces, it's just that I have other duties today.'

'You are a strong mage, young Densyr. I am not surprised you were entrusted with Dawnthief.'

Densyr felt a warmth radiating through him, calming the forces pummelling him from the outside.

'I am flattered,' he said. 'But let's raise a glass to ourselves when we're out of this. I'm tired. You must be exhausted.'

'I can take the pressure now,' said Septern. 'Release yourself. Let me work.'

'Are you sure?'

'We'll find out.' Another dry chuckle. 'Just don't go far.'

Densyr disengaged himself from the point between Heart and grid, feeling Septern take the strain. Densyr sagged back into his chair. The roar of unsuppressed mana faded but there was no peace. He became immediately aware of a low unsettling noise from behind him, to the west. And of angry shouts coming from below, inside the college.

'Sing if you need me, Septern,' he said, pushing himself to his feet.

Densyr had to cling on to the arms of his chair just for a moment while the blood rushed away from his head, threatening to black him out. When it cleared, he walked to his balcony doors, took a deep breath and threw them open.

Ten years of rebuilding and pride, wiped out in the time it took to boil a cauldron of water. Densyr felt physically sick. In his mind's eye he had seen rubble and dust but nothing could have prepared him for this. A few half walls were standing beyond the college gates but aside from that nothing remained of the entire eastern section of the city. On an arc that stretched for four miles left to right and three miles in depth, everything was gone.

'Who needs the Garonin when we have such means at our disposal?' he whispered.

Fires still raged in hundreds of places. The yellow flame of burning wood mixed with the harsh dark blue flame of mana gorging itself on any material with which it came into contact. Those flailing strands of the grid, easily identifiable now, spewing out their energy, adding final insult to the crime that had been committed on Xetesk. The Wesmen had come and been beaten off. The demons had done such awful damage. Yet no enemy had managed quite the complete desolation that Densyr and Septern had been forced to perpetrate to save . . .

Beneath him the Heart was still intact and the college walls had not been breached. But what of the body of Xetesk? He didn't even need to look west to know what the rumbling hum was. People were leaving. They were scared and they were running and they didn't even know where. The security of their college had proved not to be enough.

'Despair is the province of the weak,' said a voice behind him.

Densyr straightened his shoulders, lifted his head and turned.

'What am I saving, Dystran?' he asked. 'How am I benefiting Xetesk and Balaia?'

'Don't let what you see fool your mind,' said Dystran gently. 'When the battle is won, and it may be that it is already, there is but one beacon for the leaderless and it is here. Only one place capable of rebuilding all that we have lost. Only one place with the strength and the desire to make Balaia a power again. And only one place that can rule.

'The Heart of Xetesk still beats and it must beat on, my Lord of the Mount. It is our destiny to lead and yours to rule. And it is surely all within your grasp.'

Densyr felt almost too tired to argue. 'You know they are not beaten, don't you?'

'Perhaps, but now they have seen the extent of our power and the sacrifices they will have to make to take our Heart. Surely a negotiation is the least we can expect and a withdrawal is something for which we can now hope.'

'I wish I shared your optimism.'

'Take a look outside.' Dystran moved past him and out onto the balcony. Densyr followed a little reluctantly. 'What do you see? What do you hear?'

'I see the mess I've created in the most beautiful city on Balaia and I hear the sounds of my people panicking and running to the west.'

Densyr glanced below him and then away again, unsure whether to believe what he was seeing.

'You are being too literal. Perhaps I should have asked what you *don't* see and hear. No Garonin foot soldiers. No machine. I— Are you listening to me at all?'

'Now I really do believe I have seen it all,' said Densyr by way of a reply.

Coming across the courtyard, with guards and mages closing in, were a man being helped along by a woman and a second man. Two boys walked just in front of them. A third man walked head bowed and arms outstretched and could only be a mage. A fourth man was carrying a fifth and was surrounded by wolves. In front of them all came Brynar, his loyal apprentice, waving people aside as best he could.

'Erstwhile apprentice,' muttered Densyr. 'Little bastard.'

'Have them killed,' said Dystran, waving a hand.

'Without finding out how they survived that inferno? I think not.'

Densyr pulled the bell to summon a servant and didn't have to question the relief he felt and the smile that was fighting its way onto his lips.

'The bloody, bastard Raven,' said Dystran.

'Yes,' said Densyr. 'Amazing, aren't they?'

'They aren't just going to wave us into the tower complex,' said Sol. 'What are we going to do?'

'Get as close as possible,' said Brynar. 'Ilkar has us shielded. I don't think any guards will be drawing weapons with me here.'

'Don't count on it.'

'Move!' shouted Brynar. 'Wounded coming through.'

The courtyard was packed with the anxious, the scared and a few with the desire to organise. Thraun's wolves were keeping all but the most persistent at a safe distance. But mages were gathering at the entrance to the tower complex fifty yards ahead and guardsmen were with them in good numbers. Left and right they were being shadowed by more.

Ilkar's Mage Shelter gave them the protection they needed from targeted magical attack and no one was going to fire arrows in such a crowded space. But all it would take was a guard captain with a little courage and they would be arrested immediately. Brynar was not going to let anyone fight and for their part The Raven had neither the desire nor the capacity to do so.

It was a question of whose nerve would hold the longest.

College guards were creating a path in front of them, pushing people back on either side. The clear view it gave of the doors to the tower complex was not encouraging.

'Keep moving,' said Brynar.

Thraun came to Sol's left. 'I can scatter them.'

'Wait,' said Sol. 'Let's see their intent.'

'That's close enough!'

An old soldier moved out in front of those guarding the doors. Suarav, captain at the time of the demon invasion. General now. A much-decorated hero.

'We must see the Lord of the Mount,' said Brynar, not pausing in his stride. 'We must speak with him and with Septern.'

'Not here and not now, Brynar,' said Suarav. 'Stop. You will yield to me.'

'Can't do that, General,' said Brynar. 'There is no time left.'

'Correct,' said Suarav.

He nodded. Two mages stepped forward, knelt and cast. Ilkar gasped, stumbled and refound his footing.

'Ilkar's Defence,' he said. 'How apt.'

'Can you hold?' asked Sol.

'They aren't pushing. But there's no way I can move forward.'

To their left and right, soldiers were lining the path. Behind the wolves more came but stayed at a careful distance. Ahead and left of the complex and out towards the south walls there was a flurry of movement. Sol looked first at Diera and then Jonas. Finally, he winked at young Hirad.

'Ready to run?'

'Where?' asked Jonas. 'Trapped, aren't we?'

'Trust your old father, all right? Opportunity approaches.' Sol raised his voice a little. 'Thraun. Be ready. Allies to our left. Sirendor, don't let me fall and don't go too fast for Diera.'

'What's going on?' asked Sirendor.

'Eyes front for answers,' said Sol.

Sol never tired of watching them in action. Auum appeared from the crowds to the left. He was at head height, his left leg and arm outstretched ahead of him, right leg tucked beneath him and right arm cocked to punch. He slammed into the first of the crouching mages, cannoning him into the second.

'Defence down,' said Ilkar.

'Run, Raven,' said Sol.

Thraun's wolves split one left and two right as the motley assortment of wounded, women and children began to run towards the tower complex. The animals patrolled the flanks, snapping in the direction of any man who thought to move in.

Brynar was running hard, Ilkar behind him. Ahead, Auum landed, spun and sprinted towards the tower guards. Ghaal and Miirt powered in from the left. Ghaal dropped low, sweeping the legs from a soldier and smacking the heel of his palm into the fallen man's forehead, bouncing it from the stone steps.

Miirt ducked under a clumsily drawn sword, blocked the sword arm to the right and butted her victim in the head, sending him down in a shower of blood from his nose. Auum planted a roundhouse kick into the side of Suarav's head. The old general fell like a sack of potatoes. Auum stepped over him, spread his arms and beckoned the next men on. There were no takers.

Screams to the right took the attention of one who didn't even see the ClawBound pair striding to the tower complex doors. A fist doubled him up and a knee to the chin put him on the ground. The mages had dispersed back into the entrance hallway of the complex. The doors began to close. The ClawBound pair ran inside, quickly followed by Ghaal. The doors stopped moving and shrieks echoed out.

Sol moved as fast as his aching body would let him. He leaned on Sirendor and used Diera for balance. In front of him, Jonas was holding young Hirad's hand and the little lad was laughing with the excitement of it all.

He was too small to see Auum leap and dive over the last rank of guardsmen, landing behind them and striking out at two before any had the chance to turn. The gap he made was enough for Brynar, who darted inside. Moments later, a deep blue Ilkar's Defence thrust out, beating back any defenders from the left.

Miirt and Auum faced right. In front of them, swords had been drawn by six guards. Auum took a single pace forward, dropped to his hands and spun round, legs whipping out and in. Three men fell. Miirt moved forward.

'Time to run,' she said.

And so they did.

'Clear inside!' called Brynar.

Sol nodded to Jonas to go in. Auum and Miirt shadowed him and his brother. Sol limped in with Diera, young Hirad and Jonas, and last came Thraun and the wolves. Brynar shifted the Defence spell, placing it in front of the doors.

'Well-timed, Auum,' said Sol. 'Lucky you got here.'

'We were waiting for you. Luck was not involved. Yniss keeps all of us for sterner tests.'

Sol took a quick look round. The ClawBound pair had pinned eight mages against a wall. The panther was padding up and down in front of them, the elf studying their every twitch, looking for a reason to attack. From within the complex Sol could hear running feet and the clash of metal.

'Best you go,' said Brynar. 'I'll hold the passage up to Densyr's tower as long as I can.'

Sol unhitched himself from Diera and Sirendor and limped over to the mage.

'You have done greater service than you know, Brynar. Your masters should be proud but they are blind instead. The Garonin will be back. Get out of here. Head west with your people. If what we're attempting works, we'll find you. Don't let them get you. The world, whichever world it is, will need mages like you.'

'But what if I am merely a man?' said Brynar.

Sol tapped his chest. 'In here is where you are strongest.'

Brynar blushed. Sol turned.

'Raven,' he said. 'Raven with me.'

Chapter 30

'Get me some strong spirit.' Densyr snapped his fingers at Dystran. 'Quickly. Same cabinet where you kept it.'

Dystran huffed and walked across the room. Densyr squatted back down by Septern. He had long ago turned from the sounds of combat emanating up from below.

'Hey. Snap out if it. Don't lose yourself in there.'

'Safe inn . . . side,' mumbled Septern. 'Nottt harm we.'

'What the hell is he muttering about?' Dystran poured a clear oily liquid into a goblet and handed it to Densyr. 'Just don't let him lose the grid.'

'I'll do my best,' said Densyr.

He tuned into the mana spectrum. The shapes that signified the Heart and Septern were no longer distinct. Like the Heart had reached out and grabbed him, part-consumed him. Or that he had decided to become one with it. The Heart itself appeared normal in terms of flow and density but Septern's mind map was confused and flickering.

'Septern. Septern, can you hear me?' Densyr laid a hand on Septern's arm. 'Dystran, I think you might want to join us. Is Vuldaroq anywhere nearby?'

'In the catacomb chambers, working on resonance theory with Sharyr,' said Dystran. Densyr heard him kneel down. 'Are you going to use that spirit or . . . ? Oh dear Gods drowning.'

'Septern, what are you doing?' demanded Densyr.

'I didn't even think this was possible,' said Dystran.

Densyr shook his head. At least the remnants of the ward grid appeared to be calm. He'd done something to stop the loose ends flailing. A gentle blue pulse was running along the existing lines. A circuit had been closed, temporarily at least.

'Nor me. Septern?'

'Mmmm . . . ore control. Beauty. Form fails.'

Septern's breathing was shallow and rapid.

'He's pouring himself into the Heart,' said Dystran.

'He can't,' hissed Densyr. 'It's like making yourself the wind or fire or something. Can't be done.'

'Can we be sure?' asked Dystran. 'On the point of death, when our soul is about to leave our body, who's to say what is possible?'

Densyr heard wonder in Dystran's voice. 'I think you're missing the point, rather. He's supposed to be buffering the failing grid from feeding back into the Heart and blowing it to smithereens.'

'And who's to say he isn't doing just that? Presumably you want to know whether we should try to bounce him out using the spirit.'

'And?'

'I have no idea.'

'Smashing,' said Densyr. 'Septern. How long can you survive like this?'

'Approaching . . . near. Survival no. Change. Have seee nn . . . Nottt harm we.'

'Septern, you are making no sense. Can you keep the grid secure any more?'

'Always always. Houssssseess safe.'

'He's delusional, Dystran. If he loses his mind, he loses any hold on anything.'

'Can you be so sure? Really sure, I mean.'

'I hardly think this is the time for research and experimentation concerning the soul's ability to fuse with mana on death. We have to know if he's secure. Xetesk depends upon it.'

Dystran remained calm. 'Look at the Heart. Look at the ward grid. Steadier than you or I could achieve, no?'

'I'm aware of that,' said Densyr through gritted teeth. 'But he is surely close to death. When that happens, we might lose the college.'

'You can step in, Densyr. I can help you. What other duties must you be free for?'

'Nothing much. Organising my guard, directing my mages, securing my college and defending what remains of my city and hence Balaia. Trivial, really.'

'But nowhere are your talents more useful than in saving the Heart. Is there really anything more important than that?'

Densyr dropped out of the mana spectrum and looked at Dystran hard, searching for signs of duplicity. Any senior mage had to be considered a threat, even one who had willingly stepped aside from his post.

'It is one of a number of key areas,' fenced Densyr.

'Let me command the defence. I do have certain experience in that area.'

'Following my orders?'

'Naturally, my Lord Densyr.'

'Knowing I could pull the plug on any opportunist ambition by simply disconnecting myself?'

'That is a comment unworthy,' said Dystran.

Densyr shrugged. 'I'm Lord of the Mount. I can suspect who I damn well choose.'

Dystran chuckled. 'And a fine one you are too. And thinking clearly at last.'

Densyr was interrupted by a commotion a little way down the wide spiral stairway leading up to the chambers that had become his centre of operations.

'Ah, excellent. At least someone is capable of following my orders. I do believe the reluctant Raven are about to be presented to us.'

There was no knock on the door. Rather it flew back against its hinges so violently that a cracked decanter was upset on a nearby table, crashing to the ground and spilling fine wine over a priceless rug. Glasses rattled on the tray and a bookend fell over, disgorging some rather ancient texts onto the floor, mercifully clear of the pool of vintage red.

Auum, Ghaal and Miirt issued across the floor to stand far too close to both Densyr and Dystran. Following them came the bizarre menagerie that was The Raven, Sol's family, a trio of wolves and a ClawBound pair. Thraun pushed his way to the front and laid Hirad on the table, taking a cushion from a chair for his head.

Densyr's mouth dropped open, and when he closed it, he had to suppress what would have been an ill-timed smile.

'How did you . . . ? Oh, need I really ask; I know already. Three elves and a few dead people are plenty enough to breach Xetesk's inner sanctum these days.'

'And we should not have been forced to try,' said Sol, unhitching himself from Diera and Sirendor and moving painfully to a free arm-chair. His sons sat one on each of the leather arms and Sol put an arm around each one's shoulders. 'Ilkar, can you help me with a little pain relief? My back's the worst. Followed by my hip and then everything else.'

'What do you want?' asked Densyr. 'I haven't time to chat right now. We are unsure if the enemy are defeated.'

'You can be assured they are not,' said Auum, standing less than a pace away from Densyr and piercing his skull with those cold, hard eyes.

'All the more reason to let me get on with defending what little we have left,' said Densyr.

'You can do what you like. We only want Septern.' While Sol was speaking, he was looking at the master mage, his frown deepening. 'Is he all right?'

'That depends on your—' began Dystran.

'No. He's dying,' said Densyr. 'He's currently engaged in stopping the Heart of Xetesk from exploding. So you can't have him. Sorry.'

'But we must,' said Ilkar.

He moved towards Septern, and Densyr tensed to stop him. Auum shook his head minutely. Densyr backed off. He watched Ilkar tune into the mana spectrum and saw the disbelief register on his face.

'I think we have a problem here,' said Ilkar.

'Why?' asked Sol.

'Septern appears to be inextricably melded to the Heart of Xetesk. It's like he's poured his soul into it.'

'Is that possible?' asked Sol.

'Apparently.'

'So what do we do? We have to get him out of there,' said Sol. 'I doubt very much that we have a great deal of time.'

'Whoa, whoa, whoa. No one is getting anyone out of anywhere.' Densyr tried to talk around Auum. 'Please try to understand. Simply wrenching Septern back would be like setting the tower complex atop an erupting volcano. Ilkar will confirm, I'm sure.'

'Then you do something,' said Sol. 'Now.'

'Why, Sol? I'm not unhappy with the situation as it stands.'

'No? Really think you've turned the tide, do you? Well let me tell you something, O Lord of the Mount. While you were hiding up here, some of us, as you'll recall very well, were in the middle of the shit storm you unleashed. We saw Garonin die for sure. But we also saw their air machine rise above it all. You think it's gone? Then you are more stupid than I ever imagined. They'll be back and what do you really have left?'

'What do you want Septern for anyway?'

'He knows the ritual of opening,' said Sol, and he clutched his sons a little tighter and shared a glance with Diera.

'Commm . . . ng,' muttered Septern. 'Fsssst sss-sston.'

'What's he saying?' asked Ilkar.

'Nothing that makes any sense,' said Sirendor.

'Coming. Fist. Stone,' said Jonas. He blushed into the silence. 'Well that's what it sounded like to me.'

Distantly, an explosion was heard. Densyr's heart tolled painfully. 'Oh no.'

The flat horn tone sounded once more but this time appallingly close. Papers were picked up and shredded. The balcony doors smacked back so hard that one fell from its hinges. Miirt reacted the quickest, heading outside to look.

'It is right above us. And there are Garonin in the ruined city. Many hundreds.'

'Endgame, Densyr old chum,' said Sol. 'Your time has just run out.'

'I will not let this city fall.'

Sol stood, ignoring his pain, and marched over. Auum moved aside for him.

'Fine, but let everyone who doesn't share your vision take the chance to run if they want to.'

'No! And I'm saying that for you, Sol. Because I care. Their demand that you die is one that no friend should ask of another.'

'But they may ask it of their king, and their king agrees it is the only path.'

'You will not take Septern.'

'Watch us,' said Auum.

'Looks like you'd better be ready to fill the breach, doesn't it?' said Ilkar, already with a hand on Septern's shoulder. 'You know I can wake him.'

Combat erupted all around the college. God's Eyes, IceBlades, Winter's Touch. Spells arced away to strike the Garonin machine where it hung directly above the tower complex. Coming through the blasted streets, a large force of Garonin drew heavy fire from the east walls. Septern's face darkened. His hands twitched and a low growl escaped his mouth.

Wards triggered out to the east.

'Not appprooo . . . ch.'

'You cannot move him,' said Densyr. 'We'll all die if you do.'

'You aren't talking to a room that cares terribly much,' said Sol, but he looked over at his family and the desperation within them was clear for all to see. Young Hirad had his face buried in his mother's chest. Jonas's eyes were everywhere. And Diera was glaring at her husband.

'Sol. Don't let this be the end. Just don't. We deserve better.'

Sol stared at Densyr. 'My family are three of those you have sworn to save. Help them.'

Lines dropped past the balcony window.

'Here they come,' said Miirt.

She drew her twin short blades. Auum did likewise, giving Densyr a telling look as he turned away to join her. Ghaal moved to the opposite balcony doors, standing ready with the ClawBound pair. Thraun and his wolves gathered near the table. Sirendor moved to stand with Sol. Blades taken from college guards were in hand.

'We can get away,' said Jonas. 'Sha-Kaan will take us.'

'We cannot bring him into a battle like this,' said Sol. 'The Klene would get ripped apart. Someone tell me about Hirad.'

'Alive,' said Thraun. 'Just about.'

There was the thud of heavy boots on stone from somewhere above. Possibly on the roof, possibly an upper balcony. All eyes glanced up.

'The door,' said Sol. 'Thraun, your job.'

'I've got it.'

'Ilkar, how are we doing?'

'Not good,' said Ilkar. 'Densyr is right. Moving Septern will certainly bring mana feeding back into the Heart. Probably enough to destroy it. And even if it didn't, he's too far gone to move. He'll die.'

Sol closed his eyes briefly, and when he opened them again, Densyr saw him stare at his family. Diera was rocking young Hirad. Jonas tried to comfort them both.

Densyr began to weave a spell. 'I'm sorry, Sol. But we're all in this together now.'

'We should run for the catacombs,' said Ilkar.

'No,' said Densyr. 'That's where they'll be going to attack the Heart.'

'But well defended surely?'

'Extremely.'

'Then why—'

'Come on, Ilkar, think. Full of souls, full of mana. Full of wards.'

Outside, the lines jerked and jumped as more Garonin began the descent. There were the sounds of breaking timbers from above and footsteps on the stairs. White tears flooded down to impact the courtyard and walls. The tower complex rocked under the weight of spells and energy. A bright light flashed at ground level.

Densyr held the shape of his chosen spell and faced the door. He felt a strange calm descend on him, like a fond memory soothing nightmares away. So different yet so very much the same. Standing with The Raven, facing ridiculous odds. Backs against the wall.

And trapped with no place left to run.

Nowhere in this dimension anyway.

The call to arms rang out, bells ringing a discordant tone, a sound that was picked up across the west and north of the city. General Suarav looked to Brynar.

'Let's put this aside. We have a college to defend. Stand with me.'

Brynar, from the entrance to Densyr's tower, over which he had cast his Ilkar's Defence, took but a moment to nod his head and dismiss the spell. College guard ran at him.

'Hold!' bellowed Suarav. 'Touch not so much as a hair on his head. Secure the stairway. Guard every level. The Raven won't harm the Lord of the Mount; they'll protect him now. Trust me. Brynar, organise your mage teams. Just as we rehearsed. Someone find me Chandyr. I want lookouts stationed by the west gates. I want the citizen commanders waiting to distribute their teams to their designated tasks. I'll be outside the tower complex. Move it.'

On his way past, Suarav grabbed Brynar by the shoulder.

'I won't forget this, you little bastard. You had better prove yourself one fucking big hero today, do you understand me?'

'I will die protecting those who protect the people of Balaia,' said Brynar.

Suarav grunted. 'Good enough. Go.'

The general rubbed a hand across his face, picked up his pride from where those damned elves had left it and ran out into chaos and fear. White tears spat into the ground. Two guards were ripped apart right in front of him. Burning corpses already littered the ground. He could see spells arcing out into the ruined eastern city as the enemy closed in on the college. Stone rippled and broke under the weight of enemy fire.

Above, the bulbous machine pulsated. It was enormous, casting a malevolent shadow across the whole college. Dozens of lines hung from it and Garonin slid down them one after another, landing on towers, the dome of the complex and heading for the ground.

'Where are my defensive mages? I need the walls bound up now. And bring those bastards down to earth. Brynar, get more concentration above.'

Sliding down the lines, Garonin leaned out and triggered their weapons, showering the pure energy of the white tears over the college. Brynar, out in the open, had gathered a group of mages together. One knelt to shield the other five, who were all forming the shapes for their spells.

IceBlades raced away from open palms, spreading as they rose. Frozen shards of mana ripped into Garonin bodies, sliced through lines and plunged into the fabric of the machine. Enemy soldiers fell to the earth, and where they landed, guards swooped to finish off any survivors.

More Garonin were on the lines now. More lines were dropped from the machine, and up on the hanging carriage Suarav could see frenzied activity. Above, the clouds were beginning to build and darken. Brynar nodded at Suarav and set off with his mages to find another angle to cast.

'Keep it up, youngster,' Suarav said. 'Redemption is at hand.'

Chapter 31

Garonin swung onto the balconies. White tears flashed into the chamber, smashing portraits hung on the walls and setting fire to a tapestry rescued from the library during the demon invasion. Nothing would save it now.

Densyr held an Ilkar's Defence steady across the doorway. Garonin poured fire into it. Auum could see the sweat beading on the mage's face. Next to him, Miirt ducked a swinging weapon and planted her elbow into an enemy gut. She jumped up and reversed her fist into his helmet, knocking him back. Auum straight-kicked into his face, sending him over the edge.

'Sol, call out status,' said Auum. 'Direct us.'

'Understood,' said Sol.

The tower rocked above. Loose masonry fell past the balconies. The thud of Garonin fire could be heard and felt as it pounded into the upper floors of the tower. A volley of spells flew up from the courtyard. More Garonin lines dropped. Three more soldiers landed on the balcony in front of Auum.

'Get down inside!' called Auum.

White tears lashed into the chamber. Auum threw himself forward, cutting his blades across and out in front of him. He felt them bite deep into flesh through armour not designed to defend against blade attack. A Garonin howled in pain and fell across him. Auum rolled and kicked, shoving the wounded man aside, ramming a sword up under his chin.

A weapon was on him. Miirt's blade flashed across Auum's vision. The weapon fell, a dismembered hand still clutching it. Auum arched his back and sprang to his feet, burying his blades in the midriff of the same soldier. Miirt round-housed the third, taking him clean off the balcony.

'Holding inside,' said Sol. 'Doorway secure. Left balcony holding. No casualties.'

Auum risked a glance behind. Prone on the table that dominated the centre of the chamber, Hirad was awfully vulnerable. To the left, Sol had turned Diera's chair to the wall and she was hunched up in it, her arms covering young Hirad, who was abandoned to screaming terror. Jonas crouched next to them, sheltered by the mantel of the fire. His head was down and his hands were on his knees. Auum could see him murmuring, talking to Sha-Kaan.

Sol stood by his family. One hand rested on the back of the chair. He was finding it difficult to stand and equally difficult to be out of direct combat. The doorway was secured. Garonin moved beyond the barrier, which stretched on an arc covering the door and the entire area of wall the Garonin could attack if they chose.

Thraun stood sentinel, his wolves by him, waiting. Dystran was crouched by Septern, tuned into the mana spectrum. The master mage himself was absolutely still but for his mouth, which moved to form speech no one could hear in the tumult that echoed in the chamber.

And finally, opposite Auum, Ghaal and the ClawBound held the second balcony entrance. Sirendor was stamping the last of the embers from the tapestry, which he had ripped from the wall.

'Sol,' said Auum. 'Hirad.'

The barbarian in a merchant's broken body was stirring.

'Sirendor, Thraun,' said Sol. 'Get Hirad safer. Under the table. Anywhere. Auum, on your right.'

Auum swung back to the balcony. A Garonin soldier was swinging towards them on a line. Others followed on the same calculated arc. Arrows flew into the air from below, all missing the fast-moving targets.

'Miirt, monkey snare. Take low,' said Auum.

'Down on my mark,' said Sol. 'Enemies coming in right hand.'

Auum moved back half a pace, setting himself just behind the frame of the balcony doors. Miirt flattened herself on the floor, blades at her sides, arms ready in front of her.

'Mark!' shouted Sol.

Everybody crouched or dropped prone bar Auum. White tears flooded in, smashing into stone, punching straight through the walls in several places, leaving ragged holes that fizzed and cracked, the mana binding them ripped apart. The Garonin followed behind his fire, landing inside the chamber. He balanced quickly and raised his weapon but had no chance to use it.

Miirt reached out and grabbed both his ankles. Auum leapt onto his back, wrapping arms around his chest. He crashed to the ground. Just like bringing down a larger monkey in the rainforest. Sirendor, alive to the situation, grabbed the Garonin's head, lifted it and thrust a blade deep into his throat.

Auum nodded and rolled away. Three more Garonin came in, one after another, dropping and rolling. Auum jumped above one but was caught by the second. The third landed on his feet, brought his weapon to ready and fired in an arc right to left. A wolf blew apart, smearing gore across the chamber. The ClawBound pair reacted just too late. White tears ripped into panther and elf as they dived at the enemy, shielding Raven warrior and TaiGethen elf from the same fate.

Auum bounced back to his feet and knocked the weapon from the Garonin's hands. Miirt lashed her blades into the enemy's back and he crumpled in a welter of blood. The air stank of burned flesh and fur. Thraun and the remaining wolves pounced on one of the remaining two Garonin, exacting grim revenge.

Auum turned from the sight. The second Garonin had risen. His weapon thudded butt first into the back of Ghaal's head while the Tai was fighting another on the balcony. Auum moved to strike, but Sol was ahead of him, thrashing his blade through the Garonin's lower back.

The Garonin spun round, weapon limp in his hands. His gaze fixed on Septern and he raised a hand to point.

'You,' he said, and tried to bring his weapon to bear.

Dystran rose, stretched to place a hand up to the soldier's eye slits and let mana flame gout from his palm.

'You will not touch him.'

The Garonin screamed, clutched briefly at Dystran's hand and fell, his helmet ablaze with mana fire.

'Sirendor. Fires. Get them out. Thraun. Thraun!'

The shapechanger looked up at Sol, his eyes rimmed with tears.

'So much pain,' he said.

'Hang on, Thraun. See to your wolves. See to the ClawBound. Auum, back to your watch. I'll check Ghaal.'

The intensity of Garonin fire on the tower increased as if a message had been relayed. The structure shook as raw energy spewed into it from all sides. Slate and stone blistered, broke and fell. Huge chunks of intricately carved work teetered and fell from the highest floors, tumbling down to the ground hundreds of feet below.

On the ceiling above, the paint was darkening.

'They're coming through the roof,' said Sol. 'Densyr, we need your Defence up there if you can do it. Thraun, Sirendor. The doorway. You have to hold it.'

'I hear you,' said Densyr. 'Tell me when.'

'Now. Right now.'

Densyr moved the Ilkar's Defence spell upwards. Thraun and the two wolves rushed straight through the door. Xeteskian guards came from the left up the stairs. The Garonin fell back before the onslaught.

Sol limped over to Ghaal. The TaiGethen was moving but groggy. Sol dared a look through the balcony doorway. For now the lines were empty but the Garonin in the floors above were free to take the tower apart piece by piece.

'What the hell are they after?' asked Sol, swaying back in as more stone tumbled from the roof. 'The Heart is nowhere near here.'

'But Septern is,' said Dystran. 'And we need to bind the walls to stop the tower falling. They want him because of where he is and what he's doing.'

A thunderous crash rattled the tower to its foundations. Light flooded in from above. Densyr gasped and dropped to his knees. The upper floors of the tower concertinaed, dumping hundreds of tons of stone, furnishings and timbers onto the Defence.

'Tilt it!' yelled Dystran.

Densyr moved his right hand. The Defence moved up a fraction on that side. Enough to dislodge a mountain of ruined stone. Garonin swarmed around the outside, trampling on the Defence, dodging debris as it slipped and slid. They fired incessantly at the spell, each tear splashing white and blue as it impacted.

'Whatever Septern's doing, I suggest he does it quickly,' said Sol.

Up above, they could see the Garonin machine. It was massive, bulging under the pressure of mana stored within its bell. The clouds above it were swirling but slowly, as if something was interrupting the sucking in of fuel to the detonation area.

In his chair Septern sighed, long and feeble.

'Twocanbeone,' he said.

*

Binding spells were strengthening the walls and the damage was being limited for now. Brynar ran with Suarav and Chandyr, away from the tower complex. With them a dozen guards and six mages, all under a spell shield. Up in the machine weapons fired down. More powerful versions of those held in the hand, they tore great rents in buildings, ground and exposed walls. Anyone caught in their fire simply ceased to exist.

But on the ground the tide was going against the enemy. Fifteen groups of shielded mages and soldiers moved in and out of combat areas as the Garonin landed. The focus of the assault was the base of the tower complex, as the enemy sought access to the catacombs and hence the Heart of Xetesk.

High up above, Densyr's tower was taking a dreadful pounding. Slabs of stone were falling to the ground, dealing as much damage to enemy as to ally. Suarav wondered what it was they wanted from up there.

'Hold,' said Suarav. 'Use the angles. Garonin on the deck.'

Mages crouched and prepared. Surrounding them, guards watched outwards. Time slowed. A section of wall a hundred yards to the left burst in. Chandyr cursed.

'There next,' said Suarav.

'Ready,' said Brynar.

'Cast at will,' said Suarav.

Twenty Garonin were walking through the gap in the wall. Their weapons sprayed death in a wide arc around them.

'Wait,' said Suarav. 'New target. Our left.'

'Got them,' said Brynar. 'Cleansing Flame. Cast.'

Multiple columns of super-heated mana flame roared down from the sky. Each one sought a single target. Armour flared white, twenty suits trying to ward off the power of Xetesk's most powerful individual offensive spell. They had no chance. The deluge of fire reached inside their bodies and destroyed them in an instant. No screams, no flailing limbs. The Garonin were driven into the ground. One moment walking, the next burning and still.

'Back towards the tower complex,' said Suarav. 'Good work, Brynar.'

The group moved quickly. Across in front of them, a stretcher party of civilians wearing blue armbands ran to deal with wounded on the walls. Others in yellow, green and orange bands brought up replacement weapons, got water to any who had the chance to drink but mainly tried to patch up the wounded and clear away the dead.

Xetesk had learned from the mistakes of Julatsa and Lystern. Suarav was pleased. A long way to go yet but so far they held. Frontal defence was not the way. Fight them hand to hand. Spread your force. Keep moving and keep alive. And invest mana in your walls to stop the enemy flooding over you like a spring tide.

'General, look!'

Brynar was pointing up at Densyr's tower. A mass of Garonin fire was trained on it. As Suarav watched, he saw the pinnacle and upper floors buckle and fall. His breath caught in his throat. The weight of falling stone accelerated the collapse of the floors below. The pinnacle itself tumbled almost gracefully down on a cloud of debris, smashing into the dome of the tower complex and breaking through it.

He began to run but knew he was already too late. Nothing could save those within. And as quickly as he had started, he slid to a stop. The collapse halted right above Densyr's dining chamber. A spell flared deep blue beneath the piles of rubble, broken furniture and flapping clothing and drapes. Suarav breathed again.

'He's good, our Lord of the Mount,' said Chandyr.

But Suarav was not smiling yet. He saw the spell and the rubble begin to shift.

'Clear the complex approach. Move, move. Shields above you now!'

He was running again, waving his arms and yelling over and over for people to get out of the way. Timber and stone fell in a torrent. Where it didn't beat straight through the roof of the dome, it bounced and rolled, thundering onto the courtyard and steps in front of the complex doors.

Suarav saw men crushed, others diving and rolling away. He saw mages trying to get shields in place and he saw, from above, more Garonin dropping to the broken roof of the tower.

'Brynar, see to the wounded. Take three guards with you and get blue team to help. The rest of you, Chandyr, Densyr needs us.'

Suarav felt every one of his fifty-nine years. The breath was pained in his chest and his lungs felt clogged with dust. He lengthened his stride. The violent heaving of the courtyard under his feet took him completely by surprise and sent him sprawling on his face.

For a moment he thought he'd imagined it, but when he got

himself back to his feet, he saw cracks in the courtyard cobbles and people everywhere brushing themselves down. A curious quiet fell across the whole college. The Garonin weapons had fallen silent and all that could be heard was the wheezing of the machine and the cracks of lightning in the detonation cloud.

It was a quiet short-lived. A wailing blare came from the floating machine and a melodious call from the mouth of every Garonin. As one, their weapons turned on Densyr's tower and an extraordinary weight of fire deluged the ancient bound stone.

The courtyard rippled again, and this time, from beneath the stones, he saw a flash of blue light.

All three mages had Ilkar's Defence spells running and spread on as broad a front as they could manage. The intensity of Garonin fire scorched paper inside the wrecked chamber as the heat spiralled.

Sol tried to protect his family as best he could. Auum and his Tai had fled the chamber to join Thraun's attack on the Garonin directly above. Sirendor was trying desperately to keep Hirad from suffocating. Ilkar, Densyr and Dystran, faces drawn into rictus grins by the strain, were clinging on but the Julatsan was struggling. Ilkar was quivering all over and a strangled choke was being dragged from his throat.

'Can't do this,' he croaked.

'Hang on, Ilkar. Hang on.'

But Sol didn't know what for or for how long. In his chair Septern twitched and muttered. They had felt the heaving of the floor beneath them and Dystran had shouted something about the Heart but that was all.

'Re. Re. Pel.' Septern's eyes opened briefly, fluttered and closed again. 'Fo . . . usss.'

Blue flame encased the tower. Denser and Dystran screamed and clutched at their heads. Defence spells failed. Enemies dropped into their midst, followed by the feet and blades of the TaiGethen. A wind howled through the tower, threatening to pluck them all from their precarious perch and throw them down to their deaths.

Sol crouched and laid his arms across his family. The flame gathered density; it curled and twisted into a spire above them, wreathing and pulsing. The pressure built quickly. Septern was juddering in his chair as if shaken by unseen hands. Densyr was flat on his back, tears streaming from his eyes. Dystran was unconscious.

The Garonin fire increased but every tear that hit the mana spire deflected harmlessly away. The spire's blue deepened almost to black and a spear of mana punched upwards and crashed into the underside of the machine, knocking it sideways through the air. The carriage hanging beneath it disintegrated in a ball of flame, scattering debris and bodies to fall to the earth.

Briefly, the colour of the spire lightened. Septern squeezed his eyes shut. Another spear shot up. This one skewered the machine's bulbous bell.

'Oh dear God's falling,' whispered Sol.

The machine exploded. White, blue and grey light flashed like hot sun into a blackout room. Flame ripped across the circumference of the bell. Repeated detonations rippled its hide, sending fresh flame clawing at the sky. The shock wave reflected down, rattling the tower and sending a great swathe of heat across the college. Flame dispersed over the cylinder of mana encircling the tower.

The machine hung in tatters in the air for a moment, flaps of burning skin clinging to the ribs of its skeleton, before dipping left and crashing down onto the east walls. Sol could hear the screams of Garonin soldiers. Melodious no more but a lament just the same.

Spells still fell, taking out the remaining invaders. Sol slowly dragged himself to his feet. He could hear cheering from the courtyard. And barked orders. Suarav and Chandyr were still cautious. Sol looked down on his family. Diera was cuddling young Hirad, whose shocked white face stared into his.

'It's all right now, little one,' said Sol. 'It's all over for now.'

'We've won,' breathed Densyr. 'We've actually won.'

Jonas stirred from his slumber in the mind of Sha-Kaan and his face was full of regret.

'No, Lord Densyr, I'm afraid we haven't.'

Chapter 32

TaiGethen had found and secured the old trail that ran from the abandoned, destroyed Wesman fishing village on North Bay. It ran away through the foothills of Sunara's Teeth and down a long tree-studded valley that stretched away out of sight and led, they had to hope, through the mountains and into Wesman lands proper. The valley was broad and its slopes ran up to a jumble of outcrops and crags. It was bleak but the air was fresh. The scents of the land and of Tual's creatures gave the ClawBound panthers a strut to their stride.

While Al-Arynaar disembarked elves on the beach before moving them on in ordered groups to the first of the camps just to the south of the old village, Rebraal was with the forward party, looking for a second campsite. The day was young and the ground was easy. Panthers scouted ahead while their Bound elves ran the flanks of the force of thirty TaiGethen cells and four hundred Al-Arynaar.

Dila'heth was at his side. She, like every Al-Arynaar mage, wore the cloak of loss that Julatsa's fall had thrown about their shoulders. They could still cast, but even the simplest spell had been rendered difficult, tiring and even dangerous.

'How will it feel in our new home?' asked Rebraal.

'Different,' said Dila. 'We have little expectation of being able to cast in a wholly separate dimension. But mana is everywhere, and if it should exist there, we can eventually build a new Heart to focus it. We will have hope for the future once we have arrived home. Here, we have precious little.'

Heat blossomed to their right. The ground heaved and shuddered. Rebraal pitched forward, turning a forward roll before coming back to a crouch. Elves across the force stopped to look. A ClawBound panther's mournful warning echoed against mountain and valley side.

And there they were. Blinking out of nowhere. Standing still for a few moments before marching downslope, firing as they came. Garonin. Hundreds of them.

'Shields!' yelled Rebraal as the first teardrops tore into the Al-Arynaar. 'Dila, get your mages casting whatever they can. Al-Arynaar, we are attacked. Break and skirmish. Go!'

Explosions ripped up the ground at Rebraal's feet. He hurled himself left and rolled into the lee of a standing stone. Back along the elven line, he saw his brothers and sisters ripped to shreds by the concentration of fire from the Garonin weapons. Blood misted in the air, mingling with the screams of the injured and dying.

He drew his blade.

'How did they find us so soon?'

But there was no one to answer. The TaiGethen were on the attack. A ClawBound elf stood astride a Garonin soldier, plunging his sharpened nails into flesh again and again until the white fire blew his head from his shoulders. Time to fight. Time to die. Rebraal raced up the slope, rage blinding his fear.

'Al-Arynaar. For Tual! For Yniss and for your brothers!'

Rebraal ducked under a Garonin weapon and rammed his sword up and into the neck of his enemy. The man gurgled and collapsed. Rebraal pulled his blade clear. Left, the TaiGethen were too quick for the ponderous Garonin. Elves leapt, spun and kicked at the huge invaders. They dropped, rolled and dodged. Their strikes were fast and deadly.

Bodies littered the valley side. Small fires burned all over. Rebraal ran back into the thickening smoke at the centre of the fight. Ten Al-Arynaar were with him. Once the shock of the appearance of the Garonin force had dissipated, the elves had quickly split to surround their foe. With the TaiGethen leading the way, they had got in amongst the Garonin, making every shot they fired a risk to their own.

Ahead of Rebraal, a stream of teardrops pulsed from a weapon, deluging a pair of Al-Arynaar not quick enough to dive aside. The next instant, a TaiGethen boot had kicked the weapon aside and a jaqrui throwing crescent had lodged in its wielder's helmet. The Garonin fell, the last thing he would have seen, the blade that took him through the eye.

Rebraal ran at a tight knot of Garonin. There were five of them, back to back and tracking elves with their weapons but not firing.

Rebraal grunted satisfaction. They were conserving power, no question about it.

'Break up and move in,' said Rebraal. 'Watch them closely. Those weapons will still have plenty in them. Dila. Drop something on them. Anything.'

Dila'heth stopped running and crouched low to begin casting. Rebraal's warriors spread out in a wide arc and closed in, keeping low to the ground and moving fast. All around them weapons still fired. Smoke hung thick over the ground and the screams of the wounded haunted the air.

The enemy saw them coming and weapons were brought to bear. Rebraal prayed to Tual to guide the hands of his warriors and deflect those of his enemies. And then Dila'heth's spell struck. The cone of pure mana rammed into the Garonin. Shielded as they were from many offensive spells, they had little defence against the bludgeoning force Dila sent against them. Three were downed; the other two scrambled left and right to escape a similar fate.

Rebraal sprinted in, calling his warriors to him. They fell on the helpless enemy, leaping to hack and slash at heads and necks. This was close to frenzy and Rebraal did not like the way it felt. He saw the lust in the eyes of some of his warriors. Rebraal stooped to deal a quick killing blow to the last Garonin and stood back.

'Remember who you are,' he said. 'We are Al-Arynaar. Keepers of our faith. Leaders of our people. Fight and fight well.'

He turned to look out over the battlefield. A weapon sounded from close by. Teardrops ripped through a cloud of smoke. He dived left but one caught his right arm, sending him spinning to the ground. His sword fell from his hand and he cried out as a burning pain hit him with nauseating force.

Rebraal clutched his right forearm and brought his hand up to his face where he lay writhing on the ground. His wrist was smashed. The skin was blackened across his hand and down almost to his elbow. He could see gory daylight through the centre of his arm where the teardrop had cut straight through him. The smell of burned flesh clogged his nostrils.

He screamed until the breath left him. And then he dragged in another breath and screamed again. It was like nothing he had ever experienced. A crawling agony that filled his arm and his entire body. He barely felt the comforting hands on him. He could see nothing beyond his ruined limb. A cool palm caressed his forehead and the pain ebbed away.

Rebraal was brought to a sitting position. Dila'heth was in front of him. Behind her, another cone of mana struck the Garonin who had fired, but this time it seemed to slide past him. Yet the adaptation to the spell did not help him. A TaiGethen elf whirled past him, slicing a cut deep into his chest through his shining armour, and a ClawBound panther sprang and tore out his throat.

The valley side was silent but for the breeze blowing the smoke gently away and the cries of those still in pain. Rebraal swallowed and looked at his arm again. He felt sick. The wound, blackened and cauterised, looked even larger than it had the first time. He could not move his fingers and a dull ache was spreading down from his shoulder.

'Oh Dila,' he said. 'Look what they've done to me.'

'You'll be all right,' she said. 'In time. You still have your hand and we can make the nerves regrow. Be strong, Rebraal.'

The Garonin were in full retreat but they had nowhere to go. With the TaiGethen after them, they chose cowardice rather than valour and began to blink out of existence. Dila'heth bent to her task. She whispered words Rebraal could not understand and placed her hand around his wrist.

A moment's intense heat was washed away by a freezing cold that penetrated the wound and spread up his arm, numbing all sensation. Rebraal watched while the blackened, burned skin began to pale at his elbow and recede downwards towards the centre of the wound, turning to a healthy tone.

When he looked back up at her, Dila was done, and the slump in her shoulders and the sweat on her brow told of her efforts. Rebraal could still see the wound clearly enough. It was red raw and the ache was spreading in again. But he had some movement in his hand now.

'It will need bandaging and cleaning. I can do no more. It will heal completely, given time.'

Rebraal rose to his feet and reached out for Dila to help her up. He pulled her into an embrace.

'Tual will reward you every day for all that you have ever done in his service,' he said. 'Walk with me. I will support you.'

But there was to be nowhere to go. A flat harsh sound echoed from the mountains, pressing on the ears. The Garonin attack had been a mere prelude. From within the clouds vydospheres descended gracefully. Four of them in the valley. Rebraal stared back towards the beach and the open sea. He could count another five, hanging above the last remnants of the elven race and waiting to pounce.

Garonin soldiers appeared in their hundreds and thousands. High on the peaks and on both sides of the valley. Elves began to move back down to the centre of the path. TaiGethen and ClawBound set up a perimeter and waited for the attack, yet none appeared imminent.

'They have us,' said Rebraal. 'They must have been tracking us all along.'

'Why don't they attack? Why are they waiting?'

'I really have no idea,' said Rebraal.

'What can we do?'

'At the moment, nothing. They have the numbers to slaughter us before we get close to them. Until the TaiGethen report a weakness, we can do nothing but sit and wait.'

'For what?'

Rebraal looked at her and shrugged. 'The end.'

'Father, you have to make him listen to me,' said Jonas. 'Please, there isn't much time.'

'Jonas, we hear you,' said Densyr. 'But we have to get out of this tower.'

'But you aren't listening.'

'Jonas!' snapped Sol. 'Wait. Let me deal with it.'

Dystran and Densyr were standing over Septern.

'He's dead, isn't he?' said Ilkar.

Densyr nodded. 'A true hero. He saved all of us.'

'Forget the pathos,' said Sol. 'Now we have to find another who can perform the ritual. And we won't do so standing up here in this teetering edifice.'

Densyr straightened. 'You cannot seriously be thinking of going through with your suicide on behalf of the dead? There's no need. We've won.'

'It is a small victory in a war you will still lose,' said Auum. 'You should be listening to Jonas.'

Densyr tensed and bit down on a retort. Instead, he took a moment to calm himself.

'I am listening. But do you not agree that whether the Garonin are gone or merely pausing for breath, we need to get down from this tower with anyone who can stand the trip.'

'Not entirely,' said Dystran, his voice a little distant. 'Right now I am holding the grid from feeding back, just like before. One of us has to stay here until the other reaches the catacombs and can organise a team to dismantle the grid piece by piece.'

Sol spread his hands. 'Fine. You two sort it out amongst yourselves. But the rest of us need to go. This structure is plainly unsafe. And we need to hear from my son about why it isn't over.'

'And where exactly do you think you'll be going?' asked Densyr.

He checked with Dystran that he was acting as buffer safely and rose to face Sol.

'Where I should have gone long before you interfered. I should have listened to Hirad from the start.'

'I shouldn't have to remind you that you are the King of Balaia whether you like it or not and we have just scored a huge victory. What signal does you running west send out, do you think?'

'How about that we are still in massive danger and the king is searching for an escape route should the worst happen.'

Densyr shook his head. 'I cannot let you do that. I cannot have my people deserting this city on a fool's quest for a promised land.'

Sol straightened. He was taller than Densyr by almost a head.

'*Your* people? Since when did you own them? The days of college fiefdoms are over and have been for hundreds of years. The people will do what they want.'

'I don't think so, Sol.'

'You know, standing here all alone, with your big ally stuck next to the Heart, you are not in a position to demand or expect anything at all.'

Densyr shrugged. 'Go then. We fought well here and there are more fights to come. But if you would rather run, turn your back and flee like a coward, then do so. And take your elves and your dead with you. And the zoo animals. Xetesk needs none of you.'

Sol glanced briefly over his shoulder and stepped right up to Densyr. He could smell the other man's sweat and the taint of ash and dust on his clothes. And the acid reek of mana from recently cast magic.

'You are fortunate my family are in this room,' said Sol quietly. 'Questioning my courage is very, very dangerous. Jonas, what are you doing?'

His eye had been drawn by Jonas leading Diera and young Hirad to the door, what little was left of it.

'Mother said you are posturing and it is pathetic. I just know it won't make any difference who is braver and who stands and fights. They are coming back.'

'Let them come,' said Densyr. 'We have beaten them once already and we will do so again.'

Auum and his Tai fell into place by Sol's family. Sirendor and Thraun picked up Hirad and began a cautious descent with Ilkar walking in front of them. Auum directed Miirt and a rather shaky Ghaal to follow them down the rubble-strewn stairs. The Lord of the TaiGethen paused.

'The proud do not listen to the wise,' he said. 'Their eyes are blind to the path and the only scent in their nostrils is glory. You have done well but you have beaten nobody. Yet here you stand in the ruins of your majesty and claim victory. The proud celebrate alone and fleetingly.'

Auum spun on his heel and was gone, Sol's family following him at his nod of consent.

'I'm sorry it had to end this way,' said Sol.

'We made a fine team,' said Densyr.

'I thought so. Perhaps I was wrong all along.'

'Don't think ill of me, Sol. I have done only what I thought was right.'

Sol sighed and the regret felt heavy enough to slump his shoulders. 'Oh, Densyr, what else can I think?'

Pressure beat down. Crushing. Bowing the shoulders and weakening the knees. It funnelled into the ears and dragged at the eyes. It tightened the throat and sent the heart into arrhythmia. Densyr clutched at his chest and fell to his knees. Sol staggered, gripping on to a fallen timber and trying to look up through the ruined ceiling. He heard someone stumble and fall on the stairs not far below. Wolves whined.

A piercing sound cut through the fog of Sol's consciousness, quickly falling to a low drone and then fading away altogether. The pressure eased. Sol helped Densyr back to his feet. The two men stared at one another for a moment, Sol seeing virgin doubt in Densyr's eyes.

They looked up.

Five machines descended through the cloud to ring the college. The flat blare of their horns shivered broken glass to splinters. Densyr's mouth hung open but his lower jaw moved a little as he tried to form the word 'no'. Sol almost felt sorry for him. But not as sorry as he felt for all those people denied the chance to run west days ago. Before it was too late.

Densyr snapped quickly out of his shock and hurried to Dystran. 'You can't stay here,' he said.

Dystran, lost in the mana spectrum and embraced by the Heart, smiled. 'Nor can I leave. It is fitting. One lone soul. They will not seek me here. I will hold on for as long as I can but I will not let them take the Heart.'

'I understand,' said Densyr. He got back to his feet and turned to Sol. 'How fast can you run?'

Every pace down the stairs sent shivers of pain through Sol's back, hip and scorched scalp. He trailed Densyr by a few steps and was determined not to fall too far behind the Lord of the Mount. The air was full of screams and shouts for order and to arms. Already, the spells were flying and the white tears were crashing to the earth.

'Where are we going?' called Sol.

'The catacombs. We have to catch up with the others, stop them going outside.'

Sol imagined his family trying to escape across the college court-yard and his blood chilled in his veins. He ran faster.

'Diera!' he bellowed. 'Catacombs. Keep on going down to the catacombs.'

The tower shuddered under multiple impacts. Loose stone tumbled and bounced down the stairs after them. Round and round, down and down. Dust clogged the stairway below. Sol could smell the aftermath of fires and the sick stench of blood and innards.

They hurtled down the last few stairs, jumped a body that lay across the bottom step and out into the dome. It was carnage. Much of the roof had collapsed. Corpses were flattened and smeared beneath it. Stone was scorched and scattered, mixed with body parts.

The main doors had been splintered. Outside, defensive groups were fighting hard but the weight of enemy fire was enormous. Sol silently wished them all luck and searched the wreckage for his family. Instead, he and Densyr saw Brynar, standing by the entrance to the catacombs. He looked terribly pale and blood oozed from where he held his hands to his stomach.

'They've gone down before you,' he wheezed.

'Come with us,' said Densyr. 'We can fix you.'

'Why down there? The Heart is there. They are coming there to take it.'

'But not yet; we have a spell to cast. Get healed and help me. We have to find Sharyr quickly.'

Densyr was pushing Brynar towards the entrance. Sol came to his other side.

'Come on, lad. You can make it. Let me do the saving this time, eh?'

Brynar smiled and blood dribbled from the corner of his mouth. 'If you insist. Which spell, my Lord?'

Densyr risked a quick glance at Sol.

'The Ritual of Opening.'

Sol almost tripped on the first flight of stairs. 'When we get him to some help, you had better keep on running, Densyr. Because if I catch you I am going to flatten your stupid fucking head.'

'Promises, promises. Don't be naïve, Sol. This is a blood sacrifice. We used to specialise in this sort of thing. Borrowed it from the Wesmen a thousand years ago.'

'But I thought only Septern—'

'Not you too, Brynar. All spells that deal with the travel, transport and destruction of souls derive from the same lore. Sol, I need to tell you it is the same base theory that was behind the capture of souls in the Soul Tank for placing the Protectors in thrall.'

For the second time Sol almost tripped. He felt a cold sweat on his forehead and a numbness through his body.

'I don't want to hear this.'

'But it isn't the same. Trust me; I know how to do this. Theoretically.'

'Theoretically?'

'It's been a long time since we asked for volunteers to commit suicide.'

A chuckle escaped Sol's lips. He stopped moving, forcing Densyr to do likewise. Brynar groaned.

'And why the change of heart? What happened to selfishness and cowardice?'

Densyr winced.

'I'm sorry,' he whispered.

'Gods drowning, Densyr, thousands will die because of your stubbornness.'

'I didn't think they could continue reinforcing, Sol. I really believed they would retreat from us. But they hate us, don't they? They hate us more than they need their precious fuel, and it drives them to keep on coming back in greater numbers. I can't beat five of those things. I got it wrong.'

'Finally you open your eyes.'

'Now all I can do is help others survive. I'll face my guilt and, Gods falling, it's everywhere already.'

Sol moved on.

'My heart bleeds.' Sol grunted. 'When you make a mistake it's always a fucking belter, isn't it? Which way?'

They had reached the bottom of the stairs and entered the first of the hub rooms from which multiple passages led. The elves, the Raven and his family were waiting for them.

'Glad you could make it,' said Ilkar. 'But what's he doing here?'

'Attempting redemption,' said Sol.

'Do we have that much time?' asked Ilkar.

'No, we don't.' Densyr nodded his head. 'Straight on. We need Sharyr, Vuldaroq, a couple of old books and a mage to trip the evacuation alarm ward.'

'Where are we going?' asked Sirendor.

'To a new world via a very old one,' said Sol.

And he dared not look at Diera because he would have seen her tears start to fall.

Chapter 33

General Suarav roared with frustration when the alarm sounded. The system had been put in place after the demon wars to ensure the populace was never ensnared again as it had been a decade ago. A line of wards had been set in the city, maintained by the merest trickle of mana. The key ward was in the catacombs and it triggered the energy to release the rest.

The alarm was simple. Four tones, rising in pitch over an octave and repeating quickly until the Lord of the Mount declared the emergency ended. Suarav crouched in the shelter of one of Xetesk's long-room doorways and gazed balefully out at the Garonin machines hanging in the air above the college. He thought the alarm might well sound forever.

Every Xeteskian citizen knew what they had to do. Flee the city by whichever gate and by whichever means. Bring food, water and clothing. Bring weapons if you had them, particularly hunting weapons. Be prepared for a long time in the open and on the run. Head for your allotted rendezvous point. Do not return to the city if you value your life.

'We can still fight,' said Chandyr. 'We lost none of our teams after the initial bombardment. The shielding works and the binding on the walls is strong. Let the population run. We are sworn to protect city and college. Let us not shirk that responsibility.'

Suarav nodded. 'The Circle Seven are all still in the catacombs. I will not abandon them.'

He turned to the rest of those gathered with him. He saw fear and he saw determination.

'Are you with me?' asked Suarav. Five mages and twelve guards nodded. 'With courage we can hold them long enough.'

'Why do they wait?' asked Chandyr. 'Surely they presume their force to be overwhelming.'

The bombardment of white tears had ceased temporarily. Smoke drifted across the college from multiple fires.

'They are cautious,' said one of the mages. 'Nervous even. That we could unleash such destruction without warning.'

'The trouble is, none of us knows what the hell that blue spear was, do we?' said Suarav.

'But then, neither do they,' said Chandyr. 'And, like us, they have no idea if it is repeatable. Presumably that is why they've been targeting Densyr's tower. And it still stands.'

Suarav faced his squad. 'Then let's waste no time. Mages, I need a shield. Let's find every group we can and set up the defence of the tower complex as far as we can. You are brave people and I am proud to serve with you. Face whatever comes with spirit and we will see the enemy defeated yet or at least bring our masters to safety. And while we may all lose our lives, we must not be careless with them. Every moment we resist allows our citizens time to escape. Your loved ones and mine. For Xetesk, city and college of magic.'

'For Xetesk!'

Suarav led his team out onto open ground. The five Garonin machines hung in the sky like giant insects waiting the chance to strike. Their drones combined to form a modulating bass over which the Xeteskian evacuation alarm rose in discord. Suarav saw people emerging from every door in the college to make their escape.

There was no move from the enemy to stop them. After their initial bombardment they were, without question, waiting and assessing their options. The city of Xetesk had been rich with mana but that was now largely collected or spent. The greatest prize on the continent was ensconced deep in the catacombs and any enemy, even one as powerful as the Garonin, should be wary of the task ahead.

Assuming they could not hack straight down through the-Gods-knew-how-much-rock to expose the Heart, an assault corridor by corridor, chamber by chamber was their only option. It meant a large number of soldiers were likely to descend at any given moment and try to gain access to the catacombs by the single entrance.

'Bottleneck,' he said.

'Sir?' asked a mage running along bedside him.

'I've had an idea.'

The barrage had ceased but the tension was unremitting. Having released Brynar to a healer mage, Densyr had led them through numberless twists and turns until they stood as far from the entrance as it was possible to get while still being in habitable chambers. It felt cold and unfriendly so far from the surface.

The chambers he had brought them to were joyless. Hardly a picture hung. There were no coverings for the uneven floor, and while braziers could be lit to generate plenty of light, there was no heat here. No fireplace and flue. There were three workbenches ranged across the far wall underneath a set of blackboards. Chairs stood where they had been abandoned by mages in a hurry. A dark, heavy-timbered door was set into the right-hand wall.

'You really know how to make your guests feel at home, don't you?' said Ilkar. 'What was this, some sort of torture chamber or something?'

Densyr didn't rise to the bait. 'This was the dimensional research section. You won't fail to see the scorch marks on the walls nor yet ignore the faint scent of blood that still hangs in here.'

Sirendor stepped into the centre of the dusty chamber, which measured perhaps thirty feet on a side.

'I'll take it. When can I move in?'

Sol led his family in and took Jonas and young Hirad to a couple of high-backed dining chairs that stood on the left-hand side below an artist's impression of colliding dimensions.

'I'm failing to see anything amusing about our position,' he growled. 'Densyr, get yourself sorted as quickly as you can. There is pain here for the living and the dead.'

Auum and his Tai moved silently across the chamber to the corner opposite the door and knelt to pray. Thraun laid Hirad on one of the workbenches and signalled Ilkar to look at him. Diera did not leave Sol's side.

'With every breath I dream you'll return to your senses,' she said. 'Don't do this, Sol. Don't leave us here alone.'

'If I don't do this, there is no hope for any on Balaia,' said Sol. 'And, believe me, I would not be volunteering unless I felt we truly had no other choice.'

'That's not true. Any one can be the . . .' Diera dropped her voice to a whisper with their sons so close. '. . . sacrifice. Please, Sol, think of us.'

'I am, Diera.' Sol closed his eyes. There truly was nothing else in his mind. 'And there is no one else. This isn't to be a walk through fallen leaves: it will be challenged by the Garonin every step of the way. A leader must take those steps. I am their king. It has to be me.'

Diera threw up her hands and turned her attention on Densyr, who was looking anxious and impatient.

'And you. I thought you were on my side. You of all people know how selfish this is. How dare you change your mind and, worse, how dare you be prepared to aid my husband in his stupidity.'

Densyr let his shoulders sag a little. 'But is it?'

The door opened. In walked Vuldaroq and Sharyr, arms laden with texts. Vuldaroq's eyes blazed with curiosity.

'You know it is,' said Diera. 'No guarantee of any kind of success. In fact the only certainty is that for him there is no turning back.'

'But look outside,' said Densyr. 'We cannot defend against such force.'

'So you're prepared to take any chance to save your own skin even if it means pushing the head of a friend beneath the surface? Why aren't you putting yourself forward, O Lord of the Mount?'

'The caster cannot enter the opening.'

'How convenient.'

'You have me wrong, Diera,' said Densyr. 'I will not attempt to explain my errors of the past few days. It hardly matters now. But you should know that, succeed or fail, I am not leaving Xetesk. While anyone is left to fight the Garonin, I will stand with them. But I can no longer expect my people to do the same. I want them to escape.'

'So noble,' said Diera. 'Offering the hand of salvation to strangers and the hand of a murderer to your oldest friend.'

'Diera,' said Sol. 'Please.'

'Please what? Shut up and sit primly by my sons and watch you die?'

A heavy sound struck through the catacombs. Like a giant fist had been slammed against the upper level. Dust was dislodged.

'That doesn't sound so good,' said Ilkar.

'We're as safe as we can be,' said Sharyr, spreading out texts on a bench and beginning to pull them open.

'There is no comfort in that,' said Diera.

Sol took Diera's arm and turned her away from the awkwardness she was generating.

'I cannot let you disrupt this. I need you to be strong for the boys. Make them understand.'

'How can I make them understand what I do not?'

Sol smiled. 'You understand perfectly well. You just don't like what you're hearing.'

'Well we agree there.'

'There will be time for us. Before I . . .' Sol trailed away.

It wasn't just for her he could not finish his sentence. He was only just clinging on to his own courage too. Diera sagged and let herself be drawn into his arms. Sol looked over her head and saw the mages getting to work.

'What will happen afterwards? When you go into this opening or whatever it is?' she asked.

'I really don't know. I know where we will end up but not how it will feel to travel.'

'I don't mean that. I mean what will you actually be able to *do*.'

Sol was silent just a heartbeat too long. 'It's all about belief.'

'What's that supposed to mean? That is the lamest answer I've ever heard you give.'

'But that's the point, isn't it?' Sol began to find himself. 'Those with the belief can function. Can achieve what they intend.'

'So this is just one big leap of faith, is that it?'

Sol shrugged. 'Yes.'

He saw Diera contemplate a retort but she changed tack instead. 'How will they, you know . . .'

'The Xeteskian library of nerve toxins is extensive. It'll be quick and it'll be painless, I promise.'

'Promise me one more thing.'

'Almost anything.'

'That I give it to you. Give you the cup or whatever it is. It has to be me.'

'Why?'

She stared up into his eyes. 'Because every moment with you is a lifetime's worth.'

Densyr watched Sol and Diera's embrace. He saw the pain and the tenderness, the strength and the fear. His own mind was in turmoil. The appearance of the five Garonin machines had sent him into a spiral, he could see that now. He had rushed here, defaulted to the wisdom of The Raven and Auum as so often in the past.

'This is reckless,' he said. 'Surely it cannot work.'

Vuldaroq's shaking hands paused in the act of turning a page.

'When all other options have been exhausted, what else is there but desperation?'

'I arrested him for his own good. To stop him walking to his death with his eyes closed. Now I'm about to give him a helping hand along the road. Diera is right. I am weak.'

'What difference does it make now?' said Ilkar, moving close to him and dropping his voice. 'No way out but this. You do see that, don't you?'

'I don't really know what to think. I still don't see how doing this will get you to a new cluster of dimensions or anywhere but oblivion. I can see the conviction in your eyes and in his but I can see the sorrow in Diera's too, and I will have to face that once the ritual is complete. What can I say to her?'

'Nothing,' said Ilkar. 'Except to trust that we are right.'

'But this isn't like Sol marching off with his sword strapped to his back. He is going to die and she will never know his embrace again.'

Ilkar bowed his head, unable to hold Densyr's gaze.

'Yet it is the only way for her and the boys to live.'

Densyr's heart was pounding painfully. 'I have to be sure that is true.'

'What's done is done, Densyr, and you cannot undo what you did to us and the cost of delay. But know that we are not changing our position. We have not ever since we were thrust back here. The pain grows every day. The longer we are kept here the more attractive the prospect of letting go and disappearing into the void becomes.

'We have never looked to defeat the Garonin and we are not suddenly seeing this as our last option. It has always been the only option for the populations of Balaia and Calaius. We were never here to live again on Balaia.

'Densyr . . . it's me. Ilkar. And it's Thraun, Sirendor and Hirad too. We need your help. You've come so far down the road. Don't turn away from us again.'

Densyr looked beyond Ilkar and saw Diera. Her gaze implored him to step back. Outside, the pounding was relentless. It echoed through the catacombs and sent vibrations through the stone beneath his feet. He fancied he could hear screaming but that was surely a trick of the mind.

'We are ready, my Lord Densyr,' said Sharyr quietly, his voice clanging like a bell in the silence that had fallen.

Densyr acknowledged him with a curt nod. He bowed to Diera and looked square at Ilkar.

'Let's get started,' he whispered.

Dystran sought the purity Septern had achieved. He was only dimly aware of the pounding of weapons against the walls of Densyr's tower. In all his years he had never been so deep in the mana spectrum. He felt almost as if he were swimming, his mind was so free. It was as frightening as it was uplifting. He was unsure if he would be able to find his way back to himself.

Perhaps that should not scare him. Returning to his body was probably pointless. He could cruise here in the embrace of the Heart of his beloved Xetesk or he could die as the tower inevitably collapsed. Here he felt safe though he could not entirely divorce himself from his physical bonds.

And that was what Septern had been able to do. His soul had been clinging on to an alien body, always in pain, always at risk of being swallowed by the void. But he had found a new place to go and had used himself to focus the Heart as a weapon.

'Are you still here?' asked Dystran. 'Are you truly gone or are you part of the Heart now?'

Silence.

The Heart of Xetesk was beautiful. The hourglass shape of infinity. Glorious deep blue mana coalescing and moving in the dance of power around the dark stone. A sight only a mage could ever see. Hundreds, thousands of lines disappeared from the core. Links to everywhere and to mages drawing on the bedrock of their talent to cast. And all in defence of their college.

Dystran felt a gentle buffeting. The remains of Septern's grid were still dangerous. The power held within was not bleeding away as he had hoped; rather it was building up at critical nodes. It was an irritation in his search for a way to repeat what the master mage had done.

The fluctuation from the Heart took him completely by surprise. A mass of mana, like a skull trailing fire, burst from its centre, upsetting the dance of power. It scorched the edges of his mind as it plunged deep into the ground. Dystran tried to track its movement but it was gone so quickly. Someone was casting something ancient and terrible.

The Heart had not regained its placidity before huge shapes

appeared on the periphery of his senses. Spasmodic with clashing mana and reaching towards him with tendrils that became arms ending in claws, opening and closing, grabbing. Five of them.

They were seeking him and soon they would find him.

Dystran retreated within himself and called out for aid.

Chapter 34

The next impact cast Suarav from his feet and sent him rolling down the shattered steps of the tower complex. He scrabbled upright and backed away a few paces. His team had been scattered but all seemed to be moving. The brief hurricane of air had been forced out of the broken doors, catching them square on. Left and right, other teams still stood under their shields while mages tried desperately to shore up the weakening bindings of the towers that made up the circle of six and the seat of the Lord of the Mount.

Tower Prexys was teetering. A hole had been driven through it on a diagonal from upper chambers to servants' quarters. The pinnacle was rocking. Slate and stone was tumbling onto what remained of the complex's dome.

'Oh dear Gods burning,' breathed Suarav. He began to run. 'Cover. Cover! Prexys is falling! Shields now.'

In the darkest moments of the worst nightmares of any Xeteskian, the towers of the college would fall, signalling the end of everything. So it was that Suarav felt tears welling as he shouted his warnings. He could see it with his own eyes and still he didn't believe it.

In front of him, mages were casting. No longer were there any hands on the stonework of the complex, feeding binding spells into the towers. Instead, shield after shield ghosted into existence, hoping to shelter men and women from the falling tower. Suarav ducked back under cover by Chandyr, who sported a deep cut on his left cheek from a flying piece of debris. His expression was bleak, his eyes betraying fading hope.

'That we should see this day,' he said.

'Strength, old friend,' said Suarav, wiping the tears from his face.

Prexys bulged a third of its way down as the weight above defeated the compromised structure below. The rending sound ricocheted across the courtyard. Beams snapped, steel supports sheared. Bricks and slabs of stone broke free. The pinnacle collapsed inwards. Wood and slates thundered through the weakened structure causing fatal damage.

Slowly, desperately, Prexys toppled. Showering loose stone and glass, the top section fell to the east, its ragged end cannoning into the bottom section, ripping away what little support remained. Every head turned to watch. Chandyr clutched Suarav's shoulder.

Three hundred feet tall. Over a thousand years old in its current form and a survivor of wars, the mana storms of the last days of the One magic, and the worst nature could throw. Tens of thousands of tons of stone, flashing with the breaking of bound mana, came down. The two sections struck the complex roof one after the other, bursting through or sliding from it. A torrent of crushing weight followed by a storm of choking dust. And a barrage of noise so deep and intense it drew a scream from Suarav's mouth.

Around the edge of the complex, far from the collapse, people hugged each other until it was over. Inside the damage zone, mages fought to keep their shields strong enough to deflect even the largest slab of masonry. Not all succeeded. The sheer mass of stone sent a shock wave throughout the whole complex. Thirty yards to Suarav's left, the wall of the dome blew out, simply sweeping away the team that had been standing there. When the dust cleared enough to see, there was nothing to show that they had been there at all.

The echoes of the fall rippled away. Stones still tumbled over one another inside the dome. Everywhere was coated with a thick film of dust and more fell all the while. In the sky, the Garonin machines readied for another assault.

'What do we do now?' yelled a mage into Suarav's face. 'Look what they've done. First of seven. First of seven.'

'Control your fear. We cannot afford to lose anyone to despair,' said Suarav.

'So much for binding the walls and forcing a bottleneck at the catacombs,' said Chandyr. 'They're going straight through the ground, aren't they?'

Suarav nodded. He dared a glance up. One of the machines was all but prepared. Above it, the sky was dark with a swirling cloud, but beneath it, right below the carriage suspended underneath, a dazzling light shone. It was coiled about by mist and fog. While he watched, the light moved from yellow to white, the mist thickened and a beam struck down. It bored through the dome roof where Prexys had been and caused devastation in the catacombs that he was scared even to

consider. The beam moved in a tight circle and then shut off, leaving
an edge around his vision.

'We cannot reach them,' said Chandyr. 'Their foot soldiers are
dispersed through the city, hunting down our people. We should try
and protect those we can.'

'Our duty is here,' said Suarav.

'But we can do nothing.'

'We can bind the walls more strongly, we can invest in the stone of
the catacombs. Spread a shield across the whole damned place. I
don't know, but we have to find a way. I am not leaving here without
the Lord of the Mount.'

But as he watched the machines in the sky and saw the cloud pillar
moving ever faster as yet another detonation built within it, he
wondered at his own mind. Because this didn't smell like mana
collection any more. More like straightforward annihilation.

' "Where the door lies, the elders know, yet their voices are silent," '
intoned Densyr, reading from one of the scripts Sharyr held for him.
' "Entry is only granted to those free of their mortal shackles. Free to
travel, free to find rest. Their Gods shall guide them and their souls
shall know peace." '

He waved the parchment away.

'So speaks the lore of Xetesk.'

Densyr knelt on the stone floor facing Sol and Diera. Young Hirad
and Jonas were still in the room and Vuldaroq had managed to move
close enough to them to offer any comfort he could. Auum's Tai had
not lifted their heads from their prayer.

Densyr's back was straight and his hands rested in his lap. From
what Ilkar could gather of the technical part of the lore Densyr had
read out, this casting was as much meditation as mana shape building. Another day, in another life, Ilkar would have been fascinated by
the whole process. But right now all he wanted was for it to be over.

From the moment Ilkar had known Densyr was actually prepared
to perform the ritual, the pain in his borrowed body had deepened
and the gale trying to snatch his soul away to the void had strengthened. To such an extent indeed that he found it a challenge to hear
anything that was being said and harder still to concentrate. A quick
glance at Sirendor and Thraun told him they felt the same. Hirad
surely would not last long with his defences so low.

'I will now perform the ritual. It has no words but it requires peace. Please, then, do not speak until I do. Sol, Diera. When the ritual requires its soul of free will, the shape will be stable enough for you to have the time you need.'

Sol nodded. Diera looked blank and confused.

'If it is a lengthy process, we may need to stabilise Hirad again,' said Sharyr.

'Do it quietly, then,' said Densyr. 'I—'

The chamber shook. Braziers rattled in their brackets. One of the chalkboards broke free at a corner and leaned out from the wall. The workbenches juddered. Ilkar clutched at Sirendor to steady himself. The vibration went on and on. The sound of a huge rock fall reached them and the rumble echoed away like thunder in the Blackthorne Mountains.

'What was that?' asked Jonas.

Densyr and Sharyr both had the same thought. Sharyr put it into words.

'I fear the circle of seven is broken,' he said, his voice small.

Densyr brushed dust from his clothing. 'Then I have no time to waste. It begins.'

There was the slightest reaction on Densyr's face as he tuned into the mana spectrum. His mouth moved silently, reminding himself of the process he must follow. His head fell slowly forward towards his chest and his hands came to his temples. He pressed in with middle and forefingers.

Ilkar saw each tiny twitch in Densyr's eyelids as he drew the shape of the casting together. Ilkar had always loved to watch a consummate mage at work and Densyr was certainly one such. Efficient, economical and accurate. Every movement was precise, every slight error corrected without pause or panic.

The temperature of the chamber began to decrease. A deep grey mist formed slowly above Densyr's head.

'What—'

'Shh, Hirad,' whispered Jonas. 'Just watch.'

Ilkar thought he saw the tiniest of smiles flicker across Densyr's expression. The mist expanded, like corn seeds scattered over water separating and spreading. It was set about five feet above Densyr's face, which was turned upwards to see his work. It was no bigger than a quarter-light window.

Densyr took his hands from his temples and clasped them in front of his chest. His eyes closed and he became perfectly still. His breathing slowed and deepened and the pause between each inhalation grew. Ilkar dropped into the mana spectrum and suppressed a gasp.

It was beautiful. The mist was wreathed in strands of mana, each one pulling out at a different angle to keep the mist taut in its frame, as it were. And from Densyr's upturned face came a gentle stream of deep blue, wispy and shot through with light. It was as if he was giving of his own soul to the construct.

Ilkar nodded his appreciation and tore himself away and back to the chamber. Diera was staring at the mist while her arms clutched hard at Sol's waist. He was seated with her on the ground, stroking her hair and whispering. On their chairs, Jonas was still but young Hirad was restless with Densyr's continued meditation. He opened his mouth but this time Vuldaroq turned to him, put a finger to his lips and ruffled his hair with a stick-thin hand.

Ilkar felt a growing pull inside his body. Not painful now but a yearning to recover what was lost and an impatience to begin. He breathed out slowly and deliberately and glanced around. Sirendor and Thraun beckoned him to join them by Hirad. The yearning eased.

Densyr let his head fall forward once more and his hands dropped back into his lap. He rubbed them on his thighs and turned to Sol, his expression sorrowful.

'It is done,' he said. 'Sharyr.'

Sharyr picked up a goblet and brought it to Densyr. The Lord of the Mount held it in a hand that displayed a slight shake.

'Look at me,' he said. 'Just like the early years after the demons left.'

'A shame we can't sit and reminisce about it any more,' said Sol.

'Just one sip will do. But we have diluted the poison with some particularly fine Blackthorne red so you might feel a long draught is in order.'

'How . . . how quickly does it work?' asked Diera, voice admirably steady.

'A matter of moments,' said Densyr. 'And there is no pain.'

'Nothing physical anyway,' she said, trying to smile and bursting into tears instead. 'Sorry, sorry.'

'For what?' asked Ilkar. 'For having more courage than the rest of us put together? Or for marrying a man determined to be a hero even after he's dead?'

It was a weak attempt at humour but the tension released just a little anyway.

'I need you all to leave now,' said Diera. 'You don't have to move Hirad if you don't need to. And you might as well leave Auum too. They don't seem to be taking part any more.'

Ilkar glanced at the elves. Their heads were still bowed in prayer, their arms on each other's shoulders.

'C'mon, let's go. Through here, Densyr?'

'It is marginally more comfortable than the corridor,' said Densyr.

'Jonas, Hirad, come here,' said Sol.

Ilkar ushered Vuldaroq through the door and closed it quietly behind him.

'Jonas, you have important work to do,' said Sol.

'I know what's happening, Father. And I'll be strong and I'll look after everyone for you.'

Sol smiled and put a hand to Jonas's cheek.

'Tell me you really understand,' said Sol.

Jonas swallowed hard and blinked away the moisture in his eyes. 'I know what is in that goblet. And I know you are going to drink it. I know that means I will never see you again but —'

Sol dragged him into a crushing embrace as Jonas broke down, sobbing on his father's shoulder. So much surged through Sol. Conflicts raged within his mind, his heart and his soul. Holding his son so close, smelling his hair and feeling his heaving chest and his breath, all desire to leave deserted him. He didn't care how long he clung on to Jonas. He didn't flinch when another massive impact struck the college but he covered his boy's head to stop the dust falling in his hair.

Sol looked at the goblet placed on the ground near him. The wine and poison had a film of dust on its surface. Sol reached out a hand, ready to knock it flying, scatter the contents across the stone and bring an end to the madness. Sol felt his pulse rattling in his temple and the heat in his face. The tears flowed down his cheeks. Slowly, he pulled Jonas away from him. Their two faces were close together. Jonas wiped Sol's cheek.

'I wish with all my heart you didn't have to do this,' he said. 'But I am proud. Because you always want to save those you love and even those you do not know. Just like you taught me.'

Sol almost choked and his love for his son deepened further than even he thought possible. He saw Diera's face, admiration through the pain. She reached out a hand and stroked Jonas's hair.

'You really are your father's son,' she said. 'Gods falling, but you will keep me strong, I know it.'

'Remember this day,' said Sol. 'Remember this moment. Because it was when you became the man you were destined to be. So much important work lies ahead of you but none more than this. Contact Sha-Kaan. Tell them what we are doing. We need his help on the journey.'

'I will, Father.'

'I love you, Jonas. And from beyond death, I will always do so.'

'One day, we'll stand together again,' said Jonas. 'But I'll be old and grey like you before that happens.'

Sol chuckled. 'I am proud you are my son. And I trust no one more than you to see the family safe. No one.'

Jonas almost burst as he breathed in and stood up. 'I will not let you down, Father.'

'I know you won't.'

Jonas stepped away and let young Hirad come to Sol's embrace.

'And what about you, young man?' he asked.

Hirad's little round face was creased with the anxiety he had picked up around him but there was no genuine understanding in his eyes.

'I want to come with you,' he said brightly.

'Oh, I don't think so,' said Sol. 'Too dangerous. And I need you to look after your mother.'

'When will you be back? You promised to teach me to ride a horse.'

Sol bit his lip. 'Sometimes we cannot do everything we want to do. Sometimes there isn't enough time.'

'But when you come back,' said Hirad.

'I cannot lie to you, young Hirad. Even if you don't understand now, one day you will and it is better that the truth was not hidden from you. So listen.'

Sol shifted his body and hoisted Hirad to sit on his thigh so he could hold the boy close while he spoke.

'I have to go to a place now from which I will not be able to return. I have to go to search for a new place for you to live because it is not safe here any more.'

'But why can't you come back?' There were tears in Hirad's eyes now and a quiver to his voice as the message began to sink in.

'You remember what happened to your grandmother just a little while ago?'

Hirad nodded. 'She died.'

'Yes, she did. And . . . and for me to go to the place I must go, I have to die too. And that means I cannot come back to you because no one can come back when they are dead.'

Hirad frowned. 'Yes, they can. There are lots of them here now. You can do that too, can't you.'

'Get out of that one,' whispered Diera, her hand resting on the back of Sol's neck.

'Well, at the moment, some dead people are here again but they shouldn't be. And when you go to your new home, those people will go to their new home and they are in different places. I will be in the other place.'

'You'll be dead?' asked Hirad.

'Yes, I will,' said Sol quietly. 'So I need to tell you now how much I love you and how proud I am of you.'

'Please don't go!' Hirad threw his arms around Sol's neck and buried his face in Sol's chest. 'I don't want you to go.'

'Neither do I, Hirad,' said Sol, caressing Hirad's head. 'But I have to. Because you and Jonas and your mother have to be safe. That is why I have to go.'

'NO!' screamed Hirad, and his limbs flailed in Sol's embrace. 'You mustn't.'

'I'm sorry, Hirad.' Sol beckoned Jonas closer. 'Goodbye, little one. Remember me as I remember you.'

Sol unpicked Hirad's arms from his neck and released him to Jonas. Hirad was screaming and crying, and Sol had to look away to save himself from breaking.

'Father.'

'Yes, Jonas,' said Sol, turning back.

'Let me down!' shrieked Hirad. 'I want Father. Let me down!'

'Goodbye, Father. I will make him understand.'

'All in good time,' said Sol. 'Go on. It won't get any easier.'

Jonas nodded, smiled and walked quickly to the door, trying to calm the screaming Hirad. Sol watched them go, breathing in every last glimpse. As the door opened, Jonas turned back a final time. Hirad looked up from his shoulder and reached out.

'Goodbye,' said Sol, feeling the sobs building again. 'Know that I love you.'

The door closed on his boys. His world. Diera's hand was on his shoulder. He covered it with one of his own. He turned to look at her. She drew him slowly to his feet and they fell into a long, silent embrace.

Chapter 35

Diera did not want the dance to stop. She moved her hands all over his back and arms, feeling the strength of him and the tenderness. She touched the wound in his lower back and felt him relax into it. She breathed in his scent. Male and powerful, sweat and determination. Belief. Another day it would have been an aphrodisiac too powerful to resist.

His breath was caressing her neck and his hands were stroking her back. They swayed gently where they stood, closer than she could remember for years. Before the visions began.

'I'm sorry I didn't believe you,' she said.

'When?'

Neither of them moved to look at the other. The touch was everything.

'When The Raven came to you in your dreams.'

'I'm glad you didn't,' he said. 'Someone had to challenge me. It's always been you.'

'And are you ready now?'

'No. But I never will be.'

'I love what you said to the boys. They will hurt but they will never feel cheated.'

'I hope not. And what about you?'

'I've felt cheated of you so often it ceases to surprise me,' she said, and did surprise herself by laughing.

'What's so funny?'

'You, my hero husband. Because you ought to be a ridiculous figure but you never were and you never will be.'

'How so?'

'Men puff themselves up for all sorts of stupid things. Trying to make themselves great in the eyes of their women and their children. But you . . . well you just went and did what you had to do every time. Hardly even a backward glance and never any big words. That was hard. Sometimes I wanted you to be all grand and speak about the great good you were setting off to do.'

'You'd have seen straight through that.'

'And you always came back like you'd spent the day at the bakery or something.'

Diera could feel Sol smiling.

'Not this time. And I suppose my grand words lacked a little.'

'Well you've not had a great deal of practice.'

They fell silent again, continuing to sway. But Diera knew it could not go on. Three further impacts rattled through the catacombs, each one sounding closer and more violent than the last. She prised herself away from him and the chill that touched her body was a prelude to all that was to come.

'Come on. I don't want this to be more of a waste than it already is,' she said.

Sol took her by the hand and they walked slowly towards the goblet that sat on the floor beneath the grey, static mist. They stood staring down at it.

'That dust will seriously impair the flavour,' said Sol.

Diera punched his shoulder. 'Don't.'

Sol drew them down. He sat cross-legged on the floor. She let him go and picked up the goblet, caressing it in both of her palms. She gazed down at the liquid that was to kill her husband. A teardrop fell into its centre, rippling the dust. Everything that she had tried to shut from her mind came crashing back in and she felt the strength desert her. Sol had taken the goblet from her, replaced it on the ground and dragged her to him before she gave in. The agony washed over her and through her, wiping away her courage and leaving her only with despair and a desperate longing that felt like a shard of ice in her heart.

'I can't . . .' she began. 'I don't . . . want . . . this.'

'I know, love, I know. Lean into me, let it out.'

And she did. She tried to talk but all that came were mumbles of her anguish. Her cries came out hard, tearing from deep within her and rasping in her throat. Her body quaked in Sol's arms and she thumped uselessly at his chest.

'Don't make me . . . don't make me. Don't leave me alone.'

'My darling, you will never be alone. I will live in you and the boys for as long as you need me.'

'But I cannot reach for you in the night. I cannot feel you close to me.'

'I know, I know.'

Sol's chest was heaving and she felt dampness on her shoulder and the fall of tears on the side of her face. She forced the collision of memories, future fears and current pain from her mind and fought to regain a little control.

'How will I know you have done what you go to do?'

'Because a door will open next to you and you will walk through it and into a new world. A new home where you and the boys can be safe forever.'

'How long will it take?'

'I cannot say, my love. But trust me that I will succeed. Believe in me, and it will make me stronger on my journey. And stay hidden down here, far from the Heart and far from the surface. The enemy will not touch you here. Let Densyr keep you safe. He is returned to himself just in time.'

Diera nodded and let Sol go again. She wiped at her tears with the backs of her hands. Sol cupped her face and kissed her tenderly.

'It was always you who was the true hero,' he said. 'Wherever I was and whoever I fought, you always stood by me, gave me faith. I need you to do that one more time.'

'I will,' whispered Diera.

She leaned to her right and picked up the goblet. Her hand did not shake any more. She sat down beside him, switched the goblet to her left hand and put her right arm about his shoulders. He let out a great shuddering breath.

'I will not fail you,' he said.

'You never do,' she replied.

Diera brought the goblet towards his lips. His right hand came across and held it with her.

'Goodbye, my love. My life was ever sweetened by your presence,' said Sol.

'Goodbye, Sol. Until our souls touch each other again.'

They brought the cup to his lips and after the slightest pause he drank, not stopping until the last of the mixture was gone. Diera took the goblet and laid it on the ground. She put a hand to his cheek and turned his face towards hers. Sol placed both his hands on her, cupping her neck and she did likewise. They held each other's gaze and a lifetime flowed between them.

Sol's eyes blinked slowly. One of his hands fell to his side. She turned him then, leaning his head against her chest so that she could stroke his cheek. Her other hand lay on his chest.

'Rest now, my darling. Rest.'

Above her, the mist cleared and a warmth entered the room, caressing their bodies. Sol's chest rose and fell. It did not rise again.

'Oh Sol. My strength, my brave heart. I love you. Don't leave me. Please don't leave me.'

Diera held her to him and rocked him gently until she felt tender hands about her.

Chapter 36

He felt no pain and no regret. There was no fanfare within to mark his passing. He had no idea what to expect but the memories of words spoken by returning souls. He could see nothing and he did not feel as if he was moving. No sensations touched him and the fact of his solitude did not scare him.

Here was the place between life and death. He knew his soul had left his body, that all he was now was a soul. Slowly, his new awareness and senses, if he could call them that, brought him knowledge of his surroundings. Luminescence, like light seen through closed eyelids. Sound. A rushing, scourging noise, distant and contained. The void, he assumed.

He moved towards the luminescence. It was the only thing in his new reality. Anywhere else he cast his senses, there was nothing at all. He needed to know more. The closer he came, the greater his understanding. Here was a doorway. That meant he was floating in the chamber in the catacombs. The doorway was open. Through it, he could distinctly sense a pathway. That meant his death had indeed completed the spell.

He reached out further. Energy encased the door. Strands of it, keeping it steady while the void beating around outside it fought to snap it shut. He could sense the void more definitely now. A seething ocean of random energies revealed as flecks of yellow-gold and deep bronze in a sea of pale grey.

It was the flecks that added light to the passageway. They shone through its walls. Walls that were not solid, and if he had still possessed a body it would have been like walking on taut canvas. He came to the doorway and reached out.

For the first time he felt fear but it was ephemeral. A sudden clash of light and sound had startled him and he had no reference point for safety. But his act of reaching had triggered something. The pathway fled off to a point he could not make out. The chaotic sounds of the void became muted. And he heard voices. More shockingly, he could see his own hand and he stared down at the shapes it made as he trailed it in front of what he assumed were his eyes, or the soul's equivalent.

'Yes, yes, we all did that. Making blurry motions with our shiny new limbs.'

Sol – he thought of himself as Sol again – turned in the doorway. Shapes were approaching. Like silhouettes formed of a grey light. Slowly, they resolved themselves as they walked towards him. But even if he didn't recognise their shapes yet, he knew the voice.

'Hirad?'

'Yes. Me. Us. Ilkar, Sirendor, Thraun. And a few others who might come in handy although I don't really know how fighting is done here.'

'Where are we?' asked Sol. 'Why do you appear to be walking? I thought souls had no physical form.'

'Interesting, isn't it? I think we're still technically on Balaia at the moment, by the way.' Ilkar. 'It happened the first time I died too. I think the mind can't stop working the way it does when you're alive. Not for a while, anyway. When I got to my rest, this body stuff all faded away and everything changed to bliss.'

'Same here,' said Sirendor.

'What now?' asked Sol.

'You opened the door and you must be the first through it. Then others can follow.' Thraun.

'And it leads to Ulandeneth?'

'We'd better bloody hope so,' said Hirad. 'Or Diera is going to be seriously unimpressed with your sacrifice.'

'That is where it leads, though the pathway is dangerous.'

Another new voice. Other figures were approaching but a little distant yet.

'Then we should go,' said Sol.

He moved inside the pathway. All at once he heard a sigh as of a thousand voices finding comfort together.

'What was that?' he asked.

'You will see,' said the new voice. One he recognised but could not place. 'But we must go. The enemy will be aware of this corridor.'

Sol shrugged. Or he thought he did.

'No time like the present.'

'Raven,' said Hirad. 'Raven, with me.'

'Hold it!' roared Suarav and Chandyr. 'Hold it. You can do it.'

Tower Prexys had fallen. Tower Laryon had fallen and there was little they could do to shore up Tower Nyer now. Suarav was damned if any more would tumble. The five machines continued hovering above them. The new weapons continued to fire. The detonation clouds continued to build and burst. The machines continued to grow.

But now Xetesk was fighting back again. Beneath a cooperative Ilkar's Defence casting, thirty mages kept the weapons away from the tower complex. Another six were in reserve and supported a second shield above the working team. Twenty-five guards stood on the perimeter. The machines had fired again and again, each time leaching more strength from the casters. Even so, precious time was being bought and it was hoped fervently that people were escaping into the wild. Garonin were advancing on all sides. Perhaps because they had caught all who had tried to run. Perhaps because they had failed to do so and had been called back for the main prize.

'Clear!' shouted the lead mage, an elderly man named Gythar. 'And steady.'

'Great work, people,' said Chandyr. 'Machine four is building. Be ready.'

'Guards, look to your fronts. Enemies closing on foot,' said Suarav. 'Mage reserve, we need shields on the ground and facing out. Let's keep the dome wall at our backs.'

Inside the shattered complex more mages worked on binding what was left of the circle of seven towers and the superstructure of the dome. Suarav did not think the enemy had seen them move in.

'Come on and have a go,' muttered Suarav. 'I'm sick of using my sword as a pointer.'

Forty or fifty were advancing carefully from across the width of the courtyard. It was littered with bodies and rubble. Their weapons were trained on the small knot of defenders but they had yet to open fire. From behind Suarav, he heard confirmation of shields dropping into place in front of them.

'What are they waiting for?' asked Chandyr at his side.

Suarav shook his head. 'I don't know. Think we've scared them?'

'Well, if it helps, I think we've worried them enough for them to want to wipe us out to the last man.'

'Ever the voice of comfort, though I happen to agree.'

'They fear the Cleansing Flame,' said Gythar. 'They've countered most offensive spells. Not that one.'

'Then we should use it,' said Chandyr.

'No. They will sense the lessening of our shield cover.'

'Gythar's right,' said Suarav. 'We've got all the time in the world. It is they who are in a rush, it would seem.'

The enemy soldiers loped on, their big strides eating up the distance. At thirty yards, each slung his weapon back over his shoulder and drew what looked like a short sword though with an extremely thin blade. White light seemed to play up and down their edges.

'Well, well, what have we here?' muttered Chandyr.

'They mean to take us on hand to hand. Inside the shield.' Suarav raised his voice. 'Not one of those bastards gets past our sword line. Protect the mages. Look to your flanks. They are playing in our world now.'

At twenty yards the Garonin broke into a run, taking Suarav by complete surprise. It was not just that this was the first time they had seen any Garonin do anything other than walk, they were fast too. Very fast.

'Brace yourselves!' called Suarav and he set his sword to ready, holding it out front and in both hands. 'Blunt the charge.'

The Garonin loomed tall and powerful. The drum of their feet sent shivers through the ground and up through his body. He took his own orders and braced his feet as best he could. The Garonin soldiers struck.

Suarav ducked a flashing blade and buried his sword to the hilt in his opponent's stomach. The momentum brought the Garonin clattering into Suarav and both men tumbled to the ground. Suarav's blade was ripped from his grasp. Suarav shovelled the dying man from his legs. Right above him, a Garonin blade beat the defence of a young guardsman. It sliced straight through his neck, down through his ribcage and out of the side of his chest. The stink of cauterised flesh rose. The side of the guard's body slid away and the rest of him collapsed.

'Dear Gods falling.'

Suarav snatched up the fallen man's weapon and swiped it as hard as he could into enemy legs. He felt it bite deep despite the flaring of the armour. He dragged it clear and hacked upwards as he came to his feet, his blade meeting chest armour and bouncing clear.

Suarav backed away a pace. The Garonin had torn the guard line to pieces. Chandyr blocked a weapon aside and struck high to slide his own blade into the eye slit of his enemy. Another guard near him lost his arm to an easy swipe of a Garonin blade.

'They're amongst the mages.'

Suarav saw some space and ran into it. He carved his sword through the back of enemy legs at the knee, feeling bone collapse. He kicked the Garonin in the calves and he fell backwards, arms flailing. A guardsman ran past him and leapt onto the back of another, ramming a dagger again and again into the side of his neck.

Suarav sensed danger and ducked. A blade buzzed over his head. He saw enough of it to know it was steel but edged in mana, pure and deadly sharp. Something Xetesk had been trying to perfect for generations. Suarav spun away. The Garonin followed him, stabbing straight forward. Suarav sidestepped, grabbed the man's arm and pulled him off balance. The general brought his sword round high above his head and felt it connect with helmet and then bone.

Above him, the Defence spell flickered and steadied.

'Gythar!' he called.

The old mage was in the thick of the melee, defended by two guardsmen. One fell under a mana blade that stabbed clear through his body, spitting and smoking as it went.

'Chandyr! To Gythar!'

Chandyr nodded. He brought the pommel of his sword down on the head of a Garonin trying to rise and smashed a knee into his faceplate for good measure. Enemy slaughtered mages but some fought back, having discarded the obsolete spell shields.

Suarav saw one calm young mage leap up and grab a Garonin faceplate to feed a superheated flame of mana inside it. The Garonin screamed. Three others turned and bore down on the youngster. Suarav diverted from his course and hammered his blade into the neck of one. The second went down under another tightly cast spell but the third sheared his blade left to right and opened up the mage's back.

Gythar was still standing. Chandyr was near him. Garonin closed. A third of the defence mages were down. Above, a weapon cycled up to fire. Suarav knew they wouldn't be able to resist the impact. Garonin blades halted in the act of falling. Faceplates turned skywards. A hideous sound rang out from the machines floating above.

Suarav saw an opportunity and swept the throat out of an enemy neck.

'I didn't agree a ceasefire,' he growled.

And the next moment they were gone. All of them. The machines blinked out of existence, the detonation clouds dispersed and the foot soldiers simply ceased to be. Suarav turned a quick circle, looking for the counterpunch but there was no one to deliver it.

Xetesk was silent.

Densyr had wondered how, without screams from Diera, he would know when Sol was dead. But in the end it was as obvious as it got. Sirendor, Thraun and Ilkar dropped soundlessly to the ground, Thraun's wolves howled grief and padded across to Diera's boys, and there was an extraordinary explosion of sound from above. An alien sound like rage but metallic in tone.

Densyr opened the door and was first through it, the boys and Sharyr hard on his heels. Wolves and a more stately Vuldaroq came along behind. Diera was sitting on the floor, cradling the still form of Sol. His head was against her chest and she stroked the side of his face. Her weeping was quiet, reverential, and Densyr found a lump in his throat that would not swallow away.

Above her, the doorway was plainly open. Its properties had changed. The grey mist had cleared and a wan light shone out. He could see nothing within but there was a very slight breeze heading up into it. He found the thought that it might be returning souls a comfort.

Jonas and Hirad had run to their mother and were clinging to her. Densyr and Sharyr walked around to crouch in front of her. The sight of Sol, King of Balaia, the Unknown Warrior of The Raven, lying dead, was truly shocking. As close to an immortal as Densyr had ever considered any man. And to think he had betrayed this great man's trust.

'Diera?' said Densyr.

Both of her boys were crying too and the three of them put their faces close to one another, sharing their grief, gleaning what strength they could from each other.

'Diera, we should move him. Somewhere safe. Now more than ever he deserves our protection and our respect. Diera?'

Diera opened her eyes. They were red-rimmed and puffed.

'So brave,' she said. 'So determined and so full of belief. We must all believe that he has done the right thing. He said it would help.'

Densyr nodded. 'And I do. Belatedly, I do. I mean that. He is Raven. And they are not prone to wasting their efforts. We should remember that.'

Diera moved the boys aside just a little bit and the two wolves padded over. She looked at them briefly but realised they were no threat and laid Sol's head on a rolled-up cloak which Sharyr had placed on the ground. Diera kissed his lips and smoothed his cheek one more time.

'Don't cover his face. Let him see. Let the air pass over him. He always loved the breeze on him. When you have to take him, take him where you must but still don't cover him.'

She turned back to her sons and Densyr heard her ask a question though he only heard Hirad's over-loud reply.

'Thraun told them to take care of us. And he told us to make sure they got home,' the boy said proudly.

'What now?' asked Sharyr.

Densyr gazed about him. There seemed to be bodies everywhere. Hirad and Sol in here, the other three in the antechamber. His gaze alighted on Vuldaroq, who was bending over the kneeling forms of the TaiGethen cell.

'Poking them isn't usually advisable,' said Densyr.

Vuldaroq looked round. 'I don't think they'll notice. They're dead. All three of them.'

Densyr started. 'They're what?'

'Dead,' said Vuldaroq. 'Check if you doubt me.'

'What happened to them?'

Try as he might, Densyr couldn't get himself around this. First Sol and now Auum. Two of the finest warriors ever to grace Balaia. Both gone in moments.

'They are Ynissul,' said Vuldaroq. 'The long-lived of the elves. Immortal, actually. I mean that in its literal sense. They can be poisoned and die of an arrow or a sword thrust but, left in normal health, they do not ever have to die.'

'Well they're dead now,' said Densyr.

'Because, and this is a presumption but an educated one, they chose to die.'

'Why?' asked Sharyr.

'Presumably they felt they could be more help to Sol than to us,' said Vuldaroq.

'We could have done with them here,' said Densyr. 'Their sort of fighting is always useful.'

'But haven't the Garonin gone?' asked Sharyr. 'That sound we heard. And it's quiet above.'

'They've gone after Sol,' said Jonas. 'Haven't they? It's why Father wanted Sha-Kaan to know what he was doing.'

'I don't know,' said Densyr. 'All I do know is, the Garonin came for our mana. They want to rip out the Heart of Xetesk. That is why they are at our gates and in our skies. And whatever Sol has done, that won't change. They may have gone for now but they'll be back and we have to be ready for them.'

'We'd best get ourselves outside then,' said Sharyr. 'See what's left.'

Densyr nodded. 'Vuldaroq, if you would be so good as to see Diera and company to more comfortable quarters and organise the moving of our departed to the Master's Morgue, I'd really appreciate it.'

Vuldaroq inclined his head. 'Of course, my Lord Densyr. And anything else I can do . . . Um, one favour though?'

'Yes?'

'Dystran's condition is a concern.'

'He's top of my list,' said Densyr. He moved to go but brought himself up short before Diera. 'My Lady Unknown.'

'Only Hirad calls me that.'

'I know but . . . well, you know. Sol's sacrifice. It's the most extraordinary thing I've ever known anyone do. And I have seen some truly stunning acts.'

Diera nodded but could not raise a smile. She had a son under each arm and the wolves flanked them.

'It doesn't stop him being dead though, does it?'

'No, of course not. I just wanted you to know, that's all.'

'Thank you, Densyr. Really. It is bearable, just, to know the reasons why he has done what he has done. What would be truly unbearable, would be for it to be a waste. That means you and your college have to try and save as many souls as you can.'

'That's exactly where I'm going now.'

'And one more thing. We haven't got along well in the last few days but I won't forget what you've done for my family in the last ten years. Dismal shame though it is, you're pretty much all I've got of the old life barring my two wonderful boys. So when you go out there, be sure not to die.

'We need you. The old you. Denser.'

Chapter 37

Densyr picked his way over the rubble having already scared himself a dozen times on the way up the remains of the spiral stair to his formal dinner chambers. He was amazed the tower still stood. Holes had been blown in the walls in too many places to count. Several timber floors had collapsed, but it was testament to the original builders that all the stone floors, placed to strengthen the tower in key areas, remained intact.

He looked up to the open sky, mercifully clear of Garonin machines, and wondered at the sheer level of the destruction and whether they could possibly rebuild. A matter for the future, should they have one. Meanwhile, he and Brynar moved aside beams, shelves, burned portraits and tapestries on their way to where Dystran still sat in the chair next to Septern's abandoned borrowed body. A body that looked very suddenly about ten days dead.

'Doesn't smell too good, does he?' said Brynar.

'Strange. Presumably, the returned soul holds off decay but only to the extent of hiding it. I wish I knew how that worked.'

Dystran was partly covered by a beam that had fallen across his chair. Coming closer, Densyr could see that the beam had lodged between the back and side panels of the chair, which had broken its fall and stopped it from crushing the old Lord of the Mount's skull.

'How close we came to ultimate defeat,' breathed Densyr.

'Then you think he's still alive?' asked Brynar.

'Of course he's still alive, idiot. If he wasn't, the Heart would have been destroyed by mana feedback.'

'Oh right, yes.'

'Gods drowning, Brynar, you really ought to meet Hirad Cold-heart again. You'd get on like a house on fire with your similar-sized intellects.'

Densyr helped the young mage shift the beam and blow the dust from Dystran's face. He looked very peaceful. His breathing was deep and sure and his body was uninjured so far as they could see. Densyr knelt by him and took his hand, dropping into the mana spectrum right by him.

Dystran's aura pulsed strongly where it rested as a perfect buffer to the loose mana charging around the ruined grid. Densyr could see that Dystran had done good work in allowing some peripheral areas of the grid to feed back into the Heart under control. But still enough remained to do severe damage and most likely destroy it.

'My mother would have said it is like unpicking a woollen knit,' said Dystran, making Densyr jump. 'You have to retain the integrity of the pattern, you see, or else the whole lot just falls in a knotted heap. Something like that, anyway.'

'It's good to hear your voice,' said Densyr.

'Told you they'd not see me here.'

'Well, I'm not sure that's entirely true. Have you seen this place? It isn't how I left it.'

'A little more untidy, is it?'

'You could say.' Densyr waved in Brynar's direction. 'Have a look round, see if by some miracle any water has survived in a container.'

'Bless you, Densyr. Tell me, how are we doing?'

'Average to awful,' said Densyr.

Dystran managed a dry chuckle. 'You really must go back to your propaganda classes.'

'Only when I can issue blindfolds to all the sceptics too. The college is in ruins. Two towers are gone. This one and Nyer are on the verge of collapse. The other three are relatively sound but only because binding work went on all through the attacks. The dome is rubble, most of our outbuildings are destroyed and the population are scattered and, we presume, chased by Garonin.

'Sol is dead and, again we presume, travelling with The Raven and with Auum's TaiGethen cell, who also took their own lives down in the catacombs.'

'Oh. Ynissul deciding that enough is enough, I suppose.'

Densyr shook his head. 'You and Vuldaroq really had too little to do down in your rathole of a suite, didn't you? Too much time to study ancient elven lore and history.'

'No, no, no. We did all this during the Elfsorrow crisis, trying to work out how they manage to live so long. Not my fault if you never bothered to consult the popular texts on the matter.'

'I was otherwise engaged, if you recall,' said Densyr. 'The question

I need you to answer for me now is, can we move you? We are assuming the Garonin are chasing The Raven but we don't really know why since the mana in our Heart is enormous compared to anything they have around their souls. But in any event the Garonin will surely return to complete the job. And you have to be somewhere safer.'

'Very thoughtful of you.' Dystran's aura pulsed as he tested his mind. 'All I will say is, be gentle. And I'd like to go back to my chambers if you consider them safe enough. Rathole or not, they smell good.'

'Consider it done.' Densyr turned to Brynar. 'You heard the man. Bring up a stretcher party, though they might want to just pick up the chair with Lord Dystran in it. Less mucking about, I'd say. And ask them not to drop him. There would be . . . repercussions.'

'Yes, my Lord.'

'And Brynar.'

'My Lord.'

'Your antics out in the city earlier. With The Raven.' Densyr paused and let Brynar sweat. 'Good work.'

Brynar's smile was broad. 'Thank you, Lord Densyr.'

'Sentimental nonsense,' muttered Dystran.

'I remain lord of this pile of redesigned stone and wood,' said Densyr. 'And hence I shall be as sentimental as I like to whomsoever I choose. Thank you very much for your input. Time to relax. Help is at hand.'

'Did the young pup find any water?'

'Apparently not.'

Densyr made his careful way down the stair, already feeling nervous about Dystran's journey to the catacombs. He passed Brynar's team on the way up and favoured them with what he hoped was an encouraging smile. At the base of the tower, guards and mages were at work trying to make a path to the shattered complex doors and to clear the rubble-strewn mess that cluttered the entrance to the catacombs.

The evacuation alarm still sounded across the city, and while it had merged into the background for a while, Densyr heard it loud and clear again now. He clapped his hands for attention.

'I'm speaking loudly because the evacuation alarm is, as you are aware, intrusive. Exactly as it is designed to be. Now, as you also are aware, evacuation is a term meaning leave, run, go away, don't look back and any number of colloquialisms that put together lead to the conclusion that the city should be cleared of its entire population.

'This leads me to my question, which is: what the hell are you all still doing here?'

Densyr found it difficult to keep the smile from his face such was the pride he felt at the efforts still being made on behalf of himself and Xetesk. There was a moment when every man and woman inside the devastated complex thought his verbose utterance was in all seriousness. One by one, however, he saw them begin to relax. One spoke up.

'General Suarav asked if we would stay and help the fight. This is our college. So here we stand.'

'And I am more proud of you than I can say. Thank you for your courage and your strength. With people like you standing firm, this college and city will survive, rebuild and be great once more. But right now my advice to you is to rest. Mages, your stamina reserves must be low. Guards, your arms must be tired, your every muscle crying out for pause. There will be plenty of time to clean up this mess when our victory is complete. For now we have to assume the Garonin will return. Rest. For there is still much work to be done.'

They cheered him on his way out through the doors of the complex, and he had never felt more like a fraud in his life. Suarav was waiting for him.

'My Lord Densyr, it is joy to see you alive and well.'

'And it is joy to be so.' Densyr walked forward and clasped arms with his trusted friend. 'I always knew you to be a great man. But even I had no idea about the depths of your courage and your powers of persuasion. How is the college still standing?'

'I'll explain later, if there's time,' said Suarav. 'For now I need to give you a situation report.'

'Do I want to hear it?'

Suarav shook his head. 'You can learn most of it just by looking around you.'

There were not enough survivors to clear away the dead and the scattered body parts strewn across the courtyard. Smears of blood stained every surface that wasn't touched by the scorch-marks of Garonin weapons. Brave Xeteskians were abandoned in the grotesque poses of their deaths. Survivors were moving through them, searching for any who might still be breathing.

It would have been impossible to drive a wagon across the

courtyard to the east gates of the college, which themselves stood open revealing the destruction of the city beyond. Rubble and debris covered the ground. Two out of three long rooms were flattened. The mana bowl existed only as a crater and the living quarters, refectory and medical buildings were all holed and partly collapsed.

Densyr turned a slow circle and drew in a sharp breath at the parlous state of the tower complex. Its symmetry was destroyed by the wrecking of Prexys and Laryon. His own tower was leaning to the north and Nyer was in even worse shape.

'Only binding magic holds any of it together now,' said Suarav. 'The structure of the complex and its foundations are essentially unsound. When this is over, it will all have to come down.'

'I'm sure the Garonin will be only too happy to help in that regard,' said Densyr, feeling a bitterness that surprised him. 'So what do we have besides rubble and ruins?'

'I have twenty-seven mages able to cast. I have fifty or so fit sword guards and another thirty injured but prepared to fight.'

'That's *all*?'

'And that represents a good survival rate given where we started. Don't forget, you can add to that the entire catacomb defence. What's that: fifty personal guard, the Circle Seven and the research teams plus people like the Communion Globe team. Thirty mages in all working down there?'

Densyr nodded. 'Yes. Not as many as we'd have liked but clearly the weight of numbers had to be up here. We're going to need to be clever with spells. We can bind the catacomb ceilings and walls as far as possible and take them on down there unless you have a better plan.'

'Not on the face of it but my concern is that they will not try and walk through the front door. Looked to me as if they were trying to come straight through the top. Means that binding is all very well, but should they breach it, we have nothing because they can just reach in and grab the Heart.'

Densyr glanced up at his tower, wondering how far Dystran had got down the stairs.

'There is one thing we can keep up our sleeve. It'll stop the Garonin getting the Heart for sure.'

'There's a but, isn't there.'

'We won't have it either.'

'Still preferable.'

'Agreed. All right. Look, you've done an extraordinary job thus far, General, and I would not presume to alter your plans. Have who you need from the catacomb defence. Strengthen where you see fit and just tell us all what we need to do. Fair enough?'

'The best I could hope for.'

Densyr clasped arms with him again. 'We can do this. If The Raven are successful, we can be sure the Garonin will be weakened and it gives us a chance.'

Densyr heard his name being called. Brynar was picking his way out of the complex, waving as he came. He tripped, fell flat on his face, got to his feet and ignored the scrapes evident on his hands as he ran on.

'Good to see you looking better,' said Densyr. 'What can we do for you?'

'Brynar, take a deep breath,' said Suarav.

'Communion Globe. They're Korina, it's there them.'

'Brynar,' said Suarav, his tone commanding this time. 'I am unused to repeating myself.'

'Sorry. Sorry.' Brynar stared at Suarav and took a deliberate deep breath. And then another three. 'The Communion Globe is active, my Lord Densyr, General Suarav. Korina is still there and still fighting. They are surrounded but the enemy is not moving. They say the Garonin are waiting.'

'For what? I wonder.' said Densyr. 'Brynar, tell Sharyr I want communications open as long as is humanly possible. In fact longer. Suarav, the floor is yours. I'll be in Dystran's chambers until the Garonin return.'

'If,' suggested Brynar.

'Until,' repeated Densyr. 'Just accept it.'

Chapter 38

Sol stared at their silhouettes and felt a keen sadness. 'Why are you here?' he said. 'You didn't have to be here.'

'It is ever the way,' said Auum. 'The TaiGethen serve Yniss in whatever realm we are most needed.'

'But your sacrifice—'

'Is no greater than your own in any event. And we do not consider it so.'

'But you can never go back,' said Sol. 'You are dead, like me. Like all of us here.'

'But our work does not cease. We are Ynissul, servants of God. I have been alive for thousands of years. Now is my greatest challenge.' Auum chuckled. 'You are feeling guilt.'

Sol nodded. 'Because I am glad that you are here. And that means I am glad that you are dead.'

'Then do not think of it in those terms. Consider that together we have a greater chance of saving both our peoples.'

'That I can do.'

The dead crowded the corridor, which was no wider or higher than fifteen feet at any point thus far. All of Balaia's returned dead were thronging along it, most in a desperate hurry to reach Ulandeneth. The Raven and Auum's Tai were behind the mass by some distance now and moving with growing unease.

Sol was finding the physical laws that bound the corridor very disconcerting. The corridor itself was like walking over a huge sponge. The floor had little tension to it. It was the same if you pressed a wall. But there was no imperative to walk as such; with an effort of will it was entirely possible to float above the floor and in whatever attitude you chose, and move with no apparent motive force.

Hirad had been keen to demonstrate his skills in the area until Sol had worked out that he could also, with another effort of will, give him a thump in what had once been his gut. And it still hurt, which was completely bizarre.

'You know what really rankles with me?' Sol said. 'It's that even though I'm dead, I've still got things to learn. Worse than that, things Hirad *already* knows, which is a first.'

He didn't look at any of the others because to do so made him feel intensely sad. He had come to terms with the fact that each of them was represented by what was in effect a silhouette picked out in varying shades of bright grey. But what he couldn't get over was that, though outlines were recognisable, when any of them turned to him, all he could see was a blank canvas where a face ought to be.

'But this is not true death,' said Auum.

'How do you work that out?'

'Until all physical manifestations are cast aside and the soul rests in eternal bliss, death cannot have truly occurred.'

'Yet we cannot go back.'

'No, Sol, we cannot, but there is a place between life and death, and this is it,' said Ilkar. 'We all came back down something not dissimilar when the Garonin ripped open our resting place.'

'You're telling me you were genuinely alive back on Balaia in those alternative bodies.'

'Yes, of course,' said Ilkar. 'How else would you describe it?'

'Possession,' said Sol. 'To us, you were you all right but walking dead nonetheless.'

'Charming,' said Sirendor.

They moved in silence for a while. Sol watched the mass of the dead moving further and further ahead of them. They had become an amorphous bright blob. Sol wished he had some reference to work out how far they were ahead. All he could come up with was: out of easy reach to feel in his soul comfortably.

'There's so many things I'm not getting about all this,' said Sol.

'And that surprises you, does it?' asked Sirendor. 'I mean, you are dead. Lots to take in and all that.'

'Just ignore him and tell me what's bothering you,' said Ilkar.

'Well, for starters, why is there distance here? I thought all travel was instantaneous between dimensions and that being dead was a seamless transition.'

'Can't believe everything you read.'

'Shut up, Hirad. I've thought about this one, and it's easy really. We aren't travelling between dimensions. We're outside anything we know, both when we were cast out of our rest and right now. Ulandeneth is a place that exists beyond our sphere of comprehension. Sorry, that sounds lame, doesn't it, but it's all I can come up with.'

'It'll do, Ilkar, thanks. But given I accept that, then what are all the other dead doing here? We're here because we're hoping to find new lands beyond Ulandeneth, though God knows how that'll manifest itself. Where do they think they're going?'

'You forget that the reason any of us came back was ultimately to get all the living to leave, admittedly knowing that at least one of you had to lay down his life to open the first door,' said Ilkar. 'And now it is open and the path to salvation is ahead. I know there is no end at the moment but you must understand that the pull of this corridor is incredibly strong for a returned dead soul. Far too strong to resist if you are clinging on to a possessed body. It is what we want. The relief from pain alone makes it worth the risk.'

'What risk?' asked Sol.

'That this goes nowhere but oblivion,' said Thraun.

'Right. Well, leaving that aside for now, can someone tell me why we aren't travelling at greater speed? Presumably, we can go as fast as we can will ourselves. This is a snail's pace, is it not? And we are anticipating trouble. How in all the hells do we repel it?'

Ilkar didn't get the chance to respond. Hirad's silhouette flashed a deep gold rimmed with warm red.

'Company,' said Hirad.

Sol tensed.

'Who?' asked Sirendor.

'Take a look.'

Hirad's silhouette arm gestured at the translucent walls of the passageway. Sol stared into the maelstrom without. Grey-, white- and gold-flecked brown. A chaos of light and dark, swirling and racing. He shuddered to think of the forces at play out there, beyond the flimsy barrier.

For a while he saw nothing but the void. A ghostly wing, there and gone. The merest glimpse of a long, sinuous neck. A trailing tail, lost in the roiling space. And then there, flying by their sides, beneath them and above them, Kaan dragons. Dozens, a hundred maybe, cruising the walls of the passage, spiralling around it, enclosing it in a solid wall of dragon scale.

'We are come,' rumbled Sha-Kaan, his voice reverberating along the corridor.

Ahead Sol heard screams and saw the mass of the dead pack even more tightly together and increase their speed. He tasted their fear as if it were his own.

'We will not harm you. We have come to protect you.'

Sha-Kaan's voice stilled the panic as surely as day follows night. Now, Sol heard chatter and cheers and he felt a surge of relief that suffused his entire being. It felt wonderful, and reminiscent of a life long past.

'Oh yes, forgot to mention that. Emotionally, you'll find we are all very close indeed,' said Ilkar.

'Thanks for the warning, but this one I think I can handle. The Soul Tank gave the same sense of togetherness to the Protectors.'

'The Garonin are close,' said Sha-Kaan. 'Already, we have fought them out here. They are attracted to the mass of mana within, just as I am attracted by the touch of your mind, Hirad.'

'Good to feel you too, Great Kaan.'

'Let us make sure this ends well. The Garonin will try to breach the corridor. We will do what we can. But you must also be ready.'

'What can we do?' asked Sol.

'You will know.'

Multiple flares of light erupted outside a little way further along the corridor. Sol heard dragons roaring. Sha-Kaan beat his wings and was gone. The walls wobbled under a collision. Above their heads Sol saw a Garonin soldier bounce and roll, his body a mass of flame. A dragon's jaws came down on him, ending his pain.

'It begins,' pulsed Sha-Kaan. 'Fight hard.'

Hirad was already pulling at Sol's arm.

'We need to catch up with the rest,' he said.

'What will we do?'

'Come on, it's where the fight will play out.'

The Raven quintet and Auum's Tai soared away down the corridor. Sol forced himself to believe it could be done, and with every passing moment he found it easier to follow them. He shook off Hirad's arm.

'I'm all right,' he said.

He was certain Hirad was smiling. Seeing his face would have brought great comfort. The thousands of dead were moving as fast as their combined mass would allow. The corridor bulged as they pressed on. Outside, there were flashes like a cloud shot through with lightning. He heard solid thuds and saw the crowd swaying right, a shoal of fish trying to dodge a predator.

'They've landed!' called Hirad. 'We have to stop them. Sol, it's you we need.'

'Why? I don't understand?'

'You are the free soul,' said Auum, close by. 'You bind us all just as you bind this place.'

Sol tried to stay calm and he forged ahead. Flame splayed across the corridor. There was a scrabble of claws and the shape of a dragon's tail stabbed down almost to the heads of the dead. Sol looked right. A limp body, huge and lifeless, its wings shredded, spiralled away and was lost to sight.

'Dear Gods burning.'

Lines of harsh white light appeared on the wall of the corridor. They spread quickly, looking like a lattice of ice across a window. The wall hardened around them. Flame beat down in the same place. Garonin soldiers cried out. The light flickered briefly but was not extinguished.

'Move!' shouted Hirad from somewhere ahead. 'Move, keep going.'

The wall exploded inwards and Garonin soldiers entered the corridor on the wings of a hurricane. The noise was incredible. A harrowing whistle and a roaring gale in one. Dead near the breach were sucked out into the void. Garonin waded though the masses, striking out with the instruments they held in both hands. And where they struck, bright grey silhouettes faded quickly to black and then were gone.

Everything was being dragged towards the breach. The void was inhaling and it meant to capture them all. Flame lashed across the tear. Sol saw Auum, Ghaal and Miirt's silhouettes flash by him and slap into a Garonin soldier. Auum's hand came back across the enemy's neck and his head parted company from his body.

The shocking sight brought Sol hope and understanding. He let the gale take him and he threw himself forward, arms outstretched. They plunged into the chest of his target and he felt his hands squeeze the enemy's heart. Hirad and Sirendor were flying together. Sol saw them crash into the midst of the dead and he saw a Garonin flattened against the far wall, rebound from it and be sucked from the corridor.

The gale intensified. Garonin still came through. Braced against something Sol couldn't sense, Auum, his Tai and Thraun waited to pounce. The dead were racing away up the corridor with Hirad and Sirendor in pursuit of the enemy amongst them. Silhouettes faded with hideous regularity.

'The breach!' called Auum from across the other side of it. 'Sol, close it.'

Auum thrust his hand deep into the skull of a Garonin soldier and flung his lifeless body back into the path of others coming through. Ghaal, clutching one side of the tear, evaded a flailing weapon and smashed his free hand into the gut of another, tearing out entrails as he pulled it clear.

Sol dived for the breach. Here, the howl of the wind was extraordinary. Its pull was immensely powerful. Sol was dragged towards it off balance. He collided with a flapping section of wall and grabbed hold. A Garonin weapon swung towards him. Miirt's hand clamped on the enemy's wrist, squeezing and crushing the bone inside to dust. The Garonin screamed. Thraun completed the kill.

Sol looked at the breach. He could taste the chaos. He could feel his soul drawn to it. He reached out a shadow hand and touched the wall at the top of the breach. The two sides flowed together beneath his hand. Sha-Kaan had been right. This felt as natural as waking in the morning. A Garonin soldier thrust his upper body through the breach. Sol drew his hand quickly down. The wall knitted seamlessly together, snipping the enemy neatly in half.

The wind died but further along they could hear another tear being made.

'No rest,' said Auum. 'Not yet.'

Sol stared at his hand very briefly but could see nothing at all. He angled his body and flew on forward.

Fyn-Kaan took the full force of the concerted fire across his belly. The scales split and his body was torn apart. Sha-Kaan roared fury. He plunged through the gore being scattered into space and unleashed flame across the corridor. Five Garonin were reduced to charred remains. He angled his wing and turned along the length of the corridor. In three more places, the Garonin were forcing breaches. He called flank dragons to him and ploughed along the surface, his claws ahead of his body and his neck arched to strike.

Garonin turned their weapons and fired. White tears spanned the space and thudded into Sha-Kaan's wings and chest. He did not flinch. Snapping his neck forward he snatched two soldiers in his jaws and bit down with all his prodigious strength. The feel of bone cracking was satisfying. He spat out the remains. With another beat of his wings, he was onto more of them. His claws tore into armour, which flashed white uselessly as it was ripped aside.

Sensing danger, Sha-Kaan flipped his left wing and climbed sharply away from the corridor. A thick column of light slammed into it where he had been, searing the wing and left-hand side of one of his flankers. The dragon mourned as it fluttered away into the void, out of control and spinning to its death. The corridor was undamaged though within, the panic of the dead was evident.

Sha-Kaan sensed Hirad and his people in the heart of the fight. He pulsed to the Kaan to support him. He turned away, arcing up and left in a long looping curve that brought him above the Garonin vydosphere, which was hanging in space, loosing its huge bolts of energy and launching its teams of soldiers.

He circled while others joined him. Ten in all came to his call. Enough to do the work.

'They will sense us,' he warned. 'Loose formation, flame and claw. Pass quickly and turn sharply. Give them no target.'

He felt the warmth of their understanding.

'The Dragonene must survive or our melde will fail and with it the Kaan Brood. We must not let that happen.'

'We hear you, Great Kaan.'

Sha-Kaan tucked his wings into his body and dived. He stretched his neck out straight before him and his tail moved gently behind him, a rudder to keep him on course. The gales of inter-dimensional space clashed and pulled. Eddies appeared, strong enough to suck even a dragon off course.

He breathed in the purity of the air and let his flame ducts open. The vydosphere was taut but not bulging, a machine taken from its former task before time to come here and counter a genuine threat to the Garonin. Sha-Kaan felt satisfaction in that. This race that knew no enemies beyond its own dimension threatened by frail, primitive humans. Complacency. An enemy the Kaan had known in their past.

Kaan dragons were widely spaced about him. Below, left, right and behind. Sha-Kaan flew in close to the skin of the vydosphere. He saw streams of white tears pouring out from its underside. He opened his mouth and breathed. Flame spewed onto the skin, bubbling and melting it. Joints buckled and small sections twisted up, gouting steam into the void. He let his wings and body smash through antennae and funnels, feeling them bend and snap against his bulk.

In two beats of his wings, he was past the machine. He angled sharply down. Kaan were taking terrible damage from the weapons on the carriage slung beneath it. One of his brothers lost a wing, sheared off near the root. Another's head was destroyed, taking a thick beam of light square on.

Sha-Kaan dived hard, spread his wings and executed a sharp U-turn. A wounded membrane protested but held. The carriage was directly above him. White tears streamed from all sides. A Kaan dragon was caught in two bursts, his body rippling with the fire and his wings ablaze.

'No more,' pulsed Sha-Kaan. 'Clear and retreat.'

Sha-Kaan forced his body up. He beat his wings hard and fast. The Garonin could not see him, searching as they were for the Kaan just departed back to the corridor. He closed on the carriage, saw it looming large. With a final beat of his wings, he swung his body around. His hind claws and huge bulk slammed into the base of the carriage.

The force of his impact bent metal, splintered glass and shattered strut and fixing plate. The whole vydosphere was shunted upwards. Garonin were thrown into the void, snatched away without the means to save themselves. Sha-Kaan whipped his tail into the structure again and again, feeling parts of it weaken under the blows. His head snaked in, biting down on man and machine, tearing anything loose away and spitting it into the maelstrom.

Here and there, Garonin clung on to whatever they could. One brought a weapon to bear. The white tears caught Sha-Kaan on the side of the face, burning his scales away just beneath his eye. He roared his pain, snapped his jaws in and took the head from his tormentor.

He let go his claws and fell away, looking back to see what he had achieved. The vydosphere was drifting without apparent control. No more weapon fire came from it. Steam and smoke was pouring from gashes and holes in its skin. Funnels hung from its sides. Two Kaan dragons, standing off while Sha-Kaan attacked, flew in now, their flame encasing the front of the machine. The entire section collapsed inwards. The Kaan beat up at a steep angle. Sha-Kaan flipped his body and drove away, feeling the force of the explosion across his broad back.

'Seek more,' he pulsed to his Brood. 'You know what to do.'

Sha-Kaan saw the corridor in all its glory as he approached. A strand of light that stretched as far as he could see in either direction. A beacon of hope for man, elf and dragon, an icon of fear for their enemies. The single gossamer filament of a spider's web, shining through the swirling chaos of light and dark. Within it the dead still moved and the Garonin still stole the mana from them. And The Raven still fought.

The journey would soon be at an end. In the distance an ethereal light could be seen. Ulandeneth, the elves called it. The top of the world in dragon lore, where no single term could describe it. The Kaan could not help them in there. In there they would either believe or they would fail.

And the fate of all would be decided.

Chapter 39

The instrument in the hand of a Garonin grazed Hirad's silhouette. Weakness flooded him and he dropped. The enemy advanced on him. He scrambled backwards, soul energy deserting him. The dead had scattered in front of the soldier. The instrument was a pale ball held in the palm of the hand. It had a neck like a gourd which ended in a needle-sharp point. The point was thrust at him again. He managed to roll aside. He came up against another silhouette, and this one did not flee.

Legs straddled his body and hands lashed out. The Garonin withered and crumpled.

'I did it when I was alive and I'm still doing it now I'm dead,' said Sirendor.

'What?'

'Saving your thick hide, that's what.'

'And you're still moaning about it,' said Hirad. He flowed to an upright position and felt the strength begin to return. 'Best if you don't let one of those things touch you.'

'Valuable safety tip. Thanks, Hirad.'

Up ahead, Sol and Thraun were fighting their way towards a breach in the corridor. Auum's Tai rushed into the flanks of a group of four Garonin who had dropped through a second breach. More helpless dead were drained of mana. More souls failed as they were pierced.

'Let's go,' said Hirad. 'It would be nice if some of you others decided to fight.'

'Same as it ever was,' said Sirendor. 'Is it just me, or is this passageway starting to angle upwards.'

The pair of them flashed past the ranks of the dead, now broken into smaller groups. Some of them were trying to fight back but something was missing. Hirad ignored them. Sirendor was right. The passage had an incline to it now. Gentle here but it curved up ever more steeply.

'Up to the top of the world,' said Hirad.

A broad flash of light bathed the corridor. Hirad gazed to his left. The afterglow of an explosion lingered for a while in the midst of the void then was snatched away. Sha-Kaan's mind touched his again.

'You are close,' he said. 'The enemy is weakening.'

'It doesn't look much like it,' said Hirad.

The corridor was full of Garonin. Right behind Sol, another breach had been forged in the base of the path. Garonin surged up. Dead fell in their hundreds under the onslaught. Sirendor raced ahead, planting his feet into the chest of an enemy, swivelling and driving right through the Garonin's body.

'That I must try,' said Hirad.

The shade of the barbarian launched himself head first at his nearest enemy. The Garonin saw him coming, his hands came up, weapons in hand. Hirad was going too fast to avoid him. Sirendor washed past his vision. The Garonin stared at the stumps of his wrists. Hirad plummeted through his chest, feeling the faintest resistance and a glimmer of heat.

On the other side, he turned, feeling cold and a measure of sympathy that surprised him.

'No souls,' he breathed. 'They've got no souls.'

'Down!' called a voice.

Hirad ducked. He felt something pass over him. He swung round, saw Garonin armour large in his vision and the arm of a dead woman sinking up to her elbow in the soldier's body. She shouted her triumph.

'We can fight,' she said. 'We can fight them.'

The word spread. Hirad flew about, heading for Sol.

'They have no defence against you but your own fear,' he said. 'Go at them.'

Sol had his hands on a tear and was closing it. Garonin turned to stop him. The dead simply engulfed them. Elsewhere, knots of Garonin soldiers paused and Hirad could see the uncertainty in them. Outside, there was another wide flash of light, another machine destroyed by the Kaan dragons. Fire played over the corridor. Claws dragged along the wall right by Hirad. Garonin were swept away.

Inside, the dead surged. Garonin stabbed out, bleeding the energy from as many as they could. But for every two that fell, an enemy was downed. Unencumbered, Sol flew for the next tear. The tide had turned. Garonin were trying to escape back out to the void.

'Hold them here,' shouted Hirad. 'The Kaan need respite.'

Sol nodded. Thraun moved ahead of him. Auum came to the shapechanger's side. The shadows of the warriors struck out high and low. Garonin soldiers fell back. Auum crushed the waist of one in a killing embrace. Thraun's fists punched holes in another's chest. Ghaal crashed in to take the head from another.

The enemy began to panic.

'We have them,' called Hirad. 'Keep it going.'

The broken groups of dead moved to reform. Garonin were cut off in their midst. Sol landed at the next breach, the last breach. He laid his hand on it, fused it shut in moments. The noise of the gales was gone. The pull of the void shut off. Silence but for the dying cries of the last Garonin. The soulless sent to nowhere.

The dead were crying victory. They packed together and moved on up the incline. Far ahead, a pale glow was evident. Hirad nodded his satisfaction. The Raven and the elves came together.

'Everyone all right?' he asked.

'Never better,' said Ilkar. 'Besides being dead, that is.'

'Hardly a surprise,' said Hirad. 'I didn't see you making holes in the Garonin.'

'Fighting never was my thing, Coldheart, you know that. And magic doesn't seem to work in here. Thought I'd be better used keeping the dead moving in the right direction.'

'Will they be back?' asked Sol.

'They will not,' said Sha-Kaan. 'Not here in the void.'

Hirad sensed him very close. He looked about him. There, by the right-hand wall, the Great Kaan was cruising alongside them. He had burns the length of his body and perilously close to one of those huge glorious eyes. His wings looked in tatters.

'You look a complete mess,' said Hirad.

'At least I still live,' rumbled the dragon, a warmth filling the corridor.

'Still crap at jokes though, aren't you?'

'I had a fine tutor in that regard,' said Sha-Kaan.

'Still good at insulting you, though, isn't he, Hirad?' said Ilkar.

'What's next?' asked Sol.

'The Kaan must go to rest. We will watch Balaia when we can. The enemy still move in Beshara and we must look to defend our lands even now. They are not beaten anywhere. Do not relax.'

'And will you find us when we reach our new home?' asked Hirad.

'When Jonas reaches there, I will find him,' said Sha-Kaan. 'As I will now. The healing streams are stronger within a Klene than out here.'

'Tell him how we're doing, won't you?' said Sol.

'I will. And I will speak with your wife, Sol, if I can. Don't speak now; I know it is difficult. I know what you would wish to say to her.'

Sol's sudden grief washed through them all. Hirad felt it as keenly as if it were his own.

'Thank you, Great Kaan,' said Sol.

'This is goodbye,' said Sha-Kaan. 'Where you go now, I cannot follow.'

Hirad nodded and smiled. Though none of them could see his smile, they would be able to feel it.

'Your touch has been joy, old friend,' he said.

'For me also.'

'Farewell,' said Hirad.

'Always believe,' said Sha-Kaan.

And he was gone.

Sol bowed his head. He hadn't thought to feel grief. Perhaps there was something in what Ilkar said about the path between life and death. If that was the case, he just wanted it to be done. He gazed back the way they had come and immediately felt comfort from the closeness of The Raven.

'No way back, big man,' said Hirad. 'Only way is on.'

'I know, it's just . . .' Sol sighed. 'So much time I was away from her. And she never ever failed in her love for me. I never told her how much that meant.'

'You don't think so?' said Hirad. 'You told her every day you were with her. You didn't need words to say it, Unknown. You should have seen the way she looked at you even when she was angry.'

'Not always,' said Sol.

'Always,' said Hirad.

'I wonder how fa—'

Sol stopped in his tracks. He was standing in a wide, open, featureless place. Around him, below and above, all he could sense was a pale ivory colour. Slowly, distantly, dark specks appeared in his vision. He was here. Ulandeneth. He looked all around him and felt the crushing weight of defeat on his shoulders.

He was alone.

It was never too late to learn. Sharyr had returned to the dimensional research chambers to study what he could about the doorway through which only the dead could travel. The pale light still shone from the doorway and he could see nothing through it. Like staring into sand.

Dropping into the mana spectrum briefly, he studied the mana lattice that framed it. Densyr had created a network of fine lines that anchored in space. None of them did any more than touch the very edges of the doorway yet the frame was utterly rigid. He pushed at it with his mind. The force that returned through the spectrum was enough to sit him on his backside.

'Wow,' he said.

He brushed his hands together, stood up and had another look into the light. Garonin soldiers were clustered against the doorway. Sharyr shouted a warning but there was no one else to hear it. He backed away, still staring. Something wasn't right about this. The Garonin had their hands against the entrance. They brought curious-looking instruments to bear on it. One in particular had a blade that revolved at high speed. It was clear that this piece of equipment was being pushed against the doorway but was having no effect.

Sharyr smiled. 'Can't get out, can you?'

His smile was short-lived. They might not be able to get out, but since they had got in somehow, what was the state of any allies within? It didn't bode well at all. Sharyr moved forward again to stand beneath the opening. He pressed his fingertips against it, just able to reach it if he stood on the tips of his toes.

They could see him. He saw weapons brought to bear. He didn't move, confident in what he believed. White tears splashed against the entrance, dispersing harmlessly. Sharyr laughed and beckoned them on with both hands. Fists thumped soundlessly and uselessly against the doorway.

The Garonin withdrew a pace. One looked over his shoulder. Three of them threw themselves back against the doorway, clawing and scrabbling. Abruptly, the doorway vibrated and Sharyr feared his goading would be his undoing. He watched helplessly as the frame buckled, held for a moment and folded in on itself. He saw a last desperate Garonin fist hammering on the opening before it winked out of existence leaving nothing but the faint whiff of burnt mana.

'What was all that about?' he whispered.

Sharyr hurried back to Dystran's quarters to report all he had seen to Lord Densyr.

'How can it end here like this?' whispered Sol, fear gripping him.

He felt as if he was shaking but his shadow form revealed nothing. Ulandeneth was empty. The black flecks moved in the distance but perhaps they were a trick of his eyes this time.

'Where do I go? What do I do?'

So much he had yet to learn. So many assumptions he had made. About those who would stand by him to help him. Those who would show him the way. All gone now. He truly was alone.

'Where are you!' he shouted. 'Hirad! Raven! Where are you?'

Where are you?

A door. He needed a door. But there was none. He needed a sign, something to set him off in the right direction. All his life the path had been before him. The solution had always presented itself. He had always known when to talk or to fight or to run.

'But you're not alive now, are you? And none of the rules apply.'

Sol stood where he had appeared. He turned another slow circle. For all its vastness, the place bore down on him, closed around him, sought to smother him. He dropped to his haunches to feel the ground beneath his feet but his hands transmitted nothing to him. Neither did they sink in.

'There is substance here.'

In his mind time passed terribly quickly. Only he could help the living and the dead and he had no idea where to start. He forced his mind back over what he knew. Ulandeneth was a place where he had been. Where he had fought and lived and from where he had escaped. It was the place, so Auum and Sha-Kaan had it, that held the doorways to all other places.

It was a place where will and belief held sway over the rules of the living lands.

'You have to believe,' he said to himself, his voice swallowed up by the immensity of the space around him. 'But in what?'

The capacity to succeed and the victory of the righteous were just too huge, too imprecise. Not beliefs he could hold on his own. Not yet anyway.

'So, let us start at the beginning.'

Sol stood tall. He held his arms out from his body and in front of him as if he was about to orate. He jutted his chin and spoke loudly and clearly to whoever, whatever, would listen.

'I am Sol. I am The Unknown Warrior. I am Raven.'

The simplicity of his conviction flowed through him. He felt energy surging through the shadow. He felt warmth. His fingers began to tingle. He stared at them. Flesh burst through the shadow like he was picking his hands out of black oil. Sol saw the swirls on the tips of his fingers, the hard skin of his palms and every nick and scar that had never quite faded.

The skin flowed down over his wrists, across his forearms and round his elbows. He watched it form his shoulders, pick out the lattice of old scars on his chest and his legs. He felt it creep around the back of his shaven head. He felt a breeze on him. A glorious, beautiful, cool breeze.

'Now we're getting somewhere.'

Sol was aware of other changes in the atmosphere of Ulandeneth. His nose twitched and in that there was joy. His sense of smell had returned and with it he found an acrid, burned odour in his nostrils. His ears picked up distant sound yet though he narrowed his eyes there was nothing to see. Wait. Forms in the mist, if such it was. Unrecognisable but moving all around him.

'I am Sol,' he repeated and he smiled, feeling the familiar pull of muscles in his face. 'And I never walk outside naked.'

Clothing began to form on his body. Shirt, trousers, trail boots. The ring he wore that Diera had given him seven years ago was there on the middle finger of his right hand. A delicate piece, depicting a raven in flight.

'Almost there.'

Sol tried to remember his thoughts when last he was here. Then as a living being. Some of them eluded him. He remembered he had travelled home but now he could not think how. He supposed that was right and just. He remembered that he had been without a weapon when he arrived then too.

'That I can do something about. I am The Unknown Warrior. Sword of The Raven.'

Across his back he felt the comforting weight of his scabbard and in it his two-handed blade. Interesting. Not a weapon he would use now. His hip wasn't . . . But then of course that had been when he was alive. He laughed. Around his waist came his belt and everything that hung from it. Daggers, flint and steel.

'Now all I need is a place to go.'

Sol took a pace forward and six Garonin stood before him. He backed up and looked behind him. No one there. He turned back. Light flowed around the armour of the Garonin. Their hands rested by their sides. None appeared to be carrying the white tear weapon but something that looked like a blade hung from each waist. Sol snapped his sword from his back and held it before him.

'I believe,' he said.

In front of him the blade felt momentarily light and it all but fell from his grasp. He reformed his grip, taking careful note of how it felt, how the steel shone sharp and how even the nicks along its edge were part of its perfection. It rested balanced in his hands.

'Good. Right. I may go down here and now, but some of you fuckers are coming with me.'

Chapter 40

The dead clustered at the end of the passageway. The Raven and Auum's Tai were at the head of them. Ilkar still probed the wall. Behind them, the passageway fled off beyond their senses. Outside, the void clashed and raced. But surrounding them was an ivory light that came from beyond the end wall.

Every one of them could feel it. They were drawn to it, pulled along by it. None would so much as consider moving away from it by even a toe. Yet none of them could reach it. None, they assumed, but one.

'Where is he?' asked Hirad.

'Gone,' said Ilkar.

'Now if I'd replied that way to you, I'd be on the end of a long, long line of abuse.'

'Sorry, Hirad. Gone through here. He must have done. Ulandeneth.'

'We have to get through,' said Sirendor. 'He's going to need our help.'

'Perhaps he doesn't,' said Ilkar. 'Perhaps this is part of the whole scheme.'

'Not if Sha-Kaan is to be believed,' said Auum.

'Something must open this wall,' said Ilkar.

'Another astounding revelation,' said Hirad. 'Is it too stupid of me to ask what that might be?'

The dead surrounding them were restless and anxious. Adrift at the end of their journey. Feeling vulnerable as they stood waiting for answers in a place open to attack. They made a hum of chatter and a swirl of emotions that sometimes made coherent thought difficult.

'We must stop thinking like the living,' said Auum. 'This door will never have an iron latch.'

'Sol had an advantage over us all,' said Thraun. 'He has knowledge of this place. Did that help him travel there?'

'Well if it did, I wish he'd given us some pointers,' said Hirad. 'Unhelpful, just disappearing like that.'

'I don't think he had any choice in the matter, do you?'

Ilkar's ears would have pricked when he said that. Hirad smiled, another invisible gesture.

'No, probably not. So. Any ideas?'

'Everything so far has been an act of will,' said Thraun. 'Or a use of the soul's energy. We should start there.'

'You think we can will ourselves over there, do you?'

'Got a better idea, Hirad?' asked Thraun.

'No, it's just that it's difficult to will myself to a place where I've never been and which lies somewhere . . . you know . . . else.'

'I don't want to rush you but I think you'd better start believing as quickly as you can.'

Sirendor's shadow was facing back down the passageway. Hirad rose above the mass of the dead and looked in the same direction.

'This does not look promising.'

Three Garonin were pounding up the corridor but none of them was intent on attacking the dead. All three had eyes only for what was behind them. Panic spread among the dead. There was a concerted move to the wall, which remained steadfastly blank and impenetrable.

All the while the Garonin ran on. And well they might because the passageway was folding up behind them.

'So many problems.'

The melodious voices flowed over Sol, taking the ire from him. He lowered his blade. The Garonin were standing about five yards from him.

'We underestimated you.'

'Damn right,' said Sol. 'Lucky for you we weren't all acting together. We'd have kicked your sorry carcasses right out of Balaia.'

'We think not.' There was a susurration that Sol took for laughter. 'But we warned you that resistance forcing us to expend our resources would ultimately go badly for you.'

'I do remember that. And since then we've seen all sorts of wonderful things and bigger and nastier weapons. And yet, when last I looked, Xetesk still stood and you were denied her Heart. And here I stand once again, ready to take you on. No one who stood before me then is alive to tell you about it.'

'Ultimately.' The whispered word was discordant and sent a shiver up Sol's spine forcing him to hunch his shoulders. 'So much has been expended. So many of our people gone because of your fruitless resistance.'

'It is not fruitless.'

'No? One wrecked city still stands. Another is ready to fall. Your land is no good to you. It was ever going to be thus. And yet still you thought to fight, though to accept defeat would have been the easier option.'

'For you, perhaps. Your problem is that you have fundamentally misunderstood what drives us. It is the will to survive. The belief that we *will* survive, whatever the odds and however powerful the enemy. And we will. We will.'

Sol saw them hesitate. One of them even fell back a pace.

'You have spirit but you do not have the strength to turn us aside.' The melodious quality was back. 'You think to find a new home. We will follow you and we will destroy you there. You cannot escape us.'

'So you say.'

'It is forever the way. We need new worlds to harvest. We do not allow interference. We demand compliance.'

'Well, as my friend Hirad Coldheart would say, you can shove your compliance right up—'

'However. We respect a worthy foe and a worthy ruler of men. You are both of these.'

'I don't care for your respect,' said Sol, and he spat on the ground at his feet.

'No? When you have the lives of so many in the palm of your hand. Lives we can snuff out on a whim.'

'I'm aware of my task.'

'But not perhaps of the risks you take. Watch and . . . believe.'

The Garonin all lowered their heads. Sol felt a rush of energy in the air about him. The space above him turned black. He stumbled, almost fell. Night had fallen. From horizon to horizon it was the most complete blackness. But there was movement within it. Images resolved slowly, coming into focus like the world through a bleary eye after a long night.

Korina. The central marketplace. The Rookery. His old inn, now under new ownership but maintaining the tradition. Sol smiled at the memories. But the picture was not right. The market was empty and rubble-strewn. The inn's sign hung from one hinge and was split down its middle, ready to drop.

'What is this?'

Sol could not keep the quiver from his limbs. Dreams he could understand. This was something utterly different. The image drew away, like he was rising into the sky. Korina was slowly revealed before him. The once-beautiful capital city, the place where he had fallen in love, reduced to ruins and populated by gangs of survivors searching for scraps.

He saw whole areas barricaded off and the people within them carrying bows and spears against those without who begged for entry. He saw a man being kicked mercilessly by a gang of other men, some in ragged rich clothes, as still he tried to eat the bread he gripped with both hands.

Higher he went, and the scene or one like it was played out over and over. Shapes came into the image on either side of his view, as if he were passing between two high structures. Quickly they were revealed for what they were. Garonin machines. Vydospheres. Floating in the skies above Korina. And not just two. As the image continued to expand, he counted nine in a circle around the city. Worse, on its borders stood foot soldiers in their hundreds. Just waiting to fall on the helpless and desperate thousands within.

'We have their fate in our hands. They cannot get out. We can destroy them. We can wait for them to destroy themselves. Or we can set them free. It is the same for these people. Some friends, I think.'

The image switched, and Sol was transported to the wilds of Balaia. He didn't recognise where but he knew the faces that dominated the image he was shown and that lowered down on him. It took all his strength not to sink to his knees.

Rebraal and Dila'heth.

Their faces were grey with exhaustion and fear. Their eyes were wide and their expressions were of helplessness and despair. He saw their mouths move and knew they were speaking to one another but he could hear nothing.

'What are they saying?'

Sol tried to read their lips but the image was not quite distinct enough. Again the image pulled away. Not as high this time though it didn't have to. A few campfires sent smoke spiralling into a grey sky. In an open space stood multiple cells of the TaiGethen and a fair-sized group of Al-Arynaar. Surrounding them, a very large number of

Garonin foot soldiers. Two thousand at a quick guess. Too many even for the TaiGethen though the battle would be fierce and bloody until the bitter end.

'They have come so far to reach this dead end. We were always watching them even if they did not know it. They are tired. They need rest. You will ultimately decide whether they should get it. We are not always unmerciful.'

'Why are you doing this?' demanded Sol.

Not a head rose. There was no acknowledgement of his question. He thought about rushing them, seeing if he could take one of them down, but it seemed so futile and his emotions were churning anyway. He wasn't sure if he could hold his sword steady.

The Garonin showed him one more scene. It was of a huge fleet at anchor. Hundreds of elven vessels in the waters off Sunara's Teeth. North Bay. Wesman territory. The decks of the vessels were crowded with people. Many of the ships appeared to be riding low. Many others bore the marks of battle. There was flotsam in the water. Above them hung six vydospheres. On the peaks of the mountains stood foot soldiers. On the plains behind, a war camp.

'You thought we would not realise such a density of verrian could be taken by sea? These elves' lives are already forfeit. Long have we searched for them and we have delighted in their demise. There are over thirty thousand elves on those vessels. They are dying slowly of course. It is not in our nature to be merciful to such vermin. Yet there may be room. There may be.'

The Garonin's heads came up. The last image disappeared and the ivory sky returned. Sol sucked his lip, fighting against a rising despair. Again his sword began to feel light in his hand. He concentrated on the victory in the corridor and the familiar weight returned. And there was something else too. It gave him hope but he couldn't figure out why. Something was missing. Something had been left out.

'So you see, Sol of Balaia, despite your best efforts there really is no hope left. Even should you reach your mythical new home, there will be no living to take there; and no dead either, we will see to that. All you will have done is open fertile land for us to exploit. You have lost the war.'

'So why are you wasting your time with me?' Sol stood tall again and stared at them, each and every one. He raised his blade and pointed it at them. 'Eh? So destroy them all. Harvest your fuel and go back to where you came from to waste it on an enemy you cannot defeat. What are you waiting for?'

There was more hesitation before the reply. Sol found strength in that too.

'We are offering you and all these people salvation. It benefits you because no more of your people need die. It benefits us for the same reason. All you must agree to do is let us harvest unhindered now and at any point we choose.'

'I trust you about as far as I would trust a madman with a rapier. How can you expect me to believe you will honour such an agreement, ludicrous though it is? Effectively to allow you free access to our lands in exchange for . . . what? A few of my people being allowed to survive in a blasted country? You have no need to make such deals if your power is so great. And we all know that should you want more of your fuel you will take it without regard for the lives of my people. Gods drowning, but power comes with no guarantee of intelligence, does it? And our dead, what of them? Their resting place is destroyed.'

There was the slightest pause.

'The dead are irrelevant. There is nothing meaningful beyond life.'

Sol shook his head sadly. 'You have no souls. You do not understand.'

'Time is precious.' There was a note of stress in the mellow sound of the Garonin voice. 'Your decision.'

Sol smiled, the missing piece fitting into place.

'You're not sure you can cover your losses, are you?' He took a pace towards the Garonin. 'You don't want us to fight because you know the damage we'll do even as we are defeated. You want me to help you stop the fighting on Balaia to leave you free to plunder the Heart of Xetesk. And you didn't show me Xetesk because you damn well couldn't, could you? You are not in control. They've held you off, haven't they?'

Sol laughed. Again the Garonin displayed anxiety.

'And what happens if we choose to fight, eh? I'll tell you. You might be forced to retreat, mightn't you? To save your forces for the battles on your doorstep. Denied victory on Balaia and denied the chance to follow me to a new realm. The mighty Garonin undone by primitives. But primitives who can harness mana in a way you can never do. Let's see, shall we?'

Sol raised his blade and advanced further.

'Do not choose to fight us. You cannot defeat us.'

'Well you know what? I think I'll give it a try anyway. After all, I'm dead and I don't have anything better to do.'

'You will be responsible for the slaughter of many thousands of your people. Your loved ones, your peers. Your children. You are a man alone.'

'Don't believe everything you see,' said Sol. 'A Raven is never alone.'

The Garonin susurration irritated again. 'You are at our mercy. We know what we see.'

Sol backed away. 'Better start getting your killing sticks ready. Things are going to get bloody.'

'So be it.'

Sol spread his arms wide, his two-handed sword in his right hand, and began to turn a circle. He felt young, vital, like before the docks at Arlen, where he had seen his hip smashed beyond complete repair. Armour covered his chest, shining in the ivory light. And while the Garonin stood and watched, he raised his voice, gambling with his death and the life of everyone still living on Balaia.

'Raven! For all the times all we had was our belief, join me. For every moment we stared defeat in the face and returned victorious, join me. To avenge every one of us who has fallen, join me. You, The Raven dead. To believe is to prevail. To stand by those you love and pick up your swords one more time for Balaia and for The Raven.

'I believe in you. All of you. Hirad Coldheart, you have never run away from a fight in your life. I believe in you. Ilkar, your shield never once failed. I believe in you. And you, Thraun, who stood by us man and wolf. Belief brought you back; it can do so again. Sirendor, the warrior with a blade to mesmerise. You were stolen from us too soon. I believe in you. Auum, your whole being is belief. Your Tai will never desert you. Stand with us.'

Sol continued to turn. The Garonin continued to watch. Briefly, an image played out above. Korina under bombardment.

'Raven, where are you!' Sol shouted. 'Past and present. Believe in me. Believe in you. Believe in our fight. For the dead of Balaia, for the living of Balaia, believe in victory. Hirad, Thraun, Ilkar, Sirendor, Ras, Erienne, Will, Ren, Ark, Aeb, Darrick, Richmond, Jandyr. Whoever you are, you are Raven. Wherever you are, come to me. Stand with me. Stand with me!'

Nothing but his words echoing away into the ivory. Nothing but the susurration of the Garonin as their confidence grew. Sol narrowed his eyes and clung on to his belief.

'Don't you desert me now, you bastards. From wherever you are gone, I call you all. The Raven dead, the Tai of Auum. I call you. Stand with me. Fight with me. Raven! Raven, with me!'

The Garonin tired of watching. Weapons were drawn. Sol could hear the buzz of the white light that ran around their blades. He brought his sword in front of him and gripped it in two hands. He glared at the Garonin walking directly towards him.

'One at a time, if that's what it takes,' he said.

There was a whisper in the air. Sol felt a presence standing beside him. He breathed in a huge, glorious breath. There was no need to turn to look.

'Hirad. Just in time.'

'Never a truer word.'

In front of Sol the Garonin advance had faltered. Sol dared a glance at the barbarian. Hirad was gazing down at himself, his filthy, beaded and braided hair hanging in front of his deep-tanned face. The scar on his forehead and left cheek was plainly visible. His leather armour was a patchwork of repair. But the sword in his hand was sharp and held with total confidence.

'Don't worry about it; believe it. Work to do.'

'Where's Ilkar and Sirendor? Or Auum?'

'Plenty of time, Coldheart,' said Sol. 'Until then it's just us.'

'Should be plenty enough.'

The sound of a two-handed blade tapped rhythmically on the ground echoed across Ulandeneth.

'What do you reckon, Hirad?' said The Unknown Warrior. 'One more time?'

'You know you said that to me once before.'

'Well, this time I really mean it.'

Hirad grinned. The two men touched gauntlets.

'One more time, Unknown. Sol.'

The Unknown's blade ceased its tapping.

The Unknown thrashed his blade upwards two-handed. The edge ripped through his opponent's guard, smashing his sword from his hand. The swing continued, connecting with the Garonin's helmet. The heavy blade shattered the faceplate and tore through nose and cheek on its way out. The victim was cast back, a bubbling scream breaking from torn lips.

Before the others had a chance to adjust, The Unknown circled the blade about his head and brought its tip crashing down on the head of another. The Garonin's helmet crumpled under the force of the blow and his arms flew up as his body was driven to the ground. The Unknown roared and brought the blade through again, left to right. It buried itself in the hip of the third Garonin with a crunch of broken bone.

Hirad stepped in to block a white-edged blade angling into The Unknown's unguarded right flank. He forced the enemy sword down and away. Hirad adjusted his grip and reversed his blade high and across the Garonin's neck, finding the gap between armour and helmet. He moved his blade to his left hand.

The fifth moved in fast. Hirad spread his feet for balance and beckoned the man in. He moved to Hirad's right and struck low. Hirad turned his body sideways. The blade fizzed by his thigh. He grabbed the enemy's arm and pulled him off balance. Hirad's sword cut deep into the Garonin's back, sending him sprawling.

One man standing. The Unknown had dragged his blade from where it had lodged and began to move to the right. Hirad nodded understanding and went left. The Garonin inclined his head, lowered his blade and blinked out of existence.

The Unknown didn't pause to curse the cowardice. He ran over to his first victim and dropped down, one knee on the Garonin's chest. He pulled away the remains of the faceplate and stared into deep, dark orbs. The Garonin was bubbling blood from the slit of his nose and his cheek pumped crimson onto the ivory floor, where it faded quickly.

'You're going nowhere,' growled The Unknown.

'Impressive,' managed the Garonin.

'Just wait till we're all here,' said Hirad. 'And Unknown, we need to get the others here fast. The passageway is folding up behind them.'

The Unknown jerked his head round.

'What?'

'It started when you left. Everyone is stuck but us.'

The Unknown swore and turned back to his victim. 'Talk quickly. You want something from me. Something more. What is it?'

The susurration again. 'You already know, Sol of Balaia. You are a light to follow. Cursed to lead us to where we want to go.'

'And if I refuse to open the door?'

'Your people are already dying. It is not an option, is it?'

The Unknown stood. 'No, it's not. Hirad, join me. We can call them. Why did you come?'

'Because I was born to stand at your side to fight. I could feel your soul.'

'Exactly. Think that of the others. Bring them to us. Will you fail?'

'I will not.'

The two men spread their arms wide and called The Raven to them.

Chapter 41

Auum watched Miirt dispatch the three Garonin and felt almost sorry for them. The elves, like all of the dead, had nowhere else to run. The collapse of the passage was inexorable and unstoppable. It was folding in on itself, chasing towards where they were packed and trapped.

The Raven's dead had blinked away one by one and Auum had viewed this with some small satisfaction.

'He calls them,' said Ghaal. 'The Ravensoul is a powerful entity.'

Auum nodded. 'And so are the elven Gods. Do you believe Yniss would abandon three of his chosen to a fate such as this?'

'I do not.'

'Neither do I. Miirt. Join us.'

Miirt flew out over the heads of the dead and came to rest where her brothers were floating. The three shades bowed their heads, their arms about each others' shoulders.

'Tai, we pray,' said Auum.

'Much good will that do you,' said a voice from the crowd.

Their agitation had long since peaked and it seemed their energy had slipped away with the approach of what they assumed was oblivion. Even the sight of the quartet of Raven shadows departing had failed to lift their hopes.

'Humans despair before all is lost,' said Auum, his tone stilling the crowd. 'And you have no Gods to protect you, nothing to which to anchor your souls. For elves it is different. We will not end our journeys here. Yniss keeps us for other tasks. Any who choose to believe that might do well to form a chain of touch that begins with us.

'Tai, we pray.'

Auum bowed his head again, hearing worthless scepticism, sarcastic comment and open insult from those about to becoming nothing whatever. Such it was with humans. Offer them their only possible means of escape and their ridiculous pride would still ensure their annihilation.

'Yniss, hear your servants. From beyond the bonds of flesh, we call you. We seek that which all elves desire. To find a new place to call home. A place to bring our people where they might flourish in your glory. Where Tual's denizens might run free. Where Beeth holds mastery over all that grows and where Gyal's tears bring life. Where Shorth may speed our passing from one life to the next.

'Hear us, Yniss, your servants ready to do your bidding. To serve the purpose for which we are chosen. Hear us Yniss. Spare us for greater tasks in your name. The enemy still fights. We will cast them down.

'Hear us, Yniss. Use us, love us. Your servants ever.'

There was a brief reverential silence, broken by ignorance.

'Well, that got us precisely nowhere.'

Auum raised his head.

'If I did not respect those of your kind already fighting for you, I would cast you all aside to perish in this miserable void where your souls will find no rest for all of eternity.

'Wait.' Auum looked at the end of the passage, coming ever closer. 'Believe.'

Ilkar and Sirendor came across without difficulty. The elven mage took one look about him and sat on the ground, head in hands. Sirendor stood exactly where he had appeared, staring down at his perfect chain mail shirt and fine, tailored clothes. His blade rested in a delicately carved scabbard, its hilt freshly bound and its pommel buffed to a brilliant shine.

'Admire yourself later,' said The Unknown. 'We need to get Thraun out of there.'

Sirendor nodded. 'And quickly.'

'Ilkar. We need you.'

Ilkar raised his head. His sharp features were drawn with sadness and his dark hair lay lank across his shoulders.

'There is no mana here. Not a breath.'

'We don't need your magic right now, we need your soul,' said The Unknown.

'I feel empty.'

'Well, Thraun is going to feel pretty flat too in just a moment,' said Hirad.

Ilkar nodded. He pushed himself wearily to his feet and stood with the three warriors. Arm in arm, they bowed their heads. Ilkar leaned gently into Hirad.

'Good joke, by the way. Probably your first.'

'Concentrate,' snapped The Unknown. 'Invest your faith in The Raven. Push out with your soul. Reach for Thraun. Reach for all The Raven dead. Remember Thraun. Loyal, great heart. Whether man or wolf, Raven born and ever one of us. Stand with us, Thraun. We need you. Fight with us.'

Hirad sensed them all deep within him. The bond they had shared when they lived intensified now they stood together as souls clad in memories. The warmth and strength it brought suffused him. He cast his mind out, visualising the corridor. He thought one word and pulsed it through his soul.

'*Remember.*'

A wolf howled close by. The Raven quartet broke up. Thraun padded towards them, scenting the air. He was hunkered low as he came, semi-submissive and plainly anxious. Hirad moved to him, kneeling down in front of him.

'You're safe, Thraun. Among friends.'

'Where are we?' asked Sirendor.

'Ulandeneth,' said The Unknown.

'I've been in some dull places but this beats them all,' said Sirendor. 'Which way is out?'

'I don't know. But we're going to need more of us, to build the combined soul that has the power to sense our destination.'

Hirad looked at The Unknown and wrinkled his nose. 'I don't want to doubt you or anything but how do you know that?'

'I don't. It's a hunch. But feel us now, even with four and a wolf. You all came back to me, remember, and you were stronger when you were close to each other. Well nothing's changed except I'm dead too. The Garonin have tried to get to me twice now. There's something I can do alongside The Raven that bothers them. Something they can't comprehend or control.'

Sol had begun walking. The others fell into step with him.

'The Ravensoul,' whispered Ilkar. 'They don't possess souls. It's our one advantage up here.'

Hirad rubbed his hands over his face. 'Have any of you taken a look about? There's nothing here. I mean, I don't see a whole line of doors, do you? Where are we headed, exactly?'

The Unknown spread his hands.

'Come on, Hirad, you can't be that literal. For one thing, everything is here, we just can't see it yet. And for another, there was never going to be a line of doors, was there? This isn't one of Korina's filthy brothels.'

'Well all right then, smart-arse. What are we looking for?'

The Unknown rounded on him. 'I do not need your quick mouth and slow brain in my ear, Hirad. And aren't these questions I should be asking you? Correct me if I'm wrong, but I died at your behest, you and the rest of The Raven, to help you find a new resting place. Right, well I'm here. You tell *me* what's next. All the time we delay, the Garonin are slaughtering our people. So either make a positive comment or shut up.'

'If that's the way you want it.'

Hirad turned and wandered away in another direction.

'Gods drowning, Coldheart, you can be such a child,' said Ilkar.

Hirad's frustration boiled over. He stalked back among them and none of them would catch his eye.

'Think I want to be here in this miserable wilderness walking from one blank space to another? Seems to me I'm the only one brave enough to ask a few tricky questions. Sorry if I ask them in the wrong way but that's me, isn't it? None of us is real, all right? We do all know we're not really standing here looking ten years younger than when we died and in our old armour, don't we?

'I mean, we're here, but this is all a figment of memory or something like that. It has to be. I've just killed three Garonin with this sword and I don't want to think too hard about how that could possibly be. After all, they were actually alive, they actually bled and lost limbs, and I'm just a floating soul. Is anyone else finding this just a little bit odd? And that's even though it is unbelievable to be standing with you, fighting with you and arguing with you, and I never want it to end.

'The fact is that none of you has the first fucking clue what to do, have you? We've lost all the dead we came with. We can't help the living by standing with them any more and we haven't even got an enemy to fight. I'm happy to admit I do not know what we are supposed to do here. The rest of you seem to be relying on blind faith. Stupid. It really is.

'Well. Has any one of you got anything to say?'

Hirad's voice boomed around them as if they were in an enclosed space. Ilkar and Sirendor both looked at their boots. Thraun was prone, watching Hirad's outburst with his head cocked to one side and ears pricked right up. The Unknown had stopped his march too. He didn't turn for a while and Hirad saw him shaking his head. When finally he faced Hirad there was a smile broad enough to relax the most tense of muscles. He walked to the barbarian, took the sides of his face in his hands and kissed his forehead.

'And I love you too, Unknown, but I think the others will get jealous that you only have lips for me.'

'Hirad, as usual, in your random and confused fashion, you have come up with the answer.'

'I have?' Hirad raised his eyebrows. 'Care to point me at the cleverest bit of what I said?'

'Shouldn't be too hard,' said Ilkar. 'It'll stick out like a mage at a Black Wing party.'

'Actually, it's most of what you said in one way or another,' said Sol. 'But, in a nutshell, blind faith is exactly what it's about. Look, they had me here once before tied to a chair and I couldn't see the bonds. Only when I believed I could stand up was it possible to do so. Same as when I decided I wanted to come home. I had to *know* that was what I wanted above all else. And I had to visualise it to make it happen. This is a place beyond life or death. It's both and neither. Stop believing and you'll fade. Believe utterly and there's nothing you can't do.'

'But it doesn't get us to the door, does it?' asked Hirad.

'That's because we're trying to find it rather than let it bring us to it . . . Is anyone getting this?'

'Yes, I think I am.' Ilkar was scratching at an ear. 'After all, when you die, you travel to the last resting place without thought, it's just where you go. And when the Garonin threw us all out, we travelled back to Balaia in pretty much the same fashion, didn't we? All of us drawn by Sol or Densyr, bless his Xeteskian intransigence. And what you're saying is the same, isn't it?'

'That's about the size of it.' The Unknown frowned at Ilkar. 'You all right?'

Ilkar shrugged. He was shivering. 'I'll be fine.'

'What, so we lie down, smoke something interesting and let it happen, is that right?' said Hirad. 'Bit dull, isn't it?'

'I'm sorry but you can't always wade through rivers of blood, all right?' said The Unknown. 'And yes, we do let it happen in a sense but more along the lines of opening our souls to where the doorway is and then making our way to it.'

'Open our souls to what? When I died, I travelled, just like Ilkar said. No choice. When I came back, I recognised you, Unknown, and could follow your soul all the way home. But this new place, we know nothing about it. It's hidden from everyone and for a good reason, assuming it even exists. How do we open our souls to it?'

'I'll concede that's a good question,' said The Unknown. 'Any thoughts?'

'I've got another good question. What are they all doing?'

The Raven followed the direction of Sirendor's index finger. Indistinct, like figures in a heat haze, were people. Quite a lot of them.

'How long have they been there?' asked The Unknown, already walking towards them.

'Just caught them out of the corner of my eye,' said Sirendor. 'What are you thinking?'

'I'm thinking it looks bad. If I'm right, Garonin can travel here at will but they are also sensitive to what happens here and are drawn to opportunity,' said The Unknown.

'Which is how they got into the Balaian cluster, you think?' asked Ilkar.

'No doubt about it.'

'So, what are they drawn to this time?' asked Sirendor.

The Unknown pursed his lips. Hirad's soul was already crying out before he replied.

'Big collection of souls in the corridor, Sirendor,' said The Unknown. 'Big enough to hold a lot of mana and attract a lot of attention if the Garonin turn up here.'

'Auum,' said Hirad, and he broke into a run. 'Come on, Raven.'

Hirad heard the sound of their footsteps after him. Thraun loped easily by his side. Across the bleak land, Hirad could see the Garonin making deliberate progress, their long stride metronomic like the tapping of The Unknown's blade. In the clearing haze he could make out well over thirty.

He scanned ahead of them. Dimly he thought he could see what looked like a structure of some kind. What was definitely there was a different quality of light. He upped his pace. Curious that he felt no breath in him. And strange that there was still a limit to how fast he could run. The limit of his memories, he assumed. Still, it would be good to reach a fight on the run and not be gulping in air when he got there.

'Through the back of them or join Auum, if it is him?' asked Sirendor as they ran.

'We need to upset their attack,' said The Unknown. 'Ilkar, how's it coming?'

'Not so . . . well.'

Hirad glanced back. Ilkar was struggling. He looked as if he was running in thigh-deep mud and there was an odd quality to him, like he was shimmering or something. Hirad slid to a halt.

'Unknown. Quickly!' He grabbed Ilkar's arm and made him stop. 'Ilks. Come on, stop a moment.'

'Need to . . . get attack. In . . .'

Ilkar stumbled and fell forward, sprawling on the ivory floor. Hirad's eyes were drawn to his legs. His boots were gone and below the knee his legs seemed indistinct, grey beneath a shifting mist.

'Stay with us, Ilkar,' said The Unknown. 'Sirendor, get here. Thraun!'

'Can't find anything,' mumbled Ilkar. 'No energy. My mind is cold.'

'It doesn't matter, Ilks,' said Hirad. 'We're with you. Get your strength from us. It'll come back.'

'Listen to him,' said The Unknown. Sirendor joined them and all placed hands on Ilkar's body. It just seemed the natural thing to do. 'We know you, Ilkar. We remember your sacrifice at Understone. We know how strong you are. Believe in yourself as we believe in you. The magic doesn't matter. Your soul next to ours, that matters.'

Ilkar's shivering began to subside and the shimmering that had encased his body cleared. His boots reformed slowly over his ankles and feet. Thraun trotted up and nuzzled Ilkar's head, licking him hard across the face. Ilkar spluttered and thrashed to a sitting position.

'That is disgusting.' He stared at them as if for the first time. 'What happened?'

'We thought we were losing you, Ilks,' said Hirad.

Ilkar wiped his face. 'I have never been licked by a warrior before, in whatever shape he currently resides.'

'Well, pull a fading stunt like that again and it'll be me next time,' said Hirad.

'What more incentive could an elf want?' Ilkar held up a hand to The Unknown, who was standing. 'Can you help me up?'

'Sure you're all right?' asked The Unknown.

'Much better for the pep talk, Unknown.' Ilkar smiled.

The Unknown gathered them all close. 'Before we run, I want you all to bear in mind one thing. We cannot lose faith, not for a moment. It makes us weak and we cannot afford that. Whatever happens, we are Raven, we are strong. We have never been defeated.'

He held out his hand, palm down. One by one, Sirendor, Ilkar and Hirad placed theirs on his.

'We are The Raven,' he repeated. 'Now let's go save Auum and find ourselves a new place to rest.'

A soul-tearing scream stopped them before they had taken a single step.

Chapter 42

Two figures lay on the ivory ground not five feet from where Ilkar was standing in The Raven's huddle. Their screams called out to his soul, burying themselves in the centre of his pain. He could feel theirs so cleanly it brought him, all of them, to their knees.

He led the crawl over to them while the screaming dug at his ability to put one hand in front of the other. His teeth were gritted together and a taut sound was being dragged through them. Wreathed in flame, her hair burning like the brightest lantern on the darkest night, the little girl had her hands over her face, helpless in her agony. Arms wrapped around his head as if to protect him from whatever fell on him, the other figure, a grown man, was tucked into the foetal position. He was covered in dust as if fresh from the trail. His head was a mass of blood, his skull smashed at the back. Shards of bone had pierced the brain within.

Sol reached them first, laid his hands on the girl. The flames were extinguished immediately and her body relaxed. A shuddering sigh escaped her burned mouth and a transformation overcame her. Her body lengthened, grew. Beautiful angled features were drawn on her face. Auburn hair covered her skull and a full figure developed beneath tough trail clothes.

'Erienne,' gasped The Unknown, and she dragged him into an embrace, body shaking, her bright green eyes looking out over his shoulder, staring and confused.

Hirad hurried to the man. His screaming had subsided. Tight curls now adorned his head and the dust of the trail was gone. He wore cavalry boots and trousers, a chain mail shirt and a cloak was about his shoulders, trimmed the green of Lystern. Slowly, he straightened out and came to a sitting position. His face was pale but in his eyes shone the determination that had made him such a valuable member of The Raven.

'Thank you,' he said. 'Oh, thank you. I was lost. I heard you.' He smiled. A rare occasion when he had been alive. 'I found you across the void.'

'General Ry Darrick, late of the Lysternan cavalry,' said Hirad, holding out a hand which the other man took, shook and used to pull himself upright. 'We thought you gone forever.'

'Where are we?' Darrick asked.

'Where we should have been a long time ago,' said The Unknown, helping Erienne to shaky feet. 'Seeking our new home.'

'But there's a problem, right?' asked Darrick. 'It isn't as simple as that.'

'We are The Raven,' said Hirad by way of explanation. He turned back towards the Garonin. 'And we're late to the fight.'

'Are you all right, Erienne?' asked Ilkar, coming to her other side.

She smiled at him but there was still confusion in her eyes and the memory of agony.

'It already felt like forever,' she whispered. 'I didn't think you would ever find me.'

'What did?'

'The void. It is worse than any myth. Trapped in the moment of violent death for all time. I have been burning, my flesh melting and my bones cracking. I can still feel it, Ilkar.'

'It will fade. You're with us now,' said Ilkar. 'What's your story, Darrick?'

Darrick turned a haunted face to him. 'Even though I came back, I have been feeling the pounding of endless tons of stone on my head and across my body. Why that?'

'Perhaps it is still your most vivid death memory,' said Erienne. 'My latest most certainly is.'

Darrick nodded. 'Every moment I can feel the one that dashed my skull and the smell of the karron demons. I can see you all there on The Thread and I die endlessly, never knowing if you succeeded or not.'

'You all ready to run?' Hirad had broken into a trot. 'And as you'll have guessed, we did succeed. Couldn't have done it without your help on the way, though.'

'Thank you. Where are we running?' asked Darrick.

Hirad pointed and Darrick fell in beside him. Ilkar smiled and his body felt strengthened, more complete. Perhaps Sol was right. And perhaps more would come. Still, though, the mana spectrum was dark . . . no, not quite. Beyond the Garonin, from where the luminescence emanated, there was something.

'Souls,' said Ilkar. 'Thousands of them. We'd better make this fast or it's going to be a slaughter.'

The souls huddled together in the lee of the edifice their combined strength had created. The escape from the corridor had been close. Auum had never doubted they would make it but enough of the dead had lost faith and so had inevitably perished. They had been cast back into the void as the passage folded to nothing. The rest were scared and the crumbling of the rock, if such it was, behind them was evidence of failing belief.

None of them would help the TaiGethen. Indeed it was hard to pick out many individuals. Most had coalesced into an amorphous shifting globe, each with a voice that shouted for help. Some had remained grey shadows. All waited for Sol to appear to lead them to safety. But The Raven was nowhere to be seen and Auum had more significant and immediate problems.

'Ghaal, how many?'

'Thirty-eight. All carrying the mana drain needles. Forty yards distant.'

'Work to disrupt them. They'll try to get round us to the mass. Choose your blows.'

Auum unclipped his jaqrui pouch, loosened the swords in his twin back-mounted scabbards and thanked Yniss for his gifts. He turned to the two greatest gifts of all. TaiGethen. Souls he'd thought lost forever. Friends garbed for the rainforest and painted brown and green on their faces in the manner of Tual's children. Evunn and Duele.

'Yniss calls you for your greatest challenge, my friends,' said Auum. 'Fight with me one more time. Protect the dead. Help is coming.'

Duele and Evunn nodded. Both looked confused, fearful even. But the sight of their Tai leader brought them hope and, more importantly, faith.

'Tai to me. We pray.'

Auum knelt and bowed his head as the Garonin moved closer. He could feel their footfalls through the ground and he could hear them slapping dully on the ivory. The four knelt with him and they knew the closeness of touch.

'Yniss, we stand before an enemy that knows no mercy. Protect us. We prepare to fight in your name. Guide us. We do your work and ask only that you bless our struggle. Hear us. Ulandeneth speaks with one voice, elf and man. Join us.'

Auum raised his head and gestured to his Tai to stand.

'Ghaal, Miirt, get amongst them. Duele, Evunn, my left and right. Spread as you must. Watch your brothers. Watch your sister. Tai, we move.'

Miirt and Ghaal moved out a few paces, remaining close together. Auum, Duele and Evunn spread across the mass of souls. They couldn't hope to cover it all. The huge body of souls, thousands of them, spread over an area easily fifty yards wide and twice as high. The structure in which they huddled afforded them some protection but the anxiety spawned by the approaching Garonin increased with every moment and the walls were weak, laced with cracks and beginning to crumble.

The structure was essentially simple. A scooped-out circular over-hang, bordered by rough spires of rock and with a further tall spire rising above the centre of the overhang. It looked like an ancient weathered hand, with index finger pointing at the sky. Ivory was its colour.

The Garonin began to spread into a wide line, seeing their advantage.

'Pick your targets and work fast,' said Auum. 'Yniss will guide you.'

'I had thought myself lost in the void forever,' said Duele. 'Your call brought us back.'

'No,' said Auum. 'Yniss brought us together. Now we must show our gratitude.'

Ghaal and Miirt dropped into a half crouch. The Garonin broke into a run. Auum turned his head to face his enemies.

'Dance.'

Ghaal and Miirt sprinted forward a few paces, planted their left legs and jumped, soaring over the oncoming first line of Garonin with their bodies straight and arms ahead like a diver entering the water. Both curled their bodies, rotated and landed to run at the second line.

Auum moved a heartbeat later. A jaqrui crescent wailed away from his hand, catching his target on the wrist and chopping hard into the flesh. The Garonin's weapon fell from nerveless fingers. He turned to find Auum right in front of him. Auum's right hand came up under the enemy chin, driving his head back. His left came through, the blade in it biting deep.

Auum stepped back and ran right. The Garonin surge was fully on them. Duele swayed away from a running enemy, planting a straight kick into the side of his knee. The cracking of bone ricocheted across the edifice behind. The Garonin went down clutching at the injury. Duele ensured he was not suffering for long.

Evunn was surrounded. Garonin were unwilling to face him. Most preferred to run by, trying to get at the body of souls. He jumped. His swords whipped outwards left and right. Two Garonin pitched forward, deep cuts to their necks. Evunn brought his blades back, crossing them in front of him. The Garonin before him stumbled and collapsed. His head lolled to one side, spurting gore, all but severed. That got their attention. Three turned on Evunn and he was quickly on the defensive.

Screams rose from the mass as mana was siphoned away. Dark spots appeared briefly, fading to nothing. Too many Garonin were getting past the wafer-thin defence.

'Fight!' called Auum. 'You have to fight for your lives. For your souls.'

But their fear was too great and it played into the willing hands of the enemy. Auum ran the line of the pulsating, terrified mass of souls. Garonin were deep within it. Auum flashed a blade into the back of a Garonin, who spun round to stab his needle point into Auum's soul. Auum could see it coming as if it were being pushed through tar. He stepped to one side, grabbed the Garonin's arm and pulled the enemy onto the point of his sword.

Back out in the middle of the fight, Ghaal and Miirt were under increasing pressure. Garonin bodies fell and disappeared. Too many for them to ignore. The Tai were back to back against ten, their limbs blurring, swords tracing paths in the air. But it was all in defence.

Auum thought to help them but before him stood three Garonin. Others ran left and right of them, diving into the mana-rich souls behind him. More screams, more pleas for help. Auum drew his second blade. The three Garonin rushed him, their speed startling. Needle points flashed out from their hands, joined to their armour by lines of some kind.

Auum swayed left to dodge the first, bringing a blade through to sever the line. He ducked down as he moved, his other blade chopping into the second needle, shattering it. The third came straight for his head. Dropping the blade from his left hand he caught the needle scant inches from his forehead, hurling it to the ground, where it smashed.

Auum launched himself forward. Left fist connecting with the faceplate of the centremost enemy. His momentum carried him on. The Garonin had no chance to react before Auum's blade lodged in his gut. Auum dropped to the ground with the body and rolled aside, dragging his blade clear. The remaining two Garonin had been joined by three others.

Auum drove to his haunches and scuttled backwards, giving himself precious room. Another figure loomed over him. He glanced up into the hard black eyes of his enemy. No blow came. The Garonin toppled sideways and a human hand reached down to help him up.

'Can't have you taking all these for yourself,' said Hirad.

Auum smiled. A deep green-brown washed the ivory land to his right. Garonin by the dozen disintegrated, screaming as they went.

'Raven!' called Sol from behind him. 'Raven, with me!'

Auum sent a brief prayer of thanks to Yniss and let his blade speak again.

God's Eyes arced through the sky, falling in the midst of the Garonin blocking the mouth of the valley and the path back to the beach. Rebraal and the Al-Arynaar pushed hard up the right-hand slope, mages with them, shielding them from the white tears that blew the unwary apart. But the mages were weak and the shields fragile. The Garonin knew it too.

The attack, when it came, had been as shocking as it had been overwhelming. The valley had flooded with the weapon fire of the Garonin. Beams of energy had surged down from the vydospheres above them, obliterating those they touched. TaiGethen and Al-Arynaar rendered to so much ash in moments.

But still the Garonin could not force surrender. ClawBound and TaiGethen charged into the enemy forces. Al-Arynaar warriors and mages regrouped under shielding spells and the fightback had begun.

The God's Eyes did little but cause armour to flare. Rebraal cursed. Ahead of the surviving Al-Arynaar, perhaps a hundred and fifty of them, the Garonin were waiting, weapons raised.

'Get our shields overlapping to the front,' he called. 'The Tai have our backs. Pushing my warriors. For Yniss and our people!'

The Al-Arynaar moved forward, Rebraal at their head, Dila'heth just behind him. Down on the valley floor the TaiGethen pressed into the central mass of Garonin. The enemy pressured them at the rear, where the ClawBound and more TaiGethen were amongst them, disrupting any concerted advance.

'Slowly,' said Dila'heth.

'We cannot afford to be slow,' said Rebraal.

'My mages are weak. Concentration is fragile. We must be careful.'

But Rebraal could hear the sounds of destruction and pain from beyond the valley. He could see the bodies of his brothers and sisters littering the valley floor. Garonin weapons kicked up shards of rock and mud all around them. White tears from across the valley and from above splashed over the shields. Mages gasped under the pressure and the enemy in front still weren't firing.

Eventually, Rebraal nodded. 'Slowly, warriors! At the pace of your mages.'

'They're waiting,' said Dila. 'I don't like it.'

'They have no need to force anything,' said Rebraal.

There was a series of detonations from the foothills of the mountains. Rebraal looked up. Smoke and dust billowed out a few hundred feet above his head. A bass rumble vibrated through the rock wall that formed the valley side along which the Al-Arynaar moved. Shards of stone began to fall. Rebraal went cold. A dull thump echoed out. And another.

'Shields!' he roared. 'Shields above. Orsyn's Cocoons now. They've broken the mountain!'

The thumps had become a thundering rattle and rumble. Rebraal stared up into the dust. Boulders tumbled down the steep slopes, bouncing high and crashing through shrub and tree. They splintered on rock. Thousands of tons swept down the mountainside.

Simultaneously, the Garonin ahead began to fire. White tears washed across the front of the shield, heaping pressure on already weak mages. There was no time to split and run. Nowhere to go but into the arms of the Garonin. Al-Arynaar began to run into the lee of the valley side but the rock slewed down so quickly.

Rebraal could not take his eyes from the avalanche that rushed towards them. And when it struck, he had no idea how many mages had the strength or the skill to cast the Orsyn's Cocoons that might just save them. Not enough. Rock slammed into warrior and mage alike. Some were swept away. Others crushed, smeared into the ground by boulders the size of wagons. Screams and panic were lost beneath the tumult. Rebraal reflexively tried to shield his head with his arms. Stone slapped down towards him.

And bounced. He heard a sigh. Dila sank to her knees, holding her arms outstretched above her. The Cocoon covered at least forty elves. Some were mages keeping shields steady against the Garonin. Others were warriors praying to Shorth for swift transport of their souls. And Shorth would have to wait.

Rebraal crouched by Dila'heth, trying to peer through the dust cloud that temporarily enveloped them while he lent her the support of his damaged body. The torrent of rock had lessened dramatically but merely allowed Rebraal to hear the cries of the injured and dying.

As the dust began to clear a little, he could see three groups of elves standing beneath Cocoon castings. Down on the valley floor, the fight still raged on. TaiGethen and ClawBound fought like never before. Claws, jaws, blades and fists ripping into the enemy. But they were outnumbered by more than ten to one. It was a brave action but it could not go on forever.

The Garonin in front had ceased firing for the moment, no doubt assessing the damage their soldiers had done in causing the avalanche. A vydosphere thrummed overhead, sucking the mana from the dead and dying. Dila'heth let her spell disperse. She swept her gaze over the survivors.

'We cannot win this way,' said Rebraal. 'We are trapped.'

'But not helpless,' said Dila'heth and, bless her, she smiled. 'It's our turn now.'

Rebraal frowned. Dila'heth called a few mages to her.

'What are you—?'

'Just keep them off us. Just for a little while. And run when I say. We don't have much but what we have we're going to use right now. All of it.'

Rebraal kissed her forehead and stood. 'Warriors! Fight with me.'

He charged ahead towards the waiting lines of Garonin, caring not if the white tears tore his body to pieces. He felt his brothers and sisters with him. The enemy readied, some choosing blades above weapons as they sought to harvest mana rather than simply kill. So much the better.

The leader of the Al-Arynaar roared the name of his brother to clear his mind for the fight. Looking left and right, he guessed fifty were with him. The elves sprinted into the attack. Weapons fired. Energy seared across the diminishing space, ripping into bodies, hurling smoking corpses to the ground and blasting limbs from bodies.

Rebraal ducked, dived headlong and rolled over his left shoulder. White tears fled over his body. He came up to a crouch, jumped and smashed his sword into the face of his target. The Garonin's helmet split. Gore spilled out. The body disappeared. Rebraal gripped his blade with both hands, ignoring the pain from his damaged wrist. He stabbed straight out. A weapon blocked the thrust. Rebraal carved out and down, slicing through thigh and knee.

Al-Arynaar waded in next to him. Others hurdled him, driving feet first into the ranks of the enemy. Blood misted the air. The stench of innards rose. Rebraal surged to his feet. Directly in front of him, two Garonin. He blocked the blade of one and hacked down into the weapon of the other. Both enemies stepped back. They loomed over him, tall and powerful.

Rebraal moved into the space. He feinted to the right and brought his sword through from the left, clattering it into the shoulder of the blade carrier. Armour flared white. The other turned his weapon on Rebraal. The hand of an Al-Arynaar clamped on it, forcing the weapon down. A short blade whipped through and severed the enemy wrist.

Rebraal nodded thanks. He punched out into the midriff of the blade carrier. He dropped to his haunches and swept out his left leg. The Garonin saw the move and jumped but he landed off balance, stumbling forward. The thrust of an Al-Arynaar sword took him under the chin.

Rebraal rose again. Garonin were thick about him and his warriors. White tear weapons were useless now. He fielded a blade on the hilt of his sword and shoved the Garonin back. To his right an Al-Arynaar took a blade through his throat. Blood spurted from the wound. The elf fell yet even in the act of dying held out his sword. Rebraal took it and swept it through his killer's gut.

Blade in each hand, Rebraal moved into the space.

'Disengage!' Dila'heth's voice carried into the heart of the fight. 'Al-Arynaar. Scatter free!'

The speed of their withdrawal was as exhilarating for Rebraal as it was confusing for the enemy. Thirty warriors, maybe a few more, ran hard into open space. Rebraal headed straight for Dila's team of six mages.

'Down in front,' she said.

Rebraal hit the deck. Yellow heat flooded the air above him. The Jalyr's Sun, which normally traced an arc, barrelled straight ahead only a few feet from the ground. The Garonin had seen these before and adapted to them. But the loss of Julatsa's Heart made every casting a compromise. It made them different. Different enough.

The Sun, perhaps three wagons in diameter, exploded across the Garonin, covering dozens of them in superheated mana fire. Armour flared but could not withstand the force of the barely controlled spell. The withering flames consumed flesh and bone. Burning Garonin screamed. They fell, some trying to crawl away from the fire that ate at everything it touched.

The Garonin line holding the valley wall collapsed. Soldiers scattered before the conflagration that rolled across the ground. Some even turned and ran. Rebraal climbed to his feet and caught Dila's eye. She smiled.

'Spell Shield up,' she said.

'Our turn now,' said Rebraal.

And, calling his warriors to him, he charged across the fires and down to the unguarded flank of the fight for the valley mouth.

Chapter 43

The fighting washed around Sol, leaving him feeling detached. It all seemed sped-up to his mind and he experienced confusion and a slew of nausea. Hirad's blade crashed through the top of a Garonin helmet, beating the man to the ground and spreading his brains across the ivory floor.

The Raven, along with Evunn and Duele, had fought to form a rough circle in which stood Erienne and Ilkar. The former was causing devastation with One magic castings against which the Garonin armour had no defence. The latter seemed unable to grasp the concept of where they were. Ilkar relied on actual feelings, not memories and beliefs. Right now he was a passenger.

Outside the circle, the remaining TaiGethen weaved their unique form of death with astonishing accuracy and speed. But even they were coming under increasing pressure. The Garonin had ceased their attack on the mass of souls in an attempt to destroy the aggressive defence provided by Raven and elf.

'We need to get to the TaiGethen. Bring them into the circle,' said Sol.

Sirendor blocked a strike to his waist and stabbed out, landing a glancing blow on his opponent's hip.

'That's the third time you've said that.'

Sirendor feinted to move in and instead swept his blade low, carving deep into the thigh of his target. The Garonin staggered back. Another took his place. Sol scowled and lashed out with his blade. The Garonin in front of him blocked the strike, grunting with the effort.

'Fight me,' growled Sol.

But they would not. The Raven circle was moving steadily towards Auum. Erienne cast again. Reinforcing Garonin were hurled aside like a child discards a toy. A path opened up to the TaiGethen leader. Sol saw him surrounded. Six Garonin converging on him. Auum turned full circle, taking them all in. His movements impossibly quick and sure.

Auum crouched. Blade in one hand, jaqrui in his left. He powered to his feet, taking off and twisting his body. His left arm came round. The jaqrui howled away, slamming into the helmet of a Garonin soldier. His blade came next, spinning on the horizontal as it left his hand. It hacked deep into the arm of a second soldier. Both men fell back.

Auum landed and was running at his next target. Sol couldn't focus on him. He shook his head to clear his vision but there were clouds before his eyes. He gasped, pain gripping his soul.

'Unknown!'

Hirad's voice came from a long way off though the touch of his hand was immediate. Hands dragged Sol backwards. The circle closed. Sol could hear fighting. The clash and spark of weapons. He felt a huge pull on his body, like someone was trying to suck his heart clean out of his chest.

'I have him.' Ilkar's voice. 'Unknown, lean into me. We're still moving.'

Sol had no idea if was standing or seated. Warmth was growing around him. The light of the mass of souls burned incredibly bright in his mind, like staring into the sun. Pinpoints closer were those of The Raven and TaiGethen. He heard voices. Distant echoes of those he loved. And those of the lost seeking sanctuary.

Sol's entire body was juddering. In a brief moment's vision, he saw Ilkar's arm and clung to it. The elf's face was confused and bright, so bright.

'Keep it inside you.' The voice came from everywhere. It was Auum. 'Do not let it take you. Not yet.'

But Sol did not know how to achieve any of that. He felt as if his body were being flushed by the force of the void. A chasm had opened up between the body that had drawn around his soul and the soul itself. He reached out, trying to grip himself. He saw a spectral hand clutching at the centre of his spiritual body. He found purchase. And he found a tiny degree of calm.

The fight was raging on around him. Sol shook off Ilkar's hand and straightened his shoulders. Garonin had closed in on Miirt. Ghaal was fighting his way towards her but he wasn't going to make it. Hirad was moving The Raven's circle in the same direction. The barbarian's blade licked out, cracking against the armoured shoulder of a Garonin shoulder. Next to him, Sirendor ducked a wayward thrash and jabbed his blade up and into the gut of his opponent.

The pull on Sol's body declined. He looked about him. The soul mass was pulsating, lanterns to banish the darkest of nights. They could feel the pull.

'Enough,' he said.

'Unknown, are you . . . ?' said Ilkar.

'Let me go,' said Sol.

He walked between Hirad and Sirendor, moving them both aside. His blade was held in one hand, leaving his right hand free.

'Follow on. Keep your guard up,' he said to Hirad.

Sol strode up to the Garonin, who fell back a pace ahead.

'Fight me!' he barked at them. 'What, no guts for it? Then cease your attack. Now.'

The Garonin ahead of him stopped. Sol moved up and drove his blade straight through the soldier's chest. The man was hurled backwards, skidding across the ivory floor, blood pulsing from a deep gash.

'I can take you one at a time,' growled Sol. 'I know what you want from me. Cease your attack.'

Sol was wavering. He fought to keep his body steady while his mind was ablaze with light and a yearning that he would soon not be able to deny. The Garonin paused. All of them.

'Miirt, hold.'

Auum's voice came as if from a long distance. Sol felt The Raven move up around him again. He heard Hirad calling Miirt and Ghaal into the circle.

'What are you doing, Unknown?' asked Darrick from by his right shoulder.

'Buying time,' said Sol.

The Garonin began to move away from The Raven. Sol could hear the susurration of their conversation or laughter or whatever the hell it was. Hirad was standing close to him, as was Darrick. Close enough that he couldn't fall sideways. Thraun padded up and down in front of the Garonin lines. There was blood about his muzzle and on the fur of his shoulders.

'You accept your fate,' came the voice of the Garonin.

'We accept nothing,' said Sol. 'But that the price you have paid is far too high for the mana you have managed to harvest. We may not have beaten you but what price your failure in your own world, I wonder.'

'What's going on?' asked Darrick. 'I don't understand.'

'They know what Sol represents,' said Auum. 'What he is here to do. They wanted to take as many of us from him as they could to weaken us. To make it easier for them to gain entry to our new home through him. And in that they have failed.'

'And what do we do now?' asked Sirendor.

'Prepare,' said Auum.

Someone took Sol's arm and helped him move towards the edifice. There was comfort there amongst the thousands of souls that had survived the Garonin attack. The Raven gathered in front of him, Ilkar and Hirad helping him to a seated position with his back to the wall, directly under the finger of rock.

'Who built this?' he asked, though the answer was obvious.

'They did,' said Auum. 'The souls. To focus themselves. To give them a place to congregate and a place where you would find them.'

Outside, the Garonin mustered. More and more were appearing. They stood still for a few moments as if orienting themselves before moving forward. Darrick was standing and looking out.

'This is not a good situation,' he said. 'We may have a wall at our backs but we have an overwhelming number in front. How long will this all take?'

'I don't know,' said Sol, brightness again growing within and without him, his soul reaching out. 'But we have to hold them off until we can bring our people to us.'

'And what then?' Sirendor spread his arms. 'How can we stop them following us? How can we stop them doing exactly what they did on Balaia and following the dead to their rest and then back to the land of the living, wherever that is?'

'Have faith,' said Sol.

'Faith isn't going to be enough,' said Sirendor.

Sol climbed to his feet and grabbed Sirendor's shoulders before The Raven man began to fade.

'No, Sirendor, it is everything. Believe. You must believe. Anything less and we are lost. We will find a way to prevail.'

There were tears on Sirendor's face. 'I cannot see it. A thousand against a handful.'

'Trust me,' said Sol. 'Trust the Ravensoul. Just a little longer.'

Hirad put his arm around Sirendor's shoulders, nodding to Sol to sit back down.

'Stand by me,' said the barbarian. 'They can't touch me and I will not let them touch you. More will come.'

'How do you know that?'

'Because we always find a way,' said Hirad.

The ivory sky darkened. Garonin voices blared out across Uland-eneth.

'Do not delay us. Open the door, Sol of Balaia. Your people are dying. Their suffering is on your hands. Let us into your new home. End the pain of your people.'

Sol sat down hard against the wall of the edifice, thrust there by unseen hands. The clamour of the mass of souls was renewed inside him. Fear swept them. The sky became black again. Thraun howled. He saw The Raven and the TaiGethen putting their hands to their ears, shutting out the sounds of a gale of suffering voices.

'Now, Sol of Balaia. Now. End the agony. Bring us what we desire.'

The sky flickered. Flashes of light ran across it from horizon to horizon. Images appeared. Images to take the heart from any of them. Images to crush hope. Erienne was screaming. Ilkar was on his knees, hugging himself, his chin on his chest, body shaking. Hirad stood tall, thrusting out his chest and bawling some unintelligible cry at the waiting Garonin. Sirendor and Darrick were transfixed, gazing up at the sky and the horrors it displayed. Auum and the TaiGethen appeared locked in prayer.

Thraun howled again and Sol let the yearning in his body take him.

The east walls of the college blew apart for a stretch of over three hundred yards. Garonin soldiers poured in. Guards and mages who had been standing on the walls were lost in the cataclysmic failure of binding. At the ruins of the tower complex dome the binding work continued though the effort had become desperate.

Suarav stood with Brynar. The young mage's shield, in concert with four others, held firm against the withering fire from the six vydospheres circling above. But they could no longer defend the entire tower complex. Bindings were weakening on the remaining towers while feverish attempts to shore up the walls of the catacombs were ongoing.

The noise was extraordinary. White tears flooding over the shields set up a resonating whine while the clattering of the vydospheres' heavy weapons added a juddering roar that could be felt through the feet.

'We're surrounded,' shouted Suarav. 'Chandyr, we need swords to the east. Brynar, shields ahead and left.'

How many hundreds of Garonin advanced on them was impossible to guess. They did not close for hand-to-hand fighting, not yet at any rate. They were content to bombard the shields that Xetesk's tiring mages held against them. Not one offensive spell was being cast. There were no longer the numbers to do it. Suarav bit his lip.

'We can't hold out here,' yelled Brynar. 'We're just waiting for the end. I can feel others weakening.'

'Just a little while longer. Keep them away from the catacombs. Let Densyr complete if he can.'

Below them, the Circle Seven were placing defence around the Heart. Not enough mages remained to bury it out of the reach of the Garonin so their only chance was to booby-trap it to keep them away for as long as they could. Densyr had one last card up his sleeve, and if he meant to play it, it would be when he could inflict maximum damage on the enemy.

Somewhere, The Raven would be trying to find a way to rescue them into an uncertain future. No one knew how long they would take, or indeed if they would succeed at all. Until then, Suarav and his people hung on grimly, just trying not to die.

The moment Brynar shifted his shield across to block the fire from the advancing soldiers, the focus of the vydospheres changed. Streams of pure energy slammed into the now-unprotected towers. Bindings flashed and flickered. Stone shifted. Dark blue light rippled up and down the length of Densyr's tower. The Mount Tower. Suarav gulped in a breath.

'We have to get more focus on the Mount Tower. We have to keep it standing.'

'We aren't enough,' said Brynar. 'The bindings will have to hold.'

'They will not.'

'Then move the catacomb binders to shore it up. We can't help you here.'

As if to illustrate his point, Brynar gasped and dropped to his knees. The Garonin deluge was growing. More soldiers poured onto the courtyard, moved within range and fired their weapons. To their right a shield collapsed. White tears rampaged through the defenceless soldiers.

'We're just targets!' roared Chandyr into Suarav's face. 'We have to move now.'

From above, a flat crack echoed out over the college. Suarav saw dust rip out from the Mount Tower about a third of the way up. Blue light flared briefly. The entire tower shifted violently to the right. More Garonin fire pounded the walls. The result was inevitable. Catastrophic.

The Mount Tower, the symbol of Xetesk, fell.

Grinding and shearing, stone, metal and wood failed and tumbled. The remaining upper floors collapsed inwards, the weight of material battering through the tower, bringing the whole sliding and crumbling. Tens of thousands of tons of ancient building sent clouds of billowing dust flooding out as it thundered down on the complex and the defenders below.

Suarav just stood and stared. There was nothing else to do. Around him, people were scattering but with nowhere to go. Some ran into the teeth of the Garonin advance. Others fled into the tower complex, directly beneath the falling stone of the Mount Tower.

He saw Brynar turn to him and open his mouth to speak, but a piece of debris struck his left leg and he fell. Chandyr cannoned into him, pushing him into the lee of one of the only piece of wall still standing at their backs. Suarav snapped out of his trance. Chandyr rolled off Suarav. Pieces of the tower dashed through the complex ruins, shattered on the courtyard stone. All around them it fell.

Suarav could see Brynar writhing on the ground with stone falling all around him. He was screaming and clutching at the stump of his left leg, gone below the knee.

'Chandyr, we've got to—'

A shattered timber slammed end first into Chandyr's head. His skull was crushed. His body jerked and was flung to the side. Suarav threw up his arms. Gore and splinters sprayed across his face. He breathed in gasping breaths. Every shield was down. Every binding spell not yet complete was gone. The defenders had been blasted away from their positions by the stone of their own college.

And beyond the clouds of dust that choked his vision and clogged his lungs, dragging wracking coughs from his throat and chest, he could hear the Garonin march on the catacombs. Suarav fought the urge to panic. He scrambled back to his feet and stumbled over to

Brynar. The mage was unmoving but breathing. His ruined leg bled freely.

'Hold on, Brynar. Hold on.'

Suarav ignored the pain in his body and the protestations of his weakening muscles. He picked the young man up. He turned and moved as fast as he could through the rubble and into the complex, hoping to find the entrance to the catacombs still open. Garonin weapons were firing again. Suarav coughed up more dust and hurried away, seeking brief salvation.

Chapter 44

'Where are we going?' asked Diera.

Densyr stopped and turned to Sol's family. The three of them, and the wolves that flanked them, were scared witless by the astounding noise from above and the echoing organisation of Xetesk's last defence all around them. The continued barrage had brought down various ceilings throughout the catacombs and the place where he had been keeping Diera and the children was no longer safe. Every corridor was full of smoke and dust to a greater or lesser degree. Wounded guards and mages left blood trails on the ground. The whole maze was awash with fear.

'I have to get you to a place where we can get you out if we have to.'

'Wait, wait,' said Diera, hugging her children close to her. 'This is going back towards the main entrance, isn't it? Back towards the Garonin.'

'The only entrance,' said Densyr. 'I'm trying to give you the best chance if we're compromised here. Do you trust me?'

Diera hesitated before inclining her head. 'Do I have any choice?'

'Nowhere is safe in Xetesk,' said Densyr, feeling a weight of responsibility greater than any he had experienced in his time as Lord of the Mount. 'But I will not put you at unnecessary risk. I've made mistakes. You won't be another of them.'

Densyr looked into Diera's eyes. And then into Jonas's. He found the strength there that he needed. He turned and led them back into the centre of the catacombs. Another huge jolt shook the whole underground structure. Densyr lost his footing and stumbled into the wall at his right hand. Young Hirad had fallen and grazed his knees. Diera scooped him into her arms, letting him sob into her shoulder.

'Where are we now?' asked Jonas.

'Map room just ahead and right. Old Soul Tank chamber this door on your left. The Heart is below us now and my tower a little way ahead. Let's keep moving. Everyone all right?'

'Still alive, anyway,' said Diera.

Densyr moved on. There was a worrying groaning of stone above. Some part of the complex struggling under the Garonin assault. One of the wolves was whining. They were approaching a hub. Figures were rushing past the corridor and he could hear anxious shouts echoing down to them. A second, lesser jolt rattled through the catacombs. It was followed by a hideous cracking sound.

'Oh dear Gods,' breathed Densyr. 'Run. Quickly. Follow me.'

Densyr grabbed Diera's free hand and pulled her with him. Mages ran past them and away back towards the dimensional research chambers.

'It's coming down! Run, my Lord Densyr, run!'

'What's coming down?' demanded Diera above the groaning, cracking sounds ricocheting down from above. Plaster fell from the corridor. 'Denser!'

Densyr said nothing, dragging them into the hub room. To the right, the roots of his tower plunged deep into the ground. Passages ran down either side of the foundations. Gaping cracks had been torn in the stonework and the wall was vibrating. He led them left and away towards Dystran's chambers.

'Denser!'

'It's my tower,' Densyr called over his shoulder. 'Don't look back.'

The corridor down which they now hurried was shaking violently. Debris and plaster fell. There were small cracks in the floor at his feet. Hirad was screaming. Diera tried to comfort him though her voice was trembling. Jonas kept up a running commentary, encouraging them, keeping them running. So much his father's son.

A thunderous crash hurled them all from their feet. A torrent of stone and metal barrelled through the roof of the catacombs, sending dust rushing down all the passages away from the hub.

'Down!' yelled Densyr.

Diera covered Hirad's head. Jonas was lying half on his mother. The dust howled past them, carrying with it shards of rock and wood. The wolves ran on, away from the avalanche at their heels. The sound of the falling structure, the noise of rock on rock, splintering timbers and the grind of twisting, tearing metal, boomed around their heads. On and on it went. Densyr felt debris cover his boots and the lower part of his legs.

As the din subsided, he could hear crying. He lifted his head, relief making him a little light-headed. Diera and Hirad clung to each other, tears streaking their grimed faces. Jonas was shaking muck from his back, legs and hair. Densyr stood and held out his hands. Behind them, the hub and corridors were gone, filled by tons of rubble.

'Come on. The enemy will be down here next. We have to make one short stop and then get out of here.'

Diera got shakily to her feet and looked behind her, gasping in a breath. Hirad had stopped crying but wouldn't be put down. Diera nodded and gestured Densyr to lead on. Jonas came to his shoulder.

'What are you going to do?' he asked.

'Light a fuse, in a manner of speaking. One long enough to allow us to get out.' Densyr dropped his voice as they took a right turn then another left. 'Can you use a sword?'

'My father taught me a few things.'

'Good. We'll find you one. Just in case.'

'You will do no such thing,' said Diera.

Densyr didn't pause or look behind him. 'Sorry, Diera, but you need to know what the collapse of my tower means. The outer defence has failed. We can assume no one has survived up top. The Garonin will be down here ripping the walls out to get to the Heart. We're liable to run into some of them. Right turn, Jonas. Second door down on the left. Go straight in.

'We have little choice but to arm ourselves. Just in case.'

'Where are the wolves, Mama?' asked Hirad.

'They'll find us again,' said Diera. 'Don't you worry.'

She caught Densyr's eye and he did nothing to hide the doubt he felt. He ushered Diera and Hirad intro Dystran's chambers and closed the door on the disaster unfolding outside. Densyr cast his eyes around a dust-filled oasis of calm. A fire was in the grate. A servant was pouring tea and Vuldaroq was seated in front of Dystran, a hand on his wrist.

'How is he?' asked Densyr.

'Fading,' said Vuldaroq. The old Dordovan Tower Master took in Sol's family. His face cleared and he smiled. 'It's time, is it?'

'Yes,' said Densyr.

'He can't speak but he can hear you,' said Vuldaroq. 'But he is proud of you and the decision you're taking. As am I. It is a fitting end.'

Densyr knelt by Dystran. 'We've had our battles, my Lord Dystran. But I like to think we've carried ourselves with respect. Most of the time, anyway. The Garonin are crawling all over this place. You know what to do. Don't leave it too long. Don't build too much. You will be remembered as a hero of Xetesk for this even more than the demon wars. May your soul find peace.'

The slightest of smiles crossed Dystran's face. Densyr rose.

'Come with us, Vuldaroq.'

Vuldaroq shook his head. 'I don't think so, Densyr. I'll stay with him. We both need the rest.'

The two men shook hands. Pain flitted through Densyr's head. Dystran had begun his work.

'What's going on?' asked Diera.

Densyr smiled. 'The end of magic, Lady Unknown. Only way to make this world not worth further plundering. Come on, we've fresh air to breathe.'

The yearning was overwhelming. Sol knew there were tears falling down his cheeks. He knew he should feel the anxiety that the rest of his friends were experiencing as they awaited the inevitable attack. But he felt a joy that he could not confine. The hopes of every soul around filled him. Their lights shone so bright within him.

Sol reached out to gather in the strength of The Raven. He could touch each one of them. The huge presence that was Hirad. The determination that shone from Erienne. Ilkar's stoicism through his frustration. Sirendor's will buoyed by Hirad's refusal to let him fade. Darrick's calm purpose. Thraun's animal power. He would have wished for more of them to be with him, but they were enough.

The weight of the body of souls was his foundation. The Raven were his keystone. Sol opened his soul to the void. Warmth washed through him. He had never paused to wonder how he would find their new home. The soul searches and the soul finds, so Auum had said. And it was true. He could smell trees and flowers, sea and stone.

Yet there was nothing to see. There was no passageway down which to travel, no door that needed to be opened. There didn't need to be. Sol was all these things and he was the bridge to a place he would never see. A place where hope would be kindled by the fact of his death. Yet a place open to plunder unless the final battle was won.

Sol opened his eyes to find his vision changed. He could still make out the forms of his friends standing in front of him but they were altered. They were shadows again though now with a pulsing white soul energy that coursed around them. The Garonin too were changed. No longer the tall imposing soldiers he knew. They too were silhouettes though no energy shone from them. They were dark mist. No soul, no cohesion.

Sol breathed in the wonder of it all, forgetting for the moment that the enemy were massed to attack. The ivory of the land had gone too, so had the blackness in the sky. It was an even grey to Sol and there was what looked like dust in the air. Clouds of it. Not dust, he realised with a gasp. They were the marks of souls. Thousands, maybe millions. Travelling towards life or to their rest. Painting patterns in the comforting grey, like flocks of birds in flight.

'It's beautiful,' he breathed.

'Unknown.' Hirad's voice. Close. Sol looked and thought he could make out the barbarian's shadow. 'Unknown, can you hear me?'

'Yes, Hirad.'

'You're sounding like you drank something way too strong, old friend.'

'You can't see or sense what I can, Hirad. It's wonderful.'

'I'm sure it is. But the Garonin are getting restless; we can see our people dying in the sky, though that might be a trick. We can't see how we can stop them taking us, then you, and ripping the heart out of wherever it is you've found . . . You have found something, haven't you?'

'Oh yes, you could say that. And I can't hold the door closed any longer. My soul desires to feel a new dawn. All these souls need a berth just as yours does. Keep strong, Hirad. You're the heart of The Raven, don't forget that. Trust me. Help is coming.'

'From where?'

'From everywhere. That's why it had to be me that died for this.'

'What are you talking about?'

'Just be ready. We're going home, Hirad. Home.'

Sol closed his eyes again. Everything had become very clear. The only risk now was that the Garonin would overwhelm the defenders before he was ready. But if he trusted anyone, it was The Raven. Sol let his soul fly. The scents of life suffused him. A breath played over him, gentle caressing growing to a breeze. It was the passage of souls, flooding forward into their new lands, there to find their resting place, there to find the paths back to their loved ones. There to end the torment of those marooned on Balaia.

Yet not all the souls that flowed over Sol passed through. Again and again he felt the touch of familiarity amongst the mass. And each one responded to his call to arms. To turn from sanctuary and defend the resting place none had yet seen.

'My brothers, the world is forever in your debt,' said Sol.

'We are one,' they responded.

Sol, the bridge between worlds, the director of the souls of the dead and the seeker of the paths back to the living, opened his eyes once more and he smiled.

Rebraal smashed his sword into the unguarded flank of a Garonin soldier. The Al-Arynaar bludgeoned into the enemy force holding the valley mouth. TaiGethen attacked with renewed vigour.

'Down in front,' said Dila'heth.

Rebraal ducked, bringing his warriors with him. IceBlades whipped over their heads. From somewhere, she had found another casting. The slivers of ice as hard as diamond sliced into the helmets of the Garonin. Seventy and more held the valley mouth. Before them, the dead of the TaiGethen lay, the enemy's corpses long since claimed back to whence they came.

It sickened Rebraal to look at the dead but they gave him more energy for the fight. He surged up and chased in after the IceBlades. Dila'heth's spell had wreaked havoc in the Garonin line. They had been unable to adapt to the out-of-tune Julatsan casting. Blood poured from the split helms of dozens of soldiers. Those nearest the impact were down. Others were pierced but still standing, unsteady on their feet.

The Al-Arynaar ploughed on. White fire ripped through their ranks. Rebraal swayed outside a stream of tears, leapt high and brought his sword down onto the helmet of a Garonin soldier. The man's head broke apart under the force of the blow. Rebraal landed, rolled and came upright, in the thick of them now. He stabbed left and right.

His warriors were with him, driving a wedge deep into the enemy line. A white-edged blade came at him. He parried and thrust out, knocking his man back. The Garonin came on again. A jaqrui tore into his neck. Blood spurted from the wound. Rebraal stepped up and finished him.

Elves poured down on the diminishing knot of the enemy. Behind, further up the valley, the vydosphere's weapons were useless during the melee. And on the ground the TaiGethen and ClawBound defence kept the balance of the Garonin from joining the fight.

Rebraal punched straight out, feeling his fist crack against stomach armour. There was a flare of white. Rebraal ducked instinctively. Something had lashed out from the armour. He heard elves scream. Rebraal chopped down hard on the Garonin's right arm, battering the weapon from his hand. He reversed his blade and slashed up into the helmet, denting it deeply and sending his opponent sprawling.

Rebraal glanced behind him. Dila'heth lay on the ground, blood pouring from a gash across her face. Mages were running to her aid. Rebraal turned back. Still the Garonin fought. A TaiGethen warrior fielded a blade on his short sword but a second came round and carved the top of his skull clean off. His Tai brothers spun, leapt and kicked, feet driving into chest and gut. The two Garonin went down. Rebraal turned from the kill.

'Break their line,' called a voice from behind him. 'You're close. You're so close.'

Rebraal faced a new enemy. The soldier raised his weapon to fire. Rebraal turned sideways and grabbed at it, feeling the heat along its length as it discharged. He forced the weapon down. White tears rattled into the dirt. Rebraal bounced on the balls of his feet. He jabbed his left elbow into the soldier's faceplate and his blade through the eye slit. The man fell soundlessly.

Al-Arynaar surged around him. A ClawBound panther from the rear defence leapt over elf and enemy. She flattened a Garonin soldier, her jaws closing on his neck as he struck the ground. Rebraal followed up, hacking through the thigh of the last man in front of him as he struggled to find his blade, unable to fire for fear of hitting his own.

Rebraal was clear. He tore down the path to the abandoned village. From ahead he could hear screaming and shouting and the detonation of weapons. Spells lit up the sky in desultory fashion, impacting both the ground and the vydospheres hovering over the bay.

He rounded the last bend, ran through the village and slithered to a stop, his heart thrashing in his chest.

'Oh no,' he said. 'Dear Yniss, preserve your people.'

The sea was aflame. He watched a Garonin heavy weapon fire

from the carriage of a vydosphere. The ship beneath it disintegrated in a ball of flame. Timbers and planking were reduced to ashes in moments. Those aboard were incinerated in the blink of an eye.

Rebraal could not see beyond the fire and smoke to the open sea and the remainder of the fleet. He could not see the *Calaian Sun* and could only pray that Jevin had escaped to deep water and away to preserve the bound statue of Yniss. But he could see the staging point on the beach. Or what was left of it.

Smoke trailed over blackened sand. Remnants of marker flags blew across the shore. Three thousand he had left there. All gone, their souls cast into the void. Rebraal fell to his knees. The only thing left now was to pray.

Chapter 45

Densyr took them at a dead run on a circuitous route back towards the catacomb entrance. All around them the sounds of fighting echoed through the corridors, replacing the earlier bombardment. It was hard to hear. His guards and mages defended the Heart while he ran for his life, hoping they could delay the Garonin long enough for Dystran to complete his final task.

Diera was struggling under the weight of young Hirad. The lad wouldn't touch the floor to run or walk now. Densyr brought them to the junction of two corridors and stopped before making a right turn.

'Do you want me to take him?' he asked.

'You need your hands free to cast,' said Diera, blowing hard. 'Hirad darling, please, will you run if Jonas runs with you?'

'I can't, Mama. I'm frightened. Why aren't the wolves here?'

'They must be ahead somewhere, checking the way is clear for us. It's going to be all right. You'll see.'

Hirad clung to her neck. Diera raised her eyebrows at Densyr.

'I'll be all right. Just you look after Jonas. I don't like seeing him with that sword in his hands.'

Densyr glanced down at the blade they'd taken from one of Dystran's guards. It rested easily in Jonas's grip. He had hefted it like a veteran but Densyr knew he had only ever fenced with Sol. Real combat was horribly different. For his part, Densyr had part-cast an Ilkar's Defence. It was the best he could think of without risking his charges.

'Are you ready? We go right here, all the way down to the end of the corridor, then it's left, up a short incline, straight across the hub and up the stairs to the way out. It gets hard from here. Do what I say and we'll make it.'

'Ready,' said Jonas.

Diera nodded again and put her hands under Hirad's backside to lift him onto her chest.

'Put him on your back, Mother,' said Jonas. 'He'll be better protected that way.'

'Hirad?' asked Diera.

The boy shrugged and climbed up on Diera's back. She put her arms under his thighs.

'Thank you, Jonas.'

'Let's go,' said Densyr. 'Jonas up front with me. We'll shield your mother.'

Jonas kept pace with him. They hurried down the corridor, a long, narrow space that inclined very slightly along its length. As they approached the end, Densyr heard a sound from ahead and brought them to a sliding stop. Footsteps, heavy and deliberate.

'Be ready,' he said.

Jonas clutched his sword in both hands. The point tapped on the ground. Densyr could not suppress a smile.

'Sol used to wait until we could see them at least,' he said.

'It helps the nerves,' said Jonas.

'For us too.'

Round the corner came a figure, carrying another in his arms. Densyr sagged with relief and ran towards them.

'Suarav. Dear Gods above, man, how are you still alive?'

Suarav's face crumpled. Tears streaked down the dirt encasing his face. His shoulders shook. The head of the man in his arms fell outwards. Brynar. Behind him, Diera gasped.

'Hide your head, Hirad. Do it now.'

The whole of Brynar's left leg beneath the knee was gone. Ripped away by some huge force. Blood still dripped from the stump.

'Help him,' managed Suarav. 'He fought so well.'

'Put him down,' said Densyr. 'There's nothing anyone can do for him now.'

Suarav shook his head. 'Don't say that. So many of them out there. We held them. He deserves to live. He—'

Suarav's body juddered and blew sideways, slamming into the opposite wall of the corridor. White tears thudded into his body, ripping him and the dead Brynar into smoking pieces. Diera screamed. Densyr swore. More footsteps. Powerful and rhythmic. Two men at least, possibly three.

'I'm ready to cast. Jonas . . . Jonas, no!'

'Jonas!' shrieked Diera.

The boy had heard neither of them. He had run to the end of the corridor and was waiting just away from the turning, sword cocked back. Densyr could see his body heaving and the tremble in his legs. Densyr began moving towards him, his spell itching to be cast. It shouldn't feel like that.

A Garonin soldier appeared at the corridor entrance, stooping to squeeze his frame into the confined space. Jonas hesitated, looking up at the eight-foot-tall figure hunched under the low ceiling. But not for long. With a cry, he swung his sword round and up. The blade sheared through armour at the waist. The Garonin howled in agony and fell back.

Densyr made the end of the corridor and cast his Defence spell down it. Two more Garonin stood there. White tears played over the blue-washed barrier. Densyr could feel every impact through his arms. He clung on to the casting, finding it hard to concentrate.

'What's going on?' he asked himself.

By him, Jonas was staring at the blood on his sword. He was shivering.

'I killed someone,' he said, his voice tiny.

'And though I shouldn't say it, your father would have been proud of you. Just check your moves with me first next time, eh?'

The answer to Densyr's first question became obvious. The walls all around them and throughout the catacombs glowed deep blue and trembled. Densyr pushed hard at his casting, forcing the Garonin back along the corridor.

'Time to leave. And quickly.'

There was beauty in the way it all folded back, thought Dystran. A certain symmetry of which Septern himself would have been proud. The lines of the ward grid had gathered together when he had let go the entry point between Heart and casting. The place where he should have set his mind to keep the opposing forces at bay was now empty. There was more he could do, however, and do it he did.

Dystran imagined himself humming as he did his work. His mother used to hum when she was cooking so it seemed the right thing to be doing. Dystran did not want to let the small chance that the energies within the grid would dissipate come to fruition. So he directed the mana flow back along the grid lines, using his failing mind to force them into the shape of a rope with individual fibres spiralling together.

And when that was thick enough, for his own amusement he gave the shape of this focused mana an arrowhead. Feedback. The most terrifying force any casting mage would ever face. But at this moment, Dystran's last on this Earth, it was simply stupendous in its simplicity and its power.

The arrowhead slammed into the gentle pulsing hourglass of the Heart's mana. There really could be only one outcome. He hoped Densyr escaped it. That would somehow be just.

For Dystran the world turned a fiery blue and then to utter dark.

Densyr gathered every ounce of strength in his mind and pushed. The Garonin were shoved straight into the hub room and flattened against the wall to one side of the stairway. Surely there were many hundreds more enemy up the stairs but that was a chance they'd have to take.

Densyr held the spell a few moments more.

'Got to ask you to do something, Jonas,' he said.

'I know,' said Jonas. 'I'll take left.'

'Good lad. Don't think about it. Only consider what they have forced your father to do. Don't let them take any more of your family.'

Jonas nodded, a grim expression on his young face. The sight of it angered Densyr more than anything he had seen these past days. He gave the Ilkar's Defence another shove, batting the heads of the Garonin against the wall one more time.

'Dropping on three,' he said. 'One, two . . . three! Defence down.'

The two of them rushed the stunned Garonin. Densyr dragged a dagger from his boot sheath, reached up and rammed it into the neck of his target. Beside him, Jonas gave a wavering call and stabbed his man through the stomach. His blade ran straight through and screeched against the wall.

'And now it's time to run.'

Densyr ran for the stairs up to the ruined tower complex. He had not got two steps before he felt the air being sucked out of his lungs. A wind howled down the stairs, a mana gale that blasted through his mind. Behind him Sol's family couldn't feel it at all. He screamed and clamped his hands to the sides of his head, dropping to his knees and tumbling back.

He felt hands about him, trying to help him. All around them the blue in the walls had faded to a crisp white and frost bulged out, thick and grabbing. Ice fingers probed into millennia-old stone. The catacombs gave a death rattle. A complete silence fell.

'What's happening?' asked Diera.

'The Heart is about to stop beating,' said Densyr.

There were footsteps on the stairs. Densyr swore. Hirad screeched and clutched hard at Diera's neck. Four Garonin pounded into the hub room. Densyr wasn't ready. He had no spell prepared. His head was thumping as loud as the enemy boots. Jonas rushed in, yelling at them to leave his mother alone. A Garonin arm came round. The back of the soldier's hand clattered into Jonas's chest, sending him sprawling.

Diera and Hirad both shrieked Jonas's name. Garonin weapons trained on Densyr. He bowed his head and closed his eyes. From his left two shadows whipped by. He heard a Garonin shout. There was a howl and then the crunchy of fang on flesh and bone. A weapon was fired, dust and stone fell from the ceiling. Densyr dared to look.

Both wolves had attacked from a side passageway. Two Garonin were down. The other two trying to beat the wolves back. Jonas stormed past him and hacked his sword into an exposed back. Densyr, impelled to action, freed his dagger again. He paced forward. The one free Garonin reared back, a wolf snarling and snapping in his arms. The soldier roared with the effort.

Densyr jammed his dagger blade hard into the back of the Garonin's left thigh and kicked into the back of his knee. The Garonin pitched forward. The wolf spun in his grip. Claws and fangs lashed in. Before long, the enemy had ceased his struggle. Blood slicked across the hub room floor.

Densyr, breathing heavily, nodded his thanks at Jonas. He wiped his dagger on his trousers and sheathed it. A bass rumble rippled out from the centre of the catacombs. The hub room shook. Areas of the plaster ceiling fell in. The walls heaved. Fissures appeared within, shattering ice. The wind began to howl again but this time all could hear it.

'Run!' yelled Densyr.

He sprinted back to the stairs, trying to ignore the pounding in his head. Jonas was by his side, bloodied sword still held in one hand. They ran out into the devastation that had once been the tower complex. Nothing was left now but treacherous ruins. Ruins filled with Garonin. A hundred eyes turned on them as they fled the top of the stairs and were forced to stop by the piles of stone blocking their path. Fifty weapons were brought to bear. The wolves placed themselves in front of Hirad and Jonas, barking out warnings. Lips curled back from teeth and hackles rose.

'To me,' shouted Densyr. 'Huddle close.'

There was a growing whine in the air, replacing the silence. Densyr cast quickly and efficiently, trying not to think about the fact that it would be his last casting as a true mage of Xetesk. He had a choice to make. To deflect the Garonin weapons was one option. He chose a second. Densyr stared at the nearest Garonin as the soldier's hand rested on the trigger of his weapon.

'I'd duck if I were you,' he said.

The Heart of Xetesk exploded. The speed of the shock wave was incredible. The ground rippled underfoot, upsetting every Garonin, pitching them from their feet. It was followed by a series of detonations from deep within the catacombs. Densyr's Orsyn's Cocoon covered the four of them above and below, a seamless bubble of mana that he would cling on to for as long as his mind would let him.

From the centre of the catacombs the ground heaved in expanding concentric circles. Cracks were torn and blue fire lashed out, sending shards of stonework out in lethal clouds. Garonin, struggling to their feet, were cut to shreds in their tens and dozens. The ripple detonations thundered beneath Densyr and his charges. They were cast up eight or ten feet and dumped back down.

The ground collapsed beneath them and they fell further. All around them Garonin soldiers died. The air was full of whistling missiles. Great slabs of catacomb wall spiralled high, crashing down on the undefended. Bodies were smeared beneath falls of rock that would have crushed dragons. The ripples fled ever outwards, blue light gleaming under the surface. The wolves leapt out and bolted, howling as they went.

Densyr could just see the remaining college walls to the north judder and fall. Below, in the catacombs, nought would be left but dust. Stones and debris rattled on the skin of the cocoon. Densyr could feel his link to the Heart fade and die. An intense sadness swept into his body and the shield was gone. There was still mana here. He could feel it, taste it. But the flow he knew, the security that had always been there . . . nothing was left. Not a trickle. Mage rendered man.

'I wonder if this really was always inevitable,' he said.

'Probably,' said Diera.

She hugged Hirad close to her. The little boy was cut and crying but otherwise unharmed. Physically at least. Jonas coughed and sat up, using his sword as a prop to help him stand.

'Is it over?' he asked.

'Well, that depends whether the Garonin find us of no more use or whether they feel annihilation is fitting revenge. Either way, we should probably get out of this hole. I dread to think what it's like below us. As treacherous as shifting sands, I should think.'

'Densyr,' said Diera, feeling able to use his new name at last

'Denser, I think,' said Denser. 'That little ego trip didn't last, did it?'

'Denser, then. Sol would have been proud of you. Thank you.'

'Don't thank me. Not yet,' said Denser. 'Not until he comes for you. Come on. We need to find somewhere safer to hide.'

The doorway was open. The light that encased Sol was blinding. All any of them had to do was turn and walk towards it and they would be gone. And the Garonin would be right behind them. The pull, the temptation, was enormous. But to give in would be a betrayal of everything for which Sol had sacrificed his life.

And so Ilkar turned back, the howls of the Garonin loud in his ears, and watched them charge across the open space. There had to be two thousand of them in ranks forty yards wide. They would reach The Raven and TaiGethen in moments. They would roll over them as if they were wheat in a field and they would plunder a new set of dimensions.

Even so, Hirad, who stood a few paces in front of him, did not flinch or turn to run. And he held The Raven with him, daring any of them to weaken. Erienne was casting beside him and how he wished he could do the same, but something was still missing. It hardly mattered now, he supposed.

'Pick your targets, Raven,' said Hirad as Garonin weapons came to bear. 'Ilkar, Erienne, we need shields now. Let's keep them back as long as we can.'

Which would be a few heartbeats at best. Ilkar searched within himself for the ability to make something from this place bereft of mana. For Erienne, the task was plainly a simple one.

'Shield up,' she said.

The Garonin halted twenty yards from them. Ilkar watched them move into an arc, surrounding The Raven completely. He felt powerless, useless. With Erienne shielding them, he was the one who could actually deal damage but he had no idea how. Thraun stood stock still to Darrick's left, lips drawn back from his teeth. He snarled. Darrick, like Hirad beside him, faced the enemy with no hint of fear. But to Hirad's right Sirendor was twitchy, unsure. The TaiGethen flowed left and right along the thin Raven line, seeming far more than the five they numbered.

'Are you ready for this, Erienne?' asked Hirad.

'We're about to find out,' she replied.

'You can hold on,' said Sol, his voice around them all, comforting and strong. 'Trust me. Help is near.'

The Garonin opened fire.

White bloomed across Erienne's shield. A thundering and crackling noise built up, reaching a screaming crescendo. Ilkar couldn't see beyond the front edge of the shield, such was the density of fire. Erienne was driven to her knees. She stretched out her arms and a guttural sound escaped her throat. She gasped. Ilkar blinked. She was being pushed slowly back across the floor, and the shield would be coming with her.

'Pace back, Raven,' called Hirad into the booming noise. 'We won't see them until they step inside. Ilkar, is there nothing you can do?'

Ilkar felt the question like a slap in the face.

'There's no mana here,' he said.

'There's nothing here. No swords, no armour. Nothing,' said Hirad. 'This isn't about reality. It is about belief. You believe you see me, don't you?'

'Yes but . . .'

'It's the same for your mana,' said Hirad. 'Believe you can cast. Expect to cast.'

Ilkar shook his head. His mind remained a blank for constructing spells but there was something he could do. He hurried over to Erienne, dropped to his haunches and leaned his weight against her. Ilkar felt her move into his body. He put his arms about her stomach and held her close.

'Tell me how you're feeling,' he said into her ear.

'You ssshould, ttry, tthhis,' she said.

'I wish I could. You're doing brilliantly. Keep talking to me.'

'Ignore the emptiness,' gasped Erienne. 'Use your memories. You already are for everything you see of us. It works, I promise.'

The fire density increased steadily. Either more Garonin were attacking or . . .

'They are closing,' said Sol, his voice sounding deep in Ilkar's head.

'How are you doing that?'

'Things are a little different from where I'm sitting. You have squads of Garonin coming in at the far left and right of the shield where it touches the edifice. The main bulk are standing off and there is another force behind them. They will look to get to me. Be wary.'

Ilkar saw the TaiGethen split and move to the flanks. Within the bubble of Erienne's shield the open ground was quite limited. Perhaps only forty feet square. But the defenders were very thinly spaced.

'It will only take one to touch me,' said Sol as if reading his thoughts. 'And we are lost.'

'Where's that help you promised?' asked Hirad.

'Just around the corner,' said Sol. 'In a manner of speaking.'

'Ilkar.' It was Erienne, and her voice sounded as if she were about to break.

'Not long now,' he said. 'Be strong.'

'I need you to be able to help me,' she said. 'They are speaking to me.'

'They're what? Who?'

The sky over Ulandeneth turned black.

Chapter 46

Ark's last living memory was of the moments before the demons took his soul. Beyond that, the awful pain of their torment and, later still, the dread knowledge that even when the demons were destroyed, his soul's fate was eternity in the vast screaming purgatory of the void. Over and over, he had lived the last beats of his heart. The ice of the demons' touch. The dragging of their claws through his body and the freezing agony of a reaver's grip on his soul.

Unlooked-for and beyond his capacity to hope, the touch of Sol had found him. Somewhere a door had been opened and he had been pulled towards it, helpless to avoid its embrace whether it be fair or foul. Then had come the strength of Sol, imbuing his soul with light and hope. And with it had come the rush of voices in what he began to think of again as his mind. Comforting, supporting, powerful. As one. Their souls mingled but this time not in the thrall of the Soul Tank. No demons forced them to their work. This time they did so as free men under the banner of the first to have escaped the order of the Protectors. The first to stand in battle without a mask.

For Sol they gathered, and for Sol they would fight.

Images played out across the sky above them while the Garonin weapons blinded them head on. Erienne was groaning with effort and slowly losing her own personal battle. Ilkar prayed that she didn't look up but he could see her head moving as if someone were forcing it back.

'Don't do it,' he said. 'Face front or close your eyes.'

'I . . . No. NO!'

Erienne's arms trembled. Her whole body shook and her fingers, splayed out to keep the shield taut, began to draw into fists. Above her Xetesk destroyed. Barely recognisable. Yet in the middle of the ruined college figures ran while white tears bit at their feet and spat at the ground right behind them. Wolves flanked them, blood running from their blackened flanks.

'Please no,' said Erienne. 'Don't let it be true.'

Denser. Running for his life. And with him all that was precious to Sol and to Thraun.

'Don't believe it. Don't trust it.' Sol's voice sounded loud but even his tones carried a tremble to them. 'Be strong and we will save them all.'

Garonin burst through the opaque shield to the left, running along the wall of the edifice, firing as they came. Thraun howled and leapt to the attack. Auum and Duele closed in. Hirad made to move.

'Stop, Hirad,' boomed Sol. 'More coming at you. Hold the line, Raven.'

Ilkar stood up behind Erienne. He drew his short blade from its scabbard. The weapon felt heavy and unbalanced in his hand. Four Garonin had punched through the shield. White tears fled across the enclosed space, missing their targets. Thraun's leap took him onto the shoulders of the lead Garonin, bringing him down. Auum hurdled the pair of them. He landed, spun and kicked up and out. The sole of his right foot slammed into the chest of his target, rocking him back. Auum continued his spin. His blade snaked out, slicing into neck and faceplate. The Garonin staggered.

Duele whispered past Auum. He ducked a stream of energy fire, bounced back up and hammered his blade into the ribcage of his enemy. The man fell against the last of the four invaders. Weapons were triggered reflexively. White tears ripped into the walls of the edifice. Cracks ran away along its surface.

Auum jabbed his blade into the gut of his victim. Without pause, he grabbed a jaqrui and threw. The keening wail was brief. The razor edge sliced through the arm of the last attacker. His weapon fell from his hand. Duele leapt to carve his blade into the Garonin's faceplate. Auum followed up his jaqrui and buried his blade two-handed into the gut of the wounded man. Ilkar heard the blade shriek as it exited his back and scraped the edifice behind.

Another howl from Thraun. The wolf sprang up and ran right. Ilkar followed him. Garonin had pushed through the barrier. White light filled the space. Ghaal ducked but not quickly enough. He took the full force of two streams of fire in his face. His head was engulfed in flame. His body juddered and was thrown back to slide across the floor. Ilkar had to turn away. Ghaal's neck smoked, his skull was blasted to shards.

In front, Hirad called a warning. Ilkar heard the clash of weapons. But to the right was the greater threat. Thraun had his jaws clamped around the leg of a Garonin soldier who was beating the wolf's skull with the butt of his weapon. Evunn and Miirt surged into the attack. But one Garonin was free. He could see Sol, sitting helpless, light streaming into him and away from him. The door open to invasion. Auum, running headlong, was not going to make it in time. Ilkar hefted his blade. He was standing no more than ten yards from Sol.

'Get this wrong and it ends here,' he said to himself.

Ilkar hurled his blade. It caught the Garonin in the right thigh. The soldier stumbled, slowed and regained his feet. He ran on, a shout of victory ripping from his alien lips. He reached out to Sol, to touch him and render everything the great man had died for a waste.

The Garonin did not make contact. An axe materialised in the air before him, swinging across with frightening power. Behind it the body of a huge man in jet-black armour washed into being. The blade savaged straight through the Garonin's neck, taking his head clean off to bounce across the floor towards Ilkar.

The elf blinked to dispel the illusion but it didn't shift. There stood Ark. Protector and Raven. He was carrying the sword and axe of Xetesk's dread calling. He wore their colours but without the mask that bound them to the demons. Ark roared. His arms shook and his fists ground against his weapons. His face cleared and he stared square at Ilkar. Blood dripped from his axe.

'We are come.'

Hirad pushed the Garonin's weapon to the left and swung his sword high. The edge slid from the man's shoulder and clattered up into the side of his helmet. The Garonin stumbled. Darrick's reverse sweep carved a gash deep into his chest. The Garonin gasped. Hirad thrust up under his chin strap.

Hirad was aware of shouting from behind him and resisted the urge to turn. More Garonin came through the barrier in front of him. To his right Sirendor ducked a stream of white tears, swayed left as he came back up and jabbed up into the armpit of his attacker. Hirad paced forward. He switched his sword to his left hand, dropped to his haunches and swung the blade low across him, feeling a satisfying connection. Blood spurted from the Garonin's right shin. The soldier stumbled forward. Hirad darted right, reversed his blade and cracked it into the back of his opponent's knees.

The sound of running filled the air around him. It came from behind, to the left and the right. Sol managed a chuckle that reverberated through his head. Protectors swarmed by Hirad, forming a solid line around him and the rest of The Raven. At the centre of the masked army was a man whose face felt the air.

Garonin surged through the barrier again. Hirad smiled as they faltered in their charge.

'Good to see you, Ark,' said the barbarian. He beckoned towards the enemy. 'Come and get it, boys.'

Ark and the entire Protector line stepped forward. Axes came through left to right, low to high. Swords came the other way, chest-high. Garonin screams filled the air. The weight of fire on the shield intensified still further. Hirad felt the pressure of souls crammed into the small space. At last he turned. The shield was full of Protectors. Hundreds of them materialising in front of Sol and spreading across the space.

'Bloody hell. Brought a few friends with you too, did you?' Hirad's voice rose to a shout. 'We have to spread the shield. Ilkar!'

Abruptly, the sky darkened once more. The sound of white tears splatting against the cobbles of ruined Xetesk was replaced by silence. Simultaneously, the deluge against the shield ceased. Protectors moved out of its compass, forming a line four deep, stretching across the face of the edifice.

Hirad heard Erienne cry out. In front of him the shield flickered. He turned and ran back to her, glancing up at the images played out above them in huge hideous detail. Black Wings castle. Two boys lay on a filthy bed. It was covered with blood. The boys were unmoving, throats carved open. Hirad slithered to his knees.

'That's not the future; it's the past,' he said. 'And we all still grieve for your boys. Don't let them beat you. Don't let our new world become another graveyard for us.'

'I couldn't save them,' she said. 'I couldn't save Lyanna. I can't save anyone.'

'Erienne, you're saving us right now. Hang on to that. You're saving the future for everyone still alive and the souls of your boys.' Hirad turned. 'Raven! Get here now. Lend Erienne your strength.'

But Hirad could see she was crumbling. Above their heads images played of storms lashing the coast of Balaia and of a little girl in the centre of them, calling out for her mother. Erienne was shaking horribly. Her shoulders were hunched as if against a cold wind and her hands were closing again.

Thraun padded up behind her and sat, leaning his body into hers and nuzzling her neck. Darrick stood in front of her, looking down. He stripped off a glove and placed his hand on the top of her head. Sirendor did not come so close. Sirendor, who had never met her, stood to watch the Garonin. They were unsure for the present as they gauged the Protector force. Hirad looked for Ilkar. The elven mage was moving towards them one moment and gone the next.

For an instant Ilkar thought he had lost faith entirely and simply ceased to be in Ulandeneth. But a warming feeling washed over him, familiar and strong. A metaphorical arm around the shoulders from a huge presence.

'You need to get your brother to safety now because we haven't got much time,' said Sol.

'Where are you?' asked Ilkar. 'Where am I?'

Ilkar could see nothing but a brown and gold blur.

'Travelling,' said Sol. 'And I am where you left me. I hold the door. You and your brother must bring the elves through now. And then you have to return and play your part.'

'What do you mean?'

'Erienne cannot shield us on her own. Hirad cannot fight them on his own. Belief is only so great in any one of us. Find it in yourself. And think on this. Hirad was right. Absolutely none of what we have seen in Ulandeneth can possibly be happening. So why is it? Find the answer within you and turn this fight around.'

Ilkar wanted to ask more but the blur in front of his eyes coalesced into a scene of devastation. He was standing on the beach of North Bay. Around him the bodies of thousands of elves were scattered in the nauseating attitudes of their deaths. Ilkar tried to move but found he could do nothing but turn on the spot.

Coming towards him across the beach was a small knot of elves pursued by three Garonin firing their weapons. White tears wiped across a flaring, sputtering spell shield. The elves ran on. Not five yards from him they stopped and turned. Four of them, mages, bent to a casting. Rebraal faced the onrushing Garonin with five Al-Arynaar. Ilkar could see his brother was wounded. He held his blade in the wrong hand.

Rebraal was speaking but Ilkar could not hear the words. The Garonin stopped ten yards from them and continued firing. Other enemies were approaching. This was a fight only going one way. But not quietly. From the hands of one of the crouching mages IceBlades tore out. Garonin armour flared white. One of the enemy clutched at his helmet, blood spurting from his eye slit. But, even as he fell, a finger of white lashed out along the path of the spell and buried in the caster's chest. The mage blew apart. The spell shield flickered but steadied.

'Rebraal,' said Ilkar.

Rebraal, with his back to Ilkar, stiffened. His head turned this way and that.

'I'm behind you. Turn round and look.'

Rebraal shook his head.

'Bloody hell, little brother, do I have to draw you a map?'

Rebraal spun round, clearly surprising the Al-Arynaar warriors standing by him. His face was angry, his mouth ready to deliver a threat. But his jaw dropped and he pointed directly at Ilkar before beginning to walk towards him. His people were asking him why.

'Can you not see him? He's standing right there.'

Ilkar could not hear their responses. But he could see their expressions. Disbelief. And why not.

'Don't worry, Rebraal. They can't see or hear me yet.'

'Ilkar?'

Ilkar nodded. 'Well, sort of. I'm still dead but at least I can get you out of here. You don't need the Wesmen. Come to me, all of you, and I'll take you home.'

'We're scattered, Ilkar,' said Rebraal. 'Our people are trapped aboard ship and back along the valley behind me. I cannot leave them.'

'You won't be,' said Ilkar. 'Reach out to me. Touch me. And we will appear to each and every one of them. End their torment. Bring them home.'

Rebraal shook his head. 'I've seen too much to believe this. It cannot be you.'

'I cannot prove it but that you look at me and see me,' said Ilkar. 'You're my brother.'

'Then tell me what you always feared the most,' said Rebraal.

Ilkar still felt a twinge of pain at the memory. 'I feared walking this earth long after my friends, The Raven, had gone to their graves.

Hundreds of years of bleak grief. Lucky for me that I died in screaming agony before the lot of them, wasn't it?'

Rebraal's face cracked into a huge smile and he walked towards
Ilkar.

'You came back for me,' he said. 'After all this time.'

Ilkar shrugged. 'Someone has to look after you.'

'Where will we end up?'

'Ah, now that I can't tell you. After all, I'll end up elsewhere, being
dead and all that.'

Rebraal's smile faltered. 'So this is only to be a brief meeting.'

'The briefest. But worth the moment.'

'So it is, my brother, so it is.'

Rebraal reached out and touched Ilkar's hands. Ilkar felt the
faintest of physical contact but it was enough to last him eternity.
With that touch the doorway opened for every surviving elf on Balaia
and on Calaius. And in that same moment Ilkar was thrust back
to the desperate now of Ulandeneth but this time with an answer
shrieking for attention.

*Brothers fall. Grieve for their souls. Run hard. Strike back. Protect
The Raven. Protect Sol.*

The pulses of thought ran around Ark's head. The Protector line
forged towards the Garonin forward position. They covered the
short space quickly but the Garonin weapons were tearing his
brothers apart. Behind Ark, the shield of the One mage was guttering. Garonin were waiting for it to fail. His brothers would die to
keep them from her. From all who sheltered within it.

They still ran four deep. The white tears smashed into them. To
Ark's immediate left his brother Kol took the full force of a weapon
in his chest. His body was lifted and hurled backwards, scattering
those in his wake. Multiple tracers of energy moving right to left,
burning, gouging and blistering. Protectors fell soundlessly. Others
stumbled, limbs shorn away. Wounds to torso and head brought
down more. But the Protectors would not fold.

Reform. Run on. Close the line. Strike.

The Protectors broke across the Garonin. Ark exulted. He
smashed his axe through the chest of the first enemy. He kicked the
body aside. He thrust his sword deep into the gut of the next. Orn's
axe whipped across to block a weapon coming back up to fire. The
voices were loud in his head.

Duck low, jab up. Strike left, sword. Axe defence chest, Orn. Spin blade. Upper cut sword. Brother down. Body away. Fill. Drive axe forward, Pel. Pace up. Lower left flank block.

The Garonin were wavering in front of them. There were no gaps in the Protector defence barring those torn by the desultory white tears that some from the rear risked around the bodies of their fellows. Blank masks faced flat faceplates. Pitiless enemies squaring up. Ark buried his axe in the top of a Garonin skull, splitting it open and showering gore. He wrenched it clear. Orn clattered his axe flat into the waist of another.

Ark could see beyond them. The plain was empty. The remnants of the Garonin force broke and ran, blinking out of sight as they went.

Hold, my brothers.

Ark looked about him. The shield was thirty yards to their rear. Protector bodies covered the ground, two hundred and more taken by the white tears. He could feel Sol's tension in his mind. He asked of him.

'They are not gone. They've drawn you out a long way,' said Sol. 'Fall back.'

A shimmering in the air appeared less than twenty yards ahead. Garonin dropped into Ulandeneth. Hundreds of them. They stood like statues for a moment, gathering themselves. Weapons were raised to fire. It was going to be a slaughter.

Back, my brothers. Back to the shield.

Above, the sky was dark again. The images changed.

'Fall back.'

Sol's voice sounded through each and every one of them. Above, the black images had changed. Demons tortured souls where they stretched away from the Soul Tank. Protectors had masks ripped from their faces and they died in torment.

Strength. Move fast. Don't look back.

The Protectors turned and ran. Behind them, the Garonin unleashed a storm of raw white power.

Chapter 47

Hirad watched helpless while the Garonin slaughtered the Protectors. Erienne's shield had strengthened. The images had changed away from her personal torment, leaving her free to concentrate, with Thraun acting as strength and comfort right by her. But the cost had been savage and was worsening.

The Garonin had materialised in huge numbers just too far away for the Protectors to reach. Their only course was to try and get back inside the shield. The white tears spoke another outcome. Protectors were hurled forward. Backs of skulls were crushed in. Holes were punched through chests and legs were blasted from beneath strong bodies.

Hirad could see Ark, and now Aeb, running headlong. Arms pumping, weapons flashing in the glare of the tears. Fire was back on the shield too, rattling and fizzing, reminding Erienne of the grim task before her. Garonin closed in on all sides. He could even hear weapons fire behind the edifice now, blasting through the stone, leaching away the belief of every soul still yet to cross home.

'Be ready, Raven! Steady, Erienne. Sirendor, looking forward.' Hirad's voice couldn't cover that of Ilkar. The elf so recently disappeared was plainly back amongst them and he was raving about something. 'Ilkar! Drop the speech. Get casting.'

'No! You don't understand. Well you do but you don't. Gods drowning, what am I saying? You lot only believe so far. I see it now. I see everything. We are just spirits. They cannot even touch us if we don't believe they can. They only hurt us because that is what we expect! Listen to me. They cannot break us. They cannot!'

'We haven't time for this, Ilks. If you believe, cast something to help us.'

Hirad never took his eyes from the Protectors. White tears splashed against the few that remained. Less than fifty. A masked man fell against Aeb's legs, bringing him down. Ark stopped to drag him clear. Fire splashed across Aeb's body, tearing it apart where he lay. Ark ran on. The few ran through the barrier, stopped, turned and faced.

The mass of the Garonin surged at them.

'Listen to me, Gods drowning, listen!'

'Cast, Ilkar you bastard. Just cast!'

'All right, I will.'

Hirad drew a deep breath and picked his first target. He dared a glance left and right. The line was solid but there was precious little in reserve. The TaiGethen held the flanks by the edifice. The Raven warrior trio had the centre with Protectors filling the gaps in between. The Garonin came through the shield.

Darrick fenced a weapon aside. He found a gap in the enemy defence and slid his sword up under his arm. The soldier fell. The one behind him opened fire. White tears splattered against the shield. He closed, still firing.

Hirad tore into the Garonin ahead of him. He batted away a weapon, smashed his fist high into the soldier's faceplate and dashed the pommel of his sword into the side of his helmet. The soldier fell. Hirad leapt over him.

The Protector line struck their targets. Hirad felt the power. Axes came down in unison. Blood sprayed into the ivory sky. Swords flashed through. The Garonin juddered to a temporary standstill. The Protectors stepped up, still just inside the shield. Hirad saw an axe remove the arm of one Garonin. He saw that same axe turn out to block a thrust to a brother Protector. And he saw the Protector lose his head to a stream of white tears as it moved a fraction beyond safety.

'The line's not going to hold,' shouted Darrick.

The earth shook just beyond Erienne's shield. Garonin broke off and stepped back. The Protectors stopped as one. Hirad looked out over the juddering landscape while beneath his feet he could feel nothing at all. He glanced over his shoulder. Ilkar was casting. He watched the elven mage stare out over the Garonin and raise his hands from by his sides.

The ground of Ulandeneth heaved. Mighty spears of rock thrust up, spilling Garonin to either side. High the walls of bedrock climbed, and between them hundreds of enemy soldiers were standing and staring. The ivory mountains shuddered to a halt, loose pebbles running from their impossibly smooth surfaces. For a heart-beat the battle ceased.

Ilkar clapped his hands.

Hirad fell back a pace and had to turn his head away. The dread thump of the low mountains coming together was augmented in his imagination by the crunch of bones. Enemies, yes, but snuffed out so coldly. Surviving Garonin were too stunned to react for a moment. Above, the sky had returned to its bland ivory. Hirad turned to face Ilkar. The elf's hands were still clasped together. The clap they had made had been heard across Ulandeneth.

'That was some trick for an elf who can't see a way.'

'What did I tell you? They cannot beat us.'

But outside the survivors reformed. Still over a hundred remained. They scattered themselves across the front of the shield, raised their weapons and ran.

'Ilkar, we need another of those.'

'No time. Just believe what I say.'

'Ilkar. A shield,' said Sol. 'I need Erienne. And I need Hirad.'

The Garonin breached Erienne's shield. White tears flared across the space. Protectors fell. Darrick took a bolt across his left shoulder. Sirendor ducked and flailed his weapon. Hirad swayed and jabbed out, deflecting a weapon which fired high and wide.

'No time, Unknown!' he called.

'Make time.'

'Shield up,' said Ilkar.

Hirad was plucked away.

'Unknown, no!'

'It is our last chance. The Garonin will break us eventually. We have to complete the job and hide the door from them. First we need every soul to cross. Thousands are coming in from the void, heading for rest. Now we need the living to join them. Erienne will bring Densyr. You will bring my family.'

Sol's voice was like a warm cloak about Hirad's shoulders. He could sense Erienne but could not see her, and if he looked at all, he could see nothing but a blurred mess all around him.

'Why me?'

'Why do you think she named our son Hirad?'

'Thought that was your idea.'

'No.'

'She'll want it to have been you she saw, big man.'

'You'll understand why I cannot move.'

The Unknown's voice was leaden. Hirad felt his regret as if it was his own.

'It's probably for the best,' said Hirad.

'I can think of no scenario where that would be true. Just tell them I'll be watching over them always.'

The blur coalesced. Hirad and Erienne were standing in the ruins of Xetesk. Diera, the boys and Denser were running towards them. The wolves had peeled off and were harrying three Garonin, keeping them away. Both animals were badly wounded. Neither would last long.

Denser could feel her before she appeared before them. The four of them were running towards a temporary haven in the ruins of the refectory. Garonin still prowled the grounds of the college but the vydospheres were gone, snatched away to some other task.

Erienne stood with Hirad. Warmth flowed out from them. Diera and the boys saw The Raven duo too. Diera slithered to a stop, young Hirad still on her back. Jonas walked towards Hirad, sword still in his hands.

'Hello, Jonas.'

'You're like that painting at our inn. How can you be here?'

'It's a long story. Your father sent me. But I'm here to show you to your new home. You, Hirad and your mother. Reach out to me; let me take you there.'

Jonas turned to Diera.

'Mother?'

She looked up and there was joy in her face despite the tears. 'Why isn't he here?'

Hirad smiled. 'He's busy making sure every soul that ever was gets safely to the other side. You know The Unknown.'

Diera smiled. 'Yes, I do.'

'And he says he'll be watching over you, keeping you safe.'

'He actually means it, doesn't he?' said Diera.

'You know, I think he does.'

'Time for you to come too, my love,' said Erienne.

'Yeah, Xetesk-man. Get over here and feel my spectral boot in your arse for all the crap things you did.'

But Denser shook his head, suddenly certain of his path. 'I don't think so.'

'What?' Erienne and Hirad spoke together.

'Not because of you, Hirad. I never was scared of you, not really. But there'll be so many people left here, people that won't cross over. So much work to be done if we are to rebuild anything of our former selves. And all without the aid of magic now.'

'Are you sure?' asked Erienne.

'I've never been surer about anything,' said Denser, and he felt a weight lift from his shoulders. 'I can't abandon those who cannot leave.'

Erienne nodded. 'The words of a true leader of men. You'll make a fine king, Denser. I'm proud of you.'

'Not a king. Never that.'

Hirad chuckled. 'Good job. Come on, you lot. Time to go.'

Denser watched the three of them reach out to Hirad and disappear. Hirad nodded to him.

'I'm glad, Denser. You've restored my faith in you. Something I didn't think you could do. Never mind your college trappings. This is a destiny you can make all for yourself.'

'I'll do my best.'

Hirad vanished, leaving Erienne standing in the light alone.

'I will never cease to love you,' said Denser. 'Or our daughter.'

Erienne smiled, blew him a kiss and was gone. Denser looked about him.

'Interesting decision,' he said. 'Thoroughly thought through. Hero, king or utter fool. Time will surely tell.'

Denser ducked into the refectory ruins as a Garonin soldier thumped past his hiding place. He could still hear the wolves but they were distant now, perhaps chasing Thraun's soul. He hoped so.

The Lord of the Mount watched the Garonin soldier march away.

'Right. Well, best get started.'

The Garonin were amongst them.

'How long, Sol?' asked Ilkar. He had kept his shield up against the few enemies who remained outside but increasingly he felt it to be a waste of time.

'You'll know,' said Sol.

'We could do with the others. Why won't everyone see what I see?'

'They are coming. And your time is soon.'

Sirendor and Darrick fought back to back. Darrick's left arm hung useless at his side. He was sweating heavily and struggling to keep up his defence. But there was no doubting his courage. He jabbed and fenced, keeping enemies busy while Sirendor killed with his trademark stylish efficiency. The remaining Protectors held the line as solidly as they could but were being worn down inexorably.

Around them, the TaiGethen were a blur of ruthless murder. Every time a Garonin soldier got inside the shield, a TaiGethen was on him before he had gone five paces. Yet Ilkar could not relax. Surely the enemy were being snuffed out and indeed it did seem their numbers were thinning beyond the shield. Ilkar, though, felt the approach of something bad.

Garonin soldiers broke through on the right again. Four of them. Thraun barked a warning and leapt. White tears tracked him, searing across his flank. With a yelp, Thraun crashed to the ground and slid against the side of the edifice. His body heaved and smoked, shuddering its last.

Auum was already running, Evunn with him. The two TaiGethen rolled under streams of white tears flashing over their heads and into the backs of two helpless Protectors. Auum surged up and left the ground, going two-footed at the nearest enemy. Evunn made to do likewise, but at that moment Erienne and Hirad dropped back into the melee.

Evunn collided with the pair of them and all three tumbled and rolled. In front of them the Garonin could not believe his luck. His weapon discharged. Evunn was caught by the stream of energy and his body blew apart, spattering gore in all directions.

The Garonin hurdled his fallen body and raced towards Sol. Auum downed his man, turned and gave chase. Hirad was getting to his feet. Two other Garonin faced him. He had nowhere to run. Below him Erienne had begun to cast but would not make it.

Time slowed for Ilkar. Him again. He could stop the lone Garonin. Possibly. But the consequence was stark. Move and attack and lose the shield keeping the remaining fire from the defenders. Enough fire to wipe them all out. He heard Sol's last words repeat in his head.

'Now or never,' he said. Ilkar drove to his feet and dived headlong at the onrushing Garonin. 'Shield down! Shield down!'

White tears lashed into the open space. Protector, Raven and elf alike threw themselves to the ground. Ilkar prayed they all survived but knew they could not. His outstretched hand snagged the ankle of the Garonin. The soldier, in mid-run, sprawled to the ground. Ilkar scrambled up and dived on top of him as he tried to get back to his feet. White tears smashed all around him, ripping chunks out of the edifice but keeping well away from Sol, who held the door open, helpless to stop what came at him.

The Garonin shoved Ilkar off. Ilkar rolled and rose. The Garonin was on his feet too. Ilkar got in front of him. The Garonin raised his weapon. He fired.

'Ilkar!' Hirad was screaming at him. 'No!'

The white tears flowed into Ilkar's body. He spread his arms wide and he laughed.

'See me, Garonin? See me? You cannot hurt me. You do not know how. I have mastered you. I understand. Raven. TaiGethen. Listen to me.'

The Garonin ceased firing and made to sweep Ilkar aside. Ilkar raised a hand and clamped it under the chin of the soldier, holding him off while his blows slid from Ilkar's body.

'They can only do to you what you *expect* them to do. What you believe they can do. They cannot hurt me. You, my enemy, cannot hurt me. But I can hurt you.'

From Ilkar's hand the flame was the bright yellow of Julatsa and hot enough to melt metal. It scoured into the Garonin's neck. His armour buckled beneath Ilkar's hand. Ilkar closed it into a fist, crushing his neck like a twig, dropped the Garonin and walked into the midst of the white fire, letting it slam into his body, feeling nothing but an intense satisfaction.

'This is us, Raven! We are spirits. We are souls. We cannot be killed because we are already dead. Let them fear us. They cannot hurt us but they know that we can hurt them. They are real. They bleed. They die. For us it is only memories.

'Rout them! Rout them!'

Ilkar ran at the nearest Garonin. He saw the soldier flinch, take his hand off his weapon and take a pace back. Behind him, he heard Hirad roar:

'Come on, you fuckers! Fight us now, eh?'

Raven, Protector and TaiGethen took up the cry. The Garonin were swamped. Armour could not deflect blades. Punches found their mark. Blood was spilled. Garonin blood. And though the fire still came back at them, the defenders let it slide over them, doing no more harm than would water or a puff of air.

'Make a shield around Sol,' ordered Darrick, his wound gone. 'Let's not forget what we're here to defend.'

Hirad, standing next to Ilkar, gave the mage a shove on the shoulder. The Garonin fire battered them. The soldiers feinted to attack. Auum prowled in front of the line, daring any to come close.

'You can still feel me push you, then,' said the barbarian.

'Of course. I expect you to be able to. Be bloody boring if you couldn't. Then I couldn't do this.'

Ilkar rubbed his knuckles hard against Hirad's forehead.

'I think I preferred you lacking in belief,' he said.

'Look.'

Sirendor was pointing out at the Garonin. They had ceased firing and were moving slowly towards the defenders. One detached himself from the group of perhaps forty and walked to within a few paces.

'The day is yours,' he said, melodious voice tainted with discord. 'But your new worlds will be ours. The fight will never be over. One day we will follow an innocent soul through the doorway and your efforts will be rendered nought.'

'Not if we close it in your fat face, you won't,' said Hirad.

The sound of water over pebbles.

'How little you know, human. Your ignorance is our greatest weapon. Think on it and enjoy your rest if you can. The dead are irrelevant.'

The last echoes of the Garonin's voice rattled against the edifice. The plain of Ulandeneth was empty.

'What was he talking about?' asked Hirad.

He turned and led The Raven, Protectors and TaiGethen back towards Sol, or the shimmering luminescence that represented where he was seated. He knelt by Thraun much as Auum did by what remained of Evunn.

'Don't worry about them. Their souls rest with me for the time being,' said Sol.

Hirad smiled. 'Seems like a good place. So what about this door, then?'

'Once opened, the door can be hidden and protected but never shut. It must allow the passage of souls,' said Sol.

'So how *do* we stop them?' asked Hirad. 'After all this bother, I don't want to think we just moved our people from one dead space to another.'

'Well, we could wedge a grumpy barbarian in it, 'said Ilkar. 'That should keep it shut.'

'Funny elf,' said Hirad.

'Ilkar is more accurate than he knows,' said Sol. 'Even when hidden, the doorway is vulnerable. Witness their access into our cluster of worlds.'

Ilkar and Hirad exchanged glances.

'Are the words, "someone has to guard it" marching towards your lips, Sol?'

'As Hirad would undoubtedly tell you, Ilkar, you are sharp of mind today.'

Hirad chuckled and nodded his head. 'Funny how we never seem to reach the end, do we?'

'Indeed we don't,' said Erienne.

'What do you lot think. Darrick, Sirendor?' Hirad turned to his old friends.

Sirendor shrugged. 'Well, I didn't have a lot else planned for the rest of the day.'

'You mean eternity,' said Darrick. 'And I would be honoured to be considered a soul great enough to perform this task.'

Murmurs of agreement met his words. Hirad clapped his hands together.

'Right, well let's get comfortable. Ark? What say you and the Protectors?'

'I will stay,' said Ark. 'My brothers will travel to their rest. Should they be needed, they can be called upon once more.'

Sol's warmth spread out to cover them all. 'Then come, walk into me, my brother Protectors. Find your brother souls. Know they are safe and have gone beyond me.'

The few remaining Protectors bowed their heads to Ark and moved into Sol's compass. One by one, they disappeared.

'Which leaves you, Auum, and your TaiGethen,' said Sol. 'Three thousand years and more you've walked the earth. Twice you have saved the elves from the Garonin and never have you turned your head from Yniss, your God, or the tasks he set for you. Blissful rest is the very least you deserve in the company of the ancients.'

Auum's smile was brief. 'Yet I do not consider my tasks complete. Now I will serve Yniss through Shorth himself, securing the passage of souls on their final journeys. I will not falter. And never again will the Garonin lay claim to the lands of elves or men. For Yniss I say this: I, Auum, will stand sentinel for eternity. There can be no greater honour in the service of my Gods. My Tai brothers and sister will make their own choices. Those standing here and those resting with Sol.'

Neither Miirt and Duele hesitated to stand by Auum.

The luminescence dimmed and Sol was visible once more. The great shaven-headed warrior standing with his arms outstretched to them.

'Walk with me,' he said.

Jonas leaned back against the rough scales and wrote a few more lines. The sun was warm here on the hillside but he could not smell the grass or flowers, such were the overpowering odours of wood and oil from the dragon's hide.

'Read it to me,' rumbled Sha-Kaan. 'I enjoy your ramblings to your dead father.'

Jonas turned his head to the right. Sha-Kaan's muzzle was resting on the soft grass a few feet away. His eyelids were heavy but occasionally snapped open to reveal his startling blue eyes.

'All right. Let me know if I get anything wrong.'

'As ever.'

' "Dear Father. It's been a hundred days since we all arrived here and there still isn't a name for the place. All we know is that it has a lot of water and not a lot of land. Sha-Kaan says we all live on one big island in a scattered archipelago and then there is nothing but ocean for thousands of miles. Perhaps one day we'll explore the rest of it and find new lands. Right now, though, there aren't very many of us so it doesn't seem a good idea.

' "If there are other people here besides those that escaped from Balaia and Calaius, we haven't seen any evidence of them yet. Meanwhile, we try to organise ourselves into some sort of society. Mother says we should follow the model of Korina and make a central city state from where people can move out to live where they please. She's much respected among the survivors.

' "Of course there has been the odd bit of trouble. Once the euphoria of escape wore off, plenty of people started to regret what they'd left behind. We're all living in wooden huts here, at best. We've precious few tools, no way of quarrying stone just yet and nothing to eat but what we find in the ground and on trees. Mind you, Sha-Kaan says there are animals that might be farmed and I'm sure we'll get around to that.

' "We did a census when we got here. Everyone was counted and we carved names in strips of bark and wood. Two hundred and seventy-two thousand, one hundred and forty-one humans made it. Not many when you think about it but it's best not to dwell on the past, isn't it?

' "As for the elves, well, they are few in number. Twenty-three thousand, four hundred and five. But they seem content enough. Most of them have disappeared into the forests to build temples and settlements. We see a lot of Rebraal although he is quite busy. He seems to be the ruler of the elves, if they have such a thing.

' "Then there are the dragons. It's strange to look up and see the sky full of them. Comforting for me. Not so for others. But they are not numerous and have no access to the healing streams of inter-dimensional space. Sha-Kaan says they will have to seek new dimensions in this cluster in which to live or they'll all fade and die. That is not a happy thought.

' "By the way, Hirad is being a real pain. Remember that dragon you carved for him? He left it at home and he wants to go back and get it. He doesn't understand and it's driving me and Mother mad.

' "It's hard to say if we'll survive and flourish. There is such hope, but when I talk to Mother, there are so many problems to face. We need a government and an economy, she says. I think we need you.

' "I miss you, Father. I always will." How's that?'

Sha-Kaan was silent for a moment and Jonas thought he had drifted off to sleep. But then he opened his mouth wide and clacked his jaws together gently.

'It is perfect. Every word is from the heart. And you will survive, Jonas Solson. And the people will no longer need Sol. They will have you.'

'What we really need is a deck of cards,' said Hirad. 'You know, something to while away the centuries when we run out of things to talk about.'

'Don't be stupid, Hirad,' said Ilkar.

'Why, don't you like cards?'

'No,' said Sol. 'It isn't that. It's just that there'll never be a time when you don't have something to say.'

'You have a point,' conceded Hirad.

'And anyway, time is meaningless here,' said Sirendor.

'So?'

'So, dear barbarian soul, we cannot count the boring centuries, nor the exciting ones. We'll only know the moments when we are called to defend the door,' said Erienne.

'You aren't making our eternal task sound all that exciting,' said Darrick.

'I'm with you, General,' said Hirad. 'We should have gone to the halls of the ancients and left Auum here to see the place safe.'

'Or back to the bliss of the dead with the Protectors,' said Darrick.

'Neither of you means that, do you?' said Sol.

Hirad smiled. 'I never was one for having nothing to look forward to.'

'It really is very dull, this place, isn't it?' said Ilkar.

'It could do with a lick of paint of some other colour than ivory,' said Erienne.

'Hey, Ilks, maybe you could whistle up some more mountains, squeeze a few more Garonin and eke out some red for us.'

'Maybe if I cut out your tongue we'd get both a lovely red and a bit of peace and quiet.'

Hirad took a long look about him. The ivory expanse of Ulandeneth surrounded them endlessly. The door to the new dimensional cluster was hidden now but souls travelled it nonetheless. The threat of the Garonin would never fade though, and so the decision to remain had been an easy one.

The Raven were seated for the time being on the Ulandeneth side of the door. Their place of rest was within. Timeless sleep until the footfall of the enemy summoned them to fight.

'This must be the perfect eternity for you, mustn't it?' said Thraun, back in human form. 'Knowing The Raven will go on forever.'

'You know what,' said Hirad. 'It is.'

'While for us the thought of being saddled with you in perpetuity is nothing short of a living hell,' said Ilkar.

'Ah, but you love me really,' said Hirad.

'That is occasionally true,' said Erienne.

'When you're asleep, mostly,' said Sirendor.

'Speaking of which, come on, Raven, TaiGethen.' Sol clapped his hands together. 'Time to sleep. Hanging around out here will only garner us unwanted attention.'

Hirad stood. 'Fitting, don't you think? The Raven? Guardians of the new world?'

'Yes,' said Ilkar. 'They must all sleep so soundly knowing they are

defended by a dead barbarian. The door kept closed against the
Garonin by the sheer weight of your ego.'

Hirad's laughter echoed away into the vastness of Ulandeneth.
One by one, they faded to grey specks and disappeared inside to
enjoy comfort and rest as one. The Raven, together again. And, as
Hirad attested as they slipped into blissful sleep, as it was always
destined to be.

Acknowledgements

Thank you to Simon Spanton for wanting to see The Raven ride just one more time; to Lizzy Hill for providing insight and help every step of the way; to Robert Kirby and Howard Morhaim for their unflinching support and friendship; and to my wife, Clare, for always being there for me.

www.jamesbarclay.com